用身體學慣用語

像老外一樣說英語

編者｜于宥均 Daphne Yu・插圖｜吳榮騰 Felix Wu

楓　書　坊

CONTENTS

奇妙的BODY之旅即將開始！

動身之前，提醒您兩種不同的路線選擇：

- 依照左頁的目錄，從「頭」開始，循序漸進，直到終點的「肉和身體」。
- 參考下方的圖示，隨心所至，周遊不同的部位。

譬如：想先探訪「臉」，可直接翻至書本54頁，此外，與臉有關的「臉頰／下巴／下顎」，其相關的慣用語也都會一起出現在這個單元裡。

最後、當然也是最重要的，衷心祝福您，旅途愉快、豐收不斷！

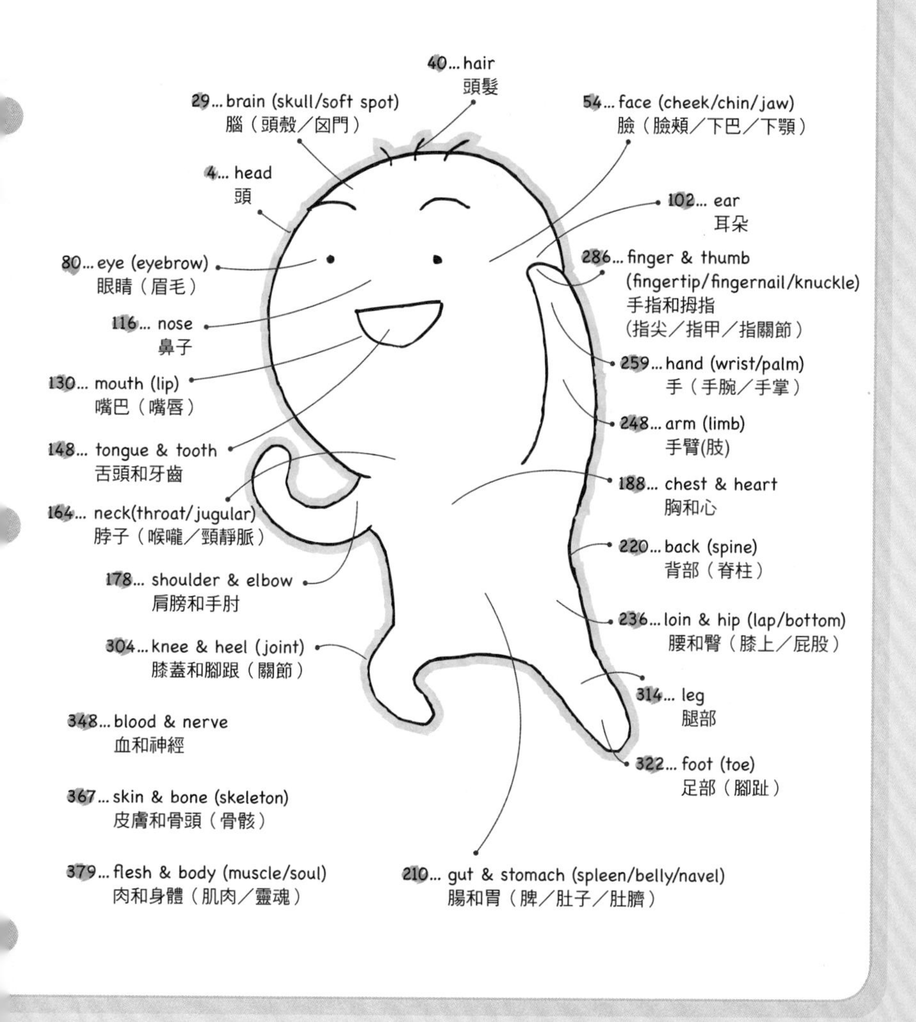

head

就讓我們從**頭**玩起吧！

HEAD（頭），可說是身體器官中最重要的一部份，手斷了還能活，但**HEAD**斷了，那就一命嗚呼沒救了；再加上**HEAD**若不是長在最頂端（如人類）、要不就是最前端（如四腳獸），這又更使得**HEAD**有了舉足輕重的象徵意義。

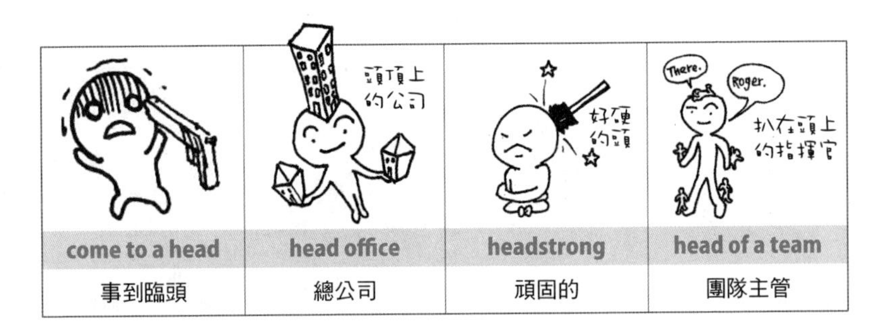

come to a head	head office	headstrong	head of a team
事到臨頭	總公司	頑固的	團隊主管

又，**HEAD**的正前方長了一張臉，除非有特異功能，否則沒有人的臉會正對後方。也因此，在**HEAD**之前多加一個**a-** → **ahead**，就意謂了「朝前地、在前地、事前地」。如：

go ahead → 往前走、儘管去做
plan ahead → 事前計畫

HEAD本身也可以當動詞使用，同樣與「前面」有關，意思是「領導、率先在前、朝（特定地方、方向）前進」，如：

head a new department → 領導新部門
head the procession → 在遊行隊伍最前方
head south → 朝南走
head for the moon → 前往月球

1

beat one's head against the wall

拿頭撞牆，白費力氣、做不可能有結果的事

to waste one's time trying hard to accomplish something that is impossible or completely hopeless

用頭去撞一面牆，即使是練過鐵頭功的人，都可能覺得危險！被撞的牆很難傷及分毫，倒是撞牆的頭恐怕傷痕累累。撞牆的動作除了用 **beat**，也可用 **bang** 或 **hit**，至於牆，磚牆（**a brick wall**）、或石牆（**a stone wall**）也都可以，就看說話當下的感覺，較想去撞什麼樣的牆囉！

- Trying to persuade him to stop smoking, you're just beating your head against the wall.

  勸他戒煙，你只是浪費力氣而已！

- Getting that hardhead to change his mind is like banging your head against a stone wall !

  想讓那老頑固改變心意，根本是在拿頭撞牆！

Write your own sentence:

- I've tried many times to ________________________,
  but I'm just beating my head against the wall !

2

bury one's head in the sand

把頭埋入沙裡，逃避現實，拒絕面對問題

to refuse to confront or acknowledge a problem; to ignore obvious signs of danger

拒絕面對問題的人，常被形容是駝鳥（**ostrich**）。如駝鳥一般把頭埋入沙裡就表示一味逃避、假裝看不到問題或危機。**bury**（埋）這個動作也可用**hide**（藏）或用**stick**表示把頭「伸」進沙裡。最後，在此替駝鳥平反一下，其實駝鳥把頭伸入沙裡，只是為了吃沙裡的碎石以幫助消化。

- Stop burying your head in the sand. The company was $50 million in the red.

  面對現實吧！公司虧損五千萬了。

- When it comes to his spoiled and untamable kid, he just hides his head in the sand.

  一說到他那被寵壞又叛逆的小孩，他就逃避。

Write your own sentence:

- I am going to ______________________________, not bury my head in the sand.

3

bite one's head off

咬掉某人的頭，兇巴巴地回應某人

to respond rudely and furiously to someone's question or comment

如果有人一開口就沒好氣，**Get out! You brain-dead**…（滾出去！你腦殘啊…）全衝出口，這是否很像一頭張著口的野獸、正準備狠狠咬掉你的頭？其實十六世紀的說法是 **bite one's nose off**（咬掉某人鼻子），不知是否人們愈來愈覺得粗暴的語言咬掉的已不只是鼻子、根本就是一整顆頭，於是從十九世紀中期開始，咬鼻就成了咬頭，**bite** 可換用 **snap**（猛咬）。

- I only asked if I could borrow your motorbike. There's no need to bite my head off.

  我只不過想跟你借個機車而已，沒必要這樣大小聲吧。

- You may have a bad hair day, but you don't have to bite my head off.

  你今天可能相當不順，但沒必要這樣跟我說話吧！

- He'll snap your head off if you ask to use his cell phone.

  你敢跟他借手機？等著被慘轟吧！

Write your own sentence:

- I'm very sorry I ______________________ but I didn't mean to bite your head off.

4

come to a head

來到頭部，事到臨頭，到達緊要關頭

to reach a crisis or a turning point

如果 **have an abscess**（長了膿瘡），長到頭部事情就大條了；如果被人用槍指著，指到頭部最令人倍感威脅。這個慣用語表示大事不妙，再不拿出辦法，後果不堪設想。也可用 **bring …to a head** 來說明是什麼原因導致事情到了不得不面對解決的地步。

- He has not expected things to come to a head so fast, forcing him to play his last card.

  他沒料到這麼快就到這個地步，逼得他不得不使出最後一招。

- The protest came to a head when the union threatened to sue the mayor.

  當工會揚言要對市長提告，這場抗爭陷入了白熱化。

- His hunger strike has brought the conflict to a head.

  他的絕食抗議使得這場衝突進入緊張狀態。

Write your own sentence:

- ____________ came to a head when ____________.

5

go to one's head

衝到頭上，使某人酒醉或自負

to make one drunk; to make one proud or conceited

當酒精一整個衝上腦袋，那就表示某人醉了；當衝上腦袋的不是酒精而是功名利祿，這人也會醉，這另一種醉就是驕傲自滿。類似說法還有 **turn one's head**，意指功名利祿將某人轉到頭昏腦脹，以致此人 **be carried away**（得意忘形、興奮到昏了頭），變得驕傲勢利、自命不凡。

- Any kind of liquor goes straight to his head.
  隨便哪一種酒都可以讓他喝了馬上醉。
- You mustn't let your promotion go to your head.
  你千萬別一升官就昏頭了。
- Winning that prize has turned his head. Now he only mixes with celebrities.
  得了那座獎後他就變了，現在他都只跟名流往來。

Write your own sentence:

- I hope ____________________ wont'go to my head.

6

get … through one's head

使…通過某人腦袋，使某人理解、相信、接受…

to manage to make someone understand or accept something

聽靠耳朵，但要聽懂，就得靠腦袋。裝有腦袋的頭意指理解，當某事通過你的頭，就表示你對這事真的想通了。類似說法還有**get …through one's thick skull**：讓某人的笨腦袋弄懂了某事；至於**over one's head:** 超出頭部，則表示超越某人的理解，於是乎**in over one's head:** 進入超出頭部的地方，就表示「處於無力掌控的境況、嘗試去做超出自己能力的事情」。

Help! I'm in over my head.
超過了啦！

This is way over my head.
太高了！不懂！

- It took her a while to **get** her feeling **through his head.**
  她花了好一會兒功夫，才終於讓他明白她的感受。

- He can't seem to **get** it **through his thick skull** that he still owes me an apology.
  他這個笨蛋好像就是不懂，他還欠我一個道歉。

Write your own sentence:

- How can I get it through your head that __________ ____________________?

7

have a good head on one's shoulders

肩膀上長了顆好頭，聰明、有見識

to be sensible and intelligent; to have common sense

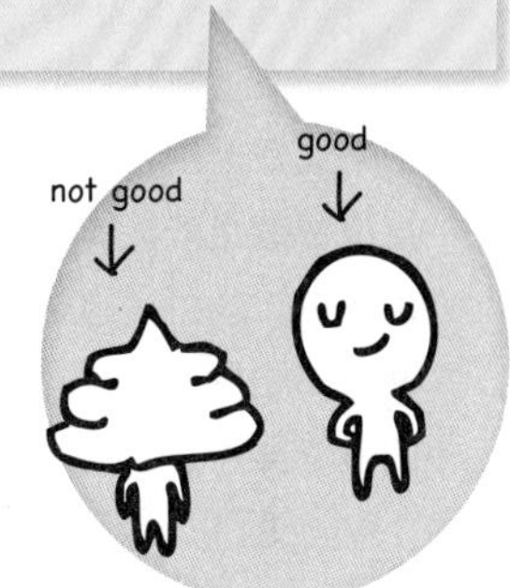

肩上長了顆好頭意指聰明，**have an empty head**則形容腦袋空空、傻乎乎。至於**have a big head**則指患了大頭症，目中無人，自我感覺良好。**have an old head on young shoulders**，年輕的肩膀卻長了顆老人頭，這表示少年老成。頭通常表示智能，所以中文說心算，寫成英文卻是**count in one's head**，在頭裡面用腦筋算哦。

- He doesn't do well in school, but he has a good head on his shoulders.

  他課業表現不是很好，可是他很聰明、很有見識。

- She has a good head on her shoulders, so you can count on her for help.

  她懂得很多，你可以指望她幫你。

- The constant flattery of his fans gave him a big head.

  他的粉絲不斷的奉承他，使得他自大驕傲起來。

Write your own sentence:

- I have a good head on my shoulders because

  ________________________________.

head

8

have a head for …

長了顆適合…的頭，有…的才能或能耐

to have a mental aptitude for something; to be able to tolerate something

中文常會用「很有…的頭腦」來表示某人擁有某種智能上的天資，這個慣用語與中文的說法不謀而合；此外，這個慣用語也可用來形容某人對某事的耐受度極佳。如果想強調其才能或能耐真的很優，可在**head**前面加上**strong**或**good**。

- He has a head for mathematics and can solve any math problem.
  他很有數學天才，任何數學題都解得出來。
- He has a good head for figures but no head for business.
  他很有數字頭腦，可是沒有經商的才能。
- She has a good head for directions and never gets lost.
  她方向感很好，從來沒迷路過。
- You need to have a head for heights to be a high-rise window cleaner.
  你必須敢站在高處才能當高樓洗窗工。

Write your own sentence:

- I have a good head for ________________ but no head for ____________________.

9

have one's head screwed on （right）

用螺絲把頭（妥當地）栓好，頭腦清醒、有判斷力

to be able to think clearly; to have good judgment

即使機器人都得把頭栓牢，何況是活生生的人？頭栓牢了才不會出差錯，一旦 **have a screw loose**，腦袋裡鬆了一根螺絲，那可會變得阿達阿達、不太正常的！

Does he have a screw loose?

- I often wonder whether you have your head screwd on.

  我常懷疑你的頭腦到底是否清醒。

- You can't take him in that easily. He has his head screwed on right.

  要騙他沒那麼容易，他腦子可是靈光的很。

- He wears a heavy jacket in the middle of summer. He must have a screw loose.

  炎炎夏日他穿了件厚外套，他八成哪根筋不對。

Write your own sentence:

- ______________________ because I have my head screwed on.

head

10

head over heels

頭朝地腳朝天，愛得神魂顛倒

to be in love with someone very much

這個慣用語原本應寫做**heels over head**，形容事物頭下腳上、顛三倒四（**upside-down or topsy-turvy**），像翻筋斗（**somersault**）一樣，有趣的是，這個慣用語後來也被上下顛倒寫成了**head over heels**，並且沿用來形容深陷在愛中的痴狂，畢竟被愛沖昏頭的時候，的確很像在翻筋斗，頭下腳上、暈頭轉向。

- They fell head over heels for one another the moment they met at the beach.

  他們一在海邊相識，隨即愛得死去活來。

- He found himself head over heels in love with her after they dated for a week.

  交往一週後，他發現自己愛她愛得無法自拔。

- John is head over heels for Mary. He is crazy about her.

  John很迷戀Mary，愛得既痴且狂。

Write your own sentence:

- I won't fall head over heels for anyone unless ______________________.

11

head and shoulders above

高出頭和肩膀，大大勝出（同類的人事物）

to be outstandingly superior to other similar people or things

如果某人或某事，整整超出了其他同類一顆頭和一雙肩，那就表示這人或這事高人一等，非常傑出。這個慣用語有時會搭配 **stand**（站立）或 **tower**（聳立）來強調高聳的感覺。但如果勝出不多只略勝一籌，可用 **a notch above**（高出一節刻度）來表達。

- This oldest basketball team is head and shoulders above the rest of the league.

  比起聯盟其他支球隊，這支最資深的籃球隊強太多了。

- This chairman stands head and shoulders above the old one.

  這名主席比起之前那個好太多了。

- This latest candidate we interviewed seems a notch above the rest.

  我們最近面試的那一個，似乎比其他應徵的人略勝一籌。

Write your own sentence:

- In my judgment, ________ is head and shoulders above ________.

12

have a head start

搶先起步，贏在起跑點，先走一步

to start early on something ahead of everyone else

head start 是賽跑時先起步的優勢，延伸用來表示贏在起跑點或先走一步。當然，**head start** 是合法的先起步，與 **jump the gun**（未鳴槍就跑）以及 **false start**（偷跑）是不一樣的。

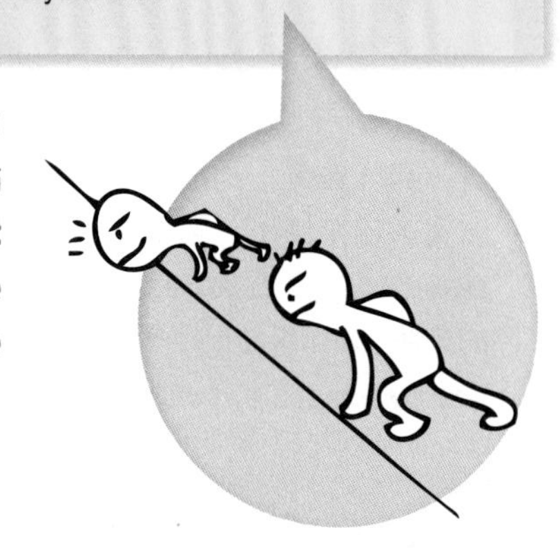

- Is it true to have a head start on life by going to the best school?
  念一流的學校，人生就能贏在起跑點是真的嗎？
- Bigger companies have a head start on the competition by running more ads.
  大公司登的廣告多，競爭上已先有優勢。
- He sent her there to give me a head start.
  他叫她去那裡，目的是為了讓我先走一步。

Write your own sentence:

- I'll try to have a head start on __________ by ______________________________.

13

have one's head in the clouds

頭在雲層裡，做白日夢，恍神

to be separate from reality; to be impractical or absent-minded

頭跑進雲裡，就表示思維離開地面，脫離了現實。這個慣用語除了形容某人滿腦子空想，也可形容某人心不在焉。用來表達「白日夢」的說法還有**cloud cuckoo land**（雲中杜鵑城）、**castle in Spain**（西班牙城堡）、**castles in the air**（空中城堡）。

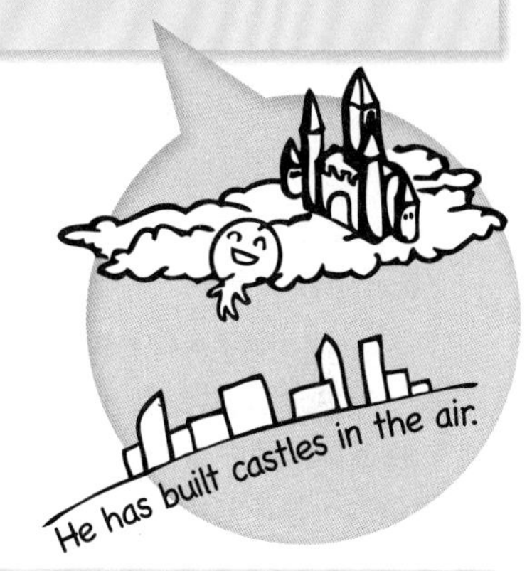

- He must **have his head in the clouds** if he thinks he is going to hit the jackpot.

  他在做夢吧，如果他真以為自己會中頭彩。

- He always **has his head in the clouds**. He never concentrates in class.

  他老是恍神，上課總是不專心。

- He walks around all day with his **head in the clouds**.

  他整天魂不守舍地走來走去。

Write your own sentence:

- I do believe I will ______________ but do I have my head in the clouds?

14

hit the nail on the head

敲在釘子的頭上，一針見血、一語中的

to do or say something exactly right

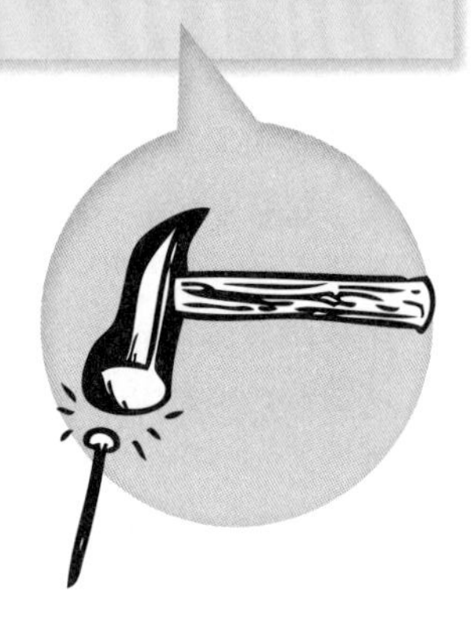

敲釘子若沒敲在釘子扁平的**head**上，不但會敲歪，還可能敲到自己的手。一旦敲在**head**上，那就表示**get to the precise point**: 說到重點、一語道破。把**nail**當動詞：**nail it on the head**也可以。要小心，這個慣用語與**hit home**不太一樣，**hit home**是指擊中要害，逼使某人面對不愉快的事，甚至產生明顯的效應。

- You have a way of always hitting the nail on the head.
  你總是有辦法說到事情的重點。
- You nailed it on the head about her. She is a high-maintenance princess.
  你說她說得對極了，她的確是個愛花錢、脾氣嬌的大小姐。
- His criticism of her appearance hit home; she decided to have plastic surgery.
  他對她外表的評語切中了要害；她決定去整型。

Write your own sentence:

- They said I hit the nail on the head when I mentioned that ________________.

15

hold one's head up high

高高抬著頭，已盡力而自豪、無愧於心

to show that one is proud and not ashamed of all the efforts

所謂抬頭挺胸，無愧天地，英雄無關乎成敗，重要的是盡全力打完人生每一場仗。反之若是做了虧心事，那就只能 **hang one's head**，頭低得不能再低，羞愧地恨不得鑽進地洞裡。另外還有一個慣用語也與抬頭有關：**a heads up**，抬起頭打個招呼，意指「事前照會或通知」。

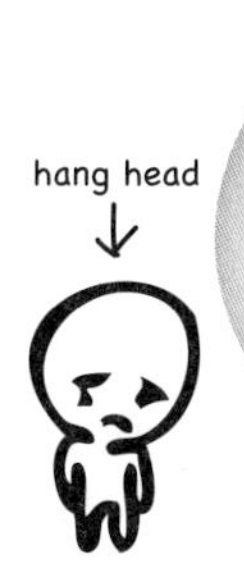

- He didn't win, but he can **hold his head up high** because he put up a great fight.

  雖然他輸了，但他無愧於心，因為他已打了一場美好的仗。

- The corrupt minister **hung his head** after being forced to step down.

  被迫下台後，這名貪腐的部長感到萬分羞慚。

- Make sure you **give me a heads up** if you decide to quit your job.

  如果你真決定要辭職，記得先跟我打聲招呼！

Write your own sentence:

- Although ______________, I can hold my head high because ______________.

16

keep one's head above water

讓頭保持在水面上，設法度過財務危機

to manage to survive financially and avoid succumbing to debt

游泳時，再能憋氣的人總還是得把頭伸出水面，一旦溺水，想盡辦法的也是不讓頭沈入水裡。讓頭保持在水面上，通常形容處在財務困境中的人，想方設法撐過去，不讓自己陷入債務的泥淖中。反之，若陷在深水中（**in deep water**），那就表示麻煩大了。

in deep water

- It's hard to keep your head above water when you don't have a regular job.

  沒有固定的工作，很難不舉債度日。

- He needs 1000 dollars this month to keep his head above water.

  他這個月需要一千元才過得了關。

- The firm is in deep water and may probably be shut down.

  這家公司有困難，說不定會停業。

Write your own sentence:

- All I can do to keep my head above water is ______________________________.

17

keep one's head

把頭保住，保持冷靜

to stay calm and retain self-control in awkward, difficult or dangerous situations

遇到問題，失去理智不但解決不了問題，還可能雪上加霜。把頭保住就表示保持住理性，不讓心火延燒，**keep a cool head**（讓頭冷卻下來）也是保持冷靜的意思。反之，**lose one's head**（失去了頭）或 **push the panic button**（啟動緊急按鈕，反應過度、驚慌失措），那就更難找出辦法解決問題了。

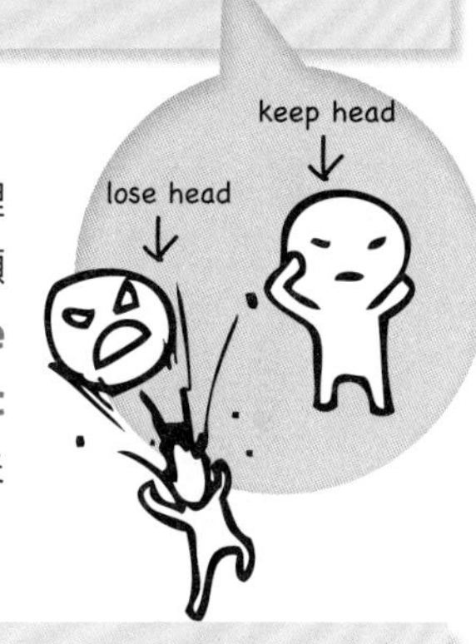

- Try to keep your head at times of pressure and stress.
  在壓力重重之時，千萬要穩住。

- When the boat capsizes, you should keep your head and hold on to the boat.
  翻船的時候，你要冷靜下來，牢牢抓住船。

- Whenever the stock market goes down sharply, people seem to lose their heads and sell.
  只要股市大跌，大家就好像亂了手腳，把股票賣了。

Write your own sentence:

- When ________________, I kept my head and tried to ________________________________.

18

knock … on the head

朝著…的頭敲下去，取消、停止原訂計畫或原本在做的事

to stop doing something

這個慣用語原本指把某人敲昏，一旦被敲昏的不是人而是事，意思就是中止了這件事的發展，使之無法如先前一樣進行。若是**knock…into one's head**（把…敲進某人頭裡），則意指想盡辦法讓某人記住或學會什麼。

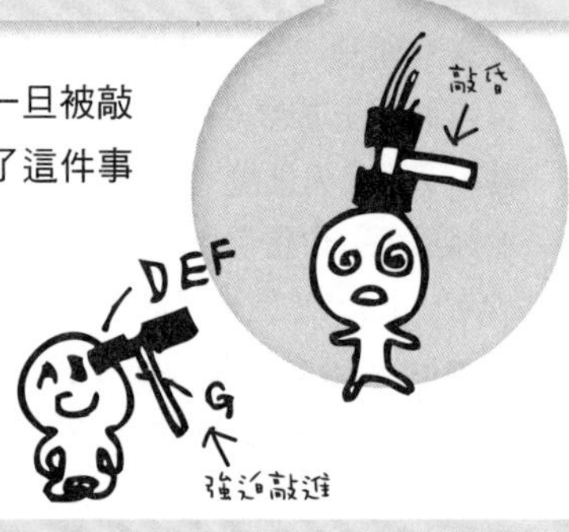

- Give me a reason why you refused my proposal and I'll knock it on the head.

  告訴我為什麼拒絕我的求婚，以後我不會再問。

- Do you still play the drums? No, I knocked that on the head a while ago.

  還有在打鼓嗎？沒，停了好一陣了。

- We can't seem to knock lessons into his head.

  我們用盡辦法就是沒法讓他記住課業的內容。

Write your own sentence:

- Give me a reason why ________________ and I'll knock it on the head.

laugh one's head off

笑到頭掉下來，狂笑不已，笑翻了

to laugh loudly and be unable to stop laughing

頭掉下來可不得了，在英文慣用語中，頭掉下來可以搭配不同的動詞，強調其強烈的程度，譬如把 **laugh** 換成 **cry**，就成了大哭不止，換成 **scream** 為尖叫不停，換成 **cough** 表示咳得很兇，換成 **eat** 表示食量驚人，換成 **lie** 表示臭蓋，換成 **talk** 表喋喋不休，換成 **work** 表示賣命工作。

- I laugh my head off whenever Bill starts telling jokes.
  只要比爾一開口說笑話，肯定讓我笑翻天。
- I had the flu. I coughed my head off for two days.
  我得了流行性感冒，慘咳了兩天。
- She ate her head off at the party.
  聚會時她拼命吃個不停。
- The girl beside me on the bus talked my head off during the whole ride.
  坐公車時坐我旁邊的女孩全程嘰喳說個不停。

Write your own sentence:

- ______________ was so funny that I almost laughed my head off.

20

can not make head or tail of …

看不出…是正面還是反面，看不懂，一頭霧水

to show that one can't understand something or someone at all

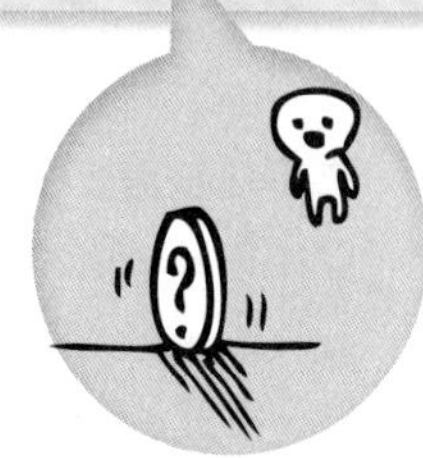

銅板正面一般都有頭像，**head** 便是指銅板的正面，**tail** 是反面。擲筊時，若看不出結果是正還是反，肯定一肚子問號、不知所措，這個慣用語表達的就是這種心情，類似台語說的「看尬霧煞煞」。不過如果有人跟你說：**Heads I win, tails you lose**（正面我贏、反面你輸），這可不是正反不分，而是表示無論如何都算他贏。**head or tail** 也可寫成 **heads or tails**；**or** 也可用 **nor**。

- People think John is a weirdo; they can't make head or tail of him.

  大家都覺得John是個怪人，沒人弄得懂他這個人。

- The way the document was worded was complicated. No one could make head or tail of it.

  這公文寫得好複雜，沒人看得懂它在寫什麼。

- The math problem that involves calculus is over my head. I can't make head or tail of it.

  這題微積分的數學太高深，我連看懂都有問題。

Write your own sentence:

- ______________________ is so difficult that I can't make head or tail of it.

21

on one's own head

算在某人頭上，由某人負責、承擔

to be at one's risk or responsibility

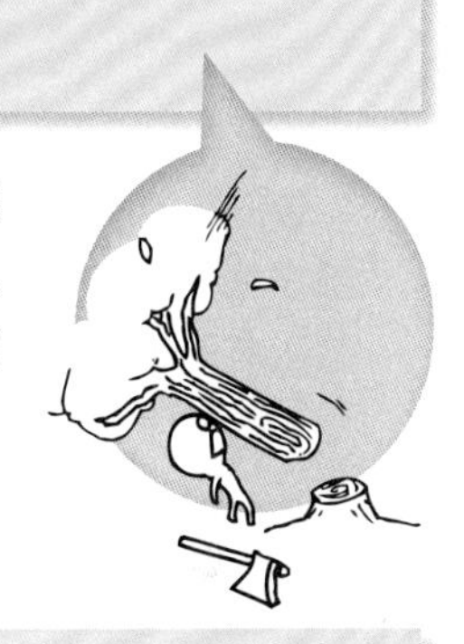

天若塌下，首當其衝的就是頭。落在某人頭上，便是指一切責任、過失、風險等皆得由此人擔負。有擔當的人，一般稱之為有肩膀的人，而 **shoulder**（肩膀）當動詞用時，正是意指承擔。若某人 **have broad shoulders**（有寬大的肩膀），即表示能肩負重任，為人有擔當。

- Your conduct is on your own head.

  你的行為你自己負責。

- If the police catch you speeding or drunk driving, it's on your own head.

  如果你被警方逮到超速或酒駕，你自己看著辦。

- If you want to go out clubbing the night before your mid-term exams, on your own head be it.

  如果你真想在期中考前晚去夜店，後果自行負責。

- The storekeeper was ready to shoulder the blame.

  店長願意承擔過失。

Write your own sentence:

- If ______________________, it's on my own head.

22

off the top of one's head

從頭頂略過，一時之間，無法多加思索

to speak something quickly without checking beforehand

僅僅與頭皮短暫接觸，當然無法深入腦部深處。這個慣用語主要表達一時間只能就眼前所想到、所知道的來回答或說明某事，無法仔細思考、仔細計算或預先考量研究。

- I don't know for sure, but off the top of my head I can give you a ballpark figure.

  我沒法確定，不過眼下我可以給你一個約略的數據。

- I can't tell you Mary's phone number off the top of my head. I'll have to check.

  一時間我沒法告訴你Mary的電話號碼，我得查了才知道。

- I didn't study last night, but today when the teacher called me to recite a poem, I did it off the top of my head. Amazing!

  我昨晚沒念書，可今天老師點我背詩，我居然不加思索背出來了，神奇！

Write your own sentence:

- I can't ______________________ off the top of my head.

23

put heads together

把頭靠在一起，一起商量（以解決問題）

to share ideas in order to solve a problem

這是個可愛的畫面，大家頭靠著頭，為共同的問題齊心協力、集思廣益，亦即所謂的 **Two heads are better than one.**（三個臭皮匠勝過一個諸葛亮）。但如果不是頭靠頭，而是 **scratch one's head**（搔頭），則表示心有困惑或不解的事。

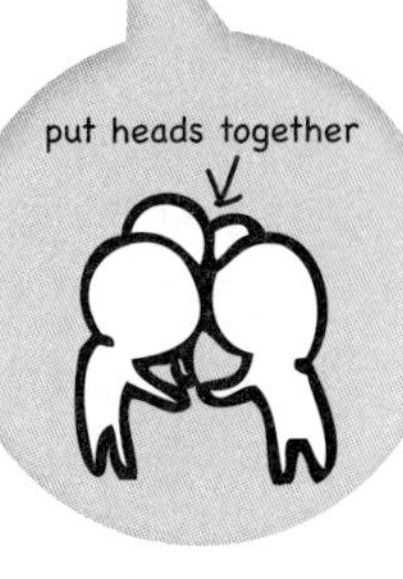

- Let's put our heads together and figure out a way to help them out of poverty.

  讓我們一起討論，找出辦法幫他們脫離貧困。

- They put their heads together and decided how the problem is to be tackled.

  他們合力商量，決定了這個問題的處理方式。

- They scratched their heads over this tough question; no one could come up with the answer.

  他們全拿這個棘手的問題沒輒，誰也想不出答案是什麼。

Write your own sentence:

- If we put our heads together, we can

  ______________________________.

24

put … out of one's head

把…從頭裡移出，斷念，試著忘掉

to stop thinking about someone or something; to manage to forget

只要記憶存在，就不可能忘記，要忘記，根除的方法當然是 **erase memories**（抹去記憶）或將記憶從頭裡移出去，當然，這並不是件容易的事。**put**的部份可換用**get**，**head**可換用**mind**。

- You had better put the idea of making a quick buck out of your head.

  你最好斷了念，別再想發橫財。

- Those starving children -- I can't get that image out of my head.

  那群饑餓的孩子——我忘不了那個畫面。

- He can't put the massacre out of his mind.

  他沒法忘卻那場大屠殺。

- He can't get his late wife out of his mind.

  他怎麼也忘不了他的亡妻。

Write your own sentence:

- I'll never put ________________________ out of my head.

brain 令人摸不著的腦

一九五五年，一名病理學家為了瞭解天才愛因斯坦的智力，竟然打開了愛因斯坦的**SKULL**（頭蓋骨），竊走了他的**BRAIN**進行解剖研究。五十多年來，科學家們發現這名天才的確擁有不同於一般人的**BRAIN**，可見得這個脆弱的器官，確實關係著人類的認知、記憶與才智。自然，談到「聰明」、「人才」就免不了用到**BRAIN**這個字，而**BRAIN+Y**成為形容詞，意思正是「聰明的」。

另外又如：**brainstorming**（頭腦風暴），意指「腦力激盪」；**brainchild**（腦生的小孩），意指「智慧結晶」。

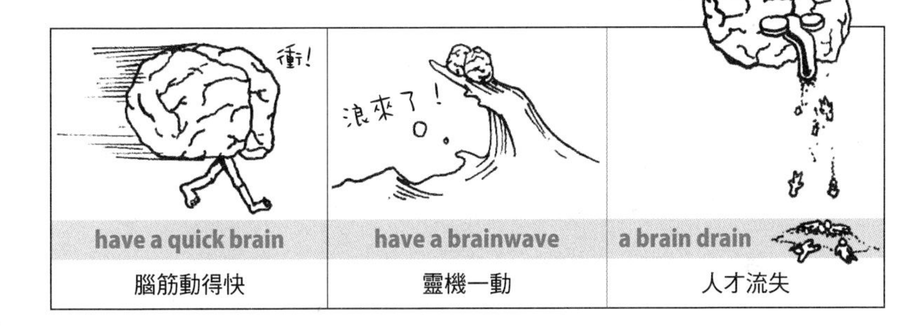

have a quick brain	have a brainwave	a brain drain
腦筋動得快	靈機一動	人才流失

雖然**BRAIN**擁有神秘的能量，但它十分脆弱，必須仰靠**SKULL**的保護，**SKULL**即頭骨，在**Jolly Roger**（海盜旗）上，經常都可見得這個象徵死亡的標誌。

skull and crossbones → 頭骨與交叉骨

話說**SKULL**雖然堅硬，但還是有其柔弱之處，此弱處即**SOFT SPOT**（囟[ㄒㄧㄣˋ]門），在新生兒的頭上最是明顯，一直到週歲前後才會閉合。因此**SOFT SPOT**不僅意指著頭頂上這一處曾經柔軟的囟門，也可用來表示一個人的弱點、罩門、致命傷。

1

be all brawn and no brains

一身肌肉沒有腦，四肢發達，頭腦簡單

to be physically strong but not very intelligent

brawn 意指結實的肌肉或肌力，換用可數名詞 **muscles**（肌肉）或 **sinews**（肌腱）也可以。許多人為了 **tone up bodies**（強化體質），每週定期 **work out at the gym**（上健身房鍛鍊），可見四肢發達其實也是一項長處。當然，如果能 **have brains and brawn**（既聰明又健壯），那就更完美了。

- I agree he has strong six pack abs but he is all brawn and no brains.

  我承認他的六塊腹肌很勇，但他實在是四肢發達頭腦簡單。

- A pork knuckle will do the job, so you have the brawn without the brains.

  找隻豬用腳都有辦法做，就說你只長身體不長腦子。

- What he lacks in brains, he makes up for it in brawn.

  他用體力彌補腦力的不足。

Write your own sentence:

- I agree he ______________________________, but he is all brawn and no brains.

2

blow one's brains out

炸出某人的腦，朝某人頭部開槍

to shoot someone in the head

blow 意指炸毀，此慣用語意指轟掉某人腦袋；但若炸的是自己的腦，便是所謂的舉槍自盡。其他幾種自殺方式的英文說法如下：**commit hara-kiri**（切腹）、**commit suicide by charcoal burning or taking poison**（燒炭或服毒自殺）、**drown oneself in the river**（投河自盡）、**hang oneself**（上吊）、**commit suicide by cutting one's own throat**（刎頸自盡）。

- He pulled out his revolver and blew her brains out.

  他掏出左輪手槍，朝她腦部開槍。

- After two unsuccessful suicide attempts, he finally blew his brains out.

  自殺兩次失敗後，他最終舉槍自盡。

- Be careful with that gun, or you will blow your brains out.

  小心那把槍，不然你可能會腦袋開花。

Write your own sentence:

- Blowing one's brains out is nothing but an act of ________________.

3

the brains behind …

…後面的腦，幕後策劃者，幕後推手

the person who plans or develops something successful

brain 代表智力，藏在後面的腦就表示在幕後出點子、統籌計畫的人，主要用於有做出成果的事，好事或犯罪都可用。**brains** 也可用 **mastermind**，**mastermind** 當名詞時，意指主謀或策劃人，當動詞時，則意指策劃或在幕後操縱。

- This film producer is the brains behind many of the top-grossing movies.

  這位電影製片是多部票房冠軍的幕後功臣。

- Someone very clever must be the brains behind such an organized group of thieves.

  這個盜竊集團組織精密，背後的主謀一定很聰明。

- The general masterminded the coup.

  這名將軍策動了這次政變。

Write your own sentence:

- ______________ must be the brains behind _____ __________________.

4

have a maggot in one's brain

腦中有蛆，腦中有揮之不去的怪念頭

to be obsessed with whims or strange ideas

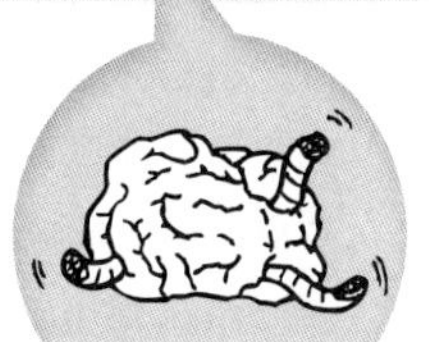

莫名其妙的恐懼、慾望、想像，常常令人不勝其擾，這些看似不重要卻纏繞不去的怪念頭，就像蛆跑進腦中蠕動一樣，讓人無處可逃。1971年一首經典的迷幻搖滾吉他曲就叫做"**maggot brain**"。近年來這個慣用語較少人用，取而代之的是**have a bee in one's bonnet**（帽子裡有蜜蜂）或**have a head full of bees**（頭裡滿是蜜蜂），表示某個念頭持續盤旋腦中，像蜜蜂般地嗡嗡嗡。

- They thought he had a maggot in his brain about the universe, but a lot of what he said has turned out to be true.
  大家都覺得他對宇宙的想法很怪，結果他說的話很多都證明是真的。
- He has a head full of bees about ghosts or spooks. He is always imagining strange noises.
  他老覺得有鬼還是幽靈什麼的；他一天到晚覺得聽到怪聲音。
- Mary has had a bee in her bonnet ever since she heard about the murder.
  Mary聽聞了這個謀殺案之後，腦子怎麼轉都是這件事。

Write your own sentence:

- Sometimes I have a maggot in my brain about ____
  ______________________________.

5

have … on the brain

…黏在腦子上，滿腦子都在想…，念念不忘…

to be very interested in something and keep thinking or talking about it

如果有什麼人事物黏在腦子上，那就表示這人或這事占據了思緒，使人成天想個不停。此處的**on the brain**也可用**on one's mind**，**brain**與**mind**都可用來表示人的心智。

- He has motorcycles on the brain and wouldn't talk something else for a change.
  他超迷重機，怎麼也不肯離開這個話題。
- He has nothing but hot girls on the brain. He is always boasting that he is a pickup artist.
  他滿腦子只有辣妹，一天到晚吹說自己是把妹高手。
- Lately she had food on her mind. That explains why she gained 5 pounds.
  她最近老想著吃，難怪重了五磅。

Write your own sentence:

- I have ____________ on the brain and I just can't stop ______________________.

overtax one's brains

對腦課稅過重，使腦負擔過重、使用過度

to make heavy demands on the brain

人人都希望稅要課的合理，腦也會希望腦力被用的合理。除了**overtax**（過度消耗）會傷腦，**brain**（當動詞用，意指朝腦部重擊）也會傷腦，另外還有**brainwash**（洗腦），強迫大腦接受某些宣傳、思想的沖刷清洗，使人失去原本的自我也一樣傷腦，這麼看來，也許洗腦的攻擊是最恐怖的呢。

- Psychologists claim that animations may overtax young brains.

  心理學家認為卡通可能會讓孩子用腦過度。

- TV commercials try hard to brainwash people into buying unnecessary luxuries.

  電視廣告想盡辦法給人們洗腦，讓大家去買不需要的奢侈品。

- I thought he was going to brain me, but he only hit me on the shoulder.

  我原以為他要扁我的頭，結果他只打我肩膀。

Write your own sentence:

- I suppose ______________________ may overtax my brains.

7

pick one's brains

採摘某人的腦，汲取某人智慧，向某人請教

to obtain information or advice from someone who knows a lot about a subject

pick通常指「摘」花「採」果，這會兒居然有人把腦當成花果**pick**？其實要採的並非頭殼裡那軟綿灰白的腦，而是腦中豐富的知識與智慧。所以如果有人問你，我可不可以採你的腦，別緊張，問你的人只是認為你在某方面很行，想徵詢你的看法。**pick**這個用手摘的動作，也可換成用口吸吮的**suck**。此慣用語若用於正面，為「請教、吸收」，用於負面則為「剽竊、拾人牙慧」。

- You can pick the brains of guys who have played against these teams before.

  你們可以去請教那些曾經打敗過這幾支隊伍的人。

- Do you mind if I pick your brains for ideas on what to see and do in Europe?

  我可以請教你，到歐洲該怎麼玩嗎？

- He is always picking the chef's brains for cooking tips.

  他老是盜用這名主廚的料理妙招。

Write your own sentence:

- I don't mind if you pick my brains about ______________ ______________________________.

8

rack one's brains

拷問某人的腦，絞盡腦汁，苦思

to try very hard to work out a problem or think of something

遇到問題、忘記事情，都得 **use brains**（動腦筋），萬一 **mind goes blank**（腦中一片空白），又或 **brain like a sieve**（腦子像篩子一樣），什麼都記不住，這時就得搬出刑具來了。**rack** 意指綁在刑架上施刑、拷問，**beat out**（敲打）也可，總之使腦子置之死地而後生，如此一來，就算是 **featherbrain**（呆瓜）或是 **scatterbrain**（糊塗蛋），絞一絞也是會有腦汁的！

- I've been racking my brains but I still can't remember who wrote the novel.

  我想了又想，就是想不起這本小說是誰寫的。

- The engineer racked his brains to find the bug.

  工程師為找出程式錯誤，可是絞盡了腦汁。

- He beat his brains out for a solution to the problem of water shortages.

  為了找出解決水荒的辦法，他簡直想破了頭。

Write your own sentence:

- I've been racking my brains trying to

  ____________________.

9

out of one's skull

沒了頭殼，醉茫茫，瘋了，腦子不正常

to be in a wandering state mentally because of the effects of alcohol or drugs; to be crazy

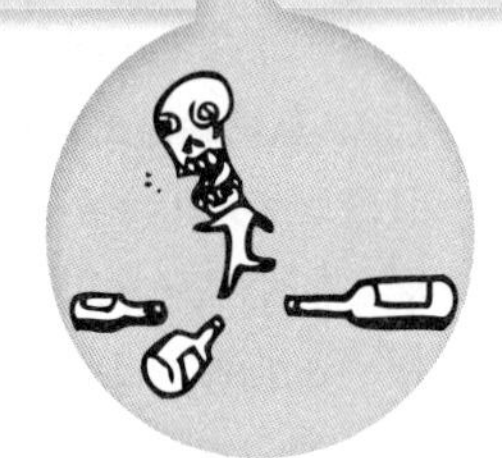

一如台語所說「頭殼壞了」，這個慣用語表示某人的行為或想法不合常理，又或形容喝了酒或嗑藥的人精神恍惚的狀態。沒了頭殼一般已到了爛醉如泥的程度，亦即**be plastered**／**be loaded**，半醉是**be half drunk**，微醉是**be tipsy**，**have a hangover**是有宿醉。但若是**bored out of one's skull**，則表示無聊到極點、無聊得要命。

- You must be out of your skull if you think I'll pay your debts.

  如果你以為我會幫你還債，那你八成是瘋了。

- He gulped down three glasses of beer and went right out of his skull.

  他一口氣喝下三杯啤酒，接著就醉得不省人事。

- He was bored out of his skull and wanted to return home.

  他無聊得要命，超想回家。

Write your own sentence:

- When I said ______________________, they thought I was out of my skull.

10

have a soft spot for…

有個專屬…的囟門（弱點），（不知為何）對…特別喜愛

to feel a lot of affection for someone or something, often without knowing why

都說人心是肉做的，再鐵石心腸（**hard-hearted**），也總會遇到使自己心軟的人事物，這就叫罩門、剋星。當我們對某人事物特別喜歡，喜歡得莫名其妙、全無招架之力，就可以用上這個慣用語，因為這就像嬰兒頭骨上有一處軟軟的囟門，只要頭骨一天沒閉合，那裡永遠是嬰兒最脆弱的地方。

- She has a soft spot for Jim, even though he always stands her up and teases her.

  雖然Jim常放她鴿子又愛戲弄她，她就是喜歡他。

- She has a soft spot for animals. She is a vegetarian and takes care of many stray dogs.

  她特別喜歡動物，她吃素，並且照顧很多流浪狗。

- Grandpa has a soft spot for my brother, his first grandson.

  阿公最疼我哥、他的長孫。

Write your own sentence:

- I have a soft spot for ___________, although ______

  ____.

hair 牽一而動全身的髮

自古以來，**HAIR**一直是人類用來區分性別、年齡、地位的方式之一。過去，男女各有各的髮型（**hairstyle**），女性甚至必須結辮或髮髻（**wear hair in a braid or bun**）才能外出，如果一頭蓬鬆亂髮（**disheveled hair**）被人看到，那是很失禮、丟臉的。

雖然到了現代再無過去種種約束，就連學校的髮禁（**hair regulations**）也都解除，但現代人依然藉由**HAIR**來表現自我，染髮（**dye**）、燙髮（**perm**）、做髮型（**set**），透過**HAIR**展現個性與心情。

說來奇妙，**HAIR**纖細又沒有神經，但只須隨手一扯卻可令人痛不欲生；而且人類的**HAIR**還會增生變質，一旦整理不好，再美的容顏也必然失色，難怪英文會以**a bad hair day**來形容倒楣、不順利的一天。

	**I think it would be a bad hair day.** 我想今天不太妙。

其實**HAIR**除了意指頭髮，也表示身上的「毛」。如：

hair-raising → 令人毛骨悚然的

a hairy chest → 毛茸茸的胸

既然毛髮會增減、會變質，於是**hair loss**（掉髮）、**baldness**（禿頭）、**gray hair**（白頭髮）種種問題無一不令人煩惱，難怪入空門第一個條件就是斬斷這三千煩惱絲：**tonsure**（剃度），一旦與**HAIR**說再見，往後就再也不必想方設法地生髮（**grow hair**）、洗髮（**shampoo**）、梳髮（**comb**）、修剪（**trim**）、剃毛（**shave**）、除毛（**wax or epilate**），倒是寒流來時別忘了**wear a scarf**包條頭巾保暖才是。

MEMO

1

by a hair

毫髮之差，差一點

by a very small distance; barely; very narrowly

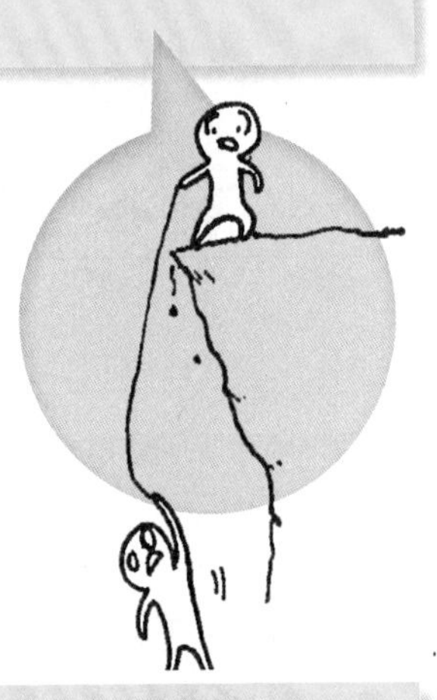

只差一根頭髮的距離，那真的是微乎其微。然而人生的得失往往就在一線（**a hair**）之間，過了關，任誰都會忍不住大呼 **That was a close call!**（好險！），但沒過關也別失意，就瀟灑地唱披頭四的 **Let it be**（順其自然）吧！同義的慣用語還有 **by the skin of one's teeth**（只差牙齒上的那層皮）／**by a whisker**（一鬚之差）。

- I got to the airport a few minutes late and missed the plane by a hair.
  我晚了幾分鐘到機場，以些微之差錯過飛機。
- He made it onto the last flight by the skin of his teeth.
  他勉強搭上最後一班飛機。
- They escaped by a whisker.
  他們差點就逃不成了。

Write your own sentence:

- I just ______________________________ by a hair.

2

get in one's hair

弄亂某人頭髮，煩擾某人

to annoy or bother someone

把手伸進別人的頭髮玩人家的頭髮，這真的是很討人厭的行為；又或是有不明物體跑進頭髮，再專心的人恐怕也會覺得不勝其擾。所以如果有人 **get in your hair**（弄得你很煩），你可以反過來告訴他：**Get out of my hair!**（別煩我！）。

- The dog barking every night is really getting in my hair.

  這隻每天晚上叫個不停的狗弄得我快煩死了。

- I wish you wouldn't get in my hair when I am dressing for the party.

  在我為參加宴會打扮穿衣時，我希望你沒事別來煩我。

- He keeps getting in my hair, always eating my food and making noises.

  他老是惹我，每次都吃我的東西，發出很吵的聲音。

Write your own sentence:

- ______________ is really getting in my hair and I'm going to ________________________________.

3

harm a hair on one's head

損傷某人一根汗毛，使某人有絲毫傷害

to hurt someone; to do harm to someone

harm 意指嚴重的損害。這個慣用語與中文一樣，皆以誇張的方式強調，只要碰到一根毛就算傷害，那麼如果有人說 **not harm a hair on one's head**，就表示不許有一點差池，連一點小傷都不許出現。其實傷害就像一個圓，最好不要有開頭，否則就會 **Harm set, harm get.** 害人終害己。

- If the kidnapper harms a hair on my daughter's head, I won't spare his life.

  如果綁匪敢動我女兒一根汗毛，我絕不饒他。

- Even if she came from the tribe that had a feud with him, he wouldn't harm a hair on her head.

  縱然她出身的部族與他有世仇，他也絕不會碰她一根汗毛。

- Harm one hair on my girl's head, and I'll carve you up into pieces.

  你敢傷害我女兒一根頭髮，我就把你剁成碎片。

Write your own sentence:

- If __________ harms a hair on my head, I will __________________________.

4

keep one's hair on

讓頭髮好好貼在頭上，沈住氣，別激動

to stay calm and not to over-react; not to get angry or emotional

雖說生氣時頭髮並不真會亂飛，但火氣一來，頭髮還真得好像就要衝起來拚命似地。這個慣用語提醒了我們，遇有爭執或問題，不要怒髮衝冠，不要情緒化，保持平常心，頭髮自然乖乖平貼。

同義的慣用語還有**keep one's shirt／pants／wigs on**，都是提醒大家，別被火氣牽著跑，莫名其妙就把襯衫長褲扒下來、或是把頭上的假髮摘了。

- It is an easy problem to fix. Keep your hair on!
  這問題很容易解決，冷靜點。
- Tell him to keep his hair on until we're all set.
  叫他耐心等到我們全準備好為止。
- Keep your shirt on! They'll be here in time for the funeral.
  別動氣，他們會準時參加葬禮的。

Write your own sentence:

- They ______________________________ but I kept my hair on.

5

let one's hair down

把頭髮放下來，放鬆做自己，不拘禮數

to completely relax and enjoy oneself freely; to behave uninhibitedly

過去，西方女子外出應酬都必須把頭髮盤起來（**put up hair**）或結辮（**braid hair**），直到晚上回家，才一根根拔出髮針（**hairpin**），放下頭髮，享受這舒服、輕鬆的一刻，再不必拘泥於世俗禮儀或世俗的眼光。這個慣用語主要用來形容身心全然放鬆的心情，不只用於女生，也可用於男生。

- Let your hair down and just have some fun.
  放輕鬆，開心玩就是了。

- Let your hair down and tell me what you really think.
  別再ㄍㄧㄥ了，告訴我你真正的想法。

- He seldom gets a chance to let his hair down and go a bit wild.
  他沒什麼機會放鬆自己、狂野一下。

Write your own sentence:

- It is nice to let my hair down once in a while and ______________________.

6

make one's hair curl

嚇得某人頭髮捲起來，令某人心驚膽顫

to frighten or shock someone with sight, sound, thought, or taste, etc.

恐懼無所不在，想到颱風、地震會怕，聞到怪味會怕，就連自願聽的故事、看的電影也讓自己怕得要命。中文常以毛毛的、頭皮發麻表達害怕的心情，英文則是怕到頭髮嚇成了QQ捲。寫成 **curl one's hair** 意思也一樣，同義的慣用語還有 **make one's hair stand on end**，恰與中文的「汗毛直豎」不謀而合。

- Any kind of siren makes my hair curl.

  不管哪一種警報聲，都會讓我頭皮發麻。

- Don't ever sneak up on me like that again. You really curled my hair.

  別再那樣偷偷靠近我，你真的快把我嚇死了。

- The horror film made my hair stand on end.

  這部恐怖片看得我汗毛直豎。

Write your own sentence:

- The scene where ______________________________ usually makes my hair curl.

7

neither hide nor hair

沒皮也沒毛，蹤影全無，連個影兒都沒有

no sigh or indication of someone or something

此處 **hide** 是名詞，意指「大型動物的皮」。如果沒見著皮，那又怎可能見得著附在皮上的毛。這個慣用語通常與否定詞（**none**／**not**／**neither** 等）搭配使用，表示毫無蛛絲馬跡可言，沒有任何蹤影或下落。

- None of his coworkers have heard hide nor hair of him since he retired last May.

  打從去年五月他退休後，他同事就再沒人有他消息。

- We don't know where he is. We haven't seen hide nor hair of him for months.

  我們不知道他在哪裡，好幾個月沒見著他的人影了。

- A button fell off my coat and I could find neither hide nor hair of it.

  我大衣掉了顆扣子，怎麼找都找不著。

Write your own sentence:

- ______________________ and I could find neither hide nor hair.

8

not a hair out of place

都在適當的位置，儀容整潔得一絲不苟

very tidy and immaculate

此處**hair**類似中文的絲毫，**not a hair**意為絲毫沒有，**out of place**意指不在適當的位置、不合適、不恰當，所以照字面解釋，**not a hair out of place**便是「絲毫沒有不當之處」。這個慣用語主要形容人的外表或儀容非常乾淨整齊、絲毫沒有可挑剔的地方。

- No matter what she is doing, she is ever neat, **not a hair out of place.**

  不論她在做什麼，她總是那麼整齊乾淨一絲不苟。

- As a socialite lady, she is as immaculate as ever, **not a hair out of place.**

  身為社交名媛，她一如以往，一身打扮完美無瑕。

- Surprisingly, the FBI agent came in out of the storm **without a hair out of place.**

  好奇怪，外面在刮暴風，這名FBI探員進來時竟一身整齊。

Write your own sentence:

- A person who usually emerges without a hair out of place must be a ________.

9

not turn a hair

連毛都沒動一根，不動聲色，面不改色

to show no surprise, anger, fear or dismay when something bad happens

此慣用語源於賽馬，若有馬匹在激烈比賽之後，一身的毛動都沒動一根，那姿態肯定從容淡定。它通常用來形容某人面對不好或意外的事情，沈著冷靜不疾不徐，一如刮骨療毒的關公，氣定神閒、泰然自若。同義的慣用語還有：**not bat an eye／eyelid／eyelash**（連眼睛／眼皮／睫毛都沒眨一下）。

- The manager didn't turn a hair during the bank robbery.

  經理在銀行發生搶案時，面不改色十分鎮靜。

- I was expecting him to be furious when he heard the cost but he didn't turn a hair.

  我本來以為他聽到這筆費用會生氣，結果他什麼反應也沒有。

- Mom didn't bat an eye when I told her I was getting married.

  我跟媽說我要結婚時，她超淡定的。

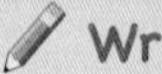 Write your own sentence:

- I didn't turn a hair during ____________________.

10

put hair on one's chest

讓某人胸口長毛，使人勇健有活力，使有男子漢的氣魄

to invigorate or energize someone; to make someone strong and masculine

西方一般都以胸毛（**chest hair**）為男人性感勇猛的象徵，也因此有了這個有趣的慣用語。若有什麼飲料或食物能讓人胸口長毛，那就表示它們具有刺激性，能提振精神與大腦。另外這個慣用語也可用來開玩笑，主要用在男性身上，表示讓男人更有男子氣概。

- Have a swig of this! It will put hair on your chest!
  大口痛飲吧！這會讓你精神百倍活力旺！
- The coffee was so strong that it could put hair on my chest.
  這咖啡好濃，喝得我整個人亢奮起來！
- This is the real soup guaranteed to put hair on your chest.
  喝了這湯保證你馬上雄糾糾氣昂昂！

Write your own sentence:

- ________________ was so strong that it could put hair on my chest.

11

pull one's hair out

拔頭髮，煩躁焦慮

to be greatly anxious, angry, distressed, or upset

抓頭髮是煩的經典動作，若有人因某事而猛拔頭髮，就表示這事令他心情焦躁、痛苦不堪。這令人想到「抓狂」一詞，情緒惡劣時會不自覺抓拔頭髮，不知是否潛意識裡是想抓住這狂的來源：腦。**pull** 也可換用 **tear**（拉扯撕裂）來表達。

- Talking to him made me pull my hair out! He is totally self-centered.

  跟他說話讓我氣到不行！他太自我中心了。

- I have been pulling my hair out to finish the proposal on time.

  為了及時完成這份企劃書，我快把頭髮抓光了。

- Yesterday when my son still wasn't home by midnight, I was tearing my hair out.

  昨天快十二點了兒子都還沒回家，我簡直快急死了。

Write your own sentence:

- ______________________ made me pull my hair out.

split hairs

切分頭髮，做不必要的細瑣分析，鑽牛角尖

to argue over small details or make trivial distinctions between things that are essentially the same

split意指劈開，倘若劈開的目標是一根根纖細的頭髮，想必會累死人。因此把力氣集中在細微又不重要的瑣事上，明明差不多的事物非要分出個東西南北，這種行為就是**split hairs**。把**split hairs**轉成形容詞**hair-splitting**，意思便是「拘泥於細節的、吹毛求疵的」。

- Could you just stop splitting hairs on things like whose name comes first on the poster?

  可不可以別再為海報上誰排名在首位這種小事囉哩八索？

- Arguing about which ring is set with the most jewels is just splitting hairs.

  連哪枚戒指鑲的寶石最多也要計較，真是雞蛋裡挑骨頭、無聊沒事做。

- No splitting hairs! Accept it the way it is.

  不許多生枝節，事情說定這樣就這樣。

Write your own sentence:

- I (don't) think ______________ is just splitting hairs.

face 面向前方、代表面子的臉

所謂相由心生，**FACE**展現的不只是容貌，它更透露了內心的喜怒哀樂、正邪善惡。根本說來，**FACE**其實是自我的表徵。因此，如果某人**blue in the face**（臉色發青），表示此人正在氣頭上，若是**red-faced**（臉紅紅的），則表示尷尬或害羞。其他又如：

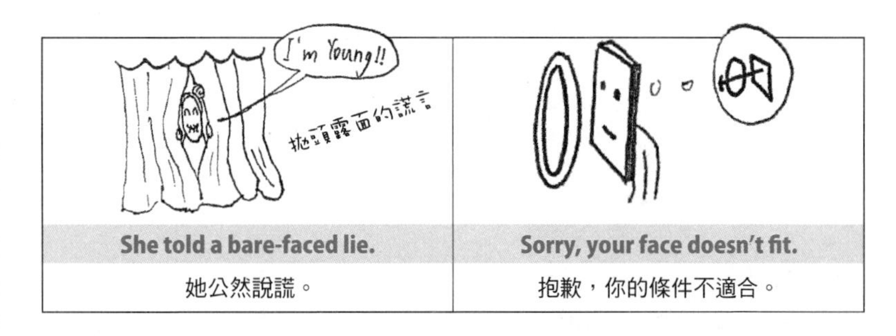

She told a bare-faced lie.	**Sorry, your face doesn't fit.**
她公然說謊。	抱歉，你的條件不適合。

又由於**FACE**長在前方，它等於是人們與世界接軌的門面，直接呈現了人們面對世界的方式。因此，當一個人**show face**（露臉），就表示現身於人群。其他又如：

face to face with a bear	**have a face-off**
與一隻熊面對面	正面對決

除了意指長在頭前的面孔，**FACE**也表示物品的表面或外觀，或當動詞使用，意指「面向，面對」。如：

the face of a building → 建物的正面

Let's face it—you had a face-lift, but you still look old.
→ 面對現實吧—你有去拉皮，但看起來還是老。

FACE的容顏除了取決於**features**（五官），由**plastic surgery**（整型手術）常見的**cheek implant**（豐頰）、**chin implant**（墊下巴）、**cheekbone reduction**（削顴骨）、**jaw reduction**（削顎骨）可知，**cheek**（臉頰）、**chin**（下巴）以及**jaw**（顎）也與面容密切相關。

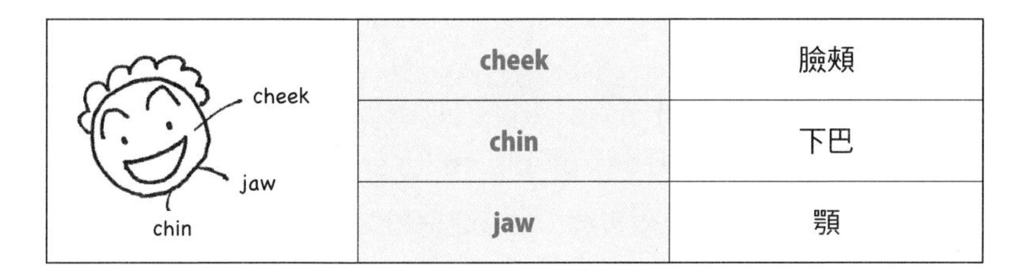

cheek	臉頰
chin	下巴
jaw	顎

與**cheek**／**chin**／**jaw**有關的慣用語將會在**FACE**這個單元一併介紹，至於**FACE**的其他五官，則將另闢單元說明。

1

a slap in the face

一記耳光打在臉上，給人難堪

an action that insults or discourages someone

臉代表面子、尊嚴，打手打腳就是不能隨便打臉。一旦打在臉上，那不只熱辣辣地痛，還會讓人顏面盡失，產生極不愉快、不舒服的情緒。這個慣用語原意為「一記耳光」，由於臉的象徵意義，「一記耳光」便被用來比喻各種帶給人傷害、侮辱、挫折、難堪等的事件或行為。

- He considered it a real slap in the face when he was blamed in front of his children.

  在自己孩子面前受到責罵，他感覺很糟糕。

- Losing the election was a slap in the face for the political party.

  輸掉這場選舉對這個政黨而言無疑是一記耳光。

- His decision to assign the patent was a slap in the face to those who had fully supported him.

  他決定讓渡這項專利，這令曾經全力支持他的人十分受傷。

Write your own sentence:

- ___________ was a real slap in the face to those who ___________________________.

2

cut off one's nose to spite one's face

切下鼻子害自己破相，一時氣不過反給自己找罪受

to hurt oneself in an attempt to punish someone else or show one's anger

為了出氣而切下自己的鼻子，弄花自己的臉，這聽起來似乎不可思議，但人在憤怒的時候，本來就很容易做出傻事，而這傻事的受害者往往正是自己。這個慣用語主要用來形容生氣的人想要出氣，反倒把氣出到了自己頭上，最後誰都沒受害，唯獨生氣的人跟自己過不去，白白傷害了自己。

- If you drop out of school because you want to make your teacher angry, you are cutting off your nose to spite your face.

  你若為了氣老師而退學，到頭來受害的是你自己。

- You would rather stay home and go hungry just because your ex-wife will be at the party? Isn't that like cutting off your nose to spite your face?

  因你前妻也參加聚會你就寧願在家挨餓，這不是跟自己過不去嗎？

Write your own sentence:

- If ______________________________,
  you are cutting off your nose to spite your face.

face

3

do an about-face

突然將臉向後轉，徹底改變想法或立場，大翻盤

to make a sudden and complete change of one's ideas, plans or positions

about-face 是軍隊裡的用語，當士兵聽到 **about-face**，就必須一個轉步，整個人轉向後方。因此 **do an about-face** 可意指行走時突然改變方向，也可形容人徹底改變了原來的立場或想法，同義的慣用語還有 **do a flip-flop**（大反轉）或 **do a one-eighty**（一百八十度大轉彎）。

- He did a quick about-face because he had forgotten to lock the door.

  他火速轉身往回走，因為他忘了鎖門。

- The witness did an about-face and gave testimony against his friend.

  這名證人大翻供，做出了不利他朋友的證詞。

- We expected him to vote for the maverick, but he did a flip-flop and cast his vote for the incumbent.

  我們本以為他會投這名獨立參選人，結果他突然改變，把票投給了現任者。

Write your own sentence:

- I did an about-face because ______________________

  ______________________________________.

4

face the music

面對音樂，承擔一切後果，好漢做事好漢當

to accept the unpleasant consequences of one's actions

這個慣用語的典故說法多種，其中一種出自某軍規：犯錯的軍人必須在鼓隊的擊樂聲中聆聽別人大聲念出自己的犯行，一邊 **face the music**，一邊面對所犯錯誤接受處罰。類似的慣用語還有 **take one's medicine**（再苦的藥也得吞下去），再糟的後果都要接受，誰教自己做了不該做的事。

- It's time for us to stand up and face the music for our bold moves.

  我們該站出來，面對我們魯莽的行徑所造成的後果了。

- The prime suspect in the murder case chose to run away rather than face the music.

  這名兇殺案的主嫌寧願逃亡，也不願出面認罪。

- He failed the test, so he had to take his medicine and went to summer school.

  他考試沒過，只好認了，去上暑修。

Write your own sentence:

- It's time for me to face the music for ______________

  ____.

5

fall flat on one's face

面朝下倒下，跌了個狗吃屎，一敗塗地

to fail completely

跌倒已經很慘了，居然還一整張臉撞在地上，弄得鼻青臉腫整個破相，於是這個原意為「臉朝下直直倒下」的慣用語，就被延伸用來形容事情做不到預想的效果或甚至敗得很慘，猶如走路時栽了個大跟頭似的，弄得一身灰頭土臉。

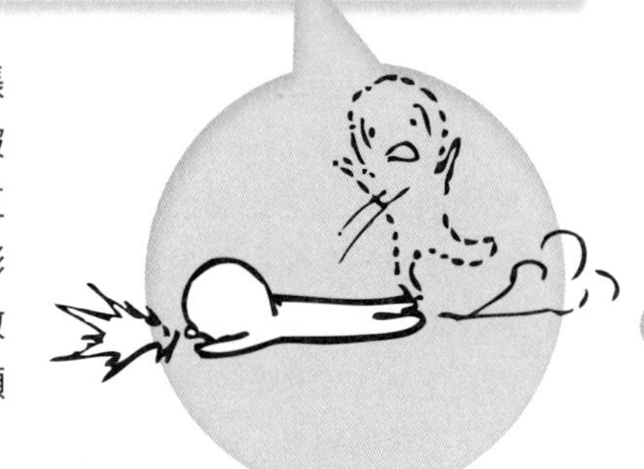

- The newscaster fell flat on his face as he got out of the car.

  這名新聞播報員一下車便跌了個狗吃屎。

- You want me to host a talk show? What if I fall flat on my face?

  你要我主持脫口秀？萬一我臨場出狀況怎麼辦？

- It used to be an amazing restaurant, but it has fallen flat on its face.

  這家餐廳以前很讚的，現在整個不行了。

Write your own sentence:

- I fell flat on my face as soon as I ______________________________.

6

have egg on one's face

臉上有蛋，當眾出醜，狼狽不堪

to be embarrassed by something one has done

吃蛋時，如果一口下去大爆漿，噴得滿臉蛋汁，這時肯定超尷尬；更糟的是，如果被人直接朝臉上丟雞蛋，那種場面肯定窘到不行。如果因為做錯事或說錯話以致於出糗、出洋相、搞得自己十分窘迫，那便是「臉上有蛋」。

- I wanted this dinner to be my treat but I had egg on my face when I found I was out of money.

  我本來想說晚餐由我請，結果發現自己身上根本沒錢，好糗。

- You'll be the one who has egg on your face if it goes wrong.

  事情若出了差錯，出糗的可是你哦。

- He boasted he could do fifty push-ups, but he ended up with egg on his face because he gave up after doing just ten.

  他吹牛說可以做五十個伏地挺身，結果糗大了，才做十下就不行了。

Write your own sentence:

- I have egg on my face in telling you that ________

  ____.

7

keep a straight face

讓臉保持直又長，板著面孔，忍住不笑

to look serious and not laugh, although one is in a funny situation

笑的時候臉會左右擴張，若把臉拉得筆直，就表示刻意不讓自己笑出來，即使心裡想笑。但不知**keep a straight face**是否會比較容易**pass the straight face test**（通過測謊）。又由於玩撲克牌時不宜透露任何情緒，所以**keep a poker face**就表示沒有表情，即使看似笑，也是皮笑肉不笑。

- He can never play jokes on people because he can't keep a straight face.
  他作弄不了別人，因為他會忍不住笑出來。
- He is so funny. It is hard to keep a straight face when I am talking to him.
  他這人很滑稽，跟他說話時很難一本正經不笑出來。
- He kept a poker face during police questioning.
  警方偵訊時，他始終面無表情。

Write your own sentence:

- I managed to keep a straight face when ____________
  ____.

8

lose face

丟臉，失去誠信

to be humiliated or come to be less highly respected

當人失去尊嚴、聲譽、無法得到別人的敬重，這就表示臉面盡失，已不只「臉上有蛋」而已了。不過既然有**lost and found**（失物招領），好運的話，失去的臉或有機會挽救，倘若**save face**，那就表示挽回了面子、保全了聲譽，沒有丟人現眼。

- He is more afraid of losing face than losing money.
  他不怕丟錢，倒怕丟臉。
- Can you explain to people where he was wrong without making him lose face?
  你能否讓大家知道他錯在哪裡，同時也保住他的面子？
- The minister is more interested in saving face than telling the truth.
  這名部長只顧保全面子，不肯說出實情。

Write your own sentence:

- I'll never ______________________ because to do so would be to lose face.

9

make a face

製造表情，扮鬼臉，做出不悅的表情

to show a funny expression in ridicule; to show an unpleasant expression

會去做表情，通常是有特別的心情。**make a face**表示開玩笑扮鬼臉，也表示想到、看到不愉快的人事物而面露不悅。同義的還有**pull a face**，把臉拉出某種表情。如果拉出了張 **long face**，便是又臭又長的苦臉，一旦長過頭，就會變成**a face as long as a fiddle**（足以跟小提琴相比的長臉）。

- The naughty children made faces behind his back.
  頑皮的小孩在他背後扮鬼臉。
- He made a face at the sight of the pile of work.
  一看到堆積如山的工作，他做了個表情。
- Why the long face? Don't talk to me with a face as long as a fiddle.
  幹嘛愁眉苦臉的？別這樣拉長了臉跟我說話。

Write your own sentence:

- I made a face at the taste of ____________________
  ____.

10

on the face of it

由表面來看

on the surface; from the way it looks

臉是一層表皮，撕開後又是另一回事。**on**表示在…的表面，**in**表示在…之中，請小心分別：**in the face of** …意指「在面臨…的情況下」，如：**in the face of danger**（面臨危險時）、**in the face of Capitalism**（面對資本主義時），而**fly in the face of** …（面對…時直接飛越），則意指公然違逆、完全不顧既定、公認或傳統的事物。

- On the face of it, the package tour seems cheap, but there could be extra expenses we don't know about yet.

  表面上看，這趟跟團旅行好像很便宜，但搞不好還有其他我們不知道的費用。

- On the face of it, he seems to be telling the truth, but I suspect he's hiding something.

  表面上看，他說的似是實話，但我懷疑他另有隱情。

- His decision flew in the face of our previous advice.

  他全然不管我們之前的忠告就做下決定。

Write your own sentence:

- On the face of it, ________________, but I doubt ____.

put on a brave face

擺出勇敢的面孔，裝出無所謂、輕鬆樂觀的樣子，強顏歡笑

to act as if something unpleasant is not as bad as it really is

put on one's makeup（上妝）= **put on one's face**，而**put on a brave face**則是另類的化妝，意指一種掩飾（**cover-up**），表示面對挫折、痛苦時，因為不想被人看出內心的脆弱或擔憂而努力讓自己看起來輕鬆自在。**put on**也有人簡化為**put**，**brave**也可用**good**或**bold**。

- He put on a brave face when he went to the dentist, but we all know he was scared.

  他去看牙齒時若無其事似的，但我們都知道他怕得要死。

- He seems all right but I doubt he is just putting on a brave face.

  他看上去沒事，但我懷疑他只是強打精神。

- He tried to put a bold face on his failure.

  他對自己的失敗裝出一副滿不在乎的樣子。

Write your own sentence:

- I put on a brave face when ________________, but actually ______________________________.

set one's face against…

把臉背向…，抵制…，堅決反對…

to oppose; to resist with determination

against表示與…逆向，如：**against the wind**（逆風），所以**set one's face against**（把臉轉開、背向）這個動作十分明顯表達出了它的意思：強烈、堅決地反對。

- If he has once set his face against a thing, nothing will change his mind.

  一旦他反對一件事，就不可能改變主意了。

- Despite fierce competition from rival companies, he set his face against price cuts.

  儘管對手公司競爭激烈，他堅決反對以削價因應。

- His mother set her face against his marrying for money.

  他母親強烈反對他為錢而婚。

Write your own sentence:

- I set my face against ____________ because ______________________________________.

13

stuff one's face

塞了滿臉，大吃特吃，狼吞虎嚥

to eat greedily; to overeat

stuff 意指填塞，吃東西如果吃到連臉都被食物塞爆，可見吃進去的量有多驚人，**stuff** 也可用 **feed**。另有兩個同義的慣用語都與豬有關：**make a pig of oneself**（讓自己像豬一樣吃得很多）以及 **pig out**（像豬一樣地狂吃）。

- When he comes home, he is apt to watch TV and stuff his face with potato chips.

  每次一回到家，他就要看電視、大嚼洋芋片。

- I really made a pig of myself at the buffet and now feel very sick.

  我在buffet吃得好撐，現在超不舒服。

- The kids pigged out on the candy they had collected on Halloween.

  孩子們狂吃萬聖節收到的糖果。

Write your own sentence:

- I am apt to stuff my face with __________ before __________________________.

throw … back in one's face

當某人的面將…往後丟，粗魯地回絕

to refuse to accept one's advice or help in a brusque way

別人好意的贈予不接受就算了，還當著人家的面把東西往後一扔，這個慣用語主要表示一個人毫不客氣地拒絕別人的好意或建議。另有一個慣用語意思類似但稍有不同：**slam the door in one's face**（當著…的面大力把門關上），意指讓人吃閉門羹、拒人於門外、將機會從某人手中收回。

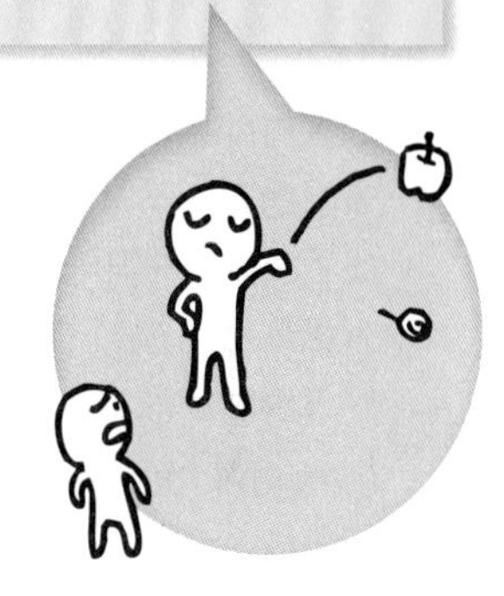

- When I gave John my suggestion, he threw it back in my face and said, "Rubbish!"

  我提建議給John，他不但不理，還說「垃圾」。

- I have given her my trust and she has thrown it back in my face.

  我對她付出了信任，結果她卻不當回事地踐踏了我的信任。

- We slammed the door in John's face since he was so rude when we interviewed him.

  我們不會給John任何機會，因為面試時他太沒禮貌了。

Write your own sentence:

- He threw my compliments back in my face. Nevertheless I ______________________.

face

15

two faces under one hood

一頂頭巾兩張臉，口是心非，虛偽雙面人

to be hypocritical and deceitful

羅馬神話的天門神**Janus**有兩張臉，一張看過去、一張看未來，於是**Janus**化身成了跨年後的第一個月**January**，而祂的兩張臉則被用來形容陽奉陰違、表裡不一，好玩兩面手法的人。類似的**run with the hare and hunt with the hounds**（一邊跟野兔逃、一邊又跟獵犬追），則形容試圖討好對立的兩邊、兩邊都支持的兩頭蛇，即所謂「放火的喊救火、打人的喊救人」。**two-faced**為形容詞，意為「雙面的，虛偽的」。

- Beware of him. He has two faces under one hood.

  當心他這個人，他這個人心口不一。

- He is totally two-faced because he is nice to your face, but says bad things about you behind your back.

  他是個不折不扣的雙面人，在你面前對你好，在你背後卻說你壞話。

Write your own sentence:

- A two-faced creep can't be trusted because ____________________.

take … at face value

依據面值接受…，只看表面就相信…

to accept and believe something or someone just as it appears

face value是指鈔票錢幣的面值，偷來的千元鈔票，與做了一天苦工的百元鈔票，究竟哪一個有價值？這個慣用語極有深意，它提醒人們不要僅以面值為唯一參考值來判斷世事，讀書考試也是一樣，分數只是表面的數值，別忘了求知的熱情與認真的態度也很重要。

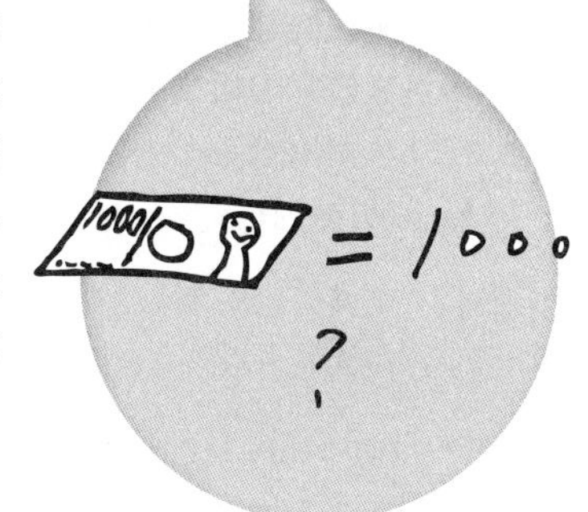

- You can't take gossip at its face value.

  別把八卦新聞當真，聽聽就好。

- You shouldn't take his promise at face value because he was just joking.

  你不該把他的承諾當真，他只是開玩笑而已。

- I take everything he says at face value because he means what he says.

  他說的話我都信，因為他一向說話算話。

Write your own sentence:

- I won't take ____________ at face value because ________________________.

cheek by jowl

臉頰挨著頷骨，緊靠在一起

to be very close together; side by side

jowl 是臉頰 **cheek** 下方的頷骨，任何人事物若像頰挨著頷那樣，就表示它們緊密相靠。這個慣用語源自莎翁的「仲夏夜之夢」(III,ii)：**I'll go with thee, cheek by jowl**. 我會寸步不離跟著你。由此 **cheek by jowl** 就形容人群、建物等的擁擠或人際關係的密切。

- The pedestrians have to walk cheek by jowl along the narrow street.

  走在這條窄小的街道，行人只能摩肩擦踵而過。

- The two families live cheek by jowl in one house.

  這兩家擁擠地住在一間房子裡。

- His house stands cheek by jowl with a convenience store.

  他家旁邊就是一家便利商店。

- They say the manager and the union are cheek by jowl.

  大家都說這名經理和工會走得很近。

Write your own sentence:

- My house stands cheek by jowl with ______________

  ____.

have the cheek to …

居然有臉敢…

to talk about a person's boldness in a negative way

中英文不約而同都以臉形容人的無恥。如：**What cheek!**（臉皮真厚）／ **I like his cheek.**（我真佩服他的厚臉皮）。此處這個慣用語，是在質疑無恥的行為，即中文所說的：你怎麼有臉去做（你應當感到羞愧的事）。形容詞 **cheeky** 正是由 **cheek** 而來，意指厚臉皮的、無恥的。

- He had the cheek to ask for a raise after only a week in his new job.

  他才工作一星期，就厚著臉皮要求加薪。

- I couldn't believe he had the cheek to ask you for help after he set you up.

  我真不敢相信，他設局陷害你之後還有臉來找你幫忙。

- I don't think these corrupt officials have the cheek to question my honesty.

  我想這些貪官應該沒什麼臉來質疑我的清白。

Write your own sentence:

- I couldn't believe ____________ had the cheek to ___ ____.

19

turn the other cheek

把另一邊臉也轉過來，打不還手，甘心承受

to respond to violence or aggressive insults with humility and passivity

這個慣用語出自新約聖經：若有人打你右臉，你要把另一邊臉也轉過來讓他打。這個慣用語的意思是遇到惡意的攻擊或謾罵時，不生氣、不還擊，心平氣和，以寬大的心來包容，畢竟以牙還牙、以眼還眼（**a tooth for a tooth, an eye for an eye**）、以暴制暴不是解決之道。

- When someone makes personal abuse on you, would you turn the other cheek?

  若有人對你做人身攻擊，你能默默忍受嗎？

- When someone is rude to you, the best approach is to turn the other cheek.

  面對粗魯無禮的人，不在意不回擊是上上策。

- There is no point in arguing with unreasonable people. Just turn the other cheek.

  沒必要和不講理的人爭辯，任由他們去吧。

Write your own sentence:

- Usually I turn the other cheek when ______________________.

20

(with) tongue in cheek

舌頭鼓在臉頰裡，並非發自真心，玩笑地

to speak insincerely or facetiously

用舌頭把臉頰鼓得突突的，一副要笑不笑的樣子，這個慣用語主要形容某人說話像在開玩笑，不是很正經。另外，如果臉頰裡放的不是舌頭而是玫瑰，如：**a brisk walk puts the roses in your cheeks**，那就表示健走能讓你的氣色看起來紅潤又健康。

- All his complimentary remarks were said with tongue in cheek.

  他說那些恭維話根本不是發自真心。

- He always speaks tongue in cheek, never takes things seriously.

  他老是說玩笑話，沒一次認真。

- Was he speaking with tongue in cheek when he told Ann to run for President?

  他叫Ann去選總統是隨便說說的吧？

Write your own sentence:

- He explained that ________________, but I know he said it with tongue in cheek.

21

keep one's chin up

把下巴抬起來，打起精神，不要氣餒

to keep one's spirits high in spite of being in a difficult or unpleasant situation

在單槓運動中，**chin up** 意指把身體往上拉、使下顎與槓齊平，於是 **chin up** 成了鼓舞士氣的精神喊話，一如中文的「加油」。遇到困難，別輕易認輸，要 **keep chin up**，積極行動，如果無精打彩、意氣消沈，**with your tail between your legs**（尾巴夾在兩腿間），那就成了夾著尾巴的小狗，灰頭土臉，那可不是好樣的。

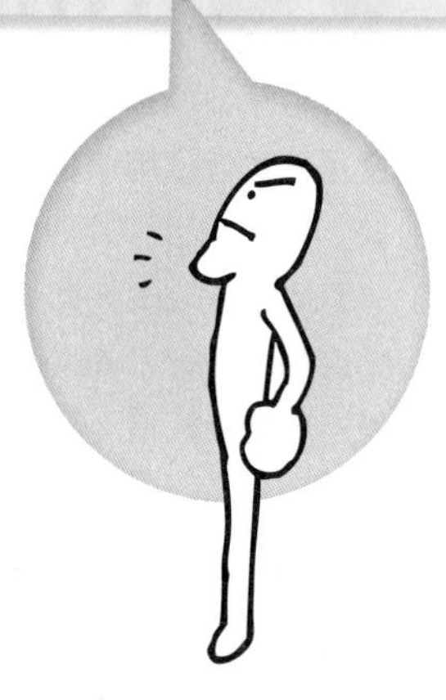

- Just keep your chin up and tell the judge all the truth.

  別氣餒，把全部事實都告訴法官就對了。

- Despite the heavy load of supporting a big family, he kept his chin up.

  儘管養一大家子很累，他還是打起精神努力拚。

- Chin up and give it another try!

  加油！再試一次看看！

Write your own sentence:

- Despite ______________________, I kept my chin up.

22

take it on the chin

用下巴來接眼前的一拳，勇敢接受不好的事情

to take something bad（adversity, criticism or defeat） directly without fuss

電影中常可見到這悲壯的一幕，通常都以慢動作呈現。這個慣用語意指面對逆境或遭人批評時，毫不囉嗦勇敢地接受、就算痛也咬著牙挺過去。**chin** 用 **nose** 也可，電影也常出現拳擊手被打中鼻子，接著 **has a nosebleed**（流鼻血）的壯烈畫面。

- He took it all on the chin but his partner was very upset by the criticism they received.

  他全然接受一切批評，但他的夥伴對這些批評十分不爽。

- He has been taking it on the chin in recent years, but he always looks on the bright side of life.

  近幾年他一直處在挨打的狀況，但他始終相信人生是美好的。

- A good baseball leader can take it on the chin when his team loses.

  好的棒球領隊能在輸球時處之泰然。

Write your own sentence:

- Do I have to take it on the chin if ______________________________?

23

flap one's jaws

擺動下顎，嘰嘰喳喳聊個沒完，閒扯

to jabber or talk aimlessly

flap 意指上下振動，如：**flap wings**（拍翅），所以下顎動個不停，便是指沒主題地閒聊，動動口、嗑嗑牙。**jaws** 可用 **gums**（牙齦），**flap** 可用 **wag**；英式另有一種說法是以 **chinwag**（搖下巴）表示聊天，可當動詞和名詞用。另外，如果 **jaw** 不擺動，而是整個 **drop**（掉下），則表示非常意外、十分吃驚。

- I can't sit here flapping my jaws all day.
  我可不能整天坐這兒閒嗑牙。
- What was that oddball flapping his gums about this time?
  那個怪咖這次都扯些什麼？
- We enjoy a good chinwag with friends.
  我們很享受與朋友開心地閒聊。
- My jaw dropped when I heard he had been admitted to Harvard.
  聽說他獲准進哈佛，我驚訝到下巴掉下來。

Write your own sentence:

- My jaw dropped when ______________________.

MEMO

eye

善惡美醜眼見為憑

EYE 是讓我們看見世界的窗戶，隨著看到的景象不同，**EYE** 往往呈現出不同的模樣。

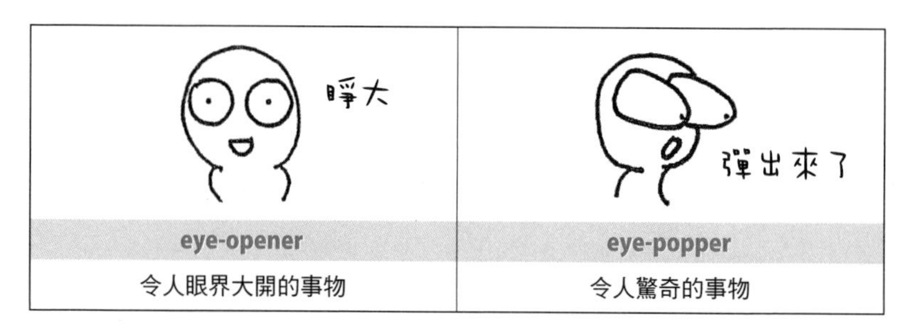

eye-opener	**eye-popper**
令人眼界大開的事物	令人驚奇的事物

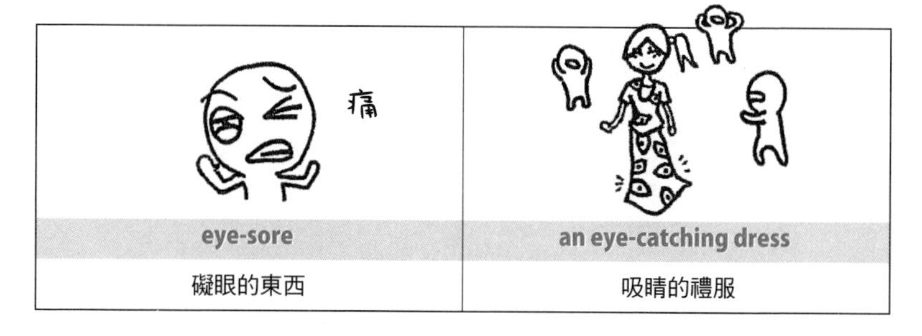

eye-sore	**an eye-catching dress**
礙眼的東西	吸睛的禮服

EYE 更是靈魂之窗，不同的眼神、眼色，透露出人的七情六慾、喜怒哀樂。如：嫉妒，中文說眼紅，英文則是眼綠，如：

the green-eyed monster（綠眼怪獸）→ 嫉妒（jealousy）

a green-eyed stare → 嫉妒的凝視

又如：

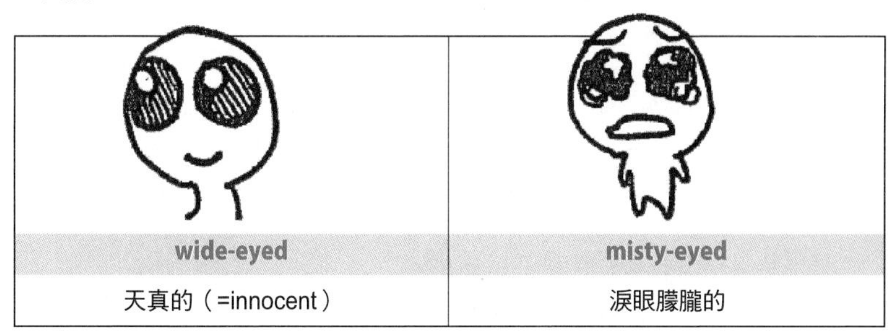

wide-eyed	misty-eyed
天真的（=innocent）	淚眼朦朧的

此外，由於搭夜間航班的人總是因睡不好而紅著眼下飛機，於是夜間航班就成了**red eye flight**，很有趣對吧。不過睡不好就容易有黑眼圈，這種熊貓眼叫做：**dark circles under eyes**，至於**black eye**，則是打架造成的「黑輪」。

身為世界與靈魂之窗的**EYE**，身邊還有好幾名護衛隨侍在旁，雖然渺小不起眼，但卻不可或缺！

eyebrow	眉毛
eyelid	眼皮
eyelash	睫毛
eyeball	眼球
pupil	瞳孔

哦對了，**EYE**並不單指眼睛，它也可以指所有「眼形狀」的事物哦！如：

hit the bull's-eye → 正中靶心

eye

1

a sight for sore eyes

可治好眼睛痛的景象，令人期待、高興的人事物

someone or something that is welcome

能讓 **sore eyes** 一看就不再痛的事物，自然是令人喜歡、渴望、願意見到的事物。另有個類似的慣用語：**the apple of one's eye**（某人眼中的蘋果），蘋果自古就是珍品，如果有什麼人事物是某人眼中的蘋果，那便意謂這是某人「非常珍愛的人事物」。

- I am starving. The meal is a sight for sore eyes.
  我餓死了，看到有飯吃超高興的。
- I have been waiting here forever. You are a sight for sore eyes.
  我在這裡等了又等，真高興終於看到你。
- His new model is the apple of his eye. He is always polishing it.
  他的新模型是他的寶，沒事就拿出來擦得亮亮的。

Write your own sentence:

- I ______________________, so _______________ is a sight for sore eyes.

2

an eye for an eye

以眼還眼，以暴制暴，以其人之道還治其人之身

punishment or retaliation similar or equivalent to the injury suffered

這個慣用語源自舊約聖經：**Life shall go for life, eye for eye, tooth for tooth**，意思是若有人傷害你，你也照他的方式傷害他。這麼做或許能消一時之恨，但馬丁路德告訴我們：**The old law of an eye for an eye leaves everyone blind**（以眼還眼最後只會讓大家全看不見），兩方廝殺，到頭來終歸是兩敗俱傷：**a no-win situation**，而非雙贏：**a win-win situation**。

- Should we forgive people who hurt us or follow the rule of an eye for an eye?

  我們應該原諒傷害我們的人呢？還是該讓他們也嚐嚐他們帶給別人的傷害？

- He believed in an eye for an eye; her cheating on him would have to be avenged.

  他相信以眼還眼是對的，她劈腿這事他非報復不可。

Write your own sentence:

- Under the rule of an eye for an eye, if a person ________, he or she deserves ________.

3

be all eyes

動用所有眼睛，目不轉睛地看

to watch intently or with a lot of interest

眼睛全數動員，表示看得非常專注，耳朵全數動員，則表示聽得十分專心。但請小心分辨 **all my eye**，話說有名水手在教堂禱告，別人念啥他就跟著亂念，聽起來像是 **“all my eye and Betty Martin”**，於是 **all my eye** 就成了“全是胡扯、瞎說”，與眼睛一點關係都沒有，真的很扯。

- The buyers at the show were all eyes when showgirls were dancing on the stage.

  展覽會上的買家個個聚精會神看著台上跳舞的表演女郎。

- He is all ears whenever we are gossiping.

  每當我們聊八卦，他都聽得超專注。

- He pretends to have great plans, but they're all my eye.

  他自稱有很棒的計畫，那些計畫全是鬼扯。

Write your own sentence:

- I was all eyes when ______________________.

4

catch one's eye

抓住某人眼睛，引起某人注意

to attract one's attention

catch 表示捉到移動中的物品，如：**catch a ball**（接球）、**catch fish**（捉魚），若有事物能抓住眼睛，就表示這事物搶眼、醒目，吸引了目光與注意。也可用 **eye-catching** 當形容詞。若有事物不只 **catch eye**，還 **kill eyes**，那就表示太精彩，精彩到連眼睛都掛了。

- I was just looking in the shop window when this brooch caught my eye.

  瀏覽街上櫥窗時，這枚胸針吸引了我的目光。

- We need more sauce. Try and catch the waiter's eye.

  我們還要醬料，設法讓服務生注意一下我們這裡 。

- Don't get a scooter that is too eye-catching. It might get stolen.

  別買太酷炫的輕機車，恐怕會被偷。

Write your own sentence:

- Out of all the __________, ________________ was what really caught my eye.

5

feast one's eyes on…

以…宴請眼睛，看…看得大飽眼福

to look at someone or something with pleasure or admiration

feast 意指盛宴，當動詞時表示設宴款待。如果受到款待的是眼睛，那就表示眼睛享盡了愉快美好的景象。也可以用 **a feast for the eyes**（眼睛的盛宴）來形容看了令人愉快滿足的事物。

- We feasted our eyes on Grand Canyon.
  我們飽覽了大峽谷的風光。
- I am feasting my eyes on the sculpture.
  我正在享受這座雕塑帶給我的視覺之美。
- He is on diet trying to lose weight, so he stopped to feast his eyes on the desserts in the bakery window.
  他正在節食減重，所以只駐足麵包店看著櫥窗裡的甜點飽飽眼福。
- The garden is a feast for the eyes.
  這花園真令人賞心悅目。

Write your own sentence:

- I am feasting my eyes on ________________.

6

have eyes in the back of one's head

後腦杓長了眼，知道身邊發生的一切

to know everything that is happening around

眼睛長在臉上，因此背後的事我們無從知曉。但如果腦門也長了眼，那就什麼事都逃不過了。有時掌握情報是有必要，但若**breathe down one's neck**（對著某人的脖子吐氣），密切地注意、監控，猶如鼻子貼在頸邊一樣，那恐怕會帶給人**breathless tension**（透不過氣的緊張）。

- Parents of teenagers had better have eyes in the back of their heads.

  家有青少年的父母最好能掌握身邊發生的所有事情。

- His wife seems to have eyes in the back of her head. She knows what he is doing when he is away.

  他老婆好像背後長了眼似的，他在外面做什麼她都知道。

- I can't work with you breathing down my neck all the time.

  你這樣時時刻刻盯著我不放，我實在沒辦法與你共事。

Write your own sentence:

- I don't need to have eyes in the back of my head because ________________.

7

have an eye for…

在…方面有一隻眼睛，獨具慧眼，有鑑別能力

to have a taste or a keen appreciation for something

欣賞或鑑別物品時，往往不自覺閉上一隻眼，因此**have an eye for**…就表示對…有"獨"到的見解與賞析。但如果是**have eyes for**…，請小心，這表示兩隻眼都只看得見…，亦即對…情有獨鍾、十分想要得到。

- He has an eye for beauty, especially for color, which makes him a great artist.

  他很有審美眼光，對色彩的感覺尤其獨到，這使他成了很棒的藝術家。

- She has an eye for curios.

  鑑別古董她很拿手。

- He has eyes only for the top award.

  他一心只想拿首獎。

- You don't need to be jealous. I only have eyes for you.

  你沒必要吃醋，我的眼中就只你一個人。

Write your own sentence:

- I have an eye for ________________, which makes me ____.

8

have eyes bigger than one's stomach

眼睛比肚子大，慾望比實際能耐大

to desire more than one can eat or handle; to be greedy

台語說「嘴飽眼睛餓」，一貪心就忘了自己的能力，一如貪心的蛇想吞象一樣。這個慣用語除了用來表達拿取過多食物，也可表達一個人不懂得量力而為。也可用 **one's eyes are bigger than one's stomach** 來表達。

- I thought you had eyes bigger than your stomach when you told me you wanted to buy a new Mercedes-Benz.

  你跟我說你想買台賓士新車，我覺得你沒考慮自己的能力。

- I can't finish the slice of pizza. I'm afraid my eyes were bigger than my stomach.

  這片披薩我吃不完，我想我點太多了。

- "Your eyes are bigger than your stomach." Father told me when I tried to get another helping.

  當我想再去拿一份食物時，父親對我說「你真是肚飽眼不飽」。

Write your own sentence:

- I was told I had eyes bigger than my stomach when I said ______________________________.

9

hit someone between the eyes

擊中某人兩眼之間，令某人震驚或印象深刻

to have a sudden impact on someone; to impress someone

如果一支箭（**arrow**）或一顆子彈（**bullet**）正中某人眉心，這經驗肯定讓人永生難忘。這個慣用語主要用來表達某事帶給某人衝擊或令某人難忘，另外，又由於衝擊往往會讓人頓時清醒，所以也可用來表達“要命！原來如此，我總算懂了”。

- When she told me she was head over heels for me, it hit me between the eyes.
  當她跟我說她愛我愛得發狂，我震驚不已。
- The song's catchy lyrics and bright melody hit me between the eyes.
  這首歌歌詞簡單好記、旋律輕快，讓我想忘都忘不了。
- His evil intent hit me between the eyes.
  我終於明白了他不軌的意圖。
- News of their divorce hit us right between the eyes.
  他們離婚的消息震撼了我們大家。

Write your own sentence:

- I remember when ____________________, it hit me between the eyes.

10

keep an eye on…

把一隻眼睛貼在…，仔細照顧、注意…

to watch or look after something or someone attentively

分出一隻眼盯著某人事物，這個慣用語表示專心照顧、避免該人事物出錯或受傷。但如果 **keep one's eye on the ball**（眼睛跟著球走），則表示明確知道自己的目標、全心全意設法達成，一如球員專注地盯著球的路徑，努力打好一場球。

- Can you keep an eye on my seat? I'll be back in a blink.
  幫我顧一下位子好嗎？我一下下就回來。
- Please keep an eye on the stove in case the beef stew scorches.
  麻煩盯一下爐火，免得這鍋牛肉燉焦了。
- You had better keep your eye on the ball to make sure nothing gets missed.
  你最好時時留神警覺，以免有什麼閃失遺漏。
- You have to keep your eye on the ball in business.
  做生意你必須看準之後全力出手。

Write your own sentence:

- I'll keep an eye on ______________ in case ______
  ________________.

11

keep an eye out for…

讓一隻眼為…凸出來，睜大眼留意…

to be watchful for someone or something

若想保持清醒警覺，首先得睜開眼睛，最好睜大到眼睛**out**出來，完全忘了**blink**（眨眼）。類此這種表示提高警覺、注意某事物的慣用語還有：**keep one's eyes peeled**（剝開眼皮，保持警戒）以及**keep one's eyes open**（睜開眼睛、隨時留意）。

- Keep an eye out for the potholes in the road.
  走在路上，要時時注意地上的坑洞。
- I'll keep my eye out for a job for you.
  我會留意看看有沒有適合你的工作。
- Be sure to keep your eyes peeled when you change lanes.
  換車道時一定要睜大眼睛多加留神。
- When cycling down a hill, you have to keep your eyes open and keep your wits about you.
  騎單車下坡時，一定要保持警覺，並且要能冷靜反應。

Write your own sentence:

- I always keep an eye out for ________ when ______
  ____.

12

make eyes at someone

對著某人製造目光，對某人放電

to look at someone amorously or flirtatiously; to ogle

所謂眉目傳情，**make eyes** 正是利用目光傳情送秋波，格調高一點的是含情脈脈地望，格調較差的則淪為拋媚眼或色瞇瞇地瞧。**give someone the eye** 表達的意思也是一樣的。

- She spent the whole evening making eyes at Joe.
  她一整個晚上都在對Joe放電。
- He is always making eyes at all the young girls.
  他總是對著年輕女孩色瞇瞇地看。
- Never make eyes at a guy who your friend has showed an interest in.
  不要對你朋友有興趣的傢伙放電。
- John kept giving May the eye. She finally got disgusted and left.
  John含情脈脈看著May，May終於覺得噁心而離開。

Write your own sentence:

- Never make eyes at a person who ________________
  ____.

13

open one's eyes to…

使某人睜開雙眼朝…看，使某人看清、明白…

to make one aware of the truth of a situation

看到了不一定知道，要看清才能真明瞭，使眼睛睜大、看清，就表示對於長久蒙昧的事恍然大悟。因此，若有人 **with one's eyes open** 地做某件事，那就表示此人完全清楚自己在做什麼、及其可能的風險與困難。

- The trip to Guinea opened her eyes to the difficulties faced by developing countries.

  去一趟幾內亞，她才明白開發中國家所面臨的困境。

- It's about time you opened your eyes to the true colors of this guy.

  你該睜大眼認清這傢伙的本性了。

- She went into the acting profession with her eyes open.

  踏入演藝界時，她已知道演藝路的辛苦。

- I'm doing this with my eyes open. Don't worry about me.

  我清楚自己在做什麼，別擔心。

Write your own sentence:

- ____________ opened my eyes to ______________

  ____.

14

shut one's eyes to…

對…閉上雙眼，對…視而不見

to refuse to see or think about; to deliberately ignore

這則恰與上則相反，事情明擺在眼前，卻彷彿沒看到。類似的還有 **turn a blind eye to…**（以盲了的那隻眼朝…看），看了等於沒看。又，如果有人 **with one's eyes shut／closed** 地做某事，就表示他完全不明白做這事的風險，又或者輕而易舉、閉著眼就能做這事，請依上下文判斷。

- The professor simply shut his eyes to students who were playing mobile games in class.
  對上課玩手機遊戲的學生，教授一律裝做沒看到。
- The management turned a blind eye to bullying in the workplace.
  管理部門全然無視於職場上的霸凌行為。
- He just met the girl and went into the relationship with his eyes shut.
  他才剛認識這女孩，什麼都沒搞清楚就與她發展起來。
- He could qualify for the semi-final with his eyes closed.
  他就算閉著眼睛也能進入準決賽。

Write your own sentence:

- I can't shut my eyes to ________ and just hope that ______________________________.

pull the wool over one's eyes

拉下羊毛蓋住某人雙眼，（以虛偽善意）蒙蔽某人

to deceive or hoodwink by elaborately feigning good intentions

遮眼為何不用 **blindfold**（眼罩）卻用 **wool**？這個慣用語源於十六世紀流行的 **woolen wigs**（羊毛假髮），意指假意示好以欺瞞別人，好似意圖遮人眼不讓看見，卻假稱幫忙整理假髮。類似的慣用語：**throw dust in one's eyes**（往某人眼中丟沙），則是指耍障眼法，故意誤導或瞞騙他人。

- The politician tried to pull the wool over the eyes of the voters with lots of promises.

  這個政客開一堆支票欺騙選民。

- The guy who claims to have supernatural powers is just pulling the wool over your eyes.

  這個號稱有超能力的人根本就是在耍你。

- The superstar's agent threw dust in the reporters' eyes, talking about a flight at the airport when he was heading for the highway.

  這名巨星的經紀人故意對記者放出某機場航班的風聲，而此時他正奔向公路。

Write your own sentence:

- Don't let ____________ pull the wool over our eyes.

  We should ______________________________.

see eye to eye

眼睛對著眼睛看，想法一致，看法相同

to think alike; to agree completely

意見不合的人通常看不對眼，因此若能**see eye to eye**看對眼，那就表示意見一致。又如果是**see with half an eye**（用半隻眼看），則表示用半眼看也知道，想都不用多想，一看便知。

- He doesn't see eye to eye with the new manager.
  他和新來的經理意見不合。
- My mom and I see eye to eye on political matters.
  在政治問題上我媽和我看法一致。
- We could never see eye to eye and argued constantly.
  我們總是意見不對盤，吵個不停。
- I can see with half an eye that grandma has a soft spot for Jimmy.
  我隨便看也知道，阿嬤最疼Jimmy。

Write your own sentence:

- I am glad I see eye to eye with ____________ on ______________________.

eye

17

be up to one's eyebrows

上昇到眉毛了，埋在一堆事裡，忙得要命

to be extremely busy with something

待完成的事堆到眉毛，那肯定有得忙。這個慣用語很有趣，**eyebrows** 可換用身體其他部位，從 **elbows**（手肘），到 **neck**（脖子）、**chin**（下巴）、**ears**（耳朵）、**eyes**（眼睛）、**eyeballs**（眼球）都有人用，基本上工作埋到手肘已夠可觀，別擔心該用哪個部位，用哪個部位意思都一樣，都很忙。

- I can't go out tonight because I am up to my eyebrows in work.

  今晚我不能出去，因為我有工作要忙。

- We are up to our eyeballs in decorating the new villa at the moment.

  眼下我們正忙著裝潢新別墅。

- She was up to her elbows in preparing dinner when the doorbell rang.

  門鈴響時，她正為準備晚飯忙得不可開交。

Write your own sentence:

- I am up to my eyebrows in ________________ at the moment.

18

raise eyebrows

使人揚起眉毛，使人訝異或不屑，引人側目

to shock or surprise people; to cause disapproval

這個慣用語意指某人事物之令人意外或驚世駭俗、又或令人懷疑、不屑、不悅等，因為這些情緒總會令人睜大雙眼、眉毛上挑。此外請注意，**highbrow** 意為高額頭，一般用來指稱自詡為有文化、高水準的人，使用此字帶有貶意。

- His early death raised many eyebrows among his fans.

  他的早逝震驚了許多粉絲。

- The highbrow woman's low-cut dress raised eyebrows at the dance.

  舞會上，這名狗眼看人低的貴婦以一襲低胸洋裝嚇到不少人。

- His seductive behavior raised a few eyebrows among parents.

  他挑逗的行為引起一些家長反彈。

Write your own sentence:

- ______________________ usually raises many eyebrows at school.

19

by the sweat of one's brow

憑著額上的汗，汗流滿面、辛勞努力

by hard work or great efforts

此慣用語源自聖經，當亞當和夏娃被逐出伊甸園，上帝對亞當說：**By the sweat of your brow you will eat your food.**（你必汗流滿面才得餬口），額上的汗表示辛苦勞動，延伸形容努力的態度。另則慣用語也與汗有關：**sweat blood**（流出血汗），意指賣命工作，但此處**sweat**當動詞用。

- He grew fruit in the country by the sweat of his brow.

  他在鄉下辛苦地種水果。

- He built the business by the sweat of his brow.

  他憑自己的努力建立起事業。

- He sweated blood over every book to earn enough money to feed his family.

  為賺錢養家，他每本書都是拼著命在寫。

Write your own sentence:

- The only way I will ________________ is by the sweat of my brow.

MEMO

ear 聆聽不可或缺的耳

身為傳導聲音的器官，**EAR**是我們接受聲音訊息的第一站。過大的音量（**volume**）或分貝（**decibel**），往往會讓我們聽力受損，所以說話一定要注意音量。

Don't shout into my ear! → 別衝著我耳朵吼！

Please whisper in my ear. → 悄悄跟我說就好。

由於聲音與**EAR**密切相關，於是幾個形容聲音或聽覺的字，就免不了用**EAR**來幫忙。

若有什麼事聽了令人高興、安慰，那便是**music to ears**，如：

The news that the castle has been restored is music to my ears.
→ 聽到古堡已修復的消息，我好高興。

其他又如：

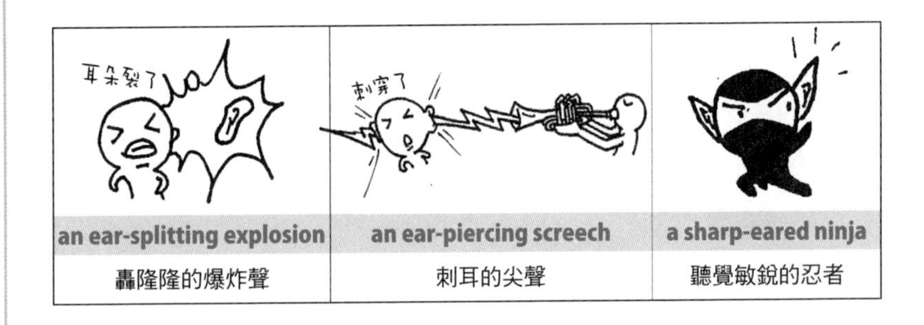

an ear-splitting explosion	an ear-piercing screech	a sharp-eared ninja
轟隆隆的爆炸聲	刺耳的尖聲	聽覺敏銳的忍者

除了意指聽覺器官，**EAR**也可用來表示任何長得像耳朵的物品。如：

the ear of a pitcher → 水壺的把手

the golden ear of wheat → 金黃色麥穗

說到水壺把手，有個諺語是這麼說的：**Little pitchers have large ears.**

為什麼說小水壺有大把手呢？其實這句話的意思是：小孩子年紀雖小，耳朵卻很靈光，所以在小孩面前說話要留神，不要以為小孩都聽不懂。基本上，**Walls have ears.**（隔牆有耳），談論重要的事情最好還是注意一下**earshot**（聽力所及的距離）。

Keep your mouth shut while they are within earshot.
→ 別說，他們聽得到。

Let's wait until they are out of earshot.

→ 等他們聽不到再說。

MEMO

ear

1

a flea in one's ear

耳中的跳蚤，刺耳的羞辱

a stinging or mortifying reproof

如果耳中有跳蚤，不但被咬了難受，還不知該怎麼把它趕走。尖酸刻薄的話語就像跳蚤，讓人痛苦難堪、反覆折磨、不知所措。但若有人 **put a bug in your ear**（在耳中放小蟲），則表示此人給你暗示或意見，就像有小蟲在你耳中嗡嗡嗡，提醒你快點有所行動。

- If you don't hand in your resignation, he will put a flea in your ear.

  如果你不提出辭呈，他一定會用話羞辱你。

- What if I come back with a flea in my ear!

  萬一我碰了釘子回來怎辦？

- I'll put a bug in her ear about keeping a pet.

  我會找機會跟她提養寵物的事的。

- John put a bug in his wife's ear about how it might be nice if he had a new golf club.

  John不時提醒他太太，如果他能換支新的高爾夫球杆該有多好。

Write your own sentence:

- If I __________________________, will you put a flea in my ear?

2

be out on one's ear

用耳朵出去，不光彩地被迫離職，被掃地出門

to be forced to leave a job because something wrong has been done

一如中文的捲鋪蓋走人，此慣用語意指被人不留情面地趕走。這類被炒魷魚的說法還有：**be fired**、**be sacked**、**get the boot**（接到靴子）、**get the ax**（接到斧頭）；反之若是老闆**give the boot**（丟靴）、**give the ax**（扔斧頭）或**show you the door**（指出門的位置），則是老闆要你走人。相較之下，**be laid off**（被裁員）、**be dismissed**（被開除）應可算是較不那麼羞辱人的說法。

- On the stage you get only one chance. If you fail, you're out on your ear.

  在這舞台上機會只有一次，失敗的話就直接滾蛋。

- You'll be out on your ear if you show up late to work again.

  下次上班再遲到，你等著回家吃自己。

- Which congressperson will get the boot from the voters in the next election?

  下屆選舉會被選民踢出去的會是哪個國會議員呢？

Write your own sentence:

- You'll be out on your ear if ________________.

ear

3

be wet behind the ears

耳後溼溼的，乳臭未乾，初出茅廬

to be young and not very experienced

馬仔出生後身體不久便乾，唯獨耳後溼溼的，若某人耳後溼溼，就表示他像新生的小馬，沒有工作經驗。由於長角動物出生時，角的根部綠綠的，因此 **greenhorn**（綠角）表示沒經驗、不懂世故或容易上當的人，如：**a greenhorn journalist**（剛入行、沒經驗的新聞從業人員）。**green hand**（綠手）與 **tenderfoot**（嫩腳）都意指 **novice**（新手），**tenderfoot** 又意指初到某環境或不習慣戶外生活的人。

- That greenhorn is fresh out of college, still wet behind the ears.
  那個生手剛從大學畢業，經驗全無。
- Those con artists thought I was still wet behind the ears. But I showed them!
  那些老千本以為我很嫩，但我讓他們領教了我的厲害。
- The old factory hands treated the tenderfoots like their slaves.
  工廠老鳥把那些剛來的菜鳥當奴才一樣對待。
- He isn't used to sleeping in a tent. He's definitely a tenderfoot.
  他不習慣睡帳棚，他肯定沒有戶外生活的經驗。

Write your own sentence:

- I am too wet behind the ears to ________________.

4

get an earful

塞滿一整個耳朵，聽上一堆不好聽的話

to have a lot of unwanted suggestions or criticism to listen to

好聽的話怎麼聽都不夠，但不好聽不想聽的話只需一丁點就覺得耳朵滿了、夠了。**earful** 意指令人不舒服的聲音或話語，不論是抱怨（**complaint**）、責罵（**scolding**），還是批評（**criticism**）都可用 **an earful** 來表達。動詞用 **get** 表示接受、聽，用 **give** 則表示發送、說。

- The general got an earful from troops because of a shortage of arms.

  由於軍備不足，部隊對將軍的怨言不絕於耳。

- I got an earful from my mom last night when I came home late.

  昨天我晚回家，被媽念翻了。

- My boss gave me a right earful because I lost the contract.

  我老闆結結實實罵了我一頓，因為我把合約搞丟了。

Write your own sentence:

- I got an earful from ______________ when ______________.

5

go in one ear and out the other

一耳進、一耳出，成耳邊風，聽過就忘

to be heard and then soon ignored or forgotten

只要有耳朵或耳朵沒生病，我們都能 **hear**。但 **hear** 並不等於主動、專注地 **listen**，所以如果 **hear without listening**，結果就會如這個慣用語所形容，聽了等於沒聽。另外如果有 **memory & concentration problem**（記憶與注意力的困擾），即使認真 **listen**，聽完也還是有可能馬上忘光光。

- Everything I say to him seems to go in one ear and out the other.

  不管我跟他說什麼，他都好像沒聽到一樣。

- I told him to get to class on time, but my words went in one ear and out the other.

  我跟他說上課要準時，但他根本沒把我的話放在心上。

- I was told a whole list of names but they just went in one ear and out the other.

  有人對我說了一串名字，但我一個都記不住。

Write your own sentence:

- I told him ________________________ but it went in one ear and out the other.

6

grin from ear to ear

從一耳笑到另一耳，咧嘴而笑，笑得合不攏嘴

to give a very wide, beaming smile

笑有很多種，**laugh**是發出聲音地笑，**smile**是微笑，**chuckle**是輕聲咯咯笑或暗自發笑，**giggle**是傻呼呼地咯咯痴笑，**smirk**是假笑或得意的笑，**roar**是狂笑，**grin**是露齒而笑。此處這個慣用語可用**laugh**或**grin**，**from ear to ear**是強調嘴巴一整個笑開，張得很大，彷彿合不起來了。

- He was grinning from ear to ear, as if he had just won the lottery.

  他笑得合不攏嘴的，好像中了樂透一樣。

- He was grinning from ear to ear when he accepted the prize.

  領獎時，他笑得嘴巴和耳朵都連在一起了。

- When we saw John grinning from ear to ear, we knew he had passed the test.

  當我們看到John笑口大開的，就知道他通過了考試。

Write your own sentence:

- I was grinning from ear to ear when ____________

  ____________________________________.

7

have an ear for …

在…方面有一隻耳朵，對…有靈敏的聽力

to have the ability to learn music or languages

　一如用眼力鑑賞會單用一隻眼，用耳朵鑑賞也用一隻耳。**have an ear for** 表示在音樂或語言等方面有獨特的聽覺；將 **ear** 換成 **eye**，則表示擁有與眼力有關的天分，如：**He has an eye for pictures.** 他懂得看畫。若用 **talent** 或 **gift** 則表示天分，不分眼或耳，如：**He has a talent for painting.** 他很有繪畫天分。

- He doesn't have an ear for music. He can't carry a tune.

  他沒有音感，他唱歌會走音。

- She has never had an ear for languages, but she has a gift for pastiche.

  她向來不是學語言的料，但她極有模仿別人作品的天份。

- She has an ear for poetry. She is excellent at writing poetry impromptu.

  她對詩的音韻很敏銳，她很擅長寫即興詩。

Write your own sentence:

- I have an ear for ____________. I am excellent at ________________________.

8

hold a wolf by the ears

抓著狼的耳朵，騎虎難下，進退兩難

to be in a dilemma or on the horns of a dilemma

此慣用語出自美國總統**Thomas Jefferson**，他認為維持奴隸制度就像抓著狼耳，抓著不是辦法、放了也不行。**catch-22**意思類似，它是小說書名也是書中的軍規：只有瘋人才能不出任務，但需本人親自申請，但申請了就等於沒瘋，因此**catch-22**表示難以解套的矛盾。另外，陷於兩難也可用**between Scylla and Charybdis**（卡在席拉岩礁與克里布地斯漩渦之間）。或**between the devil and the deep blue sea**（卡在魔鬼與藍色深海之間）。

- Telling the cruel truth is like holding a wolf by the ears.
  該不該說出這個殘酷的真相，真令人為難。
- If he adjusts the price, he will lose customers, but if he doesn't, he will lose money. How can he get out of the catch-22?
  他若調價，生意會跑掉，但若不調，他會賠錢，他該怎麼解套呢？
- He was between Scylla and Charybdis as to whether to go or stay.
  去或留他左右為難。

Write your own sentence:

- ________________________________ is like holding a wolf by the ears.

keep an ear to the ground

一隻耳朵緊貼地面，注意事態發展或最新趨勢

to be on the watch for new trends or information

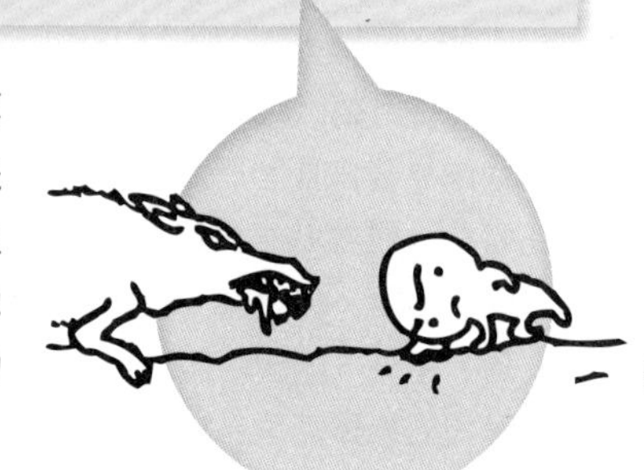

在野外生活，一定要懂得隨時把耳朵貼在地上，這樣才能知道幾哩外是否有野獸正朝自己而來。在都市生活，也要象徵性地隨時把耳朵貼在地上，這樣才能掌握先機，瞭解最新動態或潮流，為即將發生的事做準備。**keep** 也有人用 **have**，意思都一樣。

- The government should keep an ear to the ground before executing a new policy.

  政府在實施一項新政策前，應先聽取各方意見。

- There is a rumor of a new round of layoffs. Better keep an ear to the ground.

  聽說又有新一波裁員。最好隨時注意四方動靜。

- He had his ear to the ground when it came to news about the latest technology.

  只要跟最新科技有關的消息，他一個都不放過。

Write your own sentence:

- I had my ear to the ground when it came to

  ______________________________.

10

lend an ear to…

借耳朵給…，聽…說

to listen in a caring way for someone's problems

慷慨出借耳朵，表示很樂意聽，這個慣用語常用於有特別的事要說。**give ear to**…（把耳朵獻給…）也意指傾聽，反之，**have someone's ear**（得到某人耳朵），則表示得到某人的關注或垂聽。**ear**也可代表聽到的話，如：**He could hardly believe his ears.** 他簡直不能相信他所聽到的話。

- Lend your ears to me. I have an important announcement to make.

  注意，我有重要的事要宣布。

- He always lends me a sympathetic ear whenever I am feeling down.

  每次我心情低落，他都會帶著同理心聽我訴說。

- He has the boss's ear and could put in a good word about you.

  他說的話老闆都會聽，他可以幫你說說好話。

Write your own sentence:

- He always lends me a sympathetic ear whenever ______________________.

11

play … by ear

憑之前所聽到的來演奏，隨機應變，見機行事

to act according to the circumstances; to improvise

有些人聽完樂曲後即可將樂曲演奏出來，完全不需看譜（**read the score**）或事先準備，這就是**play by ear**，用在日常用語中，**play by ear**表示沒有事先計畫，總之看著辦，走到哪裡算哪裡。

- He can play anything on the piano by ear.
  只要是他聽過的旋律，他都能用鋼琴彈出來。
- I am not sure if I can go hiking with you this weekend.
  Let's just play it by ear.
  我不確定週末是否能跟你去爬山，咱們就到時看著辦吧！
- I don't know what to say in the meeting. I'll just have to play it by ear.
  我不知道開會時該說什麼，只好隨機應變了。
- If you go into the negotiation unprepared, you'll have to play everything by ear.
  如果你沒準備就去協商，屆時只能談到哪算到哪了。

Write your own sentence:

- ____________________, so I'll have to play it by ear.

12

turn a deaf ear to…

以失聰的耳朵朝向…，對…充耳不聞

to ignore something that is heard; to not pay attention to

如果某人刻意用聽不見聲音的那隻耳朵來聽你說話，那就表示他根本不想聽，就算聽了也是**go in one ear and out the other**，全成耳邊風。又如果，意見**fall on deaf ears**（掉在聾了的耳朵上），則表示這些意見並不被採納，說了卻像是沒被聽見，不被理會。

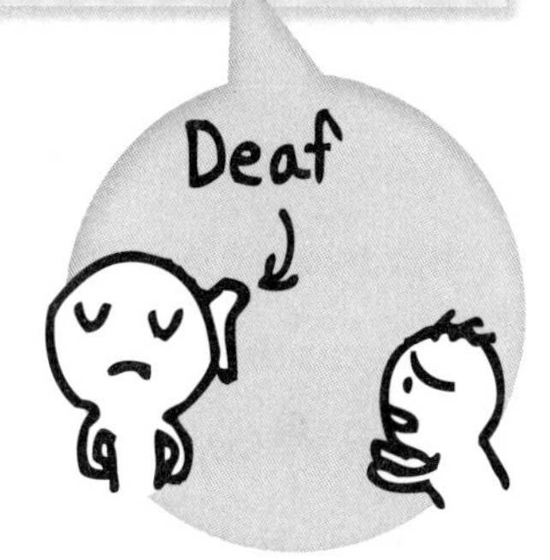

- He turned a deaf ear to any criticism of how he had mistreated his cat.

  針對他虐貓的批評他一概充耳不聞。

- How could you turn a deaf ear to her request for help?

  你怎能對她的求助置之不理?

- Any advice we gave our boss about improving QC seems to fall on deaf ears.

  不論我們怎麼建議老闆改善品管，老闆好像都聽不見。

Write your own sentence:

- Could I turn a deaf ear to ______________________

  ______________________________________?

nose 在臉中央呼吸的鼻

一整張臉，唯一突出來的地方就是NOSE，正正在臉中央，負責呼吸以及嗅聞各種氣味。即使很扁的NOSE，相信也還是很難讓人忽略，所以形容事情一清二楚，英文有一個比喻就是以臉上的NOSE作文章，另外，在許多日常用語中，NOSE也常是一種攸關榮辱、個人主見的象徵。如：

hard-nosed → 務實幹練的

plain as the nose on your face → 再明顯不過

She is a nose of wax. → 她耳根子軟，沒有主見。

Are you thumbing your nose at me? → 你是在嘲笑我嗎？

眼睛看不到時，還有耳朵可以聽，耳朵聽不到時，還有NOSE可以聞，但如果連NOSE也垮了…那小命恐怕岌岌可危，因為我們不僅靠NOSE嗅聞、更得靠它呼吸！所以NOSE也意謂著一種本能、直覺。如：

He has a nose for finding cheap items. → 他很會找便宜的商品。

狗鼻子（MUZZLE、不是NOSE）是有名的靈，而狗仔（paparazzi）是有名的愛打聽，於是NOSE+Y就成了形容詞，意指愛管閒事的，也可寫成NOSY；而NOSE當動詞用時，除了有嗅聞之意，也意指打探。如：

The hounds nosed the deer in the woods.
→ 獵犬聞到了樹林裡的鹿。

He nosed a profit in everything.
→ 任何事他都能找到對自己有利的好處。

You had better go and nose about a bit. → 你最好去打聽一下。

1

can't see beyond (the end of) one's nose
看不到鼻子（尖）以外的地方，短視近利，只考慮眼前和自己

to think too much about oneself and not see what is really important

目光停留在自己的鼻尖，眼中的世界就會只剩下局部的自己。要避免變得**short-sighted**（近視眼、短視的），就要常**see far**（看遠），**take an overall view of things**（看事情的整體），考量**long-term effects**（長期影響），才能有**broad vision**（開闊的視野），才不會變成**cross-eye**（鬥雞眼）。

- He didn't approve the investment. He couldn't really see beyond his nose.

  他沒批准這個投資案，他實在很沒遠見。

- He can't see beyond the end of his nose. He is so busy making money and pays no attention to his health and family.

  他一心只顧著眼前，成天忙著賺錢，都不關心健康與家人。

- He is very careless in this project; he has never been able to see beyond his nose.

  他處理這個案子十分草率，他向來目光如豆沒什麼遠見。

Write your own sentence:

- It surprised me that he ____________________. He couldn't see beyond his nose.

nose

2

follow one's nose

順著鼻子走，直直走，憑嗅覺找，憑感覺、本能行事

to go straight ahead; to follow a smell to its source; to make decisions by feeling or instinct

由於鼻尖指著前方，這個慣用語原意是直直往前走，又因鼻子有嗅聞的功能，順著鼻子也意指照著味道找到源頭，由此，它又延伸出了另一個意思：憑本能決定事情。

- To get to where the charity bazaar is held, just follow your nose down ABC Avenue.

  要去慈善義賣會那裡，順著ABC大道一直走就是了。

- He followed his nose toward where we were broiling fish in the grill.

  他靠著他的鼻子，朝著我們烤魚的地方來。

- I won't hold an audition. I tend to follow my nose for the part of Juliet.

  我不辦選角試演會，我打算用直覺來找適合演茱麗葉的人選。

Write your own sentence:

- As far as ______________________ is concerned, I tend to follow my nose.

3

have one's nose into …
把鼻子放進…，過度打探…

to have unwelcome interest or curiosity in someone else's business

為了打聽努力嗅，為了嗅努力靠近，結果就是鼻子一整個戳進去。這個慣用語意指某人好管別人閒事，**have**也可用**put**／**poke**／**stick**。又，如果鼻子不放在別人閒事而是放在書裡（**have one's nose in a book**），則表示埋首讀書，但小心書讀多了，**have nose in the air**（把鼻子高舉在空中），覺得自己高人一等、惹人討厭。

- Our boss always has his nose into our personal lives.
  我們老闆一天到晚打探我們的私生活。
- The girl had her nose in a book during the long train ride.
  在坐火車的漫長時間裡，女孩埋首看書。
- I wonder if she knows that she has her nose in the air.
  不曉得她知不知道她常一副自以為了不起的樣子。

Write your own sentence:

- It seems that ____________ is fond of having his/her nose into my business.

4

hold one's nose

捏住鼻子，硬著頭皮，睜一隻眼閉一隻眼

to do something unwanted; to ignore something unpleasant

捏住鼻子，通常是聞到不好的味道或進到水裡，這個動作被用來表達眼下要做的事自己其實並不願意，所以只能捏住鼻子，將就地忍過去。另外介紹幾個鼻子的動作：**blow one's nose**（用鼻子吹氣）意思是擤鼻涕，**powder one's nose**（為鼻子撲粉）其實是指要上廁所。

- This plan is better than no plan, so hold your nose and vote for it.

  有這個方案總比沒有好，就勉強投票贊成吧！

- He hated doing it, but he held his nose and signed the contract.

  他實在很不想，但還是硬著頭皮把合約簽了。

- He held his nose and quitted his job even though he needed money to pay back his loans.

  他心一橫把工作辭了，即使他需要錢還貸款。

Write your own sentence:

- I held my nose and ________________, even though ________________________.

5

it's no skin off someone's nose

沒有皮會從某人鼻上掉下來，於某人毫不相干、毫無影響

to be of no interest or concern to someone

如果某件事的發生，完全不會使某人的鼻子掉皮，那就表示這件事對於此人一點影響都沒有，好壞都與此人無關，一如中文說的，完全沒差，既不會多一條胳膊也不會少一塊肉，頗類似**It's none of my business.**（不關我的事）或**I don't care.**（我無所謂）的心態。

- I don't care if he wants to come to my wedding. It's no skin off my nose.
  他想不想來參加我婚禮我都無所謂，反正我沒差。
- It's no skin off my nose if you have a Sponge BOB tattooed on your chest.
  你想在胸前刺一個海綿寶寶就去刺啊，我又不會少一塊肉。
- It's no skin off his nose if you don't take his advice.
  你不聽他的勸是你的事，他又不會有什麼損失。
- How you managed to afford a luxury house is none of my business.
  你如何想方設法地要買一棟豪宅，那關我啥事。

Write your own sentence:

- It doesn't matter ______________________.
  It's no skin off my nose.

nose

6

keep one's nose clean

保持鼻子乾淨，潔身自愛，遠離是非

to avoid getting into trouble or doing anything illegal

中文說，碰一鼻子灰表示受冷落（**be snubbed**），但英文的用法，若是鼻子搞髒了，就表示處在不乾淨的環境或接觸不好的事物，因此讓鼻子乾淨就表示遠離不好的人事物、避免捲入是非。這個慣用語起初用 **hand**，後來改用 **nose**，畢竟手髒可以把手藏起來，鼻子髒…總不能把鼻子摘下來吧。

- Try to keep your nose clean by staying away from those rough guys.
  遠離那些狠角色，才不會惹禍上身。
- If you don't learn how to keep your nose clean, you're going to end up in jail.
  如果你不學著檢點一點，早晚要吃牢飯。
- Please keep your nose clean. I am bailing you out of jail for the last time.
  拜託別再惹事生非，這是我最後一次保你出來。

 Write your own sentence:

- Try to keep your nose clean by ________________.

7

keep one's nose to the grindstone

鼻子貼在磨石上，硬著頭皮拚命做

to work hard and steadily

grindstone 是磨刀石，鼻子都已貼在磨石上了還要磨，表示賣力做個不停、再累也要撐下去。其他像 **work one's fingers to the bone**（做到手指見骨）、**work one's head／tail off**（做到頭／尾巴都掉了）、或是 **put one's shoulder to the wheel**（肩膀貼靠在輪子上），都是用來表達持續不斷的苦幹打拚賣力工作。

- He kept his nose to the grindstone while his son was out enjoying himself.

  當他兒子在外頭逍遙玩樂，他一刻不停地在打拚。

- He has to work his fingers to the bone to feed his five children.

  他得拚命做個不停，才能養活他的五個孩子。

- Joe got the result he wanted. He really put his shoulder to the wheel.

  Joe得到了他要的成果，他真的很拚。

Write your own sentence:

- I expect ____________________ since I have been keeping my nose to the grindstone.

8

lead someone by the nose

牽著某人鼻子走，完全掌控某人

to control or dominate someone

這個慣用語出自莎翁名劇**Othello**（奧塞羅）第一幕第三景，劇中的**Iago**認為**Othello**將如驢子（**ass**）一樣地被他牽著鼻子走。許多鼻孔穿有鼻環的牲畜，常被牽著鼻環拉著走（**be led by a ring passed through the nostrils**），說巧不巧，中文也同樣是以牽鼻子這個舉動表示操控。

- Bob is a henpecked husband. His wife leads him by the nose.

  Bob很怕老婆，什麼都聽老婆的。

- You are not going to lead me again by the nose.

  你別想再牽著我的鼻子走。

- He refused to be led by the nose by his parents.

  他拒絕被他父母牽著鼻子走。

Write your own sentence:

- __________ led __________ by the nose, so ____________________.

9

look down one's nose at…

順著鼻子往下看…，鄙視，瞧不起

to regard with contempt or dislike

崇敬的目光通常朝上（**look up to**），目光朝下則表示輕視，覺得某人事物毫無價值、低人一等。鄙視之心一起，便會**thumb one's nose at**…（對著…把姆指放在鼻上），做出嘲謔或輕視的行為。至於**turn up one's nose at** …（把鼻子高高翹起），則表示因為看不起或不喜歡壓根不想多看一眼，眼不見為淨。

- He looks down his nose at people who speak with strong accents.
  他打心裡瞧不起說話口音很重的人。
- I always felt that the regular staff looked down their noses at us freelancers.
  我總感覺這些正職員工瞧不起我們自由工作者。
- He declined to accept the award in an attempt to thumb his nose at the ceremony.
  他婉拒出席領獎，藉以表示對此典禮的不屑。
- He turned up his nose at eggplant and broccoli.
  他不愛吃茄子和綠花椰菜，連看都不看一眼。

Write your own sentence:

- Don't look down your nose at people who
  ________________________.

10

pay through the nose for …

為…透過鼻子付錢，為…花很多（冤枉）錢

to pay too much for something, usually an unnecessary high price

這個慣用語的來源不可考，但極可能源自西元九世紀丹麥人在愛爾蘭所施行的 **nose tax**：若忘了繳稅或欠稅，一律要在鼻子上劃一刀（**have their noses slit**）。當然，劃了一刀之後稅還是得繳，由此來看，透過鼻子上的 **slit**（細長切口）所付出的錢，果真是令人心痛的巨額代價。

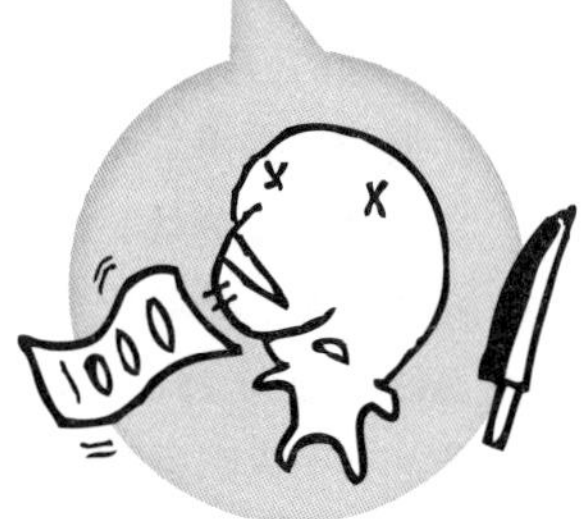

- Park legally. If your car gets towed, you'll pay through the nose.

  照規定停車吧。若是車被拖了，到時花更多冤枉錢。

- Wanting a decent meal in this fancy restaurant, you have to pay through the nose for it.

  想在這家高檔餐廳吃得像樣，就得捨得花大錢。

- He had to pay through the nose for the cell-phone part that was not covered by warranty.

  這個手機零件不包含在保固內，他只好忍痛掏錢。

Write your own sentence:

- If you ______________________________, you have to pay through the nose.

11

rub one's nose in …

使某人鼻子在…裡面搓，揭某人過去瘡疤，反覆提起某人不愉快的事

to remind one of something that one has done wrong

此慣用語源自 **housebreaking**（訓練寵物大小便）的土法：若寵物沒按規定大小便，就把牠的鼻子塞進牠拉的屎尿中 **rub**，使他牢記而不再犯。但這法子不但沒效而且還會破壞彼此之間的 **trust**。若有人犯錯或有難過往事，千萬別深怕別人忘記似地一直說，非但於事無補，還可能在人家傷口上撒鹽：**rub salt into one's wound** ，雪上加霜。

- He didn't tell her about his new relationship. He didn't want to rub her nose in it.
  他沒跟她說他的新戀情，他不想讓她想起不愉快的往事。
- I know I shouldn't have touched it, but could you stop rubbing my nose in it?
  我知道我碰了這東西很不該，但可否請你不要一直提這事？
- When I failed my exam, he rubbed my nose in it.
  我考不及格，他偏不斷提這事。
- My colleagues rubbed salt into my wound when they laughed at my defeat.
  同事們嘲笑我的失敗，更加深了我的創痛。

Write your own sentence:

- I know I ________________, but could you stop rubbing my nose in it?

right under someone's nose

就在某人鼻子下，就在某人面前，當著某人的面

right in front of someone; in someone's presence

中文的當面有兩種意思，當事情發生時你剛好在場，那麼這事就是當著你的面、在你鼻子底下發生，一如中文說的「在眼皮子底下」。另一種當面是指親自對著某人的臉：**to one's face**。另外，如果某人事物近在咫尺卻沒被你看到，那麼這人事物的所在位置就是 **under your nose**。

- I wonder how he managed to steal jewelry from the shop right under my very nose.
  我真想知道他是怎麼當著我的面把店裡珠寶偷走的。

- You should apologize to her face, not on the phone.
  你應該當面跟她道歉，不該用電話。

- He has been looking for her but she has been right under his nose all the time.
  他一直在找她，但她其實一直都在他附近。

- I thought I had lost my key, but it was sitting on the sofa right under my nose.
  我本以為鑰匙不見了，原來一直都在我眼前，就在沙發上。

Write your own sentence:

- I am amazed that __________ right under my nose.

MEMO

mouth

是非胖瘦嘴說（吃）了算

空氣、食物、水是維持生命的三個基本條件，而這三個條件都與**MOUTH**有關，因為我們由**MOUTH**吐氣、以**MOUTH**進食、靠**MOUTH**喝水，於是一張**MOUTH**就意謂著一個待養人口。

	**He has six mouths to feed.** 他有六口人要養。
	**Don't be a useless mouth.** 別吃閒飯，只吃不做。

一旦滿足基本生存需求，吃就不只為了活命，進而成了一種感官的享受。

	**mouth-watering chocolates** 令人流出口水的巧克力

除了吃，人類的**MOUTH**還有一個特別的功能：說話，所以**MOUTH**當動詞用時，意思不是吃，而是不出聲地用**LIPS**（兩片嘴唇）說話。至於**MOUTH+FUL**成名詞時，既是與吃有關的「一口量」，也是與說話有關的「長而難念的字詞」或「重要的話」。如：

He mouthed the word "LOVE". → 他以口形說“愛”這個字。

He ate the cake in one mouthful. → 他一口吃下蛋糕。

His name is a mouthful. → 他的名字好難念。

You said a mouthful. → 你說到重點了。

雖然能用 **MOUTH** 說話是人類一大福利，但說的話與存的心常常不成比例。有人說話甜滋滋（**honey-mouthed**），結果口蜜腹劍，根本是隻披著羊皮的狼（**a wolf in sheep's clothing**）；有人舌尖嘴利，說話尖酸苛薄（**smart-mouthed**），結果刀子口豆腐心，只聞嚇人的吠聲，卻沒咬人的心（**their bark is worse than their bite**）。有人心直口快，想到什麼說什麼，一根腸子通到底（**What the heart thinks, the mouth speaks.**）。不管是哪一種，總之都別忘了用嘴也用心，這樣才不會禍從口出：**Out of the mouth comes evil.**

最後不能忘了 **LIPS**，即使沒有聲音，用 **LIPS** 也可以說話，這種說話方式叫 **lip reading**（讀唇法），也因此與 **LIPS** 有關的慣用語大都與說話脫不了關係。

MEMO

1

bad-mouth…

用壞嘴巴說…，說負面的話以詆毀…，惡意重傷

to criticize or disparage, often spitefully or unfairly

bad-mouth 是動詞，對某人事物使用壞嘴巴，就表示說惡言使別人對此人事物觀感不佳。**poor-mouth** 也是動詞，意思是以窮做藉口，即中文的哭窮叫苦。至於 **mouth off**，則是以口對決，亦即頂嘴（**talk back**）。

- He persistently flatters his boss and bad-mouths his colleagues.
  他不斷奉承老闆，說同事壞話。
- He does't want to bad-mouth the dead. He wants to show some respect for the dead.
  他不想說死了的人的壞話，畢竟人死為大。
- He always poor-mouths whenever asked to donate to charity.
  只要一叫他愛心捐款，他就喊窮。
- He got in trouble by mouthing off to his superior.
  他因頂撞上司，惹上麻煩。

Write your own sentence:

- Don't bad-mouth ___________ just because ___________________.

2

by word of mouth

經由嘴巴說，以口頭知會，口耳相傳，聽別人說

in speech rather than in writing; orally, by one person telling another

此慣用語意指透過口頭相傳，而非書面文字或其他如電視、報紙、收音機等傳播途徑。一旦傳開，很容易便**from mouth to mouth**或**from lip to lip**（一傳十、十傳百），最後便會**on everyone's lips**（人人都在談論）。口傳有時會**overstate**（誇大其詞）或流於**groundless rumors**（空穴來風），千萬要小心分辨。

- He was informed by word of mouth so that no written evidence could be found later.
  當初別人是以口頭通知他，以致於後來沒書面資料可證。
- They don't advertise; they get all their customers by word of mouth.
  他們不打廣告，他們的客人都是"吃好道相報"。
- The news I learned by word of mouth spread rapidly from mouth to mouth.
  我聽別人說的那個消息，一下子就傳開了。

Write your own sentence:

- I learned by word of mouth that ____________________
  ______________________________.

mouth

3

be down in the mouth

嘴巴下垂，垂頭喪氣

to be discouraged, depressed, or sad

嘴巴下垂，大多是心情不好、**feel blue**、覺得憂鬱、沮喪的時候。如果嘴巴不下垂，而是**foam at the mouth**（口水亂噴），則表示氣得吹鬍子瞪眼，像生氣的狗或馬會唾沫四濺一樣。

- Since he lost his job, he has been down in the mouth at the thought of his future.
  失業後，他一想到未來，心情始終很低落。
- "Why do you look so down in the mouth?"
  "I was sacked yesterday."
  「你為何顯得如此消沈？」「我昨天被開除了。」
- He was down in the mouth about everything after she took French leave.
  在她不告而別之後，沒一件事能讓他心情變好。
- He was foaming at the mouth over the incompetent judge's ruling.
  他被這名恐龍法官的判決氣炸了。

Write your own sentence:

- I try not to be down in the mouth even though ______________________________.

4

keep one's mouth shut

讓嘴巴閉起來，保持緘默

to be quiet; to keep a secret about someone or something

嘴巴一開就不容易管得住，原本不該說的話常莫名地就說出了口。這個慣用語原意是閉上嘴別說話，延伸表示管好嘴巴，以免說出不該說的事。也可直接以**shut**當動詞。又，如果某人無法**shut mouth**，那就表示此人**has a big mouth**（有個大嘴巴），口風不緊。

- Be a good listener! Keep your mouth shut and let people talk.

  認真聆聽，閉上嘴巴，讓別人說。

- Should I keep my mouth shut about seeing Jason with another woman?

  我該不該說出看見Jason和別的女生在一起的事呢？

- Don't worry! I am going to shut my mouth on this issue

  別擔心，我不會在這個議題上多嘴的。

Write your own sentence:

- Should I keep my mouth shut about ________________________________?

mouth

5

leave a bad taste in one's mouth

在口中留下不好的味道，令人觀感不佳

to leave a lingering bad feeling or memory

有些東西不好吃，但吃了很快就忘；有些東西滋味不但不好，而且還留下惡臭久久不退。生活中有些事情就像後者，即使事過境遷卻留下令人不愉快的印象或感受。**bad** 可用 **nasty** 或 **bitter**，都是表達味道的糟糕。

- It was a nice restaurant, but its slow service left a bad taste in my mouth.

  這家餐廳其實不錯，可是他們服務好慢，讓我印象很差。

- When I saw the boss exploiting his employees, it left a bad taste in my mouth.

  看到這個老闆剝削他的員工，讓我感覺很糟。

- His barbaric behavior left a nasty taste in her mouth.

  他野蠻的行為讓她一想到他就不舒服。

Write your own sentence:

- When I found ____________________, it left a bad taste in my mouth.

6

live from hand to mouth

手才拿到就放入嘴裡，生活僅夠糊口，過一天算一天

to have just enough money to live on and nothing extra

沒有餘裕的日子十分辛苦，定要十分小心，才能**make ends meet**（收支相抵），一旦**live beyond one's means**（入不敷出），日子更不好過。**mouth**的慣用語常與生計有關，像是口含銀湯匙出生（**be born with a silver spoon in one's mouth**），即意謂出生富貴人家；拿走某人口中麵包（**take the bread out of one's mouth**），則表示搶人飯碗、奪人生計、讓人很難生存下去。

- His father earns very little, so they live from hand to mouth.
  他父親收入微薄，只夠他們勉強過日子。
- I keep a personal budget so that I don't live beyond my means.
  我都有作預算，所以不會入不敷出。
- He was born with a silver spoon in his mouth; he knows nothing about working for a living.
  他出生有錢人家，從不知什麼叫為生計奔波。
- Lowering wages is taking the bread out of the workers' mouths.
  降低工資會讓這些勞工無以維生。

Write your own sentence:

- Because ______________________________, he lives from hand to mouth.

7

make one's mouth water

使某人流口水，使人垂涎三尺

to make one desire or anticipate something

美食會令嘴巴 **water**（流口水），夢寐以求的東西也會令人流口水。又若食物 **melt in mouth**，既表示這食物入口即化，也意指食物很好吃，不論它是否會融。又如果某人嘴裡的奶油都不會融（**butter wouldn't melt in one's mouth**），則表示這人（尤指女生）自命清高裝得一本正經、一副端莊淑女模樣、冷冷的彷彿奶油放在口中都不會融。

- I bought a limited-edition model that would make your mouth water.

  我買了一款限量發行的模型，包準你看了流口水。

- The steak was so tender that it could melt in my mouth.

  這塊牛排好嫩，真是太好吃了。

- She looks as though butter wouldn't melt in her mouth but we know better.

  她看起來正經八百，但我們清楚得很。

Write your own sentence:

- ______________ is enough to make my mouth water.

8

put one's money where one's mouth is

把錢放到嘴巴說的事情上，以行動證明，說到做到

to back up one's opinion with action

如果願意把錢花在嘴巴所說的事情上，那就表示並非胡亂吹牛。反之，若是 **be all mouth**，則是光說不練，只剩一張嘴。至於 **lip service**（嘴唇服務），顯然只有嘴巴說得好聽，卻不見實際的行動。

- We wish the government would put its money where its mouth is and tackle metropolitan housing problems.
  我們希望政府真能拿出行動來，解決大都會的住屋問題。
- If you are really interested in helping the homeless, put your money where your mouth is.
  如果你真想幫助無家可歸的人，那就用行動證明，不要光說不做。
- He is known to be all mouth.
  大家都知道他這個人只會說不會做。
- He's not just paying lip service to the criticisms, but has truly taken them on board.
  對於批評，他不只嘴上說重視，也確實有在考慮接受。

Write your own sentence:

- Stop complaining! Let's put our money where our mouth is and ________________________.

9

put one's foot in one's mouth

把腳放進嘴巴裡，說錯話（而難堪）

to say something stupid, insulting, embarrassing, or tactless

踩進水坑令人懊惱，踩進自己的嘴…肯定後悔加三倍。這個慣用語意指失言以致場面尷尬，因此若某人有**foot-in-mouth disease**，不是有口蹄疫（**foot-and-mouth disease**），而是此人很容易出言不遜說錯話。至於口無遮攔亂說話、亂放炮，則是**shoot off one's mouth**（把嘴當槍一樣亂射），表示說話毫不知節制。

- She put her foot in her mouth when she called him by her first husband's name.
  她說錯話了，她居然把他叫成她第一任老公的名字。
- I really put my foot in my mouth when I asked a plump girl if she was pregnant.
  我問一個胖胖的女孩她是否有孕，誰知無意中說錯了話。
- He suffers a lot from foot-in-mouth disease.
  他老是說錯話的毛病相當嚴重。
- Stop shooting off your mouth about my plan to study abroad!
  別再到處跟人亂說我要出國念書的事了。

Write your own sentence:

- I put my foot in my mouth when ________________.

10

straight from the horse's mouth

直接查看馬嘴得來的，消息來源可靠

from an authoritative or reliable source

據說查看馬齒可得知馬的年齡，所以直接查看馬嘴得來的消息，就表示是第一手資料，並非輾轉得來。源自馬齒的用語還有：**look a gift horse in the mouth**，收到別人送的馬，卻要查看馬嘴以確定是老馬還是壯馬。得到東西卻挑三揀四不知珍惜，便是「查看禮物馬的嘴」，愛計較。

- They are going to get married. I heard it straight from the horse's mouth.

  他們要結婚了，我的消息絕對可靠。

- The pundit claims that he has got confidential information straight from the horse's mouth.

  這個名嘴聲稱他已掌握第一手的機密資料。

- The car is full of dents, but I shouldn't look a gift horse in the mouth.

  雖然這台車凹痕很多，但收人禮物就該心懷感恩。

Write your own sentence:

- ______________________. This comes straight from the horse's mouth so it has to be believed.

11

take the words out of someone's mouth

拿出了某人口中的話語，說出了某人心裡的話

to say exactly what someone is about to say

這個慣用語既可表示開口說出了某人心裡的想法，也可表示先一步說出某人要說的話。反之，若是**put words in someone's mouth**（把話語塞入某人口中），則表示強自把某些話語說成是某人說的、又或是自作聰明替某人說、但說的根本不是某人要說的話。

- When he said he was tired of housework, he took the words out of my mouth.
  他說他做家事做的好煩，這說中了我的心事。
- I was just going to mention that, but you took the words out of my mouth.
  我本來要提這事的，結果你先幫我說了。
- I never suggested that he should transfer. Don't put words in my mouth.
  我從來沒提議過要他轉調，不要用我的名義亂講。
- I didn't mention it. You're putting words in my mouth.
  我沒提過那事，你竟用我名義亂說。

Write your own sentence:

- When he mentioned ____________, he took the words right out of my mouth.

12

bite one's lip

咬唇，（考慮後果所以）忍住不說

to make a conscious effort not to say something

把唇咬住，一來表示忍耐，二來表示努力忍住已到嘴邊的話，因為覺得此話不該說或其實不需說。另有一個源自莎翁「亨利六世」的慣用語：**bite one's tongue**（咬住舌頭），意思也同咬唇一樣。

- She didn't reply because she was angry and was biting her lip.
  她沒回答，因為她正強忍著怒氣。

- I managed to bite my lip and waited until he confessed sleeping through the film.
  我按捺著什麼也沒說，只等他自己招認，看電影時他從頭睡到尾。

- He didn't like the way she treated him but he had to bite his lip.
  他不喜歡她對待他的方式，但他必須忍耐不能說。

- Parents must learn to bite their tongues so as not to give unwanted advice.
  做父母的要學著把話忍住，以免說出一些沒建設性的建議。

Write your own sentence:

- How I wanted to __________ but I managed to bite my lip and ______________________________.

mouth

13

button one's lip

用扣子把嘴扣起來，住嘴、閉口不談

to stop talking

button（鈕扣）當動詞，意指扣住，也可用**zip**（用拉鍊拉上），總之就是要某人封口、不要把事說出來。若某人願承諾：**My lips are sealed.**（我的嘴唇密封住了→我絕口不提），那便再好不過，就怕這承諾是**lip service**（空口說白話），結果事情就**go from lip to lip**，最後**on everyone's lips**，掛在大家嘴邊、任大家談論了。

- Tell him to button his lip about our meeting or he will regret it.

  叫他口風緊一點，別說出我們會面的事，否則他會後悔。

- You had better zip your lip about his job hopping and not say a word against it.

  他跳槽的事你最好啥都別說，反對的話提都別提。

- Read my lips! I don't want the news to get out. Be sure to zip your lip.

  給我聽好，我不希望這個消息外傳出去，嘴巴守緊一點。

Write your own sentence:

- I will button my lip about ______________ and ______________________________________.

14

keep a stiff upper lip

讓上嘴唇硬梆梆，保持堅定沈著、泰然自若

to display fortitude in the face of pain or adversity

人一慌，嘴唇就會**tremble**（顫抖），若上唇硬梆梆，就表示不為逆境所動。但為何強調上唇？因為十九世紀男人大多有留**mustaches**（小鬍子），只要嘴巴一發抖，留鬍的上唇最是明顯。這個慣用語不僅表達了**keep one's chin up**的勇敢精神，硬唇更強調了有如泰山崩於前而色不變。又，如果嘴唇不硬而且很**loose**（鬆弛），則表示說話隨便、不做考慮也不負責任。

- He is brought up with the concept of always keeping a stiff upper lip and not crying at all.
  他從小就被灌輸無論如何都要堅強、絕不能哭的觀念。
- Things are tough for you now, but try to keep a stiff upper lip.
  眼下事態艱難，但你要咬緊牙關冷靜沉著。
- The raid must be out of the blue. Loose lips can get somebody killed.
  這次突襲務必出其不意，說話不留心，有人就會因此喪命。

Write your own sentence:

- I know you are upset about ______________________, but keep a stiff upper lip.

15

smack one's lips

咂嘴，愉快地嚮往（未來某事）

to show eagerness or excitement about a future event

小孩吃東西都會發出咂咂的聲音，一副吃得很享受的樣子。這個慣用語除了意指咂嘴，也表示對未來某事的美好期待或想像。**lick one's lips**（舔嘴唇）意思與咂嘴差不多。

- Don't smack your lips while eating.
  吃飯時別咂咂地發出聲音。
- The architect begins smacking his lips when he thinks about the skyscraper being erected.
  一想到那棟摩天大樓蓋起來，建築師就開始滿心憧憬。
- The real estate agent is smacking his lips at the prospect of all the money he is going to make.
  這名房仲業者一想到可能賺到的錢，就心花怒放。
- The cartoonist's fans are licking their lips in anticipation of his new comics.
  漫畫迷們一心期待這名漫畫家的漫畫新作。

Write your own sentence:

- I am smacking my lips when I think about ________ ________________________________.

MEMO

tongue & tooth

相依互助的舌與齒

嘴巴是吃與說的重要器官，但嘴巴裡如果沒有**TONGUE**，就會食之無味、說不出話，因此**TONGUE**常代表語言或說話方式。如：**mother tongue**（母語）、**tongue twister**（繞口令）、**a silver tongue**（流利的口才），其他又如：

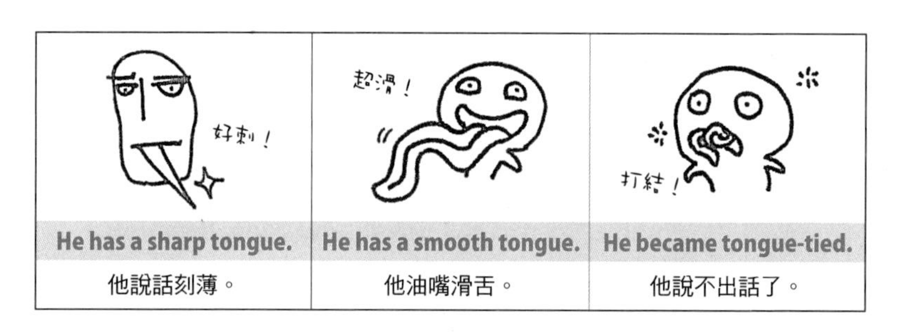

He has a sharp tongue.	He has a smooth tongue.	He became tongue-tied.
他說話刻薄。	他油嘴滑舌。	他說不出話了。

即便有**TONGUE**替我們品嚐與說話，但如果沒有**TOOTH**合作無間那也不行。我們需要**TOOTH**將食物嚼碎下嚥，也需要**TOOTH**避免空氣外洩（**leak out**），以免說話漏風；如果**TOOTH**與**TONGUE**合不來，說起話來就會大舌頭，**lisp**（口齒不清）。因此在慣用語中，牙齒意謂著效能（**power**）、又或胃口、食慾（**appetite**）。除了意指嘴巴裡的齒，**TOOTH**也意指所有齒狀的物品。

如：

Strict enforcement puts teeth in the law.
→ 要嚴格執法才有實效。（沒牙齒不給力）

He has a sweet tooth. → 他超愛吃甜食。(連牙都是甜的)

The comb has ten teeth. → 這梳子有十齒。

TOOTH也反映了人的成長，幼時是**milk tooth**（乳牙）、成年有**wisdom tooth**（智齒）或**permanent tooth**（恒牙），老年時或戴**false tooth**（假牙）或**toothless**（無牙），**TOOTH**的變遷真實反映了人的年紀。此外，由於馬的牙齦會一年年後退，年紀愈大牙齒愈長，於是**He is long in the tooth.**就等於：**He is old.**

另外還有個慣用語則是與母雞的**TOOTH**有關，問題是，母雞有牙齒嗎？是的，正因為母雞沒牙齒，所以**as scarce as hen's teeth**就意謂著十分罕見、極其稀有。如：

Convenience stores are as scarce as hen's teeth around here.
→ 這附近便利商店少得可憐。

MEMO

tongue & tooth

1

a slip of the tongue

舌頭滑了一跤，口誤

a mistake made in speaking

舌頭跑太快，一不小心就會滑倒，話就會說錯。筆跑太快，則容易寫錯、筆誤（**a slip of the pen**）。有時，舌頭太靈活以致想說的話已到舌尖，記憶卻沒來得及跟上。因此**on the tip of one's tongue**（停在舌頭尖上），就表示某事已到嘴邊，卻一時想不起來，只差一點點就想起來。

- It was just a slip of the tongue that made me say the wrong number.

  我是一時講太快，才說錯號碼。

- He intended to write "super model" but a slip of the pen turned it into "super monkey."

  他想寫「超級名模」，結果一不留神寫成了「超級猴子」。

- Hang on! His name is on the tip of my tongue. Bill something or other.

  等一下，我就快想起他的名字了，叫比爾什麼的。

Write your own sentence:

- I made a slip of the tongue when I said

  ______________________.

2

find one's tongue

找到舌頭，有辦法開口說話

to be able to talk or know what to say after being silent

驚嚇或尷尬常會讓人**lose tongue**（找不到舌頭），不知該說什麼，彷彿忘了該怎麼說話。待冷靜下來，通常很快就能**find tongue**，想起該怎麼開口或該說什麼話。另外，如果該說話時不說話，對方可能會問，(**Has the**) **cat got your tongue?**（舌頭被貓吃了嗎），就像中文說的，你啞了嗎？怎麼都不說話？

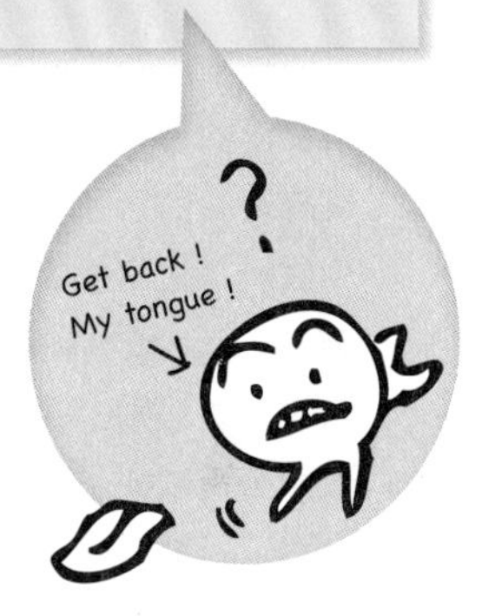

- She lost her tongue when she ran into the boy she had a secret crush on.

  她與暗戀的男孩不期而遇，不知該說什麼才好。

- "Are you surprised to see me? Cat got your tongue?" he asked.

  「看到我很意外嗎？怎麼像啞巴一樣都不說話？」他問。

- She took a step forward and finally found her tongue. "Hello!" she said.

  她向前邁出一步，終於開口說話。「你好！」她說。

Write your own sentence:

- I couldn't find my tongue when I ______________________________.

3

keep a civil tongue (in one's head)

保持文明的舌頭，說話要有禮貌

to speak decently and politely

文明的舌頭表示說話彬彬有禮，那麼像蛇一樣分叉的舌頭（**forked tongue**）又會如何說話？故事中的蛇常是魔鬼的化身，因此若有人**speak with a forked tongue**（以蛇舌說話），說出的話絕不可信。又，如果舌頭沒分叉卻成了鞭子（**lash**）去鞭撻某人，則表示對某人狠狠訓斥。

- Don't swear loudly like that. Try to keep a civil tongue in your head.

  別那樣大聲咒罵！試著好好說話。

- The politician is always speaking with a forked tongue.

  這名政客說話一向不實，不值得相信。

- His mother caught him smoking and gave him a tongue-lashing.

  他母親逮到他抽煙，狠狠訓了他一頓。

Write your own sentence:

- We must keep a civil tongue in our heads and ______________________________.

4

set tongues wagging

使眾舌頭紛紛擺動，使人們議論紛紛

to cause people to start gossiping

說閒話叫嚼舌根，若有某事引起很多舌頭嚼動，那就表示這事引起注意，成為人們茶餘飯後的話題，此慣用語也可以用 **tongues wag** 表達。此外，在酒精的催化下，肌肉放鬆，舌頭便放縱，**loosen one's tongue** 表示喝了酒後不自覺地說個不停，什麼都說，雖說酒後吐真言，但真言有時很危險。

- His late-night visit to her home has set the neighbors' tongues wagging.
  他深夜造訪她家已引起街坊議論紛紛。
- If married women date with other men, tongues will wag.
  人妻如果與別的男人約會，有人就要說閒話了。
- Tongues wagged when an SNG van was parked in front of her house.
  一輛衛星轉播車停在她家門前，引起眾說紛紜。
- The vodka loosened his tongue; then he said things that he would later regret.
  伏特加使他鬆了口，接著他說出了後來後悔不已的話。

Write your own sentence:

- I believe ______________________ will surely set tongues wagging.

5

armed to the teeth

武裝到牙齒，全副武裝，武裝森嚴

to be overly or elaborately equipped with many weapons

armed 意指備有武器，若連牙齒都佩有武器，武裝勢必萬分齊全。若把 **armed** 換成 **dressed**，連牙齒都不忘妝點，則表示一身上下盛裝打扮。全副武裝不一定會得勝，**fight tooth and nail** 的精神也很重要，用牙咬、用指甲抓，使出渾身解數全力拚搏，總之就是要全力以赴。

- As a military leader, he showed up for the inaugural ceremony armed to the teeth.
  身為軍事領袖，他全副武裝現身於就職典禮上。
- The entire country is armed to the teeth.
  這個國家武裝力量完整強大。
- She is usually dressed to the teeth in order to impress people.
  她總是盛裝打扮，好讓人對她印象深刻。
- The prosecutor fought tooth and nail against crime.
  這名檢察官全力打擊犯罪。

Write your own sentence:

- I am ____________ to the teeth in order to ____.

6

be fed up to the back teeth (with…)

連後牙都塞滿了…，對…厭倦到極點

to be unwilling or unable to put up with something

be fed up with…或**be sick of**…都表示不想或無法再忍受某事，**to the back teeth**（直到後排牙齒）則強調厭倦已達極限。又，**I've had it.**或**I've had enough.**也表示「受夠了」。但請注意，若有人問：**Would you like some more?** 還要吃點什麼嗎？可回說**I've had a lot.**表示吃夠了，千萬別回**I've had enough.**（我受夠了。）

- I'm fed up to the back teeth with your lame excuses. Cut the crap.

  我受夠了你的爛藉口，別再說那些廢話了。

- He is way out of line. I'm sick to the back teeth of his sharp tongue.

  他太過份了，我受夠了他的毒舌。

- I've had it--let's leave right now.

  我受夠了，我們現在就走吧。

Write your own sentence:

- I'm fed up to the back teeth with __________, so I decide to ______________________________.

7

cut one's teeth

長牙齒，初步磨練學經驗

to get one's first experience doing a particular kind of work and learn the basic skills

寶寶要學用牙齒，必須先讓牙齒切出牙肉長出來。

初入某行業，先設法磨練、學經驗，就像寶寶「長牙」。**teeth**也可用**eye-teeth**（犬齒）。**get one's feet wet**（把腳弄溼）意思類似但不一樣。後者是指新手上路、初步嘗試，先讓腳下水試個水溫。事總有第一次，見到老外開口說幾句，**get your feet wet**。

- He **cut his teeth** on a diner before landing a job on a five-star restaurant as a chef.
  他在一間小飯館學得手藝後才進入五星級大飯店當主廚。
- He is doing an internship in order to **cut his teeth**.
  他先實習，以磨練自己、累積經驗。
- John owns a big building company but he **cut his eye-teeth** as a cementer.
  John擁有一間大建設公司，他可是從水泥工開始磨練做起的。
- He bought just a few shares and **got his feet wet**.
  他頭一次進股市，只買了幾張股票小試身手。

Write your own sentence:

- I choose to ____________ in order to cut my teeth.

8

grit one's teeth

咬住牙齒，咬緊牙關撐過去

to summon up one's strength to face unpleasantness or overcome a difficulty

咬牙、一如療傷時沒打麻藥，硬著頭皮咬顆子彈一樣。這個慣用語與**bite the bullet**（咬著子彈）一樣，都表示無論如何忍著痛把難關渡過，打落牙齒和血吞。如果牙齒沒咬住反倒**show**或**bare**（露出來），小心，這正是猛獸攻擊的前兆，表示某人極度憤怒，準備出手一搏，豁出去拼了。

- I have to grit my teeth and come clean with him about our financial status.

  我不得不忍痛向他坦白我們的財務現況。

- Car drivers are biting the bullet after another rise in petrol prices.

  油價再度上漲，開車的人個個咬牙苦撐。

- He didn't expect Ken to show his teeth. He thought he was meek as a lamb.

  他沒想到Ken會這樣張牙舞爪的，他原以為他是個超溫順的人。

Write your own sentence:

- I can't do anything to change the situation but grit my teeth and ________________.

9

go over … with a fine-tooth comb

用細齒梳檢查，仔細檢查或搜索

to examine or search through something in minute detail

以前的人會用細齒的梳子梳頭髮，以梳出頭上的 **lice**（蝨子、複數），因而有了這個慣用語，表示嚴密仔細地檢查或搜尋，**go over** 可換用 **search**。如果不用細齒梳而是用指尖的指尖搜索（**fingertip search**），則是警方在犯罪或事件現場所做的地毯式搜索。

- My accountant went over my tax return with a fine-tooth comb, but found no errors.
  我的會計師仔細檢查了我的報稅表，沒發現任何錯誤。
- Let's go over the suitcase with a fine-tooth comb and see if we can find the ring.
  我們認真找找看這個行李箱，也許能找到戒指。
- I searched the whole place with a fine-tooth comb and didn't find my hairpin.
  我仔細找遍了這裡每一個地方，就是找不到我的髮夾。
- The police continued a fingertip search of the area yesterday.
  警方昨日持續針對這個地區做地毯式搜索。

Write your own sentence:

- Before I ____________________, I would go over it with a fine-tooth comb.

10

lie through one's teeth

露出牙齒說謊，公然撒大謊，睜眼說瞎話

to lie boldly; to utter outrageous falsehoods

謊言有很多種，像是無傷大雅的小謊（**fib**）、出自禮貌或不想傷害別人的善意的謊言（**white lie**）、或是扯的太離譜、讓人覺得誇張到不行的漫天大謊（**whopper**）。至於露出牙齒說謊，則是邊說謊邊做鬼臉，毫不顧忌，即使全天下都知道是謊言、也還是要說到底的撒賴。

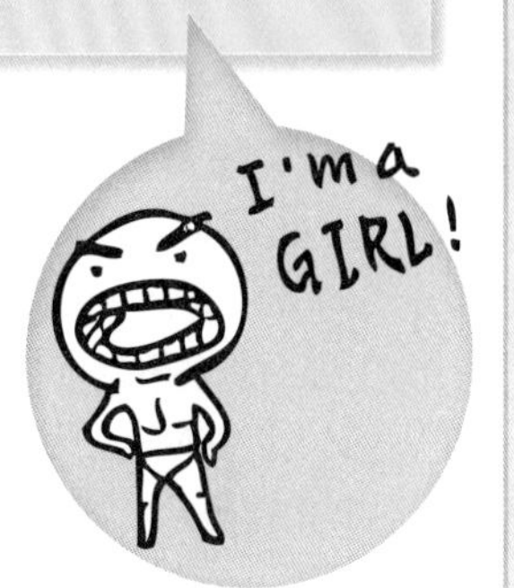

- If he denies it, he is lying through his teeth. We witnessed the car accident.
  他若否認，就是公然撒謊，我們可是親眼目睹了這場車禍。
- He was lying through his teeth when he said he had never seen me before.
  他說他從沒見過我，根本是睜眼說瞎話。
- She asked me if I liked her new hairdo, and I told her a white lie.
  她問我喜不喜歡她的新髮型，我以善意的謊言回覆了她。

Write your own sentence:

- If I ______________________________, I am lying through my teeth.

11

set someone's teeth on edge

使某人上排牙抵住下排牙，令某人不舒服到極點

to upset someone very much

edge意指邊緣或刀鋒，口語常以**on edge**或**edgy**形容焦躁不安，如：**I'm a bit on edge.**（我有點煩）或**You seem edgy.**（你好像很煩）。如果這煩竟使得牙齒也不安，以致像是吃了**acid taste**（酸味）似地緊扣在一起，那就表示這煩躁的感覺已觸動神經，令人討厭到簡直快崩潰了。

- A raucous laugh usually sets my teeth on edge.

  刺耳的笑聲總讓我渾身不舒服。

- His teeth were set on edge by the incessant screaming of the kids.

  他快被孩子們持續不斷的尖叫聲弄瘋了。

- Jumping the queue is on my list of top ten behaviors that set my teeth on edge.

  有十種行為我最受不了，插隊是其中之一。

Write your own sentence:

- The very thought of ________________ sets my teeth on edge.

12

sink one's teeth into…

讓牙齒咬進…裡，卯起勁全心投入…

to start to do something with a lot of energy and enthusiasm

當猛獸朝著**prey**（獵物）直撲而去，下一步便是使出全力、將牙齒狠狠插進獵物的身體裡。這個慣用語即源於這種畫面，意指帶著極大的熱忱，全力投入一件事，其認真、堅持、全神貫注的態度，就如猛獸用牙齒緊緊咬住獵物一樣，絕不怠忽、絕不鬆口。**sink**也可用**get**，意思一樣。

- The actor couldn't wait to sink his teeth into the role as a villain.

  這名男演員迫不及待想投入這個反派的角色。

- He is hoping for something more challenging that he can sink his teeth into.

  他總希望有什麼較有挑戰性的事能讓他全心投入去做。

- He just couldn't get his teeth into this new project.

  他就是提不起勁去動這個新案子。

Write your own sentence:

- I can't wait to sink my teeth into ________________ and see if __________________________.

13

take the bit in one's teeth

咬住齒間的嚼口，拿到掌控權，擺脫他人的控制

to put oneself in charge; to take control of a situation

身上裝了**bridle**（馬勒）的馬，口中會有一個**bit**（嚼口），當**rider**用力拉**rein**（韁繩），**bit**就會緊繃，馬頭就會受到控制無法自由轉動。然而一旦馬匹把**bit**咬住，不讓**rider**以韁繩控制牠的速度和方向，這時牠就有了自主權，猶如脫韁野馬，完全照著自己的意志走自己的路。**in**也可用**between**。

- If you want to get the civil case done, you need to take the bit in your teeth.
  如果你想搞定這個民事訴訟，你得有主見，把自主權拿穩。
- He took the bit between his teeth and now there is no stopping him.
  他不再受人擺佈，現在沒什麼事能阻擋得了他。
- He took the bit in his teeth and acted against his parents' wishes.
  他自己管自己，沒照著父母的意願行事。
- Someone was needed to direct the project, so I took the bit in my teeth.
  總得有人主導這個案子，所以我出面執掌。

Write your own sentence:

- When I really take the bit in my teeth, ____________
  ______________________________________.

MEMO

neck 使頭與身體相連的脖子

NECK連結了頭與身體，窄窄的一小截，卻是極度重要的關卡。所以如果對某人而言，某事是**neck or nothing**，就表示做這件事如同拿**NECK**來賭，孤注一擲、鋌而走險。又如果有人被形容是**NECK**以上的部份都失去了感覺，則表示此人非常蠢、蠢爆了。如：

It is neck or nothing on my side.
就我而言這事只能放手一搏了。(輸了脖子就慘了)

He acts like he is dead from the neck up.
他做起事來好像沒腦袋似的。(脖子以上石化了?)

NECK除了如橋樑一般連結頭與身，它也像是頭的方向盤，主宰著頭的動向。如果**NECK**靈活，頭就能四面八方地轉，如果脖子僵硬，頭稍稍一動都難受。但有人天生就是「硬頸」，這說的並不是脖子硬，而是脾氣硬。若是脖子硬的像黃銅，打不壞還讓人手疼，則表示此人恬不知恥，臉皮超厚。如：

a stiff-necked egghead → 固執高傲的學究

He had the brass neck to visit her. → 他竟有臉去她家。

NECK除了表示身體的頸部，也意指各種頸狀物。如：

the neck of a goblet → 高腳杯頸

當動詞用時，表示摟著脖子親吻，如：

He is necking with Mary. → 他與Mary擁吻。

說到**NECK**，絕不能忘記**NECK**內部的**THROAT**，它主掌了聲音的音量與質感，幾個與它有關的慣用語都與聲音有關。如：**deep throat**（深喉嚨、怕被人聽出聲音所以用低音嗓說話的人），意指揭發不法內幕、提供內幕消息的政府高層官員。又如：

Whenever he hums the tune, I get a lump in my throat.
每次他輕哼這首曲子，我就想哭。（喉嚨裡有團塊~哽咽~）

He is singing with a frog in his throat.
他以嘶啞的聲音唱著歌。（喉嚨裡有青蛙？）

NECK可說是生命的樞紐，它不只使頭身相連，倘若內部的**artery**（動脈）與**vein**（靜脈）出了問題，就算保住了命，身體卻可能癱瘓。因此割喉、就等於割斷生命的血脈，可見**cut-throat competition**（割喉式競爭）這種激烈的價格戰，一不小心就有可能失血過多走向滅亡。

MEMO

neck

1

a pain in the neck

脖子痛，令人討厭的人事物

someone or something that is very annoying; a nuisance

脖子痛雖不是什麼大問題，卻會嚴重影響生活，既無法自由轉頭，稍不小心還會讓人痛得嘎嘎叫。因此脖子上的痛處，就表示一切難搞難纏之流、令人頭疼的人事物；但反過來說，可千萬注意別讓自己成了別人的脖子痛。

- It is a real pain in the neck when the power or water supply is cut off.

  斷電斷水的時候真的很討厭。

- I don't want to be a pain in the neck, but can you remember to flush the toilet?

  不是我想找麻煩，但可不可以拜託你記得沖馬桶？

- He is a pain in the neck, with his constant complaining.

  他和他沒完沒了的抱怨都好惹人厭。

Write your own sentence:

- It is a real pain in the neck when ________________

  ______________________________________.

2

a millstone around one's neck

磨石掛在脖子上，沈重的負擔、拖累

a continual burden or handicap

脖子上的磨石意指難以卸除的重擔或阻礙，磨石也可用 **yoke**（牛軛）。若換成 **albatross**（信天翁），則表示害慘某人的重擔。這源自浪漫時期詩作 **"The Ancient Mariner"**：老漁夫誤殺信天翁，以致眾人認定漁夫是漁船擱淺的罪魁禍首，強迫他把鳥屍掛在脖子上，於是脖子上的信天翁便意指難以擺脫的麻煩事。

- He finds his son, who is lazy and crabby, a millstone around his neck.

  他覺得他那又懶又愛發牢騷的兒子是他的千斤重擔。

- He has a huge mortgage that has become a yoke around his neck.

  他巨額的房貸，成了他沈重的枷鎖。

- The division is an albatross around our necks, making losses of millions a year.

  這個部門每年虧損幾百萬，成了拖垮我們大家的累贅。

Write your own sentence:

- ____________________ is somewhat like a millstone around my neck.

neck

3

break one's neck

折斷脖子，拚命地做，盡力讓事情以最快的速度完成

to work very hard to accomplish something as soon as possible

動作猛或速度快都容易傷到脖子，如果做事不惜折頸，就表示十分賣力、拼命，另外也意指飛快的完成某事，因此形容詞**breakneck**便意指「速度飛快的」。但如果脖子不是折斷而是被某人擰斷（**wring**），則表示某人氣到不讓你好過。**neck**換用**back**也意指辛勞賣命，但不強調快速。

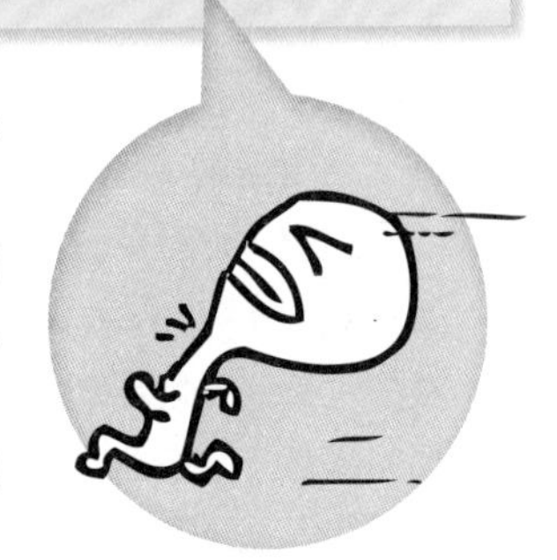

- If you don't break your neck to get there on time, she'll wring your neck.

  如果你不拚了命地準時到那裡，她肯定扭斷你脖子。

- You don't have to break your neck to fix this stereo. Take your time!

  你不用忙著趕修這台音響，慢慢來就可以！

- He is breaking his back trying to scrape up the money to start his own café.

  他為了湊足開咖啡店的錢，拚得腰都快斷了。

Write your own sentence:

- I broke my neck to ______________ for fear that ______________________________.

4

neck and neck

脖子對脖子，勢均力敵，旗鼓相當

to be exactly even, especially in a race or a contest

在賽馬中，要看哪一匹馬領先，主要看脖子。如果兩匹馬脖子的位置難分前後，就表示勝敗難分，類似的慣用語還有 **nip and tuck**（該切、該填[此源自整型用語]，勝負還很難說）。如果最後勝出的馬只領先一點點，則是 **win by a neck**，只贏了一段脖子的距離。

- May and Ben were neck and neck in the spelling contest. They tied for first place.

  May和Ben在拼字比賽中不分上下，兩人並列第一。

- Recent polls show that the two presidential candidates are still neck and neck.

  最近民調顯示，兩名總統候選人依舊勢均力敵。

- It is nip and tuck between Jack and Carl in doing foolhardy things.

  要比鹵莽的話，Jack和Carl是軒輊難分。

Write your own sentence:

- ________ and I are neck and neck all the way in ______________________________.

5

neck of the woods

樹林的峽長地帶，某某地帶，某人住的地帶

a neighborhood or region

樹林裡如脖子般的峽長地帶，是早期移民安身立命之所在。隨著城鄉發展，這個慣用語已泛指「某個地帶」，不分城鄉。與鄉村有關的脖子還有**redneck**（紅脖子），原是美國北方人對南方人的貶稱，現也通稱沒受過教育、頑固保守的鄉下人，有的人不喜歡這個稱呼，但也有南方人以身為紅脖子自豪。

- You won't find any boutiques in this neck of the woods.

  在這一帶你不可能找得到精品店的。

- I am surprised to see you in our neck of the woods. What brings you here?

  好意外在我們這一帶見到你，什麼風把你吹來的？

- Most rednecks wear plaid shirts, have blue-collar jobs, and like living in the sticks.

  大多南方農夫都穿彩格絨杉，屬藍領階級，喜歡住在人煙稀少的鄉下。

- How's business in your neck of the woods right now?

  你那一區現在生意如何？

Write your own sentence:

- There is no ____________ in my neck of the woods.

6

stick one's neck out

伸出脖子，冒著危險挺身而出

to take a risk; to make oneself vulnerable

殺雞時，屠夫都會先將雞脖子拉出來，因此，若要某人伸出脖子，就表示要這人冒著惹禍上身的危險。**put one's neck／head on the block**（把脖子[或頭]放在砧板上）意思類似，但較強調為討某人高興，明知會得罪別人也要去做。**risk one's neck／life／limb**（冒著脖子／生命／四肢的危險），則強調冒著受傷甚至沒命的風險。

- He is going to stick his neck out and expose their plot.

  他決定挺身而出，揭發他們的陰謀。

- He put his neck on the block for her but it all backfired.

  他為了她出生入死，結果惹得自己一身腥。

- They risked their necks to rescue her from the burning building.

  他們冒著生命危險將她從大樓烈燄中救出。

Write your own sentence:

- I have the courage to stick my neck out to

  ______________________________.

7

save one's neck

救了某人脖子，為某人解圍，使某人倖免於難

to save one from harm, punishment or difficulties

如果有人出手救了已架在**scaffold**（斷頭台）上的脖子，就表示為某人解除危機、使某人不致挨罰、受困或危險。把**neck**換成**skin**（皮膚）或**bacon**（培根）也可以，在以前培根可是十分珍貴的貨品。反之如果沒人救脖子，那就只能**get it in the neck**（脖子被K），等著挨罵、挨罰、慘透透了。

- While I was having trouble changing the flat tire, he came along and saved my neck.

  正當我不知該如何卸下漏氣輪胎時，他走過來幫了我大忙。

- This witness could really save your neck.

  這名證人可救你一命。

- He saved his skin by telling her he stayed with me last night.

  他跟她說他昨天跟我在一起，這才沒糟殃。

- It is always the coach who gets it in the neck when the team does badly.

  球隊表現不好的時候，挨罵倒楣的都是教練。

Write your own sentence:

- I saved my neck by __________ when____________ ________________________.

8

at each other's throats

對準彼此的喉嚨，針鋒相對，槓上了

to be in angry disagreement

一心想勒住對方的喉嚨，就表示兩人合不來，口角不斷甚至拳腳相向。如果**cut each other's throats**（割彼此的喉嚨），那就嚴重了，**cut**會流血，流血過多會傷亡，總之一旦被割了喉，就只能等著失敗、倒台、完蛋、毀滅。

- They are always at each other's throats over who is the apple of John's eye.
  他們老是吵來吵去，爭執著誰是John心愛的人。
- John and Mary have been at each other's throats since they met.
  打從John和Mary認識起，這兩人就鬥個不停。
- With their price war, the two stores were cutting each other's throats.
  這兩家店以價格戰互相殘殺。
- If I were to run for office, I would just be cutting my own throat.
  我如果參選，就是在自毀前程。

Write your own sentence:

- __________ are always at each other's throats over ______________________________________.

9

jump down someone's throat

跳入某人喉嚨，粗暴回應某人的話，過度指責某人行為

to react angrily to something that someone says or does

叫人閉嘴已夠沒禮貌了，竟還跳進人家的喉嚨，這種回應別人的方式實在粗暴恐怖。若沒人跳進喉嚨，卻覺得有什麼東西梗在喉嚨裡（**stick in one's throat**），這東西肯定是令人看不下去、難以接受。又如果梗在喉嚨裡的是話語（**words**），則表示有話要說卻說不出來。

- Even if he was wrong, you didn't have to jump down his throat.
  就算他錯了，你也不必這樣糟蹋他。
- Don't jump down my throat. I was just trying to be helpful.
  別亂罵人，我只不過是想幫點忙。
- I meant to apologize but the words stuck in my throat.
  我很想道歉，但所有話語全梗在喉嚨說不出來。
- What sticks in my throat is the way he bosses everyone around.
  他對大家發號施令、頤指氣使的樣子，讓我實在很看不慣。

Write your own sentence:

- It is ______________ to jump down others' throats.

10

ram … down someone's throat

強把…灌入某人喉嚨裡，強迫某人接受…

to compel someone to accept something

被強迫灌食，不論灌的是食物、藥物、意見、想法、還是某個人事物，都是令人不舒服的經驗。**ram** 可換成其他意指強灌硬塞的動詞，如：**cram**（塞滿）／**force**（強迫）／**push**（逼迫）／**shove**（推擠衝撞）／**stuff**（填塞）／**thrust**（用力擠塞）。

- The harsh carer forced the hot porridge down the patient's throat.
  粗魯的看護硬把熱粥灌進病患喉嚨裡。
- I don't want anyone to ram any insurance down my throat.
  我不希望有人來勉強我買保險。
- Please don't try to stuff those lies down our throats.
  拜託別再強迫我們相信那些謊話了。
- Why are you always trying to cram your political views down my throat?
  你幹嘛一直強迫我接受你的政治觀點？

Write your own sentence:

- I don't like the ______________ they are ramming down my throat.

11

go for the jugular

直取頸靜脈，直擊要害

to attack fiercely in order to have no doubt about winning

武俠片裡常見這種畫面，鋒利的劍尖抵在某人咽喉上，一動手就能置對方於死地。這個慣用語表示對準對方最弱的地方，毫不留情地進攻，一般用於運動、商業、政治、辯論等。又，如果有某事 **make one's gorge rise**（使某人咽喉上升、想吐），則表示這件事令人極不舒服，噁心想吐。

- She went for the jugular of her opponent by saying that he sponged off women.
  她犀利地直擊對手弱點，說他吃軟飯、拿女人當靠山。
- He failed to go for the jugular in the last set and the match ended in a draw.
  他沒能在最後一局直擊對方要害，比賽最終以平局結束。
- The gory sight made my gorge rise.
  這個血淋淋的畫面看了令我難過想吐。

Write your own sentence:

- Should I go for the jugular of __________ by ______________________________?

MEMO

shoulder

背扛挑的肩

& elbow

推擠撞的肘

不論是背、扛、挑，總之要將某人事物擔在身上，就少不了用到**SHOULDER**，也因此**SHOULDER**常與責任的承擔有關，如Bee Gees（比吉斯）**Rest Your Love on Me**中的歌詞：**Lay your troubles on my shoulders.**（把你的難題都交給我）；又或**stand shoulder to shoulder**（肩並肩站在一起），表示齊心協力。**SHOULDER**當動詞用，更直接意指了「肩負、擔負」或「以肩推擠」，如：

We must shoulder the future of our country.
我們應擔負起國家的前途。

He shouldered the door open. 他用肩把門頂開。

對拳擊手而言，**SHOULDER**是最重要的部位，要抬手、要格擋、要出擊，都需要靈活的**SHOULDER**。因此如果有人說：**I'll tell you, straight from the shoulder, that**…就表示這人打算直截了當地告訴你…，不想拐彎抹角，一如拳擊手由肩膀傳遞最大力道直接出擊。

SHOULDER也意指肩狀物，如：

Don't drive on the shoulder. 勿行駛路肩。

與**SHOULDER**如同兄弟般的身體部位非**ELBOW**莫屬。一如**SHOULDER**連結軀幹與上臂，**ELBOW**連結上臂與前臂，兩者都是身體移動時很容易與別人擦撞的部位。因此**elbow-room**意指能充分活動的空間，如：**There isn't any elbow-room.**（空間小的連轉身都不夠）；而**elbow bump**則表示以撞肘互相問候。至於**ELBOW**當動詞，意思是以肘推擠，如：

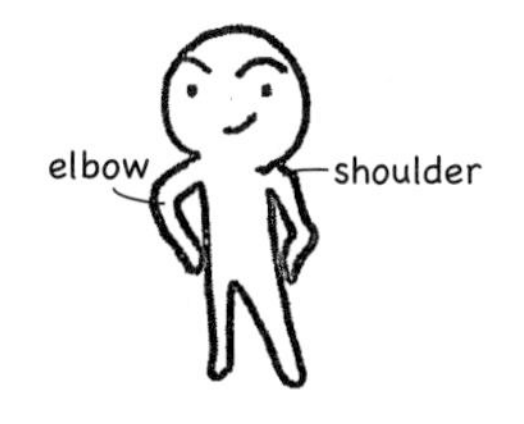

He elbowed his way through the crowd.
他一路從人群中擠過去。

MEMO

1

the cold shoulder

冷肩膀，冷淡的對待

deliberate coldness or disregard, a slight or snub

心情難過時，最需要 **a shoulder to cry on**（可靠著哭的肩膀），若得到的是 **cold shoulder**（冷肩膀），那真是雪上加霜。冷肩膀意指刻意忽略、怠慢，因為過去有個習俗，對於受歡迎的客人，主人會款待以熱呼呼的烤肉，反之，對於不喜歡的客人，則隨便以 **cold shoulder of lamb or beef**（冷掉的羊肩肉或牛肩肉）招待了事。

- When I said hello to her, she gave me the cold shoulder and looked past me.
  我跟她打招呼，結果她理都不理，裝做沒看見我。
- He used to wish me good morning, but now he gives me the cold shoulder.
  他以前都會跟我道聲早安，現在卻對我不理不睬。
- If you greet her at a party, you'll just get the cold shoulder.
  如果你在聚會上跟她打招呼，那只會是熱臉貼冷屁股。
- When he was out of town, I had no shoulder to cry on.
  他出門在外，都沒人聽我倒垃圾、吐苦水。

Write your own sentence:

- I got the cold shoulder when I ________________.

2

carry the weight of the world on one's shoulders

把全世界扛在肩上，身負重任

to be burdened with too much responsibility

這個慣用語源自希臘神話中受到宙斯懲罰、以肩頂住世界的**Atlas**，也因此**atlas**就成了代表「地圖」的單字。所扛之物可自行變化，不一定要與**Atlas**一樣扛世界。肩膀常與責任相關，**have broad shoulders**除了意指肩膀寬大，也意指有擔負重任的能力。

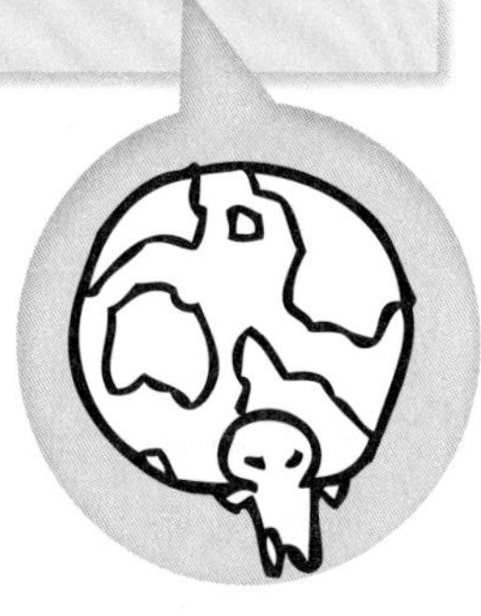

- You don't need to carry the weight of the world on your shoulders.

  你沒必要什麼責任都往自己身上攬。

- Bob is carrying the success of the conference on his shoulders.

  Bob身負重任，決定這場會談成功與否。

- We need someone who has broad shoulders to step into the director's shoes.

  我們需要一個有肩膀的人來接這位董事的位子。

Write your own sentence:

- Should I carry ______________________ on my shoulders?

3

have a chip on one's shoulder

肩上有碎木塊，（覺得不公平或不如人而）心懷不滿、耿耿於懷

to have a grievance or a sense of inferiority about something

十九世紀美國小孩打架時，會在肩上放碎木塊（**chip of wood**）問對方敢不敢踢下木塊，一旦踢下，接著就幹架起來。因此某人肩上有碎木塊，一來表示此人好鬥，動輒想找人吵嘴或打架，二來表示此人一肚子怨氣，心裡老有根刺，彷彿全世界都對不起他、都想踢下他肩上碎木與他為敵。

- He has had a chip on his shoulder ever since he was sacked for drunkenness.
  他因酗酒被炒魷魚後，火氣一直很大，看什麼都不順眼。
- He has a chip on his shoulder about not having obtained the scholarship.
  他因為沒拿到獎學金心裡很不痛快。
- He has always had a chip on his shoulder about his poor upbringing.
  他一直為自己出身貧寒心存介蒂。

Write your own sentence:

- Never have a chip on your shoulder just because ______________________.

4

rub shoulders with someone

與某人磨擦肩膀，與某人交際、往來（尤指名人）

to meet or socialize with someone, especially famous people

社交場合主要是為了 **develop connections**（拓展人脈），所以參加的人往往都是政商名流。在這種場合中總可見到一群人手拿酒杯，與人聊天，觥籌交錯。拿酒杯聊天，很容易碰撞彼此的肩膀或手肘，因此這個意指與名人交際應酬或打交道的慣用語，將 **shoulders** 換成 **elbows**，意思也是一樣的。

- At the banquet, diplomats were rubbing shoulders with heads of state from Asia.

  宴會中，外交官們與亞洲各國元首交際應酬。

- This hairdresser regularly rubs shoulders with top movies stars.

  這個髮型師平時往來的對象都是超級巨星。

- The reception offered him a chance to rub elbows with the rich and famous.

  這個接待會給了他一個認識富豪名流的機會。

Write your own sentence:

- ________________ would be a chance for me to rub shoulders with ____________________.

5

square one's shoulders

挺直肩膀，準備好面對逆境的決心

to prepare to face adversity and show fearlessness

軍士們應戰之前，如果肩膀下垂，這場戰事恐怕很難獲勝，只有挺直肩膀，才表示已準備好迎向困難。至於**shrug shoulders**（聳肩），則表示某人不在乎或下不了決定。**look over one's shoulder**（由肩膀往後看），表示某人由於憂心或沒安全感，時刻都在提防。

- The actress squared her shoulders and faced the hostile audience.
  這名女演員作好準備，面對不友善的觀眾。
- Joe squared his shoulders and re-entered the game.
  Joe拿出勇氣，再次上場比賽。
- When I asked him if he minded switching over to channel 4, he just shrugged his shoulders.
  我問他可否轉到第四台，他不置可否。
- He has paranoia. He is constantly looking over his shoulder.
  他這人有疑心病，時刻都在提防。

Write your own sentence:

- I know it won't be easy but I will square my shoulders and ________.

6

at one's elbow

在手肘邊，在某人手邊、身邊

to be close at hand; to be nearby

倘若某人或某物位於我們手肘碰得到的地方，就表示離我們非常地近。如果**out at the elbows**（手肘露出來），則表示肘部有破洞，意指某人衣衫襤褸、非常窮困。衣服容易磨破的部位除了肘部，還有**knees**（膝蓋）和**heels**（腳跟），所以**elbows**也可換用這兩個字。

- The columnist always works with a pot of coffee at his elbow.
  這名專欄作家寫作時手邊一定有壺咖啡。
- The apprentice was constantly at the master's elbow.
  這名學徒經常跟在師傅身邊寸步不離。
- When we last saw Eric, he was out at the elbows.
  我們上次見到Eric時，他看起來很潦倒。
- John strolled around out at the elbows just because he wanted to imitate a certain style of life.
  John穿得破破的到處遛達，只因為他想仿效某種特別的生活方式。

Write your own sentence:

- I always keep ____________ at my elbow while I ____.

7

bend one's elbow

彎曲手肘，不醉不歸

to drink alcohol to excess

不彎肘，就無法把酒送入口中，手肘彎不停，就表示喝很多，同義的慣用語還有**drink like a fish**（喝酒像魚喝水一樣）。有時喝酒是為了**drown one's sorrows**（借酒澆愁），有時是**social drinking**（為應酬而喝），喝酒難免會**toast**（舉杯祝賀）、喊一聲**cheers**（乾杯），若有人喊**bottoms up**，則是要喝乾見底，杯底不可飼金魚。此慣用語**bend**也可用**crook**（彎曲，使成鉤狀）。

- Her husband rather overdoes it with bending his elbow.
  她老公喝酒喝得實在太超過了。
- Your eyes look red and tired. Did you crook your elbow last night?
  你雙眼看起來紅紅的很累，昨晚喝酒了？
- I worry about Mike; he drinks like a fish.
  我很擔心Mike，他酒喝得好兇。
- Shall we stay in and drown our sorrows?
  要不要我們就窩在家裡、一醉解千愁？

Write your own sentence:

- As I know, __________ is known to bend the elbow now and then.

8

give someone the elbow

用手肘推某人，結束與某人的感情

to end a romantic relationship with someone

用手肘推撞，表示不想讓別人靠近自己，這個慣用語原本指排擠、開除某人，現常用來表示情人的分手。分手的說法還有 **break up**／**split up**／**go separate ways**／**part ways**／**cut ties**。

- She **gave him the elbow** because he was caught cheating on her.
  她跟他分了，因為他偷吃當場被逮到。
- Tom wants to **break up** with Mary because he is seeing someone else.
  Tom想和Mary分手，因為他有別人了。
- They **split up** after a year of marriage.
  他們結婚一年就分了。
- His affair had left his marriage on the line. After divorce, they **went their separate ways**.
  他的外遇使婚姻亮起紅燈。離婚後，他們即分道揚鑣。

Write your own sentence:

- I will surely give my partner the elbow if ________________________.

chest 住了心肺的胸
& heart 住了自我的心

CHEST像個小屋子，裡面住了**heart**（心）與**lungs**（肺），外面露著**breast**（胸脯或乳房）。因此心肺引起的胸痛叫**chest pains**，胸部大則是**big breasts**。正由於**CHEST**包含了心與肺，一旦有心事、胸就容易悶，除非**get…off one's chest**（一吐為快），把心事一掃而空，胸口自然不再鬱悶。

像個小屋子的**CHEST**也意指有蓋子的大箱或櫃子，如：

an oak chest → 橡木箱　**a chest of drawers** → 五斗櫃

bosom也意指胸，但**bosom**常用於抽象觀念的「心胸、胸懷」，如：

a bosom friend → 知心朋友

再來，讓我們談談住在**CHEST**裡面的大人物：**HEART**。身為器官的**HEART**，為了輸送血液不停地跳動。然而當情緒出現，心跳（**heartbeat**）往往跟著變化。所以心常象徵情感或情緒，一如頭之象徵理智，如：

My head says no but my heart says yes.
→ 理智上我知道不可以，但情感上卻想要。

又如：

a heart-throb →
令人心跳加快的男人，也就是所謂的萬人迷、女性殺手。

a heart-breaking／heart-rending news
→ 令人心碎或心痛的消息

He left her with a heavy heart. → 他帶著沈重的心情離開她。

由情感延伸，**HEART** 也代表心的意向、想法，若某事離心很近，就表示這件事對自己而言很重要，自己十分重視或關注，然而一旦心變了，就意謂著感情或想法改變了，如：

Animal rights is an issue very close to my heart.
→ 動物權是我十分關注的一個議題。

He had a change of heart at the last minute.
→ 他在最後一分鐘改變心意。

又由於 **HEART** 位居身體中樞地位，它也代表中心或核心。如：

agricultural／industrial heartland → 農業／工業重鎮

get to the heart of the matter → 切入事情的核心

此外還有信心、良心也都需要心，因此 **HEART** 也意指勇氣、熱忱、真心。**take heart**（抓住心）就是要拾起勇氣，**a half-hearted attitude**（半顆心的態度）則表示隨便、不認真的態度，**cry one's heart out**（把心都哭出來了）表示嚎啕大哭，哭得椎心泣血。

HEART 也意指心形物，如：
I have the king of hearts. → 我有紅心老K。

把 **HEART+EN** 即成動詞 **hearten**，把真心信心傳給別人，就表示鼓勵、使他人振奮，如：

I was heartened by his success.
→ 他的成功令我大受鼓舞、感到振奮。

chest & heart

1

beat one's chest

敲胸，捶胸頓足，強調自己極度悲痛或遺憾等

to make an exaggerated display of one's feelings of guilt, remorse, grief, etc.

捶胸頓足、主要是為了讓別人看見自己如何痛心疾首、悲傷懊悔，但誰都知道那不過是做做樣子。**chest**也可換用**breast**。事實上，如果真有什麼事**break one's heart**（傷透某人的心），不需刻意敲個不停（**beat**），心早就已碎成片片。

- The executive is beating his breast about the latest round of layoffs.

  執行長對於最新一波裁員深表遺憾。

- He is beating his chest about her death, but actually they were never friends.

  他對她的死深表痛心，但事實上他們並沒交情可言。

- If the verdict is guilty, it will break her mother's heart.

  如果判決有罪，肯定令她母親心碎。

Write your own sentence:

- There is no point in beating our chests about

  ______________________________.

2

get … off one's chest

卸下胸中的…，一吐為快，放下心上一塊石頭

to relieve one's mind by confessing something that has been repressed

胸如同貯藏心事與秘密的櫃子。太重的事放在櫃子裡，櫃子早晚會被壓垮。把心事說出來，救了櫃子，也讓自己鬆一口氣。除了**chest**，**breast**（胸部）也可藏放心事，若放了不好的事，最好清除掉它：**make a clean breast of…**（坦白認罪、和盤托出），讓**breast**保持清潔為上策。

- Is there something you want to get off your chest?
  你心裡可有什麼話不吐不快？
- You will feel better if you find a bosom friend and get it off your chest.
  找個知心朋友說出你的心事，這樣你會好過一點。
- I am tired of you telling me what to do. I am glad to get this off my chest.
  我受夠你老是告訴我該怎麼做，我好高興終於把這話說出來了。
- He decided to make a clean breast of the incident to his parents.
  他決定對爸媽老實說出這起事件的始末。

Write your own sentence:

- I have been worrying about ______________. I need to get it off my chest.

3

play one's cards close to one's chest

讓牌緊靠胸口，行事小心以免洩密

to be secretive or cautious; to give nothing away

玩撲克牌時，為免別人看到而把牌緊靠胸前，表示此人行事隱密、不輕易透露事況。**chest**也可用**vest**（背心），**cards**可簡縮成**it**。這種作風易給人深藏不露的感覺，但小心，此慣用語強調行事小心縝密，而**Still waters run deep.**（靜水流深）則表示安靜少言、卻深謀遠慮，是另一種深藏不露。

- We never know his next move because he always plays his cards close to his chest.

  我們永遠不知他下一步要做什麼，因為他這人行事作風一向縝密。

- The company is legendary for playing its cards close to its chest in terms of new product development.

  這家公司在推出新產品這個環節上十分謹慎小心，保密到家。

- The agent is playing it close to his vest as to when the band will begin their world tour.

  經紀人完全不願透露這樂團何時開始世界巡迴演唱。

Write your own sentence:

- I have no idea of ________________. They play it close to their chests.

4

at heart

內心裡，實際上

in one's innermost or hidden nature; secretly or fundamentally

人的內心世界常常和外在表現大不相同，難怪需要 **at heart** 來註明某個從心發出的訊息，因為它們很難由外表看得出來。因此，**at heart** 也意指「本質上；其實」。又，如果是從肺部最高處發出：**at the top of one's lungs**，則表示用盡肺活量盡可能地大聲、聲嘶力竭地。

- His academic adviser has his best interests at heart.
  他的指導教授心裡都在為他的利益著想。
- Although many people dislike him, he is a nice person at heart.
  雖然很多人不喜歡他，但他其實是個很好的人。
- He is a conservative good fellow at heart.
  基本上他是一個保守的好人。
- Those grandmas are young at heart, cheering wildly at the top of their lungs.
  那些阿嬤仍有赤子之心，一個個扯著喉嚨瘋狂歡呼。

Write your own sentence:

- I ______________________ at heart.

5

be after one's own heart

跟隨某人的心，與某人意氣相投

to one's own personal liking; with similar preferences, feelings or ideas

跟在後面表示同方向，心的方向相同，表示兩人合得來，興趣、觀念、感受都相似。這個慣用語源自聖經（Samuel 13：14），可用來指意氣相投的人，也可形容合心意、投所好的人事物。順著心表示投合，如果是對心有助益：**do one's heart good**，則表示使心感到十分快樂。

- Lee is a man after her own heart. They both live a simple life and enjoy it.

  Lee和她很合，兩人都過著簡樸的生活且樂在其中。

- He is very patient with slow pupils; he is a teacher after my own heart.

  他對反應遲緩的學生很有耐心，正是我心中好老師的樣子。

- It does my heart good to see the young couple so happy.

  看到這對年輕人這麼幸福，我心裡真高興。

Write your own sentence:

- ____________ is a man after my own heart because ______________________________.

6

cross one's heart

在心上畫十字，發誓、保證

to attest to the truth of something solemnly

cross 意指十字架，當動詞用表示「交叉、畫十字」。左手放心上或畫十字、右手指著天空，這是發誓時常有的動作，表示敢讓天地神明共鑒自己所言不假，皆出自真心。所以若要某人 **put hand on heart**（把手放在心上），就是要這人發誓、保證所說的一切都是真的、並非謊言。

- I did hand in my assignment – cross my heart.

  我真的有交作業，我發誓。

- Bob, it wasn't me who revealed the secret -- cross my heart!

  Bob，洩密的人真的不是我，我發誓！

- Can you put your hand on your heart and say you've never loved anyone else?

  你敢發誓你從沒愛過別人？

Write your own sentence:

- I did ________________________ --
  cross my heart.

7

have a heart

長顆心，發發慈悲、行行好

to show kindness and pity; to be merciful

無情的人常被形容沒心肝，要求某人長顆心表示希望他有同情心，發發善心，通常用在拜託別人的時候。但如果有人對你說**You're all heart.**（你真好心），有可能表示你心好得不得了，但也可能語帶諷刺。另外注意，**have the heart**（to V）意指有勇氣（敢做某事），與好心沒關係。

- Have a heart — I can't repay you until next month.

  拜託做做好事，錢我下個月才能還你。

- If she had a heart, she would volunteer a statement to the police.

  如果她有良心，她就會主動向警方供出情況了。

- A: Eve can't bear to see anyone upset.
  B: She's all heart.

  A：Eve受不了看到有人難過。
  B：她還真好心。

- How could we have the heart to disobey Mom?

  我們哪有膽子敢不聽媽的話？

Write your own sentence:

- Hey, have a heart and ________________.

have a heart of stone

長了顆石頭心，冷酷無情，鐵石心腸

to have no feelings of kindness or sympathy; to be cold and unfriendly

心若成了一顆冷硬的石頭，就表示此人冷酷無情，不知同情為何物。但有時心並非鐵石，卻必須狠下心，那就只好 **harden／steel one's heart**（讓心變硬）。但要小心，有的人心是熱的，冷的只是手。**cold hands, warm heart**（冷手、熱心）形容一個人不常表達感情，但內心其實飽含感情。

- Her landlord has a heart of stone. He was cruel to every tenant.

  她房東很沒良心，對每個房客都很壞。

- He found it difficult to harden his heart against his wife.

  他發現他對他老婆就是狠不下心說不。

- He rarely sends flowers or anything, but he is a case of cold hands, warm heart.

  他很少送花什麼的，他這人是外冷內熱。

Write your own sentence:

- I don't think I have a heart of stone because ______________________.

9

have a heart of gold

長了顆黃金心，本性良善、菩薩心腸

to be generous, sincere, and kind in nature

有顆閃亮的金心，表示心腸好、樂於助人。若**heart in the right place**（心長對了地方），也表示此人心眼好，宅心仁厚。但若善良過頭使心流血，那就成了**bleeding heart**（濫好人）。又若心跑進嘴巴或靴子裡（**in one's mouth or boots**），則表示此人六神無主，驚慌失措，因為心跑去了不該去的地方。

- He often plays a villain in movies, but in real life he has a heart of gold.
  他常在電影中演反派，但實際生活裡他是個大好人。
- He is a bit annoying sometimes but his heart is in the right place.
  他這人偶爾有點盧，但他心地很善良。
- His heart was in his boots as he waited for news of the plane crash.
  在等空難消息的時候，他六神無主、不知所措。

 Write your own sentence:

- I have a heart of gold and I ______________________________.

a heart-to-heart talk

心對心的交談，認真、坦誠的談話，談心

a candid and sincere talk

說話只動口不用心，就不真心。雙方都有用「心」來談話，就表示彼此的談話誠懇坦白。心對心的交談，前提要把心打開，**open one's heart to…**（對…打開心房）就表示說出心中的想法、感受等。**pour out one's heart to…**（把心往…倒出去）意思一樣，把像水一樣的心事一股腦倒出去，傾訴出來。

- Let's sit down and have a heart-to-heart talk about your coming marriage.
  咱們坐下來，好好聊聊你即將舉行的婚禮。
- We met in the guest house for a heart-to-heart talk about the conduct of the business.
  我們約在招待所，以便就企業的管理深談一番。
- Feeling upset over the school grades, he poured out his heart to his mother.
  他為成績的事心好煩，便向母親吐露了他的心聲。

Write your own sentence:

- ________ and I may need to have a heart-to-heart talk about ________________.

11

learn … by heart

用心學…，將…背誦下來，牢記在心

to memorize something

心不在焉是記誦的大敵，心在，記憶才不會**good-bye**。**learn**用**know**也可以，同義的慣用語還有**commit…to memory**（將…交給記憶）。小心，記住和記得（**remember**）不一樣，記住是隨時都能喚出記憶朗朗上口，記得是**keep in mind**，將某事放心上以免忘記又或無意間自然地想起來。

- All the cast members have learned their lines by heart before the dress rehearsal.
  所有演出人員都已在彩排之前將台詞背熟。
- He had trouble committing the text to memory, but his teacher insisted on it.
  這篇課文他怎麼背就是背不起來，但老師非要他背出不可。
- I just remembered that it's your birthday today.
  我剛剛才想起來，今天是你生日。
- Remember to learn these legal terms by heart by tomorrow.
  別忘了明天以前要把這些法律用語記熟。

Write your own sentence:

- Before I learned ________ by heart, I went over it many times.

12

lose one's heart to…

把心輸給了…，愛上或超喜歡…

to fall in love with someone or something

情住在心房裡，一旦投降開門、讓對方進駐，就表示深愛某人或某物。但若有人 **steal one's heart**（偷走某人的心），則表示悄悄取得了某人的感情。勇氣也住在心裡，一旦 **can't find it in one's heart**（在心裡找不到），就表示提不起勇氣做某事；甚者，若 **lose heart**（失去心）就表示灰心失意，沮喪氣餒。

- I totally lost my heart to the puppy.
  我被這隻小狗打敗了，我超喜歡牠的。
- Never lose heart even if you're far behind.
  即便你遠遠落後，也千萬別灰心。
- The married man stole her heart but she couldn't find it in her heart to hate him.
  這個已有家室的男人設法讓她愛上了他，但她就是無法恨他。

Write your own sentence:

- I lost my heart to ____________ when I was ______________________________.

chest & heart

13

one's heart stood still

嚇得心都停住了

to be frightened, shocked, or startled very much

stand still 意指站著不動，心停住不動，就表示受到驚嚇又或極度興奮，總之情緒十分強烈。類似的慣用語還有：**have heart failure**（心臟麻痺）、**one's heart skips／misses a beat**（心跳瞬間漏掉一拍）。

- When the bear appeared in front of me, my heart stood still.

  當這隻熊出現在我面前，我嚇得心跳都沒了。

- I just about had heart failure when I heard about her accident.

  聽到她發生事故，我擔心得差點得心臟病。

- My heart skipped a beat when I heard my name called out in the list of finalists.

  聽到自己的名字出現在決選名單，我的心猛跳了一下。

 Write your own sentence:

- My heart stood still when

  ______________________________.

14

one's heart goes out to someone

心發向某人，同情或憐憫某人

to feel sympathy or have compassion for someone

此慣用語意指對某人有同理心、即心有戚戚焉。另一個慣用語 **one's heart bleeds**（心在滴血），原本也是指覺得某人可憐，深感憐憫，但現在較常用於反諷或玩笑，亦即故意以「我的心好痛哦」、「你好可憐哦」來表示根本不覺得對方有何值得同情之處。

- My heart goes out to the victims and their families of this tragedy.

  我好為這場悲劇的受害者以及他們的家人難過。

- My heart bleeds for her as I see her toiling along on her weary feet.

  看她拖著疲憊的腳步艱辛地前進，令我感到好不忍。

- He only got you a luxury handbag for your birthday? My heart bleeds for you.

  妳生日他只買名牌包送妳？我好替你難過哦！

Write your own sentence:

- My heart goes out to ______ who ______________________.

search one's heart

往心搜尋，自省反思，捫心自問

to examine one's conscience, innermost feelings, and motives

搜尋是為了找回遺失之物，搜尋自己的心，就表示想找出深層的關於自己的真相，誠實地問問自己，了解自己。**heart** 換用 **soul**（靈魂）也可以。**heart-searching** 或 **soul-searching** 是名詞，意為省思，也可當形容詞，意為反省的、自我檢討的。

- If you could search your heart, you would know you were equally to blame.
  如果你能反省一下，你就會明白自己也有錯。

- He searched his soul trying to decide if he had been fair to all his children.
  他捫心自問，想確定自己是否有公平對待所有子女。

- After much heart-searching, he was assured that he had a clear conscience.
  他深自檢討一番之後，確信自己問心無愧。

Write your own sentence:

- I will search my heart and ask if I ________________________.

16

set one's heart on…

把心安裝在…上，打定主意要得到…或做到…

to be determined to get or do something

把心裝上，表示一心一意想得到，不達目的不輕易罷休；若是 **put one's heart into…**，則指把心投入於…，充滿熱情與衝勁。做任何事都需要有心才提得起勁，若 **have no heart for…**（無心於…），就表示沒了想做…的熱情、興緻，就算勉強去做也是意興闌珊（**half-heartedly or with half a heart**）。

- He has set his heart on a vacation in Mexico.
  他決心非要到墨西哥度個假不可。
- She has set her heart on a big and romantic wedding.
  她已決定一定要把婚禮辦得盛大、浪漫。
- He put his heart into his teaching. His heart just wasn't in his father's business.
  他全心投入教學，他的心不在父親的事業上。
- After getting married, he had no heart for playing in a band.
  結婚之後，他就無心玩團了。

Write your own sentence:

- I have set my heart on ______. I won't quit until ______________________________.

17

take … to heart

將…帶到心上，將…（忠告、批評等）放在心上

to consider or think about others' comment, advice, or criticism seriously

聽過的話若沒一耳進、另耳出，那就表示被帶往心之所在。此慣用語既意指把別人的建言認真聽進去，也意指太在意某件事或某些話，以致放進心裡，想不開、無法釋懷。至於**take heart**（抓住勇氣），則表示打起精神、拾起信心。關於**heart**意指勇氣的片語，可另參考HEART 07 & 12。

- I will take these comments about my screenplay to heart.

  我會認真看待這些就我的電影劇本所發出的意見。

- He really took that college rejection to heart.

  他真的很在意被那所大學拒收的事。

- I hope you will take heart from the story of the Paralympic athletes.

  我希望這群殘奧會選手的故事可以讓你振奮起來。

Write your own sentence:

- I listened to ______________________ and took it all to heart.

18

warm the cockles of one's heart

溫暖某人的心窩，使某人感到窩心

to cause a feeling of affectionate happiness

cockles 意指心的最內部，內心深處因為深，最容易感到冷清寂寞，能使內心深處都感覺到暖意的事，肯定令人感到幸福滿滿、溫馨美好。又，內心深處也因為深，有時連自己都覺得遙遠；**in one's heart of hearts**（在某人內心深處），表示依照某人內心最真實的想法。

- The thought of Mother's embrace is enough to warm the cockles of his heart.
  想到母親的擁抱，就足以讓他心頭暖暖的。
- It warms the cockles of my heart whenever I hear the folk song.
  每次聽到這首民謠，都讓我覺得好溫馨。
- It warms the cockles of my heart to hear you say that.
  聽你那麼說 ，我覺得好窩心。
- It's a great job offer, but in my heart of hearts I don't want to leave my hometown.
  這是個很好的工作機會，但在我內心深處，我並不想離開家鄉。

Write your own sentence:

- It warms the cockles of my heart to see ______________________________.

19

wear one's heart on one's sleeve

把心佩掛在衣袖上，真實坦率地表露情感，直言不諱

to display one's feelings or emotions openly

這個慣用語源自中世紀的傳統，騎士比武時會將心儀的淑女所贈的緞帶繫在衣袖上，以此公開自己的愛慕之情。於是把心戴在衣袖上，就表示不掩飾自己的情感，愛恨之意表露無遺，喜怒哀樂全寫在臉上，另外也可用來形容某人公然表露自己的想法、意見，直言不諱，想到就說。

- You couldn't help but see how he felt about her; he wore his heart on his sleeve.

  你要想看不出他對她的心意都難，他表現得太明顯了。

- He was ambitious for power and never wore his heart on his sleeve.

  他對權勢充滿野心，但他從沒讓人看出來。

- I always wear my heart on my sleeve, so there's no doubt where I stand.

  我向來不刻意隱瞞我的想法，想也知道我站在哪一邊。

Write your own sentence:

- I always wear my heart on my sleeve so that

  ______________________________.

20

with all one's heart (and soul)

以某人全部的心（與靈魂），全心全意，真心誠意

very earnestly; fully devotedly; with great willingness

用盡全心，表示毫無保留，絕非勉強或造做。類似的慣用語還有：**from the bottom of one's heart**（從心底深處），表示由衷、衷心。對別人真誠以待，對自己要讓心開懷。如果做某事做到**to one's heart's content**（讓心滿意），就表示十分盡興、痛快，盡情地讓心得到最大的滿足。

- With all my heart, I wish you both a long and happy life together.
  我真心祝福你們兩個白頭偕老、幸福美滿。
- They thanked us with all their heart and soul for the gift.
  他們衷心感謝我們所送的禮物。
- I am grateful from the bottom of my heart for your kindness.
  我打心底感激你的深情厚意。
- Let's drink and sing to our hearts' content!
  讓我們盡情暢飲、唱到爽吧!

Write your own sentence:

- I hope ______________________________ with all my heart.

gut & stomach

壯大肚子的腸與胃

GUT意指「腸」，如：**the large／small／blind gut**（大／小／盲腸）；**GUT**也泛指「肚子」，如：**beer gut**（啤酒肚）；**GUT+s**，則表示肚裡的「內臟」；若當動詞用，表示取出內臟。如：

Scale and gut fish before you cook it.
→ 料理前先把魚的鱗片和內臟清乾淨。

沒了內臟，肚子就成了沒作用的空殼子，也因此**GUTS**象徵了「膽識」與「內容」。如：

He has no guts. → 他沒膽識。

His book has no guts. → 他的書沒內容。

醫學上對於肚子的正式稱法為腹部（**abdomen**），肚子（**gut／belly／stomach**）是通俗的說法。肚子裡除了有**GUT**（腸），還有**STOMACH**（胃）。由於**STOMACH**位於腹部且負責消化，表達「空腹」這個詞既可用**belly**也可用**STOMACH**。如：

Don't exercise on an empty stomach. → 不要空腹運動。

STOMACH要有容量才裝得下食物，所以當動詞時，它意指能吃得下或忍受，如：

I can't stomach rich, creamy food.

→ 味道太重又奶滋滋的食物我吃不了。

位於**STOMACH**後方有個器官叫脾（**spleen**），主要負責過濾與儲存血液。由於古人認為許多壞性子都是由脾而來，於是**spleen**也意指壞脾氣、惡意。

包容著各種內臟的肚子最常用的字算是**belly**，如肚皮舞就叫**belly dance**。鮪魚肚叫**pot-belly**（鍋子肚），若某人肚子黃黃（**yellow-bellied**），表示此人膽小怯懦，因為**belly**如同**GUTS**，也象徵膽識，而在英文中，黃色本來就意指「懦弱的」（意指「猥褻的、下流的」的顏色是藍色）。此外，又由於柔軟的下腹部（**underbelly**）是易受攻擊的薄弱地帶，因此**underbelly**便意指較脆弱或較難防守的部位，如：

For them, the soft underbelly is the costs.

→ 他們的弱點在於成本。

那麼**belly button**（肚子上的鈕扣）又是什麼呢？

答案是：肚臍（**navel**）。

MEMO

gut & stomach

1

a gut feeling

肚子的感覺，直覺、預感

a personal, intuitive feeling or response; a hunch

為什麼要**feel in the gut**（用肚子感覺）？根據研究，肚子是人的第二大腦；人體神經網絡最密集的地方，第一在腦、第二就在肚子。所以心情不好就吃不下，擔心恐懼就容易消化不良甚至胃痛。此外，靜坐冥想（**meditate**）也強調集中意念於丹田（**pubic region**），即下腹部、臍下三寸之處，也因此，肚子的感覺便意味「直覺」。

- I have a gut feeling that they are going to get back together again.

  我有預感他們會再次復合。

- My gut feeling told me not to hire Ken for the job.

  我的直覺告訴我這份工作不要聘用Ken。

- When I first met him, I had a gut feeling that he had evil intentions.

  我第一次見到他，不知為何就覺得他心不正。

Write your own sentence:

- I have a gut feeling that ____________________.

2

hate someone's guts

恨某人的內臟，對某人恨之入骨

to hate or despise someone strongly and thoroughly

中文表示恨透一個人叫恨到骨子裡，英文則是恨到肚子裡的內臟全都恨。難怪中世紀會有**disembowel**（挖出內臟）這樣的酷刑，並且衍生出**have one's guts for garters**（拿某人的腸子去做吊襪帶），用來比喻嚴厲地懲罰、狠狠地教訓，類似**tear…limb from limb**（大卸八塊）這類誇張說法。

- She hates Tom's guts for his treating her sister badly.
  她對Tom恨之入骨，因為Tom對她姐很壞。
- Should you hate my guts just because I like to gamble on horse races?
  只因為我愛賭賽馬，你就要那麼鄙視我嗎？
- If I catch you street racing again, I'll have your guts for garters.
  下次再讓我抓到你在街頭飆車，我絕對抽你的筋、扒你的皮。

Write your own sentence:

- I wonder if somebody hates my guts just because I ________________.

3

vent one's spleen on …

將脾臟的惡氣發送到…，將怨氣發洩在…身上

to express freely an emotion like anger or rage

西方認為 **ill humor**（壞脾氣）是由脾臟而來，因此這個慣用語意指把心中的不爽、怒氣發洩在其他人事物上。又如果是 **bust a gut**（一根腸子破肚而出／**bust** 是 **burst** 的變體），除了表示氣炸、笑爆，另外也可表示竭盡心力、拚命地把一件事做好，即鞠躬盡瘁、爆出腸子而後已。

- He vented his spleen on his car by kicking it when it broke down.

  車子故障，他便踢車出氣。

- He vented his spleen about spoon-feeding education by kusoing.

  他藉由惡搞，發洩對填鴨教育的不滿。

- He busted a gut to please his wife, trying hard to imitate the incredible Hulk.

  他極盡所能地討好太太，努力模仿浩克給她看。

Write your own sentence:

- I may vent my spleen about ______________ by ______________________________.

4

butterflies in one's stomach

胃裡面的蝴蝶，忐忑不安

fluttering sensations caused by a feeling of nervous anticipation

活生生的蝴蝶在胃裡面啪嗒嗒地拍著翅膀，這種胃部持續翻騰、緊張不安的心情，總會出現在考試、比賽、表演、演講這類事情之前。另有一種緊張是**ants in one's pants**，倘若褲子跑進螞蟻，那肯定坐立不安，這種坐不住的焦躁通常是因為等得不耐煩又或是興奮地等不及。

- Whenever I need to speak in public, I get butterflies in my stomach.

  每次得在大庭廣眾下說話，我都緊張得七上八下的。

- He always has butterflies in his stomach before giving an English presentation.

  每次做英文簡報前，他都緊張得不得了。

- I've got ants in my pants. When is my turn?

  我等不下去了啦，什麼時候才輪到我？

Write your own sentence:

- It always gives me butterflies in my stomach to ________________________.

5

have no stomach for…

對…沒胃口、沒興趣，沒膽子做…

to dislike or be unable to tolerate something

吃要有胃口，吃下之後還要有胃容量。因此，對…沒有胃，一來表示沒慾望、不想要，另一方面則表示容不下、受不了。英女王伊莉莎白曾於1588年的演講中，說自己身軀雖是弱女子，**but I have the heart and stomach of a king**（但卻有國王的心與胃），此處**stomach**即含有野心、氣魄、膽識、肚量等多層涵義。此慣用語也可寫成**not have the stomach for…**。

- I have no stomach for greasy food and violent movies.

  我受不了油膩食物和暴力電影。

- Depressed and exhausted, he didn't have the stomach for a quarrel.

  心情沮喪加上力氣耗盡，他實在不想和任何人吵架。

- Do you have the stomach for a fight?

  敢不敢比試一下？

- I have no stomach for this trip.

  我對這次旅行沒什麼興趣。

Write your own sentence:

- I just don't have the stomach for ______________.

6

turn one's stomach

令人倒胃，令人噁心、討厭

to make someone feel sick; to disgust someone; to upset someone

想像胃在吃飽的狀態下（**on a full stomach**）坐上雲霄飛車？結局肯定是**throw up all over**（吐得到處都是）。反胃可指生理上想吐的反應，也可指精神上厭惡已極的心情。類似的慣用語還有**get sick to one's stomach**，後者泛指各種因悲傷、煩憂、惱怒等所帶來的不舒服感。

- The sight of Ben eating raw beef is enough to turn my stomach.

  看到Ben生吃牛肉，有夠讓我想吐的。

- Vast riches have turned his head, and the way he acts really turns our stomach.

  鉅富沖昏了他的頭，他的行徑令我們厭惡到極點。

- Seeing his wife make a scene at the airport, he got sick to his stomach.

  看到他太太在機場大吵大鬧，他整個人超不舒服。

Write your own sentence:

- ______________________ always turns my stomach.

7

go belly-up

肚子朝上，翹辮子，（公司行號等）破產倒閉

to be dead; to fail; to go bankrupt

魚若肚子朝上，就表示沒了命，因此**belly-up**意指掛了，用在公司行號上表示倒閉，畢竟公司倒閉就如同人之死亡。**kick the bucket**（踢掉桶子）也意指掛掉，這說法源於上吊的人以踢開腳下桶子結束生命。踢桶子或肚朝上都是俚俗說法，類似中文兩腿一伸、一命嗚呼等，要注意使用場合與時機。

- During the global financial crisis, eight out of ten businesses went belly-up.
  全球金融風暴期間，十間公司行號倒了八間。
- Rumor has it that this government enterprise is about to go belly-up.
  有謠傳說這個國營企業就快倒了。
- Before I kick the bucket, I want to be the greatest diva of all time.
  我希望我能在掛點之前成為史上最偉大的歌后。

Write your own sentence:

- The company ______________________ before it went belly-up.

8

gaze at one's navel

盯著肚臍看，耽溺於自我

to spend too much time thinking about oneself and one's own problems

肚臍是生命的中心，因為**umbilical cord**（臍帶）是胎兒與母親唯一的連結。盯著肚臍看原是修行者冥想生命的方式，延伸表示過度沈溺於自己的世界，**navel-gazing**則為「光想沒行動、紙上談兵」。注意另種自戀者：**Narcissus**（納西塞斯）是指為自己美貌陶醉的人，猶如納西塞斯迷戀自己水中倒影一樣。

- The novelist is famous for gazing at his own navel; he only uses I-statements.

  這個小說家以自戀聞名，他寫的東西全都“我”個不停。

- A narcissist likes to be admired from afar, and then complimented up close.

  自戀的人喜歡被人遠遠崇拜，近距離讚美。

- He is working hard to change the navel-gazing academic culture.

  他努力想改變學術界坐井觀天的風氣。

Write your own sentence:

- Instead of gazing at my navel, I ________________.

back 提供支持與依靠的背

BACK是生命的支柱，**BACK**上的**spine**（脊柱）之於身體，就像樹幹支持一棵大樹一樣。人體內的臟器全都沿著**spine**而生，**spine**若歪了，不僅影響體態，臟器也會受損。

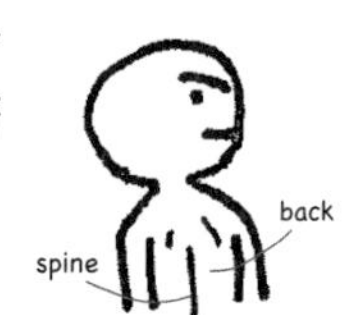

所以若是有人**at your back**（在你背後），就表示這人挺你、支持你，是你的後盾、靠山。也因此**BACK**當動詞時，其中一個意思就是支持。如：

Will you back (up) my plan?
→ 你支持我的計畫嗎？

BACK除了指身體的「背部」，也意指所有事物的「後面或背面」，又或當形容詞用，意指「後面的」，甚至當動詞用，意指「倒退」，如：

He signed his name on the back of the check.
→ 他在支票背面簽名。

He entered Harvard through the back door.
→ 他走後門進了哈佛。

The traffic was backed up to the side streets.
→ 車流回堵到小路上。

又，如果有人**back-bite**，並不是真的叮咬你的背，而是背後中傷。如果有工作**back-breaking**，讓人背都快斷了，那就表示這工作很累人、很艱辛。如：

He often backbites others. → 他常在背後說人壞話。

Working in the sun is back-breaking.
→ 在太陽底下工作很艱苦。

接下來談脊椎，**spine** 是較正式說法，**backbone**（背骨）是口語說法。**backbone** 另外也意指主幹、主力或骨氣。如：

They are the backbone of our company.
→ 他們是我們公司的中堅。

We expect him to show some backbone in dealing with affairs of state.
→ 我們希望他在處理國事上拿出強悍的魄力來。

當然，如果一個人沒有 **backbone**，就表示 **spineless**（沒脊骨的），也意指沒骨氣、優柔寡斷的。

此外，**spine** 不僅是身體的脊，也意指書的脊或某些動植物的針、刺。如：

a cactus with red spines → 長著紅刺的仙人掌

the spine of a book → 書脊

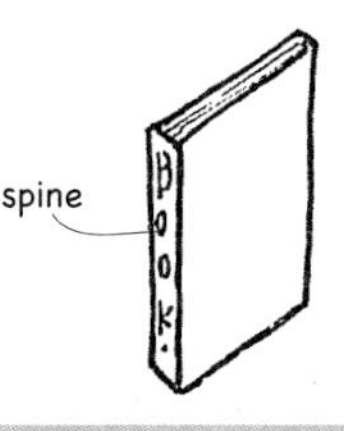

MEMO

1

a pat on the back

輕拍背部，稱讚鼓勵

a gesture of support, approval, or praise, etc.

這是個常見的畫面：輕輕拍一下背、順帶說句做得好，因此拍背意指支持、讚美、或認同。**pat** 換成 **slap**（用力拍），熱情有力但意思不變，此外用力拍背還又有賀喜（**congratulations**）之意。

pat 也可直接當動詞，**pat yourself on the back**（輕拍自己的背）意指自己給自己鼓勵一下。

- The bonus he gave his assistant was a pat on the back for doing a good job.
  他發獎金給助理，讚許他表現得很好。
- The coach gave him a good slap on the back for coming in first.
  教練大大祝賀他勇奪第一。
- We were patting each other on the back for winning when the final whistle blew.
  當哨聲響起，我們為贏得比賽彼此歡呼讚許。

Write your own sentence:

- I think I deserve a pat on the back for
  ______________________________.

2

back to back

背靠背，接連不斷

with backs close together; consecutively, one after another; in a row

這個慣用語可用來形容位置的背貼背，如：背靠背站著、座位背靠背安排，也可形容事物一個接一個、緊接不斷。**back-to-back** 是形容詞。如果背貼不到，還跑到了遠方：**back of beyond**（遠方的背面），就表示位在遠離人煙的偏遠地區。

- The seats in the boat are back to back.
  這艘小船上的座位背靠著背。
- We are going to have four tests back to back tomorrow.
  明天我們連考四科。
- The batter hit back-to-back homeruns in the 9th inning.
  在第九局，打擊手連續兩棒擊出全壘打。
- He is about to move to some tiny island at the back of beyond.
  他即將搬到很遠很遠的某個小島。

Write your own sentence:

- I am going to have ____________ back to back next weekend.

3

behind one's back

在某人背後，背地裡，暗中秘密地

out of one's presence or without one's knowledge

除非背後長眼睛（見 EYE 06），否則發生在背後的事我們很難得知。在某人背後就表示某人不在場或不知情。又如果有人 **with one arm tied behind one's back**（把一隻手綁在背後）地做某件事，則表示這事對此人易如反掌，再簡單不過，根本是 **a piece of cake**（小事一樁）。後者慣用語 **one arm** 也可用 **one hand** 或 **both hands**。

- I often wonder what they say about me behind my back.

  我常好奇他們都在我背後說我什麼。

- She pawned her jewelry behind her husband's back.

  她瞞著丈夫偷偷把珠寶當了。

- I can assemble that model plane with one arm tied behind my back.

  我輕而易舉就能把那架模型飛機組裝起來。

Write your own sentence:

- Please don't ________________ behind my back.

4

break the back of …

折斷…的背，擊潰…的勢力，突破…最難的一關

to destroy something; to get through the hardest part of something

背是重要的支柱，折斷某人的背意指某人賣命工作，折斷某事的背則表示擊倒某事，讓某事即使殘存，也只能苟延殘喘，又或克服某事最艱難的部份，即使未完成，也只剩簡單的部份。既然背是重要的支撐，若能讓背整個投入於某事（**put one's back into…**），則表示多加把勁、努力撐下去。

- The new medicine should break the back of the epidemic.
  新來的這種藥應可遏止這種流行病擴大蔓延。
- The air force might break the back of the offensive.
  這隊空軍或能粉碎這場攻勢的主力。
- We have broken the back of this journey and reached the halfway point.
  我們已熬過這趟旅程最難的部份，走到一半了。
- If you put your back into this report, you can finish it today.
  如果你能再加把勁做這份報告，你今天就能做完。

Write your own sentence:

- I manage to break the back of ______________ before ______________.

5

cover one's back

遮住某人背部，袒護某人免受責難

to protect one from criticism or future blame

不敢面對只好背對，而且還想方設法把背蓋起來，這個慣用語意指設法掩護，使之不受責罵。如果是**scratch one's back**（抓背），則表示希望得到回報而幫忙，亦即我幫你抓背、你也要幫我抓。正面來說，這叫投桃報李、魚水相幫，但若做壞事，那就成了狼狽為奸、串通一氣。

- The employer covered her back by passing the buck to the employees.
  這老闆為了掩護她自己，把責任全推給員工。
- She was careful to cover her back when dealing with the lawyers.
  與律師交涉時，她小心掩護自己以免罪名落到自己身上。
- I don't mind doing the laundry. You have scratched my back plenty of times.
  要我洗衣服沒問題，你也常幫我啊。
- The contractor has been scratching the treasurer's back.
  這名承包商一直都和會計有勾結。

Write your own sentence:

- Do I need a friend who always covers my back or ________________?

6

flat on one's back

仰面朝天，臥病在床，無助、無奈

to be sick in bed; to be helpless without recourse

此處**flat**意指「平直地，仰臥地」。相較於俯臥（**lie on one's stomach**）或側臥（**lie on one's side**），仰臥較難起身；相較於面朝地倒下，跌個狗吃屎很糗（FACE 05），面朝天倒下顯得孤立絕望。因此仰面這個慣用語常被用來形容孤立無援，又或臥病在床。

- If you sleep on your back, use a pillow for neck support.
  如果你睡姿是仰臥，用個枕頭支撐脖子。
- Acute pneumonia has put him flat on his back for two weeks.
  急性肺炎已讓他躺了兩個禮拜。
- He was flat on his back during his illness.
  生病期間他臥床不起。
- I wish I could help but the recession has put me flat on my back.
  我很想幫忙，但景氣不好我實在無能為力。

Write your own sentence:

- As I know, ________ has been on his/her back with the flu for ________.

back

7

get off one's back

從背部下來，別再一直唸或煩

to leave one alone; to stop harassing or picking on one

若有人扒在背上叨唸，走到哪都甩不掉，任誰都會希望快快甩開此人。**back** 可用 **case**。若背上是隻皮猴，那絕對是個超級麻煩，非短時間能解決。背上的猴子若能下來，長久鬱悶肯定一掃而空，因此 **get the monkey off back** 意指除去心頭大患或不快。猴子又指「毒癮」，背上有猴也指染上毒癮，究竟背上的猴是困擾還是毒癮，請依上下文判斷。

- I wish Mom would get off my back about going on a blind date.
  我希望媽別再對我碎碎唸去相親的事。
- The divorce proceedings are a monkey on her back.
  這件離婚官司讓她傷透了腦筋。
- Their seven-game losing streak was a monkey on the back of the famous baseball team.
  連吞七敗使得這支著名的棒球隊鬱悶到極點。
- By winning the championship, he has finally got the monkey off his back.
  由於贏得冠軍，他終於一掃過去的悶氣。

Write your own sentence:

- I will tell ______ to get off my back about ______.

8

get one's back up
使某人背部拱起，觸怒某人

to make one get angry; to annoy

當貓把背拱起，就表示惹毛他了。這個慣用語意指使某人心裡昇起一把無名火，氣壞了。**back**也可用**dander**（源自荷蘭語**donder**，意指**thunder**[雷；怒嚇]）。**get**也可用**put**或**set**。同義的慣用語還有：**get one's goat**（拿走[安定情緒]的山羊，此說法源自賽馬的馬廄裡常會放隻山羊以安定馬的心神）／**raise one's hackles**（使某人頸毛豎起）。

- The way he leaves his books on the floor really gets my back up.

  他常把書亂丟在地上，這點總惹得我很火。

- What really put my back up was her claiming to have done most of the work.

  讓我很不爽的是，她對外宣稱工作幾乎都是她做好的。

- He is quick to get his dander up.

  他很容易動怒。

Write your own sentence:

- ______________________ really got my back up.

9

give … the shirt off one's back

脫下背上的襯衫給…，竭盡所能地幫…，傾囊相助...

to give anything that is asked for, no matter the sacrifice required

如果有人為了幫你，連身上最後一件襯衫都願意脫下，這表示他真的傾其所有、用盡全力在幫忙，這已不只是**lift a finger**（抬根手指，舉手之勞），更不是**fair-weather friend**（酒肉朋友）做得到的。此外，如果因為賭博或投資失利，以致於**lose one's shirt**，連最後一件襯衫都保不住，則表示失去所有財產，賠得精光、一點不剩。

- He is always ready to give any of his old army buddies the shirt off his back.
  他隨時可為軍中老友兩肋插刀、在所不辭。
- He is the kind of person who would give you the shirt off his back.
  他就是那種會盡力幫助朋友的人。
- We are sworn friends. We would give each other the shirt off our backs.
  我們是結拜好友，有難時一定傾力相助互挺到底。
- I lost my shirt on the deal. I should have invested more wisely.
  這筆買賣賠光了我的錢，當初投資如果聰明一點就好了。

Write your own sentence:

- When I am in trouble, I know ________________ would give me the shirt off his/her back.

10

have one's back to the wall

背抵著牆，處於絕境

to be in a difficult situation with very little room for maneuver

武俠或軍事片中常見到這個畫面，節節敗退的一方，最後走到絕路、無處可逃。這個慣用語表示走投無路、幾已無計可施，**to** 也可用 **against**。倘若背部沒被牆堵住，卻被捅了一刀（**stab**），則表示遭人背叛，中了暗箭。為安全起見，最好 **watch your back**，以免有人在暗中搞鬼，對你不利。

- Should I give in when I **have my back to the wall**? Can I begin again?
  走到這個地步，我該認了嗎？還可能東山再起嗎？
- Success always invites jealousy. You should **watch your back**.
  樹大招風，你一定要多加注意身邊的人與事。
- My friend **stabbed me in the back** even after I helped him get a job.
  我朋友竟在我背後中傷我，虧我還幫他找到工作。

Write your own sentence:

- After ______________________, the soldiers had their backs to the wall.

11

like water off a duck's back

像鴨子背上滑落的水，（批評、警告、建議等）起不了作用，毫無影響

（criticism, warning, suggestion, etc.） without apparent effect

從水中出來的鴨子，總是抖一抖身上的水珠，身體就好像沒碰過水似的，這是因為鴨子的羽毛表面有一層天然油脂，能有效防止水分滲入。如果任何批評、忠言、提醒等像鴨背上的水，抖一抖就甩落了，那就表示這些言論絲毫不起作用，因為聽者全把它們當耳邊風，一耳進另耳出。

- I keep telling him to cut down on sweets but it is like water off a duck's back.
  我一直叫他少吃甜食，但我有說跟沒說一樣。
- All the negative reviews rolled off him like water off a duck's back.
  排山倒海而來的負面評論，完全影響不了他。
- I've told him that he is heading for trouble, but it's just like water off a duck's back.
  我早跟他說他這樣會惹上麻煩，可說了也沒用。

Write your own sentence:

- ____________________, but it is like water off a duck's back to me.

12

see the back of …

看見…轉身離去的背影，終於得以擺脫…

to get rid of someone or something

當我們目送別人離開，眼中所見自然是此人的背。這個慣用語以此象徵動作，意指終於可以擺脫某人或結束某事，不必再和此人或此事糾纏、打交道。同義的慣用語還有：**see the last of…**（最後一次見到…），後者慣用語也可與**hear**搭配：**hear the last of …**（最後一次聽到…）。

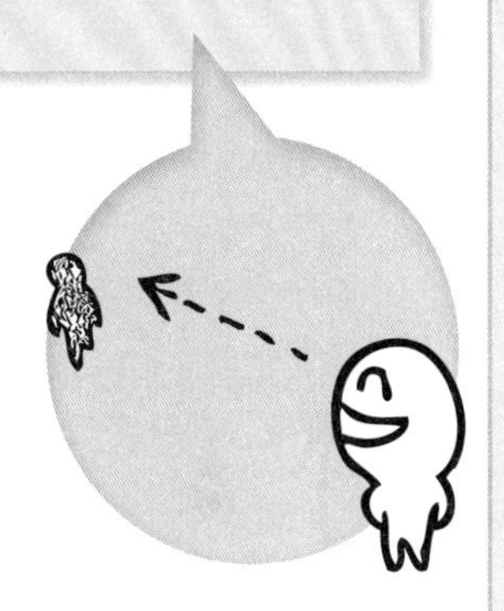

- I should be glad to **see the back of** her. She is a real pain in the neck.

  我巴不得她快點離開，她實在很討人厭。

- I hope I have **seen the back of** this thesis. It has been going on far too long.

  希望這篇畢業論文到此結束，實在寫太久了。

- You haven't **heard the last of** the harassment case! I'll see you in court.

  這個騷擾案不會到此就算了的，咱們法庭見。

Write your own sentence:

- I will be pleased to see the back of ____________ because ______________.

13

turn one's back on someone

把背轉向某人，轉身不理，拒絕伸出援手或有任何瓜葛

to refuse to help or be involved

當某人不願與你正面相對，就表示這人翻臉不認人，不但不願回應你的請求，甚至不想承認認識你。但若是無心的背轉則另當別論：**when one's back is turned**（當某人轉身之時），這指的是在某人不注意、沒看到、或不在場的時候。

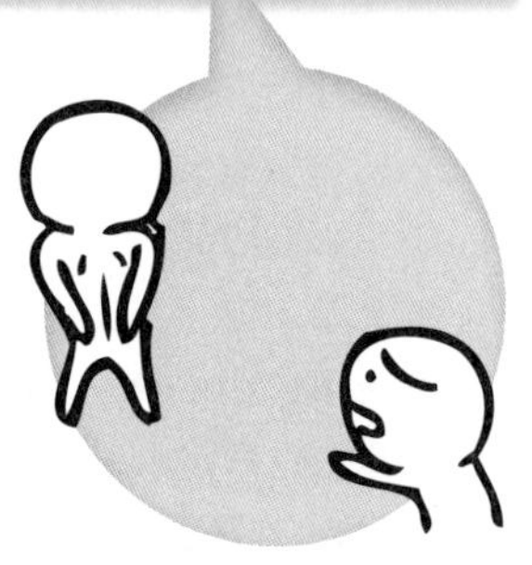

- I can't turn my back on my daughter, no matter what she has done.

  我不能放我女兒不管，不論她之前做了什麼。

- He turned his back on me when I just got out of jail.

  我剛出獄那時，他根本不想和我有任何牽連。

- When my mom's back is turned, grandpa will give me pocket money.

  阿公都會趁媽不注意時給我零用錢。

 **Write your own sentence:**

- How can we turn our backs on people who ____________________?

14

send chills up one's spine

使寒氣沿著脊柱上昇，令人不寒而慄

to horrify one and give a chilling sensation

chill 意指寒冷，這個慣用語主要形容某件事令人感到恐怖或極度不舒服，**chills** 可用 **shivers**，**up** 可用 **down**。同義的慣用語還有 **freeze one's blood**（使血液凍結）、**make one's blood run cold**（使血液變冷）、**make one's skin crawl**（使皮膚起疙瘩）、**make one's flesh creep**（似有東西爬上來，使肉毛毛的）。

- The way he looked at me **sent chills up my spine.**
  他看我的樣子令我全身發冷。
- Movies about vampires always **freeze my blood.**
  吸血鬼的電影總嚇出我一身冷汗。
- The scene where a zombie arose from the grave **made his flesh creep.**
  墳墓裡冒出一隻殭屍的畫面令他全身發毛。

Write your own sentence:

- ______________________________ sent chills up my spine.

loin 肉肉的凹腰
& hip 與凸臀

LOIN 是下背的腰部，一般說的「里肌肉」指的就是這個部位，至於 **tenderloin** 是小里肌、腰內肉，**waist** 則是指腰圍、腰身。在沒有鈕扣與拉鍊的年代，衣裝的整齊全靠束腰的帶子（**girdle**），可想而知，在古時候若要外出或行動，**gird up one's loins**（束緊腰帶）當然是重要的行前準備動作，到後來就被用來形容「做好準備以面對重要行動」，如：

The athletes are girding up their loins for the race.
→ 運動選手們個個為比賽蓄勢待發。

由於腰位於人體中間，中文裡便以「折腰」表示一個人辛苦賣命，但在英文，這種拚命的動作折的並不是腰，而是頸或背，如：

He is going to break his back working for $100 a day.
→ 他決定為一天一百的工資拚了。

LOIN 再往下是 **HIP**，**HIP** 介於 **waist** 與 **upper thigh**（大腿上部）之間，現代流行的 **hip-hop**（嘻哈），強烈的節奏總會使 **HIP** 不禁想 **hop**（跳躍）。

坐下的時候，人體與底部接觸的部份叫 **buttocks**（屁股），正面位於 **waist** 與 **thigh** 之間的L型則是 **lap**（懷抱）。意指「底部」的 **bottom** 也可用來意指 **buttocks**，若有某物 **as smooth as a baby's bottom**，就表示這東西很光滑，像嬰兒的小屁股一樣。

說到小嬰兒，令人不禁想到母親的**lap**，**lap**可抱或放東西，被抱在母親懷中很舒服，若在奢華的懷裡則表示很優渥，又若在眾神的懷裡，則表示一切操之在神，人無力決定。如：

The baby was asleep in her lap.

→ 寶寶在她懷裡睡著了。

He lived in the lap of luxury before 10.

→ 十歲以前的他生活很優渥。

The weather is always in the lap of the gods.

→ 天氣如何通常得看老天的臉色。

又，便於攜帶的筆電由於尺寸如同書本一般，看似可放在**lap**上，因此稱為**laptop**。但千萬注意，**desktop**（桌電）雖可放在**desk**上，但**laptop**（筆電）卻萬萬不能放在**lap**上，一不小心大腿可是會燒傷的。

MEMO

loin & hip

1

gird up one's loins

束緊腰帶，準備就緒

to prepare oneself for something difficult

這個慣用語出自聖經，由於古人身穿長袍（**robe**），腰間須束上帶子行動才便捷；此外，藉由束腰這個動作也可鼓舞自己、調整心情。於是束緊腰帶就表示為了重大或困難的事，把自己身心都準備到位，一如出征之前，先整裝以待發。**gird up** 可省略寫成 **gird**。

- He girded up his loins and walked in for this crucial interview.
  他準備就緒，走進去面對這場關鍵的面試。
- Now both sides are girding their loins for the long-running legal battle.
  目前兩方都束緊腰帶，準備為漫長的官司長期抗戰。
- Spider-man began to gird up his loins and went out to meet Doctor Octopus.
  蜘蛛人著手做好一切準備，出去迎戰八爪博士。
- Wherefore gird up the loins of your mind, be sober.
  因此，把心準備好，儆醒自守。（摘自彼得前書1:13）

Write your own sentence:

- I am presently girding up my loins for ________________.

2

drop into one's lap

落入懷中，（好事、美物）意外降臨

（something valuable） to be given to someone by chance or without making any effort

老天爺應是人們最常祈求的對象，心有所冀望時，人們常會合掌、望天，期盼老天爺把人們想要的東西往下一扔，落入祈求者的懷中。這個慣用語主要表示美好、珍貴的事物在沒有刻意經營、努力的情況下意外降臨，**drop** 也可用 **fall**。

- Get a life! Don't sit there all day hoping opportunities will drop into your lap.

  認真點過日子！別整天坐在那裡等機會掉下來。

- A fulfilling marriage does not magically drop from heaven into your lap.

  美滿的婚姻並不會神奇地從天上掉下來送你。

- These toffs never had to work hard. Everything seemed to fall into their lap.

  這些公子哥兒從不需打拚，他們好像要什麼就有什麼。

Write your own sentence:

- I can't expect ________ to just drop into my lap. I have to ____________________.

3

be joined at the hip

臀部相連，同進同出，關係密切

to be so closely connected as to be inseparable; always together

這個慣用語衍生自連體嬰：**Siamese twins**（暹羅雙胞胎），這個名稱源自1811年於**Siam**（暹羅）誕生的一對連體兄弟，只是這對兄弟相連的部份並不是臀而是胸。如果有人或機構好似連體嬰一樣地臀部連在一起，那就表示他們的關係已緊密到難以切割的程度。

- Tom and Meg are joined at the hip. They are more like soul mates than lovers.
  Tom和Meg到哪都在一起，他們不只是戀人、更是心靈上的伴侶。
- The law will keep unhappy couples joined at the hip for the sake of their kids.
  這條法律恐將使怨偶不得不為了孩子繼續被綁在一起。
- The two companies that John invested in have been joined at the hip.
  John投資的這兩家公司關係十分密切。

Write your own sentence:

- ____________ are joined at the hip. They even share ______________________________.

4

shoot from the hip

從臀部開槍，直來直往，不經思慮就說、就做

to speak directly and frankly; to speak or act recklessly or impulsively

槍套通常掛在臀部，此慣用語原意是一抽出槍套裡的槍就直接從臀部的位置射擊，不拿到眼前瞄準也不管姿勢，延伸用來形容人言行直接，不拐彎抹角、不圓滑、不講究姿態，動作反應快但卻可能失準。同樣是不經思慮發話，**shoot one's mouth off**（MOUTH09）是不該說的話揚揚得意說個不停，注意兩者不同。

- He means no harm. It's just his nature to shoot from the hip.

  他沒惡意，他這個人就是這樣，說話都不修飾的。

- She usually jumps quickly into a project and shoots from the hip.

  她做案子常常火速投入，想到什麼就行動。

- Don't go shooting your mouth off about how much bonus you're getting.

  別再拿你領了多少獎金的事到處說個不停。

Write your own sentence:

- He is known for shooting from the hip because ________________.

5

get to the bottom of …

到達…底部，追究…到底，弄個水落石出

to discover the truth about something

bottom意指屁股、底部，搜身的最底限是屁股，找東西也得找到最底部才算看清全部。有重量的東西總容易沈在底部，**at the bottom of**…表示在…的底部，至於**at bottom**，則表示基本上（**basically／fundamentally**），亦即底子裡的實質狀態。

- They finally get to the bottom of why their parents were murdered.
  他們終於查清了父母慘遭謀殺的真相。
- How will he get to the bottom of the unsolved case with so little evidence?
  證據這麼少，他該如何追查這個懸案？
- At the bottom of the trunk are a few tools.
  行李箱最下面有幾件工具。
- He may speak bluntly, but at bottom he is always honest.
  他說話是很直，但他說的倒都是真話。

Write your own sentence:

- I am going to get to the bottom of ____________ and find out ______________________.

6

hit (rock) bottom

碰到(岩石)底部，跌到最低點，跌到谷底

to reach the lowest or worst point

跌入水中，屁股撞到底部即表示落到最低點。若往地下鑽，穿過土層來到 **rock bottom**(岩石底)，那就真的來到了最底層。以 **bottom** 當動詞，**bottom out**(見底)就成了同義詞。人生、氣溫、利率…多少都有跌到谷底之時，只要不輕易放棄，再也無處可跌的最低點往往正是向上攀升的起點。

- Our profits peaked in June and **hit bottom** in October.
  我們的利潤在六月達到最高峰，十月跌到最低點。
- He **hit rock bottom** last year when he was forced to begin a drug rehab program.
  他去年被迫開始勒戒，人生跌到谷底。
- The stocks **bottomed out** before the general election.
  大選前，股票跌到最低點。

Write your own sentence:

- Has ____________ hit bottom and how fast will it recover?

7

knock the bottom out of …

打掉…的底部，破壞…的根基，使…無法成立

to undermine; to render invalid

一如沒了地基的房子會倒塌，任何事物如果沒了基礎，就算其他部份還在，也是岌岌可危。打掉底部就表示削弱對方根本，讓對方站不穩以致崩塌。然而這麼做是造成破壞、還是破舊以建新，就要看是什麼樣的事情以及以何種角度來看了。類似慣用語：**knock the props out from under...**（從...底下打掉支柱），意為打擊某人信心，使某人情緒崩潰或財務崩塌。

- His skilled debating knocked the bottom out of his opponent.

  他無礙的辯才以釜底抽薪之計，令對手毫無反擊的餘地。

- His strategy of mass production knocked the bottom out of market prices.

  他大量生產的策略，嚴重打亂了市場價格。

- The discovery of another planet knocks the bottom out of many theories.

  新的行星的發現，讓許多理論再也站不住腳。

Write your own sentence:

- My ______________ knocked the bottom out of ______________________________.

8

scrape the bottom of the barrel

往酒桶底部刮一刮，將就一下，無魚蝦也好

to select from among the worst; to choose from what is left over

barrel 是裝酒的大圓桶，想喝酒、偏偏桶裡只剩底部一點酒，這時只好退而求其次，往桶底刮一刮，撈起那些混著沈澱物、木屑的酒，真是萬般無奈！由此刮桶子底就表示想要的都被別人拿走了，只好降低標準遷就一下，說服自己有總比沒有好（**It's better than nothing.**）。

- Having Tom in the team proves that you are scraping the bottom of the barrel.

  會找Tom加入，可見你們這隊是濫竽充數。

- Get a jump on the clearance sale, or you will scrape the bottom of the barrel.

  搶購清倉特賣品動作要快，要不然你只能揀別人挑剩的。

- You really scraped the bottom of the barrel to nominate him.

  你真的是沒人才了才會提名他。

 Write your own sentence:

- Do I need to scrape the bottom of the barrel and ______________________________?

9

down to one's bottom dollar

只剩最後一塊錢，財務已達山窮水盡，很窮

to be broke, penniless, poor; without money

此處**bottom**是形容詞，意指「最底下的」，口袋裡只剩**bottom dollar**（最後一塊錢），那景況大抵已是身無分文、極度的貧窮。倘若有人願意以最後一塊錢來打賭（**bet one's bottom dollar**），則表示此人對某事確信不疑，以致敢拍胸脯打包票，絲毫不擔心會失去這僅有的、最後一塊錢。

- He has been out of work for years and now he is down to his bottom dollar.

  他多年沒工作，如今身上沒剩幾塊錢。

- Although he is down to his bottom dollar, he tries to grin and bear it.

  雖然他窮得不能再窮，但他努力一笑置之、苦中作樂。

- You can bet your bottom dollar that John will be in charge of this case.

  你大可放心，這個案子肯定由John負責。

Write your own sentence:

- I hope ______________________________ and nobody is down to their bottom dollar.

MEMO

arm 攻擊與自保的臂膀

人的身軀，主要由**body**（軀體）與**limb**（肢）組合而成，而**limb**則有上身的**ARM**與下身的**leg**。

這個單元先談**ARM**。

ARM的伸展，關係著人與人之間的距離與關係。當我們伸出**ARM**，使某人與我們之間隔著**arm's length**，就意謂著我們試圖與此人保持距離。相對於**arm's length**，**arm in arm**則顯得親近。

如：

I always have the feeling that he is keeping me at arm's length.

→ 我總感覺他在和我保持距離。

They went off arm in arm. → 他們挽著手離開了。

ARM也象徵手臂狀的物品，像是**arm of a chair**（椅子的扶手）、**one-arm bandit**（獨臂大盜、意指「吃角子老虎」，因為兩者同樣“搶錢”，獨臂則指機器旁的拉桿），又或**long arm of the law**（法律的長手臂，意指法律無遠弗屆的力量）。如：

He believes that the long arm of the law will eventually nab the bad guys.

→ 他相信法網恢恢，法律終究會把壞蛋都抓起來。

又由於武器大多需以**ARM**攜帶，於是**arm**便成了意指武器的字根，當動詞用時則意指「（使）武裝」，許多與武器、武裝有關的字，都可看到**arm**的身影。如：

arm（使武裝）：
The gangster was armed to the teeth. → 這名歹徒全副武裝

arms（兵力、槍械）：
take up arms against the enemy → 拿起武器對抗敵人

army（軍隊、陸軍）：
join the army → 入伍從軍

armor（盔甲）:
fight in armor → 穿戴盔甲作戰

armored（裝甲的）:
an armored vehicle → 裝甲車

armaments（軍備）：
expand the armaments → 擴充軍備

dis**arm**（解除武裝）：
disarm a robber → 解除一名強盜的武裝

fore**arm**（預先武裝、預作準備）：
Forewarned is forearmed. → 有備無患

MEMO

1

a shot in the arm

手臂上的一針，一劑強心針，一股新血，振奮、振興的力量

a positive influence; a stimulus or booster

shot 是 **injection**（注射）的口語說法，健康的人總希望打一針讓身體更勇，生病的人則希望打一針讓身體復原，虛弱的人希望打一針恢復元氣，任何事物如果能帶來嶄新的、推進的能量、使人事物振作、成長，那便是手臂上的一針。

- Getting a grant was a needed shot in the arm for the theatrical company.

  拿到補助，對這個劇團而言真是一場及時雨。

- The young recruits provided a shot in the arm for the veteran baseball team.

  新加入的年輕隊員為老棒球隊注入新血。

- They lowered the interest rate trying to give the economy a real shot in the arm.

  他們降低利率，試圖刺激經濟使其復甦。

Write your own sentence:

- ____________________ will be a big shot in the arm for me.

2

be up in arms

拿起武器準備拚了，極度憤怒不滿

to protest angrily; to be angry and rebellious

武器通常由**arm**攜帶，此處**arms**意指武器。這個慣用語意指對某事不滿、反感到極點，氣到簡直想抄起傢伙站起來開打似的，這種憤慨帶了強烈抗議的火藥味，不同於把背拱起來的惱怒（BACK 08）以及有理說不清，無力改變的怒火中燒（BLOOD 09）。**have/get up in arms**意指「使...十分火大、憤怒、不滿」。

- The students **were up in arms** over the school's plan to raise tuition.
  對於校方計畫調漲學費一事，學生們群起反對。

- He **was up in arms** about the council's decision to close the road.
  他得知市議會決定封路後十分不滿。

- Flagrantly disregarding the law, the gang leader **had** the drugs squad **up in arms**.
  這名角頭老大公然漠視法紀，惹得掃毒小組十分光火。

Write your own sentence:

- I was up in arms when I found out that ______________________.

3

cost someone an arm and a leg

價值某人的一條手臂與一條腿，使某人花掉一大筆錢、荷包大失血

to be very expensive; to cost someone a fortune

沒有相機的年代，留下身影全靠肖像（**portrait**）。只畫頭的肖像最便宜、加畫手臂的貴些、畫了腿的完整肖像最貴。話說倘若真有什麼事物得讓人付出一條手與腿的代價，那還真貴到嚇死人。總之一手與一腿表示高昂的價格，可搭配**charge**（索價），表示某人或某機構為其服務或產品索取天價。

- I want to travel all over Europe, but the air fare might cost me an arm and a leg.
  我想遊遍歐洲，但飛機票錢恐怕很可觀。
- I forgot to cancel roaming and it cost me an arm and a leg.
  我忘了關掉漫遊，結果讓我荷包大失血。
- The dentist does good work and he won't charge you an arm and a leg for it.
  這牙醫技術好，而且不會收取天價般的費用。

Write your own sentence:

- I have to ______________________. It is costing me an arm and a leg.

4

give one's right arm

獻出右手臂，（為得某事物）做什麼都願意

to go to any lengths to obtain

由於右手使用率高，獻出右手表示甘心犧牲一切或付出極高代價以得到想要的事物。說到手，歷史上曾有**Kildare**王為了中止戰爭，在**Ormond**王躲藏的教堂門上切出小洞、伸手進去，讓**Ormond**王決定是要與他握手言和、還是切掉他的手，也因此，**chance one's arm**便意指為完成某事不惜冒險一搏。

- He would give his right arm to see his dead father again.

  他願意付出一切，只要能再見到死去的父親一面。

- She would give her right arm for an uneventful day.

  只要能換得風平浪靜的一天，要她做什麼她都願意。

- Shall I chance my arm giving up a secure job to start a Bed-and-Breakfast?

  我該冒險放棄穩定的工作去經營民宿嗎？

Write your own sentence:

- I would give my right arm if I could

  ______________________________.

5

keep … at arm's length

與…保持一定的距離

to avoid intimacy with someone; to avoid connection with something

伸出手臂，可以擋住別人靠近自己，因此，與某人或某事之間、間隔一隻手臂的長度，就表示不想與這人太過親近或與某事有明顯的關聯。相較之下，**arm in arm**（臂挽著臂）則是手臂勾著手臂，中間零距離。

- He always refuses our invitations and keeps us at arm's length.
  他很少接受我們的邀約，刻意和我們保持距離。
- They kept each other at arm's length lest tongues should wag.
  他們對彼此敬而遠之，以免引起流言蜚語。
- The lawmakers are keeping the issue of tax reform at arm's length.
  立委們明顯不願與稅制改革這個議題沾上邊。
- The newly-wed couple are strolling arm in arm along the beach.
  這對新婚夫妻正手挽著手沿著海邊漫步。

Write your own sentence:

- It is wise to keep ______ at arm's length because ______________________.

6

lay down one's arms

放下手中的武器，棄械、投降

to stop fighting; to surrender

槍械大多拿在手裡，放下雙手，就表示放下武器，不再繼續戰鬥，準備投降。又，如果像土匪一樣，用手架住某人的頸子呢？源自強盜搶錢動作的 **put the arm on someone** 原意指施加壓力跟對方要錢，後來也用來廣義表示強迫某人、非要某人做某事不可。

- The war ended when the liberation organization finally laid down its arms.

  戰爭結束了，解放組織終於停戰投降。

- He asked the guerrillas to lay down arms and surrender to the government.

  他要游擊隊放下武器，向政府投降。

- He has been putting the arm on a rich alumnus for donations.

  他一直要求一名有錢的校友捐款。

Write your own sentence:

- ________________ were instructed to lay down their arms and surrendered.

7

twist someone's arm

反轉某人手臂，對某人施加壓力，非要某人去做某事

to coerce or persuade someone to do something

twist 意指扭轉，抓住某人手臂朝背後扭轉，戲劇中，這個強迫的動作總會搭配「答不答應？」這句說詞。強迫的方式有很多種，吵打哭鬧、威脅利誘、打口水戰等，不管哪一種，總之就是非要某人答應才肯罷休，也正是這個慣用語所表示的意思。

- He might help us with the project if you twist his arm a little.
  如果你稍稍拜託一下，他應該就會幫我們處理這個案子。
- She didn't really want to go to the theater, but he twisted her arm.
  她並不很想去看戲，但他非要她去不可。
- Yon don't have to twist my arm to make me stay for a drink. I'd love to.
  要我留下來喝一杯，不須你勸說，我樂意得很。
- Ann's son has been twisting her arm to get him a new cell phone.
  Ann的兒子一直吵著要她給他買支新手機。

Write your own sentence:

- If you twist my arm, I will ____________________.

8

with open arms

以張開的雙手，熱情地

with enthusiasm or obvious pleasure

張開雙手是擁抱（**embrace or hug**）的前導動作，因此張開雙手，就表示非常親切熱情。但若兩手交疊放在身前（**with folded arms**），除了指「抱著胳膊」這個肢體動作，也可搭配**stand by**（站在旁邊）或**look on**（觀望），意指袖手旁觀；**stay on the sidelines**（站在界外）意思類似，意指「置身局外」。

- The author was welcomed **with open arms** when arriving at the book signing.

  作者來到簽書會現場，受到熱烈歡迎。

- The officers received the delegation **with open arms**.

  官員們熱情接待使節團。

- He **looked on with folded arms** as she was viciously attacked.

  當她遭人毒打，他袖手旁觀。

✎ Write your own sentence:

- I was greeted with open arms when I ______________________.

9

tear … limb from limb
使…斷手斷腳，將…撕成碎片

to rip someone or an animal into bits

此處**tear**當動詞，意指撕裂，**limb**意指人或動物的肢，這個慣用語意指撕扯人或動物的肢，使其肢體分離、殘缺不全。**limb**也意指樹的主枝，若某人**go／climb out on a limb**（爬上樹枝末端），則表示此人由於支持或承諾了某事，結果讓自己卡在尷尬、不利的處境，有如掛在樹梢頂上隨時擔心樹枝折斷。

- The crocodiles attacked the wading zebras and tore them limb from limb.
  鱷魚們攻擊涉水過河的斑馬，將牠們撕咬成碎片。
- I'm sure if he got hold of that fraud, he would tear him limb from limb.
  我敢說要是讓他逮到那個詐欺犯，他肯定將他碎屍萬段。
- The candidate climbed out on a limb with promises he could not keep.
  這名候選人開了無法兌現的支票，弄得自己處境狼狽。
- His image might suffer if he went out on a limb too often with remarks he couldn't prove.
  若他老說些無法證明的話而使自己處境尷尬，將有損他的形象。

Write your own sentence:

- If you dare ________________, I will tear you limb from limb. Just kidding!

hand 是拿、是給都得有一手

HAND以wrist（手腕）與手臂相連，它包括了palm（手掌）、thumb（姆指）、以及fingers（眾手指）。

手臂如果沒了HAND，就無法拿取東西，拿不住東西，就無法遞送、呈交，無法拿或給，做起事來就不順手。因此談到做事，經常離不開HAND，如：

He baked a cake with his own hands for my birthday.
→ 他親手烤了個蛋糕慶祝我生日。

He made these drawings by hand.
→ 這些作品都是他手繪出來的。

He seized the thief with his bare hands.
→ 他赤手空拳抓到這個小偷。

With magic sleight of hand, he produced two pigeons out of his top hat.
→ 他以不可思議的手法，從大禮帽變出了兩隻鴿子。

He rules the country with a heavy hand.
→ 他以嚴厲的手段統治這個國家。

正因做許多事都得用到HAND，因此HAND也意指人手、人力。如：a green hand（綠手）代表青澀的生手，dab hand或old hand（老手）則意指行家、熟手。既然做事常得用到HAND，要想幫人一把，自然也得用到HAND，因此HAND也與幫助有關，如：

We are short of hands today. → 我們今天人手不足。

Do you need a hand? → 你需要幫忙嗎？

hand

拿取東西當然不一定全得靠HAND，但若要將東西握住，沒有HAND就很難做到。因此HAND常與掌控、支配有關。如：

He put the matter in the hands of his lawyer before it got out of hand.
→ 他趁事情還沒變得難以控制，將它交給律師負責。

It is now out of my hands.
→ 此事現在已不歸我管、我也管不了。

除了拿取、掌握，必須靠HAND做的事還有寫字，於是HAND也有筆跡的意思，如：**write a beautiful hand**（寫得一手好字）。另外玩牌時，我們常說某人拿了一「手」壞牌（**have a poor hand**），可知HAND也意謂牌戲時手中的牌。著名的梭哈英文正是**Show Hand**。

指揮交通時也會用到HAND，因此HAND也表示方向或方面，如：

on the right hand of this street → 在這條街的右手邊
又如：

On the one hand, cars are useful but on the other hand, they cause air pollution.
→ 就某方面來說，汽車很有用，但另一方面來說，汽車也帶來了空氣污染。

不可免地，HAND也意指手形的物品，最主要表示鐘錶的指針，如長針（**long hand**）、短針（**short hand**）、秒針（**second hand**）等。

由於拿取東西得用到HAND，因此HAND當動詞使用時便意指傳遞，如：

hand me the pepper → 把胡椒拿給我

hand in your application → 交出你的申請書

hand out the pencils → 把鉛筆發下去

hand down the ring to the children → 把這枚戒指傳承給子女

由此也就衍生出了複合字如：**hand-me-down**（舊衣服、別人用過的舊東西）、**handout**（傳單、講義）。

至於**HAND+Y**成形容詞**handy**當然也與**HAND**有關，它意指就近的、在手邊的、方便的。

HAND+LE所成的**handle**，當名詞時意指「把手」、當動詞表示「處理、應付」。還有**HAND+SOME**的**handsome**（英俊的），這個字在古時候表示手很靈巧的，可見手巧的男人最英俊。

談**HAND**不能忘了手掌、手腕及眾手指們，有關手掌與手腕的慣用語也將在本單元一併介紹，至於眾手指們，敬請期待下一單元。

MEMO

1

at hand

在手邊，在附近，在近期

within easy reach or nearby in time

這個慣用語表示在近處，可用於時間、意指即將到來，或空間、意指方便拿得到或去得了的附近。**at first hand**（第一手）則表示直接地、親自地、不假他人之手。第一手的消息表示直接來自當事人，反之，**at second hand**（第二手）則表示間接地、輾轉地。

- I don't happen to have the photo album at hand, but I'll show it to you later.

  這本相簿偏巧不在我手邊，我以後再拿給你看。

- He believes the goal of his career is at hand.

  他相信他長期奮鬥的事業就快達成目標了。

- I visited Egypt and experienced at first hand the splendor of the ancient civilization.

  我走訪埃及，親身體驗這個古文明的風采。

- I learned of his accident at second hand.

  我從別人那裡得知他出事。

Write your own sentence:

- I don't have ______________ at hand, so I will ______________ later.

2

bite the hand that feeds one

啃咬餵養的手，恩將仇報，以怨報德

to show ingratitude and do harm to a benefactor

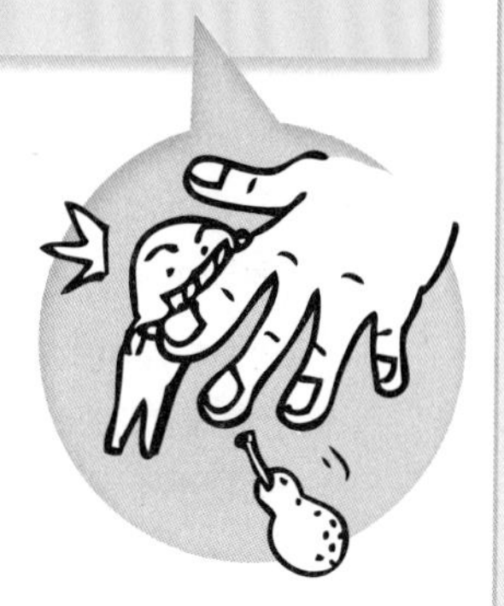

這個慣用語意指某人不但不感謝有恩於自己的人，還做出傷害恩人的事。這種行為實在可惡，但做壞事，弄髒的其實是自己的手。因此**dirty one's hands**或**get one's hands dirty**除了依原意表示弄髒雙手，也意指做了有損名譽或違法的事。反之，**one's hands are clean**則表示此人是清白的。

- Our parents may not be perfect, but never bite the hand that feeds us.

  我們的父母雖不盡完美，但絕不可恩將仇報。

- He refused to dirty his hands by giving away political favors.

  他拒絕分送政治利益，以免髒了自己的手。

- He was involved in the questionable land deals and got his hands dirty.

  他涉入這幾筆可疑的土地交易，毀了自己的清白。

Write your own sentence:

- ______________________, so I should not bite the hand that feeds me.

3

catch someone red-handed

抓到手染鮮血的某人，當場逮到某人（做壞事）

to catch someone in the act of doing something wrong

若在兇殺現場當場抓到正在犯案的兇手，想來該兇手必是雙手沾滿鮮血，因此這個慣用語便被用來表示當場將現行犯逮個正著。但若是**be caught with one's pants down**（褲子還沒拉上就被撞見），則表示某人難看的一面措手不及地被人看到，十分尷尬。

- He tried to cash a forged check, and the teller caught him red-handed.
  他想兌現偽造支票，被行員當場識破。
- They caught him red-handed dipping into the till.
  他挪用公款，被他們當場逮個正著。
- He was caught red-handed trying to cheat on the exam.
  他被當場逮到試圖作弊。
- I was caught with my pants down when I was picking my nose.
  我在挖鼻孔時剛好被看見，超尷尬。

Write your own sentence:

- ____________________ when the police drove by and caught them red-handed.

4

eat out of someone's hand

吃某人手上的食物，完全聽任某人擺佈

to do exactly as someone says or wants; to grovel to someone

許多人喜歡讓小鳥或小兔子這類溫馴的小動物（**tame animal**）來吃自己手裡的食物，但應該沒什麼人會以這種方式餵食老虎、獅子這類猛獸（**beast of prey**）。因此會去吃某人手中食物，表示被馴得服服帖帖、不敢造次。但要小心，如果 **get out of hand**（從手中跑出去），則表示 **get out of control**，不受控制或失去了控制。

- By giving them money, the tycoon had the press eating out of his hand.

  這名企業巨頭送出錢後，新聞界就完全聽他指揮了。

- She is so pretty and intelligent that most boys eat out of her hand.

  她長得漂亮頭腦又好，大多數男孩都對她唯命是從。

- You have to handle the angry crowd before they get out of hand.

  你得好好處理這群憤怒的人，以免他們失控。

Write your own sentence:

- I will eat out of your hand if only

  ______________________________.

5

force one's hand

強使某人出牌，逼某人提前出手或做某事

to compel someone to do something sooner than planned

此處**hand**意指玩家手中的牌，這個慣用語據說源自撲克，意指某人原本不想做某事，卻因故不得不改變計畫提早說出或做出什麼，一如玩家原本不想打某一手牌，卻礙於某些因素不得不將這手牌打出來。此外**hands**也意指支配掌管（要用複數），因此**change hands**表示轉手、換主人。

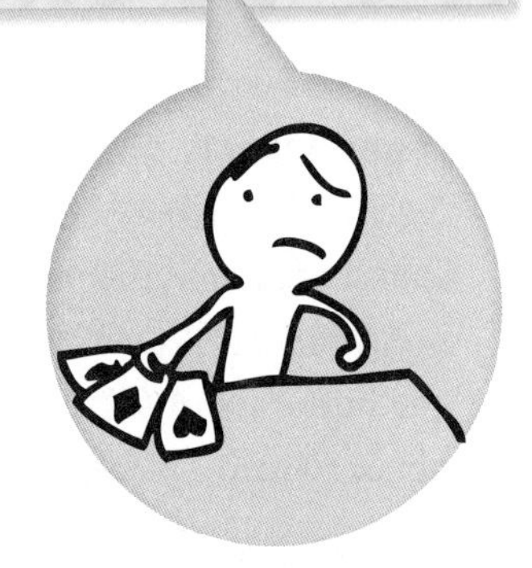

- He planned to keep his land until prices went up but his wife forced his hand.

  他原本計畫把地留到價格上揚再賣，可他老婆逼他把地賣了。

- The rebels forced his hand. He decided to go to war.

  叛軍一再相逼，他決定開戰。

- The ancient manuscript has changed hands twice since 2000.

  自2000年來，這份古代手稿已轉手兩次。

Write your own sentence:

- I didn't want to ____________________, but __________ forced my hand.

6

get the upper hand

抓到上端，佔上風，佔優勢

to have power and control over someone or a situation

大多人認為這個慣用語源於一種遊戲：兩人同時握住棍棒底部，誰的手搶先握到棒子頂端，誰就贏。其他說法還有 **arm-wrestling**（比腕力）或情侶握手，誰的手先壓在上面誰就佔上風。不管典故為何，總之得到 **upper hand** 就表示掌控了局面，位於有利的位置。**get** 可用 **have** 或 **gain**。**have/hold the whip hand** 為同義慣用語。

- He let his emotions get the upper hand and ruined his whole life.
  他感情用事，毀了他一生。
- The reformers have finally got the upper hand over the conservatives.
  改革派終於贏得優勢，壓過保守派。
- The fire fighters finally gained the upper hand on the forest fire.
  在這場森林大火中，消防隊員們終於控制住火勢。
- He had the whip hand throughout the debate.
  他在這場辯論賽中始終佔上風。

Write your own sentence:

- I hope _____ can have the upper hand over __________ in __________.

7

give someone a hand

給某人一隻手，助某人一臂之力，幫個忙

to help someone（to）do something

做許多事都需用到**hand**，所以**hand**也意指幫助。**give**或**lend**都可，反之需要幫忙則是**need a hand**。小心分辨：**give someone a free hand**表示給某人作主的權力，因為**free hand**不受約束，至於**give someone a big hand**則表示給某人熱烈掌聲，因為**big hand**拍得響（例句見HAND 19）。

- Could you give me a hand with the refreshments at the conference?
  你可以幫我準備會議時的餐點嗎？
- He is expecting his children to lend him a hand in the kitchen.
  他等著孩子們到廚房來幫他。
- Do you need a hand to remove the heavy chest?
  需要幫忙搬這只沈重的箱子嗎？
- The manager gave her assistant a free hand to reorganize the department.
  經理放手讓她的助理去整頓這個部門。

Write your own sentence:

- I am always willing to give a hand in/with _______.

8

hat in hand

帽子拿在手裡，恭敬地，謙卑地

with humility; in a humble way

帽子象徵尊嚴，中外皆然。因此摘下帽子拿在手裡，就表示極度恭敬，放下了自尊。**hat** 也可用 **cap**（無邊帽）。但帽子拿在手裡的人至少還站著，一旦 **on bended knee**（單膝跪下）或 **on hands and knees**（雙手雙膝貼地），那就真的完全不顧尊嚴、把尊嚴全丟到一邊了。

- He came back with hat in hand when he ran out of money.
  錢用完了，他就畢恭畢敬地回來了。
- They went hat in hand to the committee to ask for allowance.
  他們卑微地向委員會要求津貼。
- He was standing hat in hand before the professor.
  他低聲下氣地站在教授面前。
- He got on his hands and knees and begged his wife to come back home.
  他伏地跪求太太回家。

Write your own sentence:

- Should I go to ____________ hat in hand and beg for ________________________________?

have a hand in …

將一隻手伸進…，參與…

to be involved in or take part in something

做事常要用到手，因此放一隻手進去就表示有參與，成為其中一份子。如果用了雙手，而且**have hands full**（雙手都滿的，騰不出來），則表示要做的事很多，忙得抽不出一點空。其他表示很忙的慣用語可參見EYE 17。

- He works as screenplay writer and director. He has a hand in every aspect.

  他身兼編劇與導演，每個環節他都參與。

- He could have had a hand in designing the garden, but he missed it.

  這個花園的設計他本來也有份，但他錯失了機會。

- The garden party was basically John's idea but Mary said she had a hand in it too.

  這個園遊會基本上是John的點子，但Mary說她有出主意。

- He has his hands full with managing the store.

  他忙著經營這家店，完全空不出時間。

Write your own sentence:

- I would like to have a hand in ________, if possible.

10

have…on one's hands

有…在手上，有…需要照顧、處理

to be responsible for someone or something

允許某物放在手上就表示接受，一旦接受就有責任。因此，在手上就表示得照顧、處理、管理。

又，如果在手上的是時間，則意指可隨意使用的閒餘時間很多。倘若時間 **hang heavy**（沈重地垂下），彷彿鐘擺無力擺動，則表示時間過得很慢、令人悶得發慌。

- If the police carry on like this, they will have a riot on their hands.

  如果警方持續這樣下去，他們就等著處理暴動吧。

- His wife left a large family and an empty house on his hands.

  他太太留了一大家子和一棟空房子要他照顧處理。

- In the nursing home, he has a lot of time on his hands but time hangs heavy.

  在安養院，他手頭沒事、時間倒有一大把，但時間過得好慢、好難打發。

Write your own sentence:

- Because ________, I have ________ on my hands.

11

in hand

手中，眼前所擁有或正待處理，掌控中

to be accessible at the moment; to be in process; to be under control

握在手中，表示擁有，而握在手中的工作或問題則意指正在進行或正待解決。握在手中就跑不掉，因此它也意指掌握、掌控某人事物。如果**in good hands**（落入好的手中），則表示得到很好、很令人安心的照顧。

- The company has very little cash in hand. That is the problem in hand.
  這家公司手邊幾乎已無現金，這是眼下亟待解決的問題。
- The arrangements for the conference are all in hand.
  會議的籌備工作都在安排了。
- I thought I had my destiny in hand, but then fate played a trick on me.
  我原以為命運掌控在我手中，可後來命運卻捉弄我。
- Your car is in good hands. My mechanics are factory-trained.
  你的車會被照顧得很好的，我的師傅都有經過實務訓練。

Write your own sentence:

- I am trying to give full attention to ______________________ in hand.

12

keep one's hands off…

使雙手離開…，把手拿開，別碰、別去動或管…

to refrain from touching or handling something

這個慣用語意指不觸摸某物、不處理、不碰觸某事。**keep** 也可用 **get** 或 **take**。反之，若是 **take … off one's hands**（使…離開某人雙手），則表示從某人手中接管照顧…。**off one's hands** 表示脫手、不管，因此形容詞 **hands-off** 意指不干預的，如：**a hands-off foreign policy**（不干預他國事務的外交政策）。

- Get your hands off that plate. That's my cake.
  別去碰那個盤子，那塊蛋糕是我的。
- We hoped that the oil company would keep their hands off the wetland.
  我們希望石油公司能放手，別去動這塊溼地。
- Keep your hands off, so your son can learn to be independent.
  放手別管，這樣你兒子才能學會獨立。
- The government is going to take the troubled assets off their hands.
  政府將從他們手中接管這些問題資產。

Write your own sentence:

- I am glad to keep my hands off ________________.

13

know … like the back of one's hand

瞭解…就如瞭解自己的手背，瞭若指掌，知之甚詳

to know someone or something extremely well

此慣用語正如中文的「瞭若指掌」，同義的慣用語還有：
know…backwards and forwards／know…inside out
know…like a book。

但若有人給予手背的讚美（**back-handed compliment**），這可不是瞭解，而是表面讚美實則挖苦，這種間接諷刺的讚美也叫左手的讚美（**left-handed compliment**），因為拉丁文的「左」（**sinister**）意指邪惡陰險的。

- I can show you around. I know this town like the back of my hand.

  我可以帶你走走看看，我對這地方熟得不能再熟。

- He knows the author's life story backwards and forwards.

  他對這個作者的生平太瞭解了，倒背都沒問題。

- He said I looked smarter than I was. I thought it was a back-handed compliment.

  他說我看起來比實際聰明，我覺得這不像讚美、較像在罵人。

Write your own sentence:

- After ________________, I know ________________________ like the back of my hand.

14

lay one's hands on…

把雙手放在…上，逮到…（以處罰整治），找到並拿到…

to get hold of someone to punish; to locate and obtain someone or something

想抓人或拿東西，至少得先讓雙手碰到，因此這個慣用語既意指捉住某人以便修理一頓，使飽嘗苦頭，也意指找到並獲取某人或某物。由此便衍生出形容詞**hands-on**，表示「親自參與的、動手實做的」，如：**hands-on operations**（實務操作）／**a hands-on boss**（親力親為的老闆）。**lay**也可用**put**。小心，**lay a hand on someone**意指「傷害某人」。

- When I lay my hands on Joe, he will be sorry he ever lied to me.
  等我逮到Joe他就慘了，他絕對會為他撒的謊後悔。
- I am trying to put my hands on the music album you recommended.
  我正設法在找你推薦的音樂專輯。
- I never laid a hand on them.
  我從沒傷害過他們。
- As a hands-on manager, he has his hands full.
  他是個什麼都親力親為的經理，忙得不可開交。

Write your own sentence:

- As soon as I lay my hands on ________________,
  I will call you.

15

lift one's hand against…

舉手作勢要打…，威脅要打或真的打下去

to threaten to hit or actually hit someone or something

通常狗一看到人舉起手立刻就跑，因為舉手是打或揍的前置動作。**lift** 也可用 **raise**。但若 **lift a finger**（抬起一根手指），則表示「舉手之勞」，因為抬指頭對大多數人來說實非難事。又或指頭不抬起，而是 **lay on**（放在…上），則表示碰觸某人或某物，延伸表示意欲侵犯傷害此人此物，與 **lay a hand on** 同義。

- Don't you dare lift your hand against my brother again.
  你敢再放話威脅我兄弟你試試看。
- A gentleman would never lift his hand against a woman.
  君子不會動手打女人。
- If you lay a finger on me, I'll sue.
  只要你動我一下，我就提告。
- He wouldn't lift a finger to help them financially.
  他連小小幫他們紓困一下都不肯。

Write your own sentence:

- Would you lift your hand against ____________?

16

one's hands are tied

雙手被綁起來，心有餘而力不足，束手無策，愛莫能助

one is not free to behave in the way that he／she would like

所謂助一臂之力，手常代表幫忙，所以雙手被縛，就表示使不上力、幫不上忙。但若綁手又綁腳（**bound hand and foot**），除了表示身體行動受限、也可表示行事被綁死，難有自由的發揮空間。**single-handed** 雖只有一隻手，但至少有手，意指單獨、獨力的／地；**short-handed** 有手但不長，表示人力不足的。

- I would like to admit you into his office, but my hands are tied by the rules.

  我很想放行讓你進他辦公室，但礙於規定，我實在無能為力。

- The funds have me bound hand and foot. I will film it single-handed.

  經費問題讓我很難做事，我會自己獨立完成拍攝的。

- We are short-handed today. Do you mind helping us out?

  我們今天人手不足，你可以過來支援我們嗎？

Write your own sentence:

- I would like to ______________________________,
  but my hands are tied.

hand

17

play into someone's hands

跑進某人的手裡去玩，使某人有機可乘（自己還不知道）

to give someone an advantage without realizing it

手意謂著掌控，進到別人手裡，無異是在給別人機會，做出不利於自己的事，結果自己還渾然無知。又，若是 **take the law into one's hands**（把法律握在手裡），則表示不屑或不信法律，覺得自己可以代替天道或法律，以私人之手執行法律的公權力。

- You should have faith in us, not play into the hands of our enemies.
  你該相信我們，別讓敵人有可乘之機。
- If you allow him to be alone with you, you are just playing into his hands.
  如果你讓他跟你單獨相處，你就是在給他機會對你不利。
- If you get furious, you will play into the hands of your political opponents.
  你若發飆，那可正中政敵們的下懷。
- The mother took the law into her hands and killed the kidnapper.
  這位母親自己私了，殺了這名綁匪。

Write your own sentence:

- ________ played right into the hands of ________ when ______________.

18

show one's hand

把手牌露出來，過早透露意圖或計畫，攤牌

to reveal one's plans, intentions, or resources when they should be hidden

此處**hand**意指手牌。玩牌時手上的牌若被別人看光，這場牌戲恐怕很難再玩下去。這個慣用語意指露出底細、以致計畫提早曝光，或許是故意、也可能是不小心。**show**用**tip**（使傾斜）也可，因為牌放太斜就會被看到。小心分辨：**show of hands**（把手露出來）意指舉手表決。

- If you want to get a raise, don't show the boss your hand too soon.

  你若想加薪，別太急著跟老闆攤牌。

- The journalists tried to get him to tip his hand but he left them guessing.

  媒體記者們希望他能透露一點風聲，但他讓他們自己去猜。

- How many of you rub hands when feeling satisfied, show of hands?

  你們有誰在心滿意足時會做出搓手的動作，是的請舉手？

Write your own sentence:

- Rumors abound about ________________ but I have refused to show my hand.

19

sit on one's hands

坐在手上，不鼓掌，沒反應，沒行動

to fail to applaud; to take no action

把雙手壓在臀部底下，當然無法鼓掌，這個慣用語原本用來表示對於表演或藝術作品沒有掌聲、鼓勵，後來也用來表示沒有作為、按兵不動。

相較於把手壓在臀下，**give someone a big hand**則表示為某人大聲喝采，**get a big hand**則表示得到熱烈讚賞。

- The audience sat on their hands for the whole performance.
  整場表演下來觀眾都沒掌聲。
- When I needed help from John, he just sat on his hands.
  在我需要John幫忙時，他卻毫無動靜。
- We are facing serious brain-drain but he seems content to sit on his hands.
  我們正面臨嚴重的人才外流，但他似乎樂於維持現狀。
- She got a big hand for marvelous aerial acrobatics at the show.
  節目中她精彩的空中特技表演贏得如雷掌聲。

 Write your own sentence:

- We can't just sit on our hands and wait until

  ______________________________.

20

throw in one's hand

丟下手中的牌，放棄、退出、認輸

to abandon or give up; to admit defeat or failure

把牌丟下，表示不玩了，決定從牌局退出。同義的用語有**throw in one's towel／sponge**，因為在拳賽中，若教練把拳擊手擦身用的毛巾或海綿丟進場中，就表示這位拳擊手輸了，不再需要毛巾。

請注意，**throw up one's hands**（雙手高舉）意指沮喪、挫敗、無奈等無語問蒼天的心情。

- He left the kitchen and threw in his hand. He couldn't even beat an egg.
  他走出廚房，認輸不玩了，他連打個蛋都做不好。
- It is too early for you to throw in the towel. Hang in there!
  現在還不是認輸的時候，再撐一下！
- He threw his hands up because they wouldn't let him see his fiancée.
  他絕望地不知該怎麼辦，因為他們不讓他見他未婚妻。

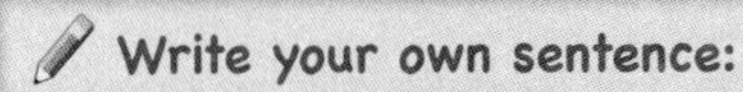

Write your own sentence:

- I was forced to throw in my hand and ______________________________.

hand

21

wash one's hands of …

清洗沾染了…的雙手，與…劃清界限再也不管、不擔相關責任

to refuse to take responsibility for someone or something

這個慣用語源自聖經（Matthew 27:24），當巡撫 **Pilate** 不得不應眾人要求判耶穌死罪，他在眾人面前洗手，聲言義人耶穌流的血與他絕無關係。因此若想聲明自己與某個人事物再沒任何關係，請別人切勿為此人事物找上門來，就可以用這個慣用語表示。

- She washed her hands of him once she realized he just wanted someone to wait on him hand and foot.
  明白了他只是想找個能將他服侍得妥妥貼貼的人，她於是與他切割，再也不管他。
- I washed my hands of politics long ago after realizing how corrupt and selfish politicians were.
  瞭解政客的貪腐與自利，我早就不再過問政治方面的事了。
- I decided to wash my hands of the whole affair and let someone else deal with it.
  我決定這事我不再過問，交給別人來處理。

Write your own sentence:

- ________________, even though I have washed my hands (of ________________________________).

22

work hand in glove with…

戴上手套與…共事，與…密切合作，緊密結合

to do something on intimate terms with someone or something else

手套是給手戴的，手放入手套，表示合作關係密切。**work**也可用**go**。但若是**go hand in hand**（手牽手一起走），則意指共存的兩個事物彼此互有關聯，有一即有二、有二即有一。又若絲絨做的手套裡（**a velvet glove**）卻有一隻鐵手（**an iron hand**），則表示外寬內嚴或先用軟的再用硬的，即軟硬兼施。

- We are glad to see that universities work hand in glove with industry.
  我們樂見大學與產業合作無間。
- The Navy and the Coast Guard work hand in glove to prevent and combat smuggling.
  海軍與海岸巡邏隊密切合作，查緝走私。
- Drug trafficking usually goes hand in hand with other sorts of crime.
  販毒常與其他型態的犯罪脫不了關係。
- She runs the town with an iron hand in a velvet glove.
  她治理這個城鎮的方式，表面看起來很鬆，實質上很嚴。

Write your own sentence:

- I am working hand in glove with __________ to ____________________.

23

a slap on the wrist

輕拍手腕，溫和、輕微的責罰

a mild or light punishment

slap打在臉上痛又羞，打在手腕則不痛也不羞。又，若是**rap on the knuckles**（輕敲指關節），則表示訓斥，也同樣算是輕微的懲處。但若**get a knuckle sandwich**（吃了一記指節三明治），則表示有人朝臉狠K一拳。又若有人揚言要**tan your hide**（鞣你的皮），則是要揍你屁股或痛打一頓。

- He committed a heinous crime but he only got a slap on the wrist from the judge.
  他犯下滔天大罪卻只受到法官輕判。
- The coach gave me a slap on the wrist for arriving rate.
  因為遲到，教練對我略施懲戒。
- I got a rap on the knuckles for not finishing my essay on time.
  我沒準時完成論文，被狠狠訓了一頓。
- Ann gave Jim a knuckle sandwich when she caught him peeping at her.
  Ann發現Jim在偷窺她，往Jim臉上賞了一拳。

Write your own sentence:

- I thought I would get a slap on the wrist for ________, but I ____________.

24

grease someone's palm

在手掌上抹油，給錢求方便，行賄

to give someone money in exchange for a favor; to bribe someone

這個慣用語意指給人油水以換取自己的方便或好處，情節輕者算給個小費（**tip**），情節重大者則屬行賄罪（**bribery**）。一般來說愛財的人掌上若沒油水手就會癢，因此**itchy palm**就表示愛錢、貪財。又，由於以前看手相者（**palm reader**）會要求客戶先付錢再服務，因此在掌上置枚銀幣（**cross one's palm with silver**）便意指為得到服務先付費、又或為額外服務付費。

- The drug baron tried to grease the police chief's palm and ask a favor of him.

  這名毒梟試著用錢疏通警察局長，要他給點方便。

- The local political boss is known for his itchy palm.

  大家都知道這名地方上的政治大老向來貪財愛收賄。

- The porter refused to carry heavy luggage before I crossed his palm with silver.

  付了費後，這名腳夫才願意幫我扛重的行李。

Write your own sentence:

- If I want ______________, do I really need to grease ______________'s palm?

finger 手指家族 & thumb 拇指老大

FINGER是手的前鋒，專責指引、抓拿，必須非常靈活，更要有犧牲小我的精神，因為手若受傷，傷點最容易落在**FINGER**上。因此若有人不小心吃虧受苦，那便是**burn one's fingers**（燒到手指），因為將手伸入險境，首當其衝正是**FINGER**。又若是**work one's fingers to the bone**（幹活到手指見骨），則表示做個不停、十分拚命。此外，若有人能使某種角色（律師、醫生、英國人）**to one's fingertips**（直到指尖），那就表示此人可說是這角色的典型，因為舉手投足之間，連指尖都呈現出這個角色的特質，如：

He is an artist to his fingertips. → 他是個十足的藝術家。

FINGER家族的成員有食指（**forefinger／index finger**）、中指（**middle finger**）、無名指（**ring finger**）、小指（**little finger／pinky finger**）。食指常被用來沾嘗食物或指出人事物，中指可做出中外皆公認不雅的動作、即**give the finger**（比中指）、無名指用來套婚戒、小指則擅長做繞轉的動作。

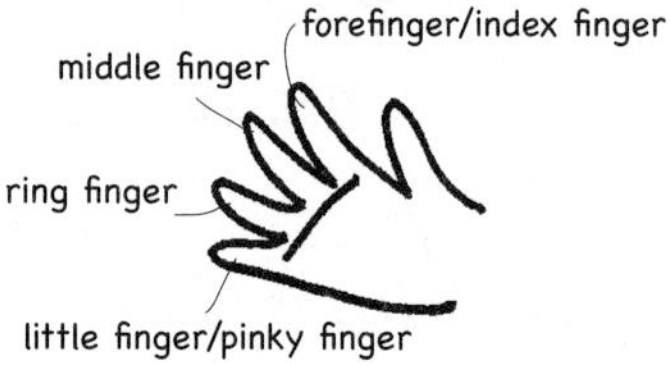

至於老大**THUMB**，它可豎起來比讚、也可倒豎表示噓，由於它粗短顯眼，一旦受傷肯定引人注目，因此人們常以**stick out like a sore thumb**來表示某人事物十分引人注意，如：

That pimple really sticks out like a sore thumb.
→ 那顆青春痘實在很難不讓人注意。

此外，據說以前的人習慣以**THUMB**中間的指關節（**knuckle**）到指尖（**tip**）這一段距離來做測量單位，因為成年人的這截拇指大多是一英吋。也因此**a rule of thumb**就表示根據經驗所得出的法則或竅門。如：

As a rule of thumb, I have three bowls of water for one dose of herbal medicine. → 我的經驗是，一帖中藥對三碗水。

在莎士比亞的「馬克白」中，為馬克白預言的巫婆們曾說：

By the pricking of my thumbs, something wicked this way come. → 根據我拇指感覺到的刺痛，壞事就要降臨。

於是**by the pricking of one's thumbs**就表示根據某人不祥的預感。

THUMB當動詞用自然與拇指有關，一則表示以拇指翻閱，如：**thumb through a phone book**（匆匆翻閱電話簿），另外也表示為搭便車翹拇指，如：**thumb a ride to Paris**（搭便車到巴黎）。

至於**FINGER**當動詞，則表示以手指撫摸或彈奏，如：
finger a keyboard（撫弄鍵盤）

---

knuckle 連結了**FINGER**與手、以及手指的兩個指節。**crack knuckles**會製造出咔咔的聲音，很有威嚇的意味，如果有人送出**a knuckle sandwich**（指節三明治）就表示朝嘴或臉揍一拳；又若坐雲霄飛車坐到指節發白（**a white-knuckle ride on a roller coaster**），表示十分驚險刺激。至於如果某人的笑話或言論**near the knuckle**（離指節很近），則表示夾有色情、兒童不宜，為什麼呢？因為尺度太過，幾乎已到了令人想活動活動指節的地步。

1

burn one's fingers

燙到手指，嘗到苦頭、吃虧上當（才學乖）

to learn caution through an unpleasant experience

此慣用語源自一則小故事：話說有隻貓在猴子的拐騙下冒險去拿火裡的栗子，結果栗子沒拿到反卻燙傷貓掌。這個慣用語意指做某些事由於粗心、鹵莽、貪心、傻傻或不聽勸等，以致害慘自己，但燙一次痛一次，人有時候就是要真正痛到才會記取教訓（**learn a lesson**）。也可寫成 **get／have one's fingers burned**。

- I'm staying away from risky stocks; I've burned my fingers often enough.
  我現在絕不碰風險大的股票，我吃的苦頭夠多了。
- He burned his fingers in the casino; he swore never to gamble again.
  他在賭場吃了大虧，發誓從今以後再也不賭。
- He got his fingers burned on master paintings that turned out to be fakes.
  他投資的大師名畫結果全是假的，真是上一次當學一次乖。

Write your own sentence:

- I burned my fingers on __________ and don't want __________________________ again.

have green fingers

長了綠手指，擅長園藝

to be good at keeping plants healthy and making them grow

這個慣用語意指某人很有園藝天分，彷彿手上直接帶有葉綠素，能點「植物」成綠，因此能種出漂亮的植栽。**have a green thumb**是美式說法。又，若手指不綠卻很**sticky**（黏黏的），到處黏走人家的東西，則表示有順手牽羊的毛病、偷竊的習慣、手腳不乾淨。**sticky**也可用**light**（輕快的）。

- I'm afraid I don't have green fingers. I've killed every plant I've ever grown.

  我想我沒園藝天分，我種的植物每種必死。

- She has a green thumb when it comes to potted plants.

  說到盆栽植物，她可拿手了。

- He has sticky fingers and is always taking his classmates' small change.

  他手腳不乾淨，老是偷拿同學的小零錢。

Write your own sentence:

- If I have green fingers, I will ____________________.

3

have a finger in every pie

每塊派都要沾一下手，什麼事都要管，參與各種不同活動

to meddle in everything; to be involved in many different activities

這個慣用語既可意指某人管太多，每塊派餅都要品嘗一下、指導一番，也可意指某人同時涉獵或參與多種事情或活動，每種口味都想試一下。**every pie** 可依情況換成 **too many pies** 表示某人同時兼做的事太多，又或換成 **the pie** 表示某人特別對某件事感到興趣，也想試一下。

- We can't make a decision without him being here. He has a finger in every pie.

  沒他在這裡我們不能做決定，他向來什麼都要有意見。

- Teaching, writing, and dancing -- she likes to have a finger in every pie.

  教學、寫作、跳舞，她喜歡多方嘗試。

- I was assigned to cover sports news and Joe wanted to have a finger in the pie.

  我被指派去報導體育新聞，Joe也想來試試看。

Write your own sentence:

- It looks as if ________ had a finger in every pie because ______________________________.

4

have one's fingers in the till

把手指放在櫃台錢箱裡，竊取上班公司或商店的公款

to steal money from the place where one works, usually from a shop

till 是櫃台裡裝錢的抽屜，這個慣用語意指某人偷錢，且下手目標正是自己任職的公司行號。**fingers** 可用 **hand**，**till** 可換用 **cookie jar**（餅乾罐子）。如果手正在錢箱或餅乾罐子裡時被抓到（**be caught with one's hand in the till**），就表示偷錢之時被人看到或當場抓包，尤指偷公家的錢。

- We suspected he had his fingers in the till but there was no evidence.

  我們懷疑他偷公司的錢，可是沒證據。

- He had his fingers in the cookie jar. That is why he lost his job.

  他偷公司的錢，難怪工作沒了。

- He was caught with his hand in the till and was fired immediately.

  他偷公司的錢當場被逮到，馬上被開除。

Write your own sentence:

- I was outraged when I found ________ had ______ fingers in the till.

5

cross one's fingers

中指疊在同手的食指上，祈求好運，為善意謊言求原諒

to wish for good luck; to ask for pardon for a white lie

希望好運發生、又或已發生的好運延續，西方的習俗是將中指疊在同手食指上代表十字架，祈求好運降臨，也寫成**have／keep one's fingers crossed**。若說了無傷大雅的謊言，他們也會把手伸到背後做此手勢，以免被上天處罰。又由於古代人認為摸樹可以驅走邪靈惡運，**touch／knock on wood**（摸或敲木頭）也意指祈求上天保佑。

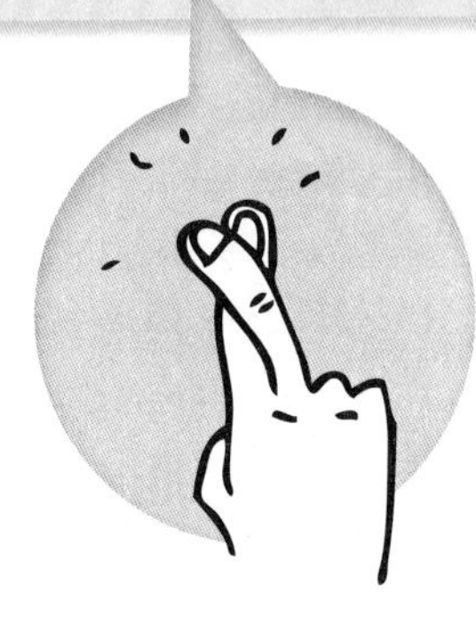

- Let's cross our fingers that the tornado goes out to sea.
  讓我們祈求龍捲風出海去吧！
- Good luck with your driving test; I'll keep my fingers crossed for you.
  祝你考駕照順利，我會為你祈禱的。
- I got a pass in English. Knock on wood.
  我英文及格了，謝天謝地。
- I told Mom I didn't get a ticket this month but I had my fingers crossed.
  我跟媽說這個月沒接到罰單其實是騙她的，希望老天別罰我。

Write your own sentence:

- I am crossing my fingers that ____________.

6

point the finger at someone

把手指指向某人，將矛頭指向某人，認為是某人的錯

to accuse or blame someone

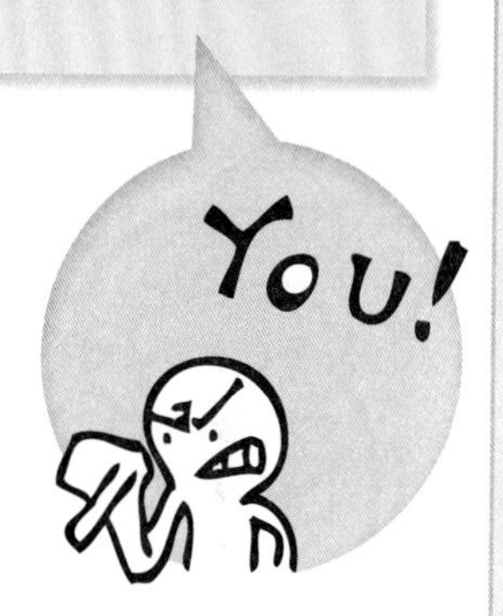

將手指（尤其是食指）朝著別人（**at someone**），是指責、怪罪的典型動作，但別忘了一指指向別人時，其實也有好幾指指著自己。又若食指放在某人身上（**on someone**），則表示指認出某個特定的人，尤指向警方密告或指證犯人或兇手等。若是食指放在某問題上（**on something**），則表示能確切說出該問題癥結所在或原因、位置等。

- He pointed the finger at the teacher when his boy was charged with blackmail.

  他兒子向人勒索被控，他把錯怪到老師頭上。

- The witness put the finger on the defendant.

  證人確切指證出被告來。

- Something is wrong with the taste but I can't put my finger on what it is.

  這味道怪怪的，可我就是說不上來怪在哪裡。

Write your own sentence:

- ________ was/were quick to point the finger at ________ when ______________________________.

7

snap one's fingers at …

對著…彈手指，瞧不起、不把…看在眼裡

to treat someone or something with contempt, scorn, or disregard

雖說彈手指這個舉動可表示助興、贊同，但用於慣用語卻意謂著蔑視、不以為然。又，**bite the thumb at** …（對著…咬姆指）也表示侮辱，嚴重性可與**give the finger**（比中指）相比，在羅密歐與茱麗葉開場，一場爭鬥就因咬姆指引起。另外把姆指放在鼻上扇動手指也表示輕蔑，參見NOSE 09。

- He snapped his fingers at the speed limit and drove as fast as he liked.

  他完全不把速限當一回事，高興開多快就開多快。

- Do you bite your thumb at us, Sir? (Romeo and Juliet [1:1])

  你這是表示看扁我們嗎？先生？（摘自「羅密歐與茱麗葉」第一幕第一景）

- He thumbed his nose at any suggestion we made.

  不管我們提什麼建議他都看不上眼。

Write your own sentence:

- The student activists snapped their fingers at ____________ and ____________________________.

8

slip through one's fingers

從指縫間溜走，錯失良機，沒留住某人、讓某人跑了

to miss an opportunity; to fail to get or keep something or someone

明明已在手中有如囊中物，卻從指縫間滑落，這個慣用語用在事情上表示就快達到的事卻錯失，如同想搭的車從眼前開走。用於人則表示讓某人跑了，明明想抓住、想尋覓、想獲得的人就在眼前，卻眼睜睜看著此人離開自己的視線終致消失。

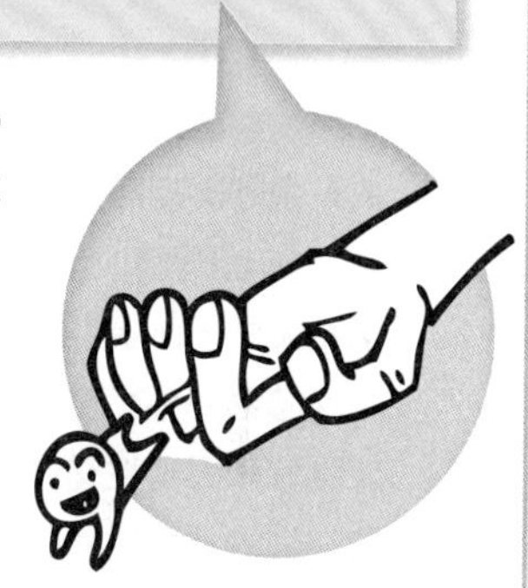

- He has seen the world championship slip through his fingers twice.

  他曾兩度看著世界冠軍與自己擦身而過。

- He has only himself to blame after letting a lead slip through his fingers.

  沒把握住演主角的機會，他只能怪他自己。

- He made miscalculations and let a potential player slip through his fingers.

  他判斷錯誤，放走了一名有潛力的選手。

Write your own sentence:

- I could have ____________________ but I let it slip through my fingers.

finger & thumb

9

twist someone around one's little finger

把某人纏在小指頭上，要某人往東、某人絕不敢往西

to exert complete control over someone

因為喜歡或依賴，以致甘願讓人綁在小指上，做什麼都願意，即使小指挖鼻孔也沒關係。**twist**也可用**wrap**／**wind**。此外，如果某人成了你手中的**putty**（灰泥），表示這人很容易受你影響，對你百依百順，因為灰泥既軟、可塑性又佳，在你手中，想捏成圓的或扁的、全都隨便你。

- Ann could twist her boss around her little finger. He really fell for her.

  Ann有辦法把她老闆吃得死死的，他超迷戀她。

- Mom has wrapped John around her little finger. He is dependent on her.

  John對媽媽言聽計從，他事事依賴她。

- Ken's wife is putty in his hands. She never thinks for herself.

  Ken的太太完全任Ken擺佈，從不替自己設想。

Write your own sentence:

- I can twist ________ around my little finger because ______________________.

have … at one's fingertips

把…放在指尖，隨手可得，(精通某事所以資料)隨手捻來

to have something ready at hand, immediately available

這個慣用語可依原意表示東西拿取容易，彷彿指尖一伸即可到手；延伸表示某人精通某領域或熟知某狀況，因此許多相關知識彷彿只需指尖一點就可調出資料。這原本只是古人的想像，但網路實現了古人的夢想，如今果真指尖一點就能取得一堆資料呢。**have** 也可用 **keep**。

- The dashboard design keeps all the vital controls at the driver's fingertips.

  這款儀表板將所有重要的操控裝置都設計在駕駛人手邊。

- He has the whole body of laws at his fingertips. Go and pick his brains.

  所有法律條文他瞭如指掌，快去請教他吧。

- He always keeps some spicy jokes at his fingertips.

  他隨時端得出幾個低級的黃色笑話。

Write your own sentence:

- I hope I can have ______________________________ at my fingertips.

hang on by one's fingernails

靠著手指甲緊緊抓住，勉強撐著、勉力維持

to manage to avoid danger or failure

吊掛在懸崖邊，唯一只剩手指甲仍與地面相連，只要一個不小心，隨時都可能墜入萬丈深淵，一切休矣。這個慣用語意指在絕困處境中，勉力維持著一線生機，但求活著、維持著，不要大敗、倒閉、或死絕。

hang 也可用 **cling**，**fingernail**（手指甲）也可用 **fingertip**（手指尖）。

- He lost his daughter. He felt as if he were hanging on by his fingernails.

  他失去女兒，覺得自己只是勉強維持著生命。

- The owner of the café is just hanging on by his fingernails.

  這家咖啡館的老闆努力讓店還能開得下去。

- The crops have failed this year. He is clinging on by his fingertips.

  今年收成不好，他勉強撐著過日子。

Write your own sentence:

- I am hanging on by my fingernails and hoping that ______________________________.

12

be all thumbs

全是拇指，手腳笨拙

to be very awkward and clumsy, especially with one's hands

如果五根手指全長成拇指的樣子，想必織毛衣、彈鋼琴、下廚房、做木工等，都會變得很不順手。這個慣用語意指手腳很笨、不靈活、不俐落。**butterfingers**（奶油手指）則表示笨手笨腳的人，指頭好像塗了奶油，拿什麼掉什麼、接東西總接不到。注意，單複數用同一字。

- He **is all thumbs** around the house. He can't even change a light bulb.
  他做起家事笨手笨腳的，連換個燈泡都不會。
- Can you thread this needle for me? I **am all thumbs**.
  可以幫我把這根線穿過這根針嗎？我的手不是很巧。
- I **am all thumbs** when it comes to shuffling cards.
  我手不夠靈活，沒法俐落地洗牌。
- He is such **a butterfingers** that he always drops a plate or a cup.
  他手腳實在很笨，老要掉個盤子杯子的。

Write your own sentence:

- I am all thumbs when it comes to ______________.

finger & thumb

13

turn thumbs up

豎起兩隻大拇指，贊成、認同、接受

to accept or approve someone or something

這個動作對應的語言是「讚」，因此這個慣用語意指接受、同意、認可。反之，倒豎大拇指則表示「噓」，意指不認同、反對、不接受。此慣用語重點在於**thumbs up／down**，動詞可用**turn**或**give**或**say**。

- Only those who really matter will turn thumbs up on the plan.
  只有真正關心的人才會對此計畫表示贊成。
- The committee turned thumbs up on my proposal and voted to fund the project.
  委員會接受我的提案，投票決定撥款資助這個計畫。
- The boss turned thumbs down on Joe. So Ben has replaced Joe as CEO.
  老闆不喜歡Joe，結果由Ben取代Joe成為執行長。
- Mom gave us thumbs down on serving beer at our slumber party.
  媽反對我們在睡衣派對上喝啤酒。

Write your own sentence:

- When ________ turned thumbs up on ____________, I knew everything was OK.

14

twiddle one's thumbs

搓拇指，無事可做，無所事事耗時間

to have nothing useful to do

做事常會用到手，拇指不做事卻拿來搓，一來可能是等候某人事物閒得無聊、白讓時間耗掉；另外也可能是懶惰閒散，不想找事做，任光陰蹉跎。閒散太久，小心腳底長出草來，**let the grass grow under one's feet**意指由於怠惰懶散或拖拖拉拉以致浪費了許多時間。

- I spent four hours twiddling my thumbs while you made one call after another.
  你電話一通接著一通打，四個小時裡我只能搓拇指空等。
- He was just sitting in the office twiddling his thumbs until he retired.
  他整天坐在辦公室裡啥都不做，就這樣一直到退休。
- She twiddled her thumbs all year and flunked out of college.
  她遊手好閒了一整年，結果成績太差被勒令退學。
- Don't let the grass grow under your feet. Sign the contract today.
  別再拖了，時間不等人，今天就把合約簽了吧。

Write your own sentence:

- Don't sit around twiddling your thumbs.
  Go ______________________________.

15

under one's thumb

在某人拇指下，在某人勢力下，徹底受到某人控制

to be under one's control and manipulation

有人認為這個慣用語源於 **falconry**（獵鷹訓練術），因為訓練師都把線纏在拇指上以控制獵鷹。另有一說認為這純粹是個手勢，若某人甲只需一根拇指就能壓住管制某人乙，可見乙如何受控於甲。其他與控制有關的慣用語還有 **under one's heel**（在某人腳跟下）及 **in the palm of one's hand**（在某人手掌中）。

- Ned is a bully. He keeps many dropouts under his thumb.

  Ned是個惡霸，他控制許多中輟生讓他們聽命於他。

- By the early twentieth century, Ireland was under the heel of Britain.

  二十世紀初期之前，愛爾蘭由英國統治。

- He had the audience in the palm of his hand.

  觀眾的情緒全掌控在他手中。

Write your own sentence:

- I don't want to be under anyone's thumb because ________________________________.

16

knuckle under

將指關指朝下，屈服認輸

to yield or give in to someone or something; to acknowledge defeat

人一跪下就表示屈服、投降，跪下時不論雙手垂在兩側還是貼著膝頭，指關節都是朝下，因此**knuckle under**意指認了、被迫接受。**knuckle down**也是指關節朝下，但此處並非跪下，而是握拳準備行動，手指的指關節朝下，因此**knuckle down**意指即將展開行動、認真工作。

- We want to reach an agreement but we refuse to knuckle under to these demands.

  我們很想達成協議，但我們拒絕屈從這些條件。

- You should not knuckle under to your boss all the time. He can't always be right.

  你不該老是讓你老闆，他不一定總是對的。

- You have just got to knuckle down and concentrate on what is important.

  你實在應該動起來，把心思放在重要的事情上。

Write your own sentence:

- Will I be forced to knuckle under before ________________________________?

knee & 屈膝蓋求饒？
heel or 拔足跟快跑？

KNEE連接著大腿（thigh）與小腿（leg），與KNEE最直接有關的動作就是跪，而KNEE+L當動詞，意思正是跪下。如：

The knights had to kneel before the king.
→ 在國王面前騎士們必須下跪。

說到KNEE，很難不想到knee-jerk reflex（膝蓋被敲之後自然彈起的反射動作），因此knee-jerk reaction便意指未經仔細思考、僅憑情緒作出的反應，如：

It's not a knee-jerk reaction to yell at a slow waiter. It's bad manners.
→ 對動作慢的服務生大吼才不是下意識動作，那叫沒禮貌。

至於knee-slapper（讓人拍膝蓋的事），則是指超好笑的笑話，但有時這個詞也會用來反諷，用「好好笑的笑話哦」意指根本不好笑。

---

knees-up則意指大家都會把膝蓋往上提起的場合，亦即舞會又或是有人跳舞的party。

由**KNEE**順著**leg**往下，是連接**leg**與**foot**的**ankle**（足踝），**ankle**再往下是**HEEL**。不論走、跑、跳，只要身體動起來，**HEEL**就得離開地面，若沒保持好距離，離地的**HEEL**很容易與別人的**HEEL**擦撞在一起，也因此**HEEL**的慣用語經常與「跑」或「跟隨」有關。

此外，談到人事物的致命弱點或關鍵也與**HEEL**有關，即**Achilles' heel**（阿基里斯的足跟）。**Achilles**是希臘神話中鼎鼎有名的大英雄，他是海洋女神Thetis與國王Peleus的兒子。她的母親為了使他與自己一樣永生不死，在他一出生就將他浸入冥河（**Styx**）使之刀槍不入，但最後**Achilles**卻被射中**HEEL**而死，因為當初母親正是抓著他的**HEEL**將他身體浸在河中，因此**HEEL**並沒浸到河水，以致成了他全身唯一的弱點、也成了他致死的關鍵。而**Achilles**被射中的部位也因此被稱為**Achilles tendon**（跟腱），亦即位於腳跟與小腿之間俗稱「腳筋」的那條肌腱。

與**Achilles' heel**同樣表示弱點的還有**feet of clay**（泥土腳）。「泥土腳」源自聖經故事（Daniel 2:31-33），話說巴比倫王Nebuchadnezzar（尼布甲尼撒）夢到一巨人雕像，有金子做的頭、銀做的胸與臂、銅做的腹與大腿、鐵做的小腿、以及鐵與泥土混合的腳與趾。結果一塊石頭擊中巨人雙腳，強大的金屬巨人因而整個粉碎。於是先知解夢表示，泥土腳便是巨人唯一致命的弱點，由此便衍生出了這個慣用語。但注意：「泥土腳」只用來表示人的弱點，尤其用於有身份、地位的人；「阿基里斯的足跟」則可表示人事物的致命弱點或罩門。如：

Being overstaffed is the company's Achilles' heel.
→ 冗員過多是這個公司的致命傷。

The popular idol has feet of clay. He drinks a lot.
→ 這名當紅偶像有個要命的弱點，酒喝太兇。

knee & heel

1

bring … to one's knees

使…跪下，打敗…，削弱…的力量

to defeat or destroy someone or something

要跪下勢必得彎曲膝部（**bend the knee**），但人云膝下有黃金，不能隨便跪，若硬是被迫彎下膝蓋，那就表示被打敗了，不得不屈服。人生難免有吃敗仗之時，也許是比賽被對手打敗、打仗被敵人打敗、甚或是自己被孤獨打敗，但這回屈膝輸了，下回設法**regain feet**（重新站起）就是。

- You cannot expect a prince to bend the knee to an ordinary man.

  你不會指望王子向平民屈膝跪下。

- The visiting team brought the home team to their knees.

  客隊打敗了地主隊。

- The fuel shortage could bring our economy to its knees.

  燃料短缺會為經濟帶來不利影響。

- Losing his beloved wife brought him to his knees.

  失去摯愛的妻子使他大受打擊。

Write your own sentence:

- __________ usually brings __________ to their knees.

2

at someone's heels

緊跟在後

closely behind; in close pursuit; soon after something

兩人行走，腳跟緊貼腳跟，肯定一前一後貼得很近。這個慣用語可依原意表示身後緊緊跟隨著某人（或某物），又或延伸表示後面緊跟著競爭對手隨時準備超過你或取代你的位置。若表示某件事緊跟在另一件事之後，較常用 **on the heels of…**。

- He walked through the square with a group of followers at his heels.
  他走過廣場，後面緊跟著一群擁護者。
- Bad luk followed at her heels all her life.
  她這輩子倒楣事不斷。
- He always felt many promising young competitors were at his heels.
  他老覺得後面有許多年輕有為的對手隨時會趕上他。
- There was a flood on the heels of the windstorm.
  暴風才過緊跟著又淹水。

Write your own sentence:

- ______________________________
  followed at my heels.

3

cool one's heels

讓腳跟冷涼，苦苦等候

to wait or to be kept waiting

　走路腳跟會熱，停下不走腳跟就會冷。這個慣用語意指苦等、久等、坐冷板凳。等得不耐煩許多人會踢腳跟，因此 **kick one's heels** 意指等得十分不耐煩。但若 **kick up one's heels**（把腳跟高高踢起），顯然心情很好，這表示要去做讓自己快樂開心的事。

- He was left to cool his heels in the lobby while waiting for the job interview.
  他被留在大廳，苦苦等候面試。
- Let him cool his heels in the outer office for 3 hours.
  就讓他在外間辦公室等上個三小時吧！
- He kicked his heels for hours outside the Embassy last night.
  他昨晚在大使館外不耐煩地等了好幾個小時。
- He plans to travel and kick up his heels after the entrance exam.
  他計畫入學考試結束後，要出門旅行輕鬆玩一玩。

 Write your own sentence:

- I am cooling my heels until ____________________.

4

dig in one's heels

把腳跟戳進土裡，堅持到底、絕不妥協

to adopt a firm position and stubbornly refuse to change

往前走，腳跟會離開地面，腳跟不離開地面，甚至戳入土中，則表示打定主意站在原地，堅決不願改變原有位置或立場。又若腳跟雖移動，卻拉長了腳步慢慢**drag**，這顯然在刻意延遲行動、施展拖字訣。**drag one's feet**同義，也意指做事故意拖延、採取緩兵計。

- The band dug their heels in over the idea of making commercial music.
  對於製作商業音樂這個想法，這個樂團表明立場絕不接受。
- The employees wanted higher wages, but the CEO dug in his heels over their idea.
  員工們希望提高工資，但CEO絲毫不願妥協。
- He dragged his heels when told to turn off the computer and go to bath.
  叫他關掉電腦去洗澡，他拖拖拉拉。
- The authorities are dragging their feet in making a decision to reduce budget.
  當局遲遲未做下減少預算的決議。

Write your own sentence:

- I am digging in my heels and I am not ___________.

5

set one back on one's heels

使某人往後倒，使某人大吃一驚、慌了手腳

to surprise, disconcert, or shock someone

遇到出乎意料的狀況，人的肢體反應大多是後退、站不穩、甚至真的昏暈往後倒下，這個慣用語即意指這種驚訝萬分的情狀。同義詞還有**knock one off one's feet**（使某人跌倒）、**make one jump out of one's skin**（使某人從皮裡跳出來，即靈魂出竅）。使用時注意主詞。

- The bill for the repairs set me back on my heels.
  這張修理費帳單嚇得我差點昏倒。
- His decision to withdraw from the election set the press back on its heels.
  他決定退選，令新聞界大吃一驚。
- He was knocked off his feet when he learned about her death.
  一得知她的死訊，他幾乎無法站穩。
- The movie was so scary that I nearly jumped out of my skin.
  這電影實在恐怖，嚇得我魂都沒了。

Write your own sentence:

- I was set back on my heels when ______________.

6

show a clean pair of heels

露出一雙乾淨的腳跟，溜之大吉，逃之夭夭

to run faster than those who are chasing

如果有人跑在前面，快速交替的一雙腳跟想必最是醒目。這個慣用語意指快跑、且跑得比追的人還快，將之遠遠甩在後面，只能眼睜睜看著前方一雙光亮的腳跟；**show one's heels**意思一樣。**take to one's heels**不強調誰快誰慢，僅意指逃跑。**turn on one's heels**也是跑開，強調突然且快速地掉頭就走，轉身就跑。

- Bob showed his heels to us as he raced for the finishing line.
  Bob將我們遠遠甩在後面，朝終點線飛奔而去。
- I showed him a clean pair of heels before he had a chance to ask me out.
  趁他還沒機會開口約我，我先溜為妙。
- The smugglers took to their heels as soon as they saw the police coming.
  走私販們一見警察來了，拔腿就跑。
- When I inquired about his partner, he turned on his heels and ran away.
  當我探問起他的合夥人，他突然一個轉身說跑就跑。

Write your own sentence:

- As soon as ______________________, ______________ showed a clean pair of heels.

7

out of joint
脫臼，失序

to be dislocated; to be out of order

joint意指接合點、身體的關節。**out of joint**表示關節沒接合好，即脫臼，也可延伸表示事物失序、混亂。但若有人**nose out of joint**（鼻子脫臼），那畫面想必好笑。若因被人取代或感覺受到不平待遇而受挫、惱怒，這時的臉色看起來就會像鼻子脫臼。

- I had a bad fall, which put my shoulder out of joint.

  我重重跌了一跤，肩膀脫臼了。

- The delays put the whole schedule out of joint.

  一再的延遲打亂了整個行程。

- The time is out of joint. (Hamlet[1:5])

  時代動盪啊！（摘自「哈姆雷特」第一幕第五景）

- We're going camping, but he has put Ann's nose out of joint by counting her out.

  我們打算去露營，可是他沒把Ann算在內，把Ann氣得臉都歪了。

Write your own sentence:

- Trying to ______________, I put my ______________ out of joint.

MEMO

leg

站得住腳的腿

介於**knee**與**ankle**之間的**LEG**意指小腿。若以柱子為比喻，**foot**（足部）就像基座、柱腳，而**LEG**則是柱身。站立雖是以**foot**觸地，卻也需要**LEG**的肌肉收縮才能蹬地走路。也因此，表示「站立」、「支持」的用語，經常都與**LEG**以及**foot**有關。如：

He is standing on one leg. → 他單腳站著。

I have been on my feet all day.
→ 我站了一整天。

除了站，人體的移動、運動都會用到**LEG**，像是游泳、騎馬，尤其需要小腿傳送力量。因此**leg up**除了意指小腿抬高這個動作，也意指**boost**，幫忙拉一把。如：

I gave him a leg up, and soon he was on his horse.
→ 我幫了他一把，他很快便坐在馬身上。

LEG除了代表人的腿，也意指動物可供食用的腿部，如：**chicken leg**（雞腿）、**boneless leg of lamb**（去骨羔羊腿）。

LEG也意指腿狀的物品，像是桌腳、椅腳等支撐物。如：

One leg of the table is missing. → 這桌子缺了一隻腳。

中文以「行腳」表示遊走四方，而英文的**LEG**正好也意指旅程、競賽中的其中一程。如：

I boarded the plane for the last leg of the trip.
→ 我登上飛機，踏上最後一段旅程。

又，如果有人有條**hollow leg**（中空的腿），這代表什麼呢？這表示此人不僅有個胃在裝食物，甚至有支空心的腿，吃喝多少都填不滿，尤其是酒，彷彿喝下去都從**LEG**流掉了似的。如：

He has a hollow leg. He never gets drunk.
→ 他酒量驚人，千杯不醉。

此外，英式有種幽默的說法也與**LEG**有關，他們會這麼形容話很多的人：**They can talk the hind leg off a donkey.** 為什麼話不停會與驢子腿扯上關係呢？因為驢子向來很少彎下後腿、讓身體坐下，如果有什麼人連珠炮一樣地說個不停，說到能讓驢子忍不住屈下後腿一屁股坐下來，足可見此人「話功」了得，**thumbs up**，厲害！

MEMO

1

a leg up

腿抬高，幫忙拉一把（使更順利、成功）

to help or support someone to get higher or to advance

上馬時，如果有人願意伸出膝蓋或以雙手交握，讓上馬的人踩著翻上馬身，上馬的人不但不必擔心跌倒，而且還更平順容易。由此，這個慣用語便延伸表示幫忙拉拔、使某人做事更有進展。此外**have a leg up**也意指具有別人所沒有的優勢。

- My uncle is an actor. It gave me a leg up when I began my career in show business.

  我叔叔是演員，這對於我的演藝事業有如順水推舟。

- Ann gave the chef a leg up when she taught him to cook her signature dish.

  Ann教這名主廚做她的招牌菜，幫忙拉抬他的地位。

- Celebrities seem to have a leg up on life; in fact, they stub their toes on life's vicissitudes too.

  名流的生活似乎優於常人，但事實上，他們一樣逃不過人生浮沈中的挫敗。

Write your own sentence:

- ________________ but it didn't give me a leg up when I ____.

2

break a leg

摔斷一條腿，祝（即將上台演出、報告等的人）好運

good luck; an imperative for a performer about to go onstage

過去的人認為對即將上台的人說 **good luck** 反會為對方招厄運，因此反向思維，祝對方跌斷腿，好為對方招好運。**shake a leg**（抖動一條腿）是要對方 **hurry up**，動作快點。**show a leg** 是叫人起床，以前水手可帶女眷上船，晨起時，巡邏會喊 **show a leg** 以查看是否有水手賴床，若露出的是女腿，便允許 **sleep in**，繼續賴床。

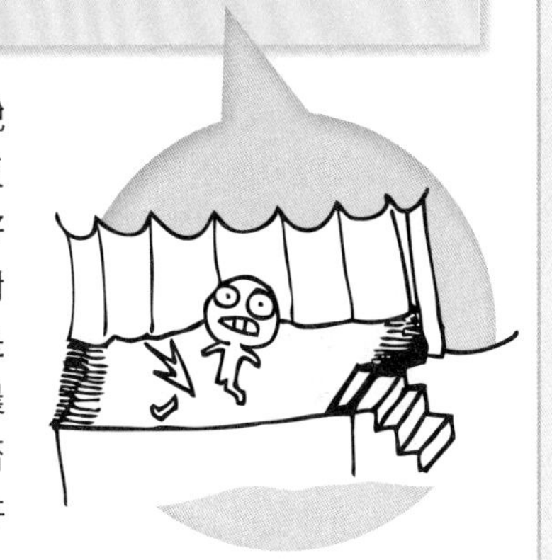

- Play well, BOB! Break a leg!
  好好演啊，Bob, 祝你好運！
- Shake a leg or we'll miss the train.
  快點，再拖就坐不上火車了。
- Show a leg! It's half past ten.
  起床啦，都十點半了。

Write your own sentence:

- "Well, break a leg!" I shouted to ____________ who ______________________________.

3

not have a leg to stand on

沒有支托讓人站，站不住腳，無法令人相信

to have no support

此處**leg**意指支柱。這個慣用語意指某人說的話或做的事缺少實質的證據或合理的解釋、條件，以致得不到支持。**not hold water**（盛不住水）意思類似，表示理由、論點等不合情理、經不起檢視，好像裝水的容器有漏洞一樣。請注意，兩慣用語意思一樣，但前者主詞是人、後者是事。

- If you don't have an airtight alibi, you don't have a leg to stand on.
  你若拿不出無懈可擊的不在場證明，很難讓人相信你。
- He sued the host, but he found himself without a leg to stand on.
  他對這名主持人提告，但他發現自己沒什麼勝算。
- There are holes in your argument. It simply doesn't hold water.
  你的論點有漏洞，根本說不過去。
- His account of the accident doesn't hold water.
  他對這起意外的說法漏洞百出，不合情理。

Write your own sentence:

- Once ___________, he won't have a leg to stand on.

4

on one's last legs

以最後的腿站著，快不行了

to be very tired; to be going to die soon; to be close to wearing out

腿撐不下去、就站不起來，繼而便會倒下去。這個慣用語可表示體力耗盡、很累，或生命已到盡頭、奄奄一息，又或物品用到瀕臨報廢。**leg** 既意指腿、也意指旅程、競賽中的一段，如：**the final leg of the race**（比賽最後一程），由此來看這個慣用語，意義更是明顯。

- He looks like he is on his last legs. I don't think he can make it to the top of the hill.

  他好像累到沒力了，我覺得他到不了山頂。

- Our old family dog has been ill quite a while. He is on his last legs.

  我們家這隻老狗病了好一陣子，大概活不久了。

- My old car is on its last legs. It's high time I got a new one.

  我的舊車已用得差不多，該換台新的了。

Write your own sentence:

- I have been ________________ all day and I am on my last legs.

5

pull one's leg

拉某人的腿，開某人玩笑

to tease someone or play a joke on someone

過去人們會用棍子絆住別人的腿，使人跌跤以捉弄別人。如今這個慣用語僅意指說些話唬弄別人，開開玩笑，並沒真的讓人摔跤。許多人看到這個慣用語總想到「扯後腿」，扯後腿意指阻擋某些事的發生，可用 **hold back**（阻擋）或 **be a hindrance**（成為拖累、阻礙）來表達。

- Are you serious about moving out or are you pulling my leg?
  你說要搬出去是說真的、還是在開我玩笑？
- She was pulling my leg when she told me she was pregnant.
  她跟我說她懷孕，原來是在耍我。
- Could a strongman hold back the extremists from further attack?
  政治強人是否阻擋得了極端份子進一步攻擊？
- She is more of a hindrance than a help.
  她非但幫不了我，反讓我處處難做。

Write your own sentence:

- ______ was pulling my leg by telling me __________.

6

with one's tail between one's legs

尾巴夾在兩腿間，灰頭土臉，垂頭喪氣

to be dejected or ashamed after a defeat

這個慣用語主要形容一個人沮喪、慚愧的樣子，一如狗兒們被打、被罵、或得不到想要的東西，便夾著尾巴走掉。如果不夾尾巴，而是 **stretch one's legs**（伸展雙腿），則表示久坐之後站起來、走一走、動一動。

- They were forced to retreat with their tails between their legs.

  他們被迫狼狽撤離。

- He lost the competition and came back with his tail between his legs.

  他比賽輸了，垂頭喪氣地回來。

- He was forced to leave the company with his tail between his legs after lying about expense accounts.

  他報假帳，最後灰頭土臉地被迫走路。

- Let's go stretch our legs during the intermission.

  趁中場休息，我們起身走動一下吧！

Write your own sentence:

- After ______________________, ____________ walked off with their tails between their legs.

foot 踏實地、跑跳走的腳

FOOT是leg的末端，一如leg的基座，FOOT的複數是feet。站立時通常兩腳踏地，走路、跑步則一腳在空一腳在地、兩腳前後交替，因此**on foot**意指走路，**on one's feet**則意指站立、又或進一步表示生活上的「站起來」。如：

There is no road to his manor. We have to get there on foot.
→ 到他的莊園沒道路，我們得走過去。

Get on your feet. They are playing the national anthem.
→ 站好，在奏國歌。

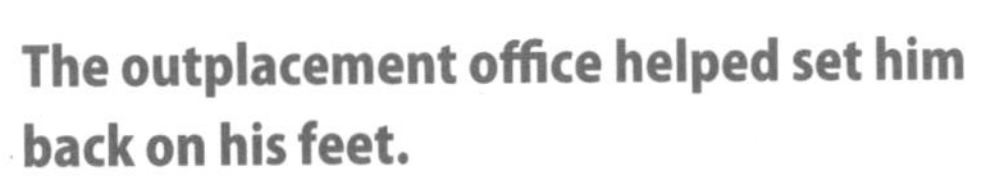

The outplacement office helped set him back on his feet.
→ 轉職就業服務處幫他重新站起來。

雖說同樣是FOOT，但左腳和右腳並不一樣，若有人兩隻腳都是左腳，既無法左右平衡，加上西方傳統向來視「左」（sinister）為邪惡的、不祥的，這便意謂此人十分笨拙。如：

I can never get the hang of this dance; I have two left feet.
→ 我老抓不到跳這支舞的竅門，我手腳很遲鈍。

兩隻左腳是笨手笨腳不靈活，癢癢腳（itchy feet）則表示蠢蠢欲動，想離開原有地方，或換工作、或旅行、或移民。如：

I am getting itchy feet. It's time to move on.
→ 我的腳躁動不安，該出發往前走了。

說到腳癢，就會讓人想到香港腳：**athlete's foot**（運動員腳）。其實就算沒得香港腳，由於**FOOT**使用度高，若不包在鞋襪裡，要不就是與地面為伍，幾乎可說是全身上下最容易髒臭的地方，難怪老外一吃到難吃的東西，就會說味道跟腳一樣（**The food tastes like feet.**）。

由於**FOOT**位於身體下盤，坐下時往往隱而不顯。這時若有人在桌下**play footsie with someone**（用腳去碰某人的腳），即表示對某人有好感、秘密地示好、調情。

除此之外，**play footsie**也表示私下、秘密的交易。如：

The councilor has been playing footsie with a powerful syndicate.
→ 這名議員與一勢力龐力的財團檯面下一直都有往來。

又，常有人走動的地方，草通常長不起來，因此閒不下來、總會找事情做的人、又或是行動果決、不會把時間浪費在磨蹭猶豫的人，通常是不會讓腳底長出草來的。如：

He is always doing something. He never lets the grass grow under his feet. → 他總有事情做，沒一刻閒著。

另外，**my foot**除了可照字面表示「我的腳」，也可用來表達不相信、不以為然，一如中文說「才怪」，但現在**my foot**愈來愈少人用，**my ass**成了較普遍的說法，唯**my ass**著實不太雅。如：

You're his brother, my ass! You look nothing alike.
→ 你是他哥，屁啦！你們看起來一點也不像。

FOOT除了指人的腳，也意指尾端或底部，如：

at the foot of his bed → 在他床尾

at the foot of the mountain → 在山腳下。

FOOT的長度大約是30公分，因此**FOOT**也意指一呎（30.48公分）。如果有人對於某人事物，**not touch with a ten-foot pole**（就算拿著十呎長的竿子也絕不碰），那就表示此人絕對不想沾染這人事物、不想有任何一點關係。又若有人身在六呎之下，則表示此人已埋在黃土之下。如：

He wouldn't touch orange foods with a ten-foot pole.
→ 橘黃色的食物他絕對不碰。

You can't read my diary—not until I'm six feet under.
→ 不可以看我日記，我死了以後才可以看。

FOOT當動詞，常見的意思是支付帳單或費用，**foot the bill**（踩住帳單）的人即付錢的人，如：

Let me foot the bill for lunch today.
→ 今天午餐我來付。

footing意指立足之處，要站穩就要**get a footing**（取得立足點）；此外，**footing**也意指地位、基礎，如：

His business is on a firm footing. → 他的事業基礎穩固。

---

footstep是腳步，**follow in one's footsteps**表示照著某人留下的腳步走、接班、接下某人手中的棒子。如：

He hopes his son will follow in his footsteps and become an astronaut. → 他希望兒子繼承他的衣缽，當個太空人。

如同手有指頭，**FOOT**也有**toe**（腳趾）。腳趾雖小小一截，踩到卻特別痛，因此要小心別踩到別人的腳趾；此外，踩腳趾（**step on toes**）也意謂著由於影響、干預到某人的權限、地盤，以致惹得某人不高興，彷彿朝某人腳趾狠踩了一腳，使某人恨得牙癢癢。如：

You can't make changes without stepping on a lot of toes.
→ 要改變、難免得罪一票人。

---

toe當動詞用表示用腳尖踩，**toe the line**表示嚴守規定，一如起跑時，腳尖絕不超過起跑線一分一毫。如：

He might not like the rules but he'll toe the line just to avoid trouble.
→ 他或許不喜歡這些規定，但為免麻煩，他會小心遵守不讓自己越線。

MEMO

foot

1

at someone's feet

在某人腳邊，(受某人吸引而甘願)受某人影響、支配

to be fascinated by someone and under someone's influence

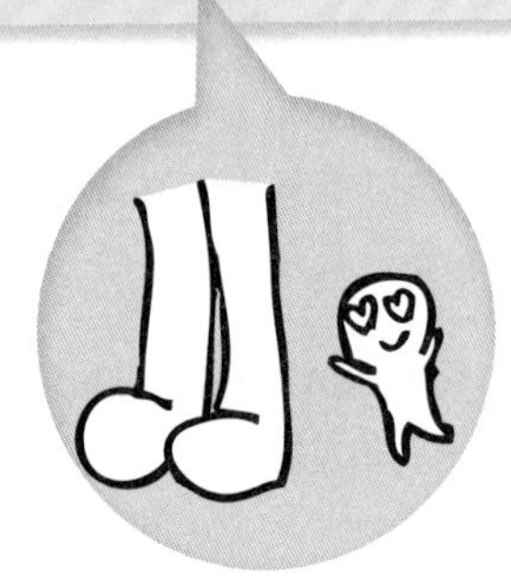

願意窩在某人腳邊，表示深為某人著迷，不惜放低身段。此慣用語若搭配**sit**：坐在某人腳邊，則表示虔敬、崇拜地追隨某人。又若某人把自己丟往別人的腳邊(**throw oneself at someone's feet**)，則表示此人卑微地乞求腳的主人能施捨愛情、祝福、慈悲、原諒等。

- Dozens of boys are at her feet.
  一堆男生拜倒在她石榴裙下。
- When Mary entered school, many boys threw themselves at her feet.
  Mary一入學，好多男孩就拜倒在她石榴裙下。
- He sat at the mentor's feet for years before he was disillusioned and left.
  他拜在這名導師門下多年，後來醒悟離去。
- He threw himself at the feet of the judge and begged for mercy.
  他千拜託萬拜託，乞求法官開恩。

Write your own sentence:

- I have ___________ at my feet but _______________.

2

be swept off one's feet

被吹得腳離地，飄飄然、魂不守舍

to be overwhelmed emotionally

這個慣用語可意指女性愛得忘了自己，也意指某人為某事著迷、興奮，以致像要飛上天一樣。**sweep** 也可用 **knock** 或 **carry**。但若是 **be run／rushed off one's feet**（被催趕得腳無法踩在地上），則表示馬不停蹄地忙著做事，如：**I've been rushed off my feet all afternoon**（整個下午我忙得腳底朝天。）

- She was swept off her feet when the handsome dude started flirting with her.
  這個帥哥一對她調情，她就像被灌了迷湯一樣。

- With his fine speech and gallant behavior, he swept her off her feet.
  他談吐優雅、風度翩翩，令她傾心不已。

- He was swept off his feet when he won first prize.
  拿下頭獎讓他整個人都快飄起來了。

Write your own sentence:

- I am swept off my feet whenever
  ________________________.

3

catch someone flat-footed

抓到腳還踏在地上的某人，令某人措手不及

to be taken by surprise because of being unprepared

起跑前，運動員都以腳尖觸地準備，若腳還平放在地上沒做好準備，此時起跑槍響，肯定反應不及。**flat-footed**也可用**on the wrong foot**，如同舞者沒準備好就開始，結果踏錯了腳。又，若有人始終不曾左右腳不分，亂踩一通，**not put a foot wrong**，則表示從不曾出錯、失誤。

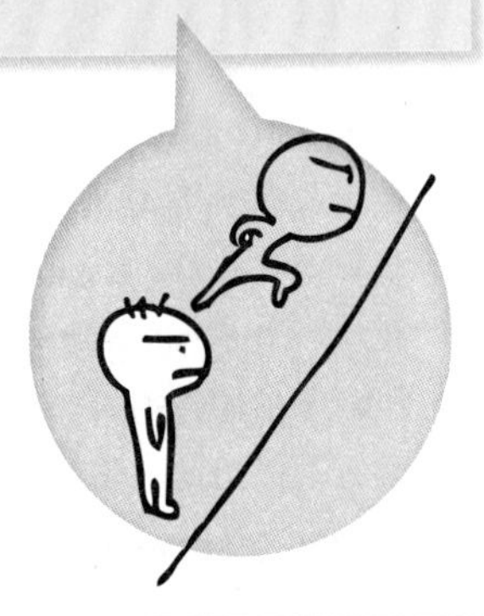

- The reporter's question caught the President flat-footed.
  記者的提問讓總統一時間無法反應。
- The new product caught our competitors on the wrong foot.
  這個新產品使我們的競爭對手措手不及。
- If you go to the party too early, you will catch the hostess on the wrong foot.
  你太早去宴會現場的話，會讓女主人措手不及。
- This is a tangled tale but the author never puts a foot wrong.
  這故事錯綜複雜，但作者完全沒出錯。

 Write your own sentence:

- I was caught flat-footed when ______________.

4

find one's feet

找到雙腳站好，站穩腳步，適應新環境或新事務

to become used to a new situation or experience

陌生環境總會令人緊張得站不住腳，要適應當然得先站穩腳步。一旦站好、適應了，不妨試著**get a foot in the door**（製造機會），如同推銷員，伸一隻腳進門裡，總好過被擋在門外毫無機會開口。機會有了，千萬別臨陣打退堂鼓：**get cold feet**（雙腳發冷），讓計畫好要做的事，卻因臨場膽怯突然不做了。

- I'm still finding my feet, but I believe I'll do a good job.

  我還在調適中，不過我相信我可以做得很好。

- New employees need a little time to find their feet.

  新進員工需要一點時間來適應。

- This part-time work has allowed Carl to get his foot in the door.

  這份兼差讓Carl邁出第一步，有了個好的開始。

- He was going to marry Ann, but he got cold feet.

  他本來要和Ann結婚，卻突然恐慌起來說不結了。

Write your own sentence:

- I was __________ when ______________ but I am finding my feet now.

5

get off on the wrong foot

起腳就錯了，一開始就給人壞印象，才開始就搞砸

to make a bad start with someone or something

跳舞第一步就踏錯，即便立刻調整回來，那錯誤的第一步恐已令人印象深刻。此慣用語用於人際，表示留下不好的第一印象；用於事則表示一開始處理方式就錯了。**wrong** 換成 **right** 則是有好的開始。開始對了，別忘了 **put one's best foot forward**（伸出最好的腳），全力以赴，盡力做到最好。

- My secretary got off on the wrong foot by being rude to visitors.

  我秘書一開始就把事情搞砸了，因為他對訪客很沒禮貌。

- We hope we got off on the right foot with our son's in-laws.

  希望我們有給兒子的親家留下好的初次印象。

- Make sure you put your best foot forward for today's audition.

  今天的試鏡千萬要全力表現出自己最好的一面。

Write your own sentence:

- I got off on the wrong foot with ______________ by ____.

6

have one foot in the grave

一腳放在墳墓裡，一腳已踏入棺材，情況不妙

to be close to death or in terrible condition

不論是棺材（**coffin**）或是墳墓（**grave**），進了一腳，下一腳難保不久就會跟著下去。此慣用語意思再明顯不過，它可表示人的身體狀況不好，有如風中殘燭、行將就木、離死不遠；也可表示人事物處於危險的境況，有如 **skate on thin ice**（在薄冰上溜冰），隨時都有可能死亡、結束。

- He has terminal lung cancer and feels as if he had one foot in the grave.

  他罹患末期肺癌，覺得自己似乎離大去之日不遠了。

- The corporation had one foot in the grave when the $10 billion investment went down the drain.

  這家公司一百億投資泡湯，狀況很糟。

- You're skating on thin ice by borrowing money from a loan shark.

  向放高利貸的人借錢，你這麼做真是太冒險了。

Write your own sentence:

- I don't think ____________ has one foot in the grave even if ______________.

7

have both feet on the ground

雙腳踏地，腳踏實地，不因名利而得意忘形

to be practical or down-to-earth; to remain stable after being successful

人一做夢或得意，最容易雙腳離地飛起來。此慣用語可形容某人處事實際，想法或行動都重視實效，也可形容某人未因突然的功成名就而站不穩，離開了原本的自己。**have** 可用 **keep**，**both** 可省略，因為 **feet** 是複數，寫了 **feet** 自然是雙腳。反之，若是沒站穩腳步而被名利沖昏了頭，可回頭參考HEAD 05。

- He has both feet on the ground. He will surely find a sensible solution.

  他做事很實在，他一定會找到有效的解決方案。

- My head is in the clouds, but I walk with my feet on the ground.

  我是愛做白日夢，但我很務實的過生活。

- He has kept his feet on the ground. Fame hasn't changed him.

  他始終保持平常心，名氣沒讓他變樣。

Write your own sentence:

- ______________________________, but make sure you have your feet on the ground.

8

jump in with both feet

以雙腳跳入，迅速全部投入

to enter into an activity or venture quickly and completely

跳水（**dive**）一般都是頭與手先下，以便入水後控制方向。除非有十足把握，較少人會以腳下水。由此這個慣用語意指做事情很快就整個投入，全心全意、義無反顧。也可寫成 **jump in feet first**。相較於此，**get feet wet** 則是先讓腳沾沾水，先以簡單的事初步嘗試，可回頭參考TONGUE 07。

- When making a decision, he either jumps in with both feet or drags his feet.

  做決定時，他要嘛火速定案、要不就拖了又拖。

- Take time to weigh the pros and cons before jumping in feet first.

  花點時間權衡利弊得失，再投入全部的心力。

- I can't wait to get behind the steering wheel and get my feet wet.

  我迫不及待想坐到方向盤後面牛刀小試一下。

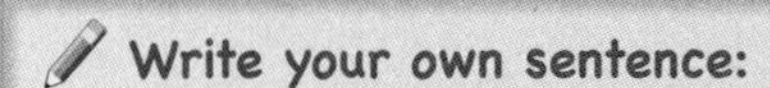

Write your own sentence:

- ____

  before we jump in with both feet.

9

keep someone's feet to the fire

把某人的雙腳放在火邊，對某人施壓（直到目的達成）

to exert pressure on someone

這個慣用語源自中古世紀逼犯人招供的酷刑，如今當然沒真的用火燒腳，而是運用法律、人情、社會、政治等各種勢力對某人或機構團體施壓，直到達成所要的結果為止。**keep** 也可用 **hold** 或 **put**。類似的慣用語有 **hold a gun to someone's head**（把槍對著某人的頭），意指用威脅、恐嚇等方式達到目的。

- She was keeping the lawyer's feet to the fire until he agreed to button his lip.

  她持續向這名律師施壓，直到他同意封口為止。

- You should hold the principal's feet to the fire about incompetent teachers.

  關於不適任教師的問題，你們應持續向校長施壓。

- Who held a gun to your head and made you consent?

  是誰威脅你，逼你點頭答應？

Write your own sentence:

- ________ should keep ________'s feet to the fire about ______________________________.

10

keep a foot in both camps

一腳進兩個軍營，腳踏兩條船，兩邊的人都熟

to be connected to two groups with opposing interests or opinions

兩軍對峙通常壁壘分明，若某人同時進出兩軍營地，也許手腕高明，也或許三心二意。此慣用語意指同時與兩個壁壘分明的人或機構團體打交道，意思可褒可貶，依上下文判斷。**keep** 可用 **have**。此外，騎牆派（**fence-sitter**）則不選邊站，他們坐在中間的籬笆觀望形勢，可說是保持中立、也可說是牆頭草。

- You can't keep a foot in both camps. Now is the time for a decision.

  你不能一腳踏兩船，現在該做決定了。

- He had a foot in both camps, making donations to both parties.

  他兩邊都下注，兩陣營都有拿到他的捐款。

- I had better sit on the fence and not offend either of them.

  我最好保持中立，兩邊都別得罪。

Write your own sentence:

- ________ had a foot in both camps because ____.

11

land on one's feet

雙腳落地站好，逢凶化吉，化險為夷

to be lucky and restored to a sound condition after a difficult experience

從高處跳下，若能雙腳著陸且完好無缺，除了技術好，運氣也很重要。這個源自貓的動作的慣用語，意指雖遭逢困境，卻能有驚無險，幸運地過關斬將、倖免於難。**land** 也可用 **fall**。

至於 **stand on one's own feet**（用自己的腳站好），則表示為人處事能獨立自主，完全不需仰賴別人。

- He got into so much trouble that he was never able to land on his feet again.

  他惹的麻煩實在太多，沒法再安全過關了。

- Don't worry about his going bankrupt! He always seems to fall on his feet.

  別為他破產的事擔心，他這人一向大難不死。

- Learn to stand on your own feet and not always listen to your peers.

  學著獨立靠自己，別什麼都聽朋友的意見。

Write your own sentence:

- It may take a few months to ______________________ ________, but I'm sure I will land on my feet.

12

on one's feet

站立，（身或心）康復，經濟自立

to be standing; to be well after illness; to be stable in a financial or emotional sense

走路時一腳離地一腳踩地，因此是**on foot**；站立時兩腳踩地，所以是**on one's feet**。此慣用語除了意指站立，也可延伸表示病後身體回復健康、或經歷困境後在經濟或心理上重新站起來，可加**back**加強口氣。至於**dead on one's feet**（站著死去），則表示很累、累到沒法再動了。

- Take more rest and you'll soon get back on your feet.
  多休息，你很快就會好起來的。
- After the death of his wife, it took several years for him to get back on his feet.
  妻子過世後，他過了好些年才振作起來。
- I cannot afford a house until I get a job and get back on my feet.
  我得找到工作、經濟沒問題之後才能買房子。
- I stayed up late studying all night. Now I am dead on my feet.
  整晚熬夜念書，我現在累到快癱了。

Write your own sentence:

- I will __________ as soon as I get back on my feet.

put one's foot down

放一隻腳落地，表明立場、堅持到底

to take a firm stand and assert something

猶豫、心軟時站姿會比較鬆垮，落腳踩地則意謂著「定案、就是這樣」。此慣用語意指下定決心堅持某事、某決定。英式用法另有突然踩下油門加快車速的意思。又，若把**foot**放進嘴巴，則表示驚覺嘴巴說了不該說的話，又或傷了人、又或使自己出糗、狼狽。可參見MOUTH09。

- His mom put her foot down and grounded him until his grades improved.
  他母親鐵了心，不准他出去玩，除非功課有進步。
- He didn't want to take piano lessons, but his mom put her foot down.
  他不想學鋼琴，但他媽堅持要他學。
- He put his foot down and tried to overtake the truck in front.
  他加快車速，想超過前面的卡車。
- I put my foot in my mouth by praising his hair. It was a wig and he was bald.
  讚美他的頭髮反弄得我好糗，那其實是假髮、他頭是禿的。

Write your own sentence:

- I'll have to put my foot down and ______________.

14

put one's feet up

將雙腳平放，坐下或躺下休息，放鬆

to rest, sit down, lean back, or lie down; to relax

這個慣用語意指休息，尤其強調讓腳休息。站立或走路，腳或膝承受著體重兩倍的壓力，因此**take a load off one's feet**（移除腳上的重擔）也意指休息，尤其指坐下，所謂的重擔正是指身體，**one's feet**可省略。休息過後站起來，就得再用到腳，**get to one's feet**意指站起來，即**stand up**。

- Put your feet up for a few minutes after a long day's cycling.
  騎了一整天腳踏車，坐下來休息幾分鐘吧！
- I enjoy putting my feet up and going on FB after working all day.
  上了一天班之後，坐躺著休息、上FB，真享受。
- I'm going to make myself some coffee and take a load off for half an hour.
  我要泡個咖啡坐下來休息半小時。
- We all got to our feet when the Pope came in.
  當教宗進來，我們大家全站了起來。

Write your own sentence:

- It is nice to put our feet up after ________________.

foot

15

shake the dust off one's feet

抖落腳上的塵土，急著離開再也不想回來

to depart or leave with a measure of disgust or displeasure

腳步匆忙總使得腳邊塵土起又落，因此這個源自聖經（Luke 9:5）的慣用語意指憤然離開某個不喜歡的地方。又若是 **shake／get the lead out of one's feet**（甩掉腳上的鉛）則要人動作快點，別像是腳綁了鉛似的慢吞吞。**get／have a lead foot** 表示開車開很快，腳上像綁了鉛，踩油門老踩到底。

- He was glad to shake the dust off his feet when he left this snobbish place.
  他真高興能趕快離開這個勢利的鬼地方，他絕對不會再來。
- I couldn't wait to shake the dust off my feet; I never wanted to see either of them again.
  我迫不及待想趕快離開，我再不想看到他們倆其中一人。
- Get the lead out of your feet, or we'll be late.
  走快點，要遲到了。
- I won't carpool with him. He's really got a lead foot.
  我不要和他共乘一車，他車開得好快。

Write your own sentence:

- I can't wait to shake the dust off my feet when I ____________________.

16

set foot in／on

把腳放進／上，進入，踏上，來到，造訪

to enter; to visit

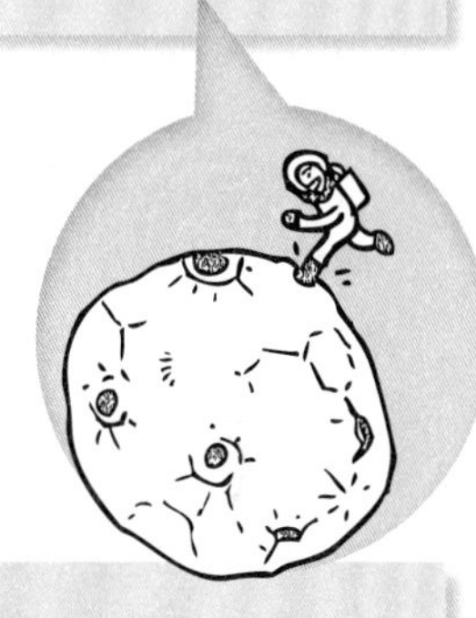

　腳到表示人到，由此，這個慣用語意指到達某個地方，用**in**或用**on**端看後面所到之處，如國家、城市、地區、建築物等強調進入內部者用**in**，如：**in Britain**（在英國）；土地、島嶼、星球等強調踩在表面者用**on**，如：**on British soil**（在英國）。

- The judge ordered him never to set foot in her house again.
  法官下令，不許他再踏進她家大門。
- In 1969, Neil Armstrong became the first human to set foot on the moon.
  1969年，Neil Armstrong成了首度踏上月球的人類。
- The overseas are happy to set foot on their homeland.
  華僑們開心地踏上家鄉的土地。
- He has never set foot in the capital ever since he was born.
  打從他出生後，他從沒到過首都。

Write your own sentence:

- I was very excited to set foot in / on ____________ to ____.

the shoe is on the other foot

鞋已穿在另一隻腳上，風水輪流轉，不可同日而語

the circumstances have reversed; the participants have changed places

原本一腳有鞋、另一腳沒鞋，如今情況反轉，沒鞋的有了鞋，弱的變強、劣勢的取得了優勢。**shoe** 換用 **boot** 為英式說法。**turn the tables** 意思一樣，下雙陸棋（**backgammon**）的人對換棋台，使得情勢反轉，逆轉勝。難怪諺語說每隻狗都有得意之時（**Every dog has its day**），人生不會永遠得意、但也不會永遠失意，人人都有時來運轉的機會。

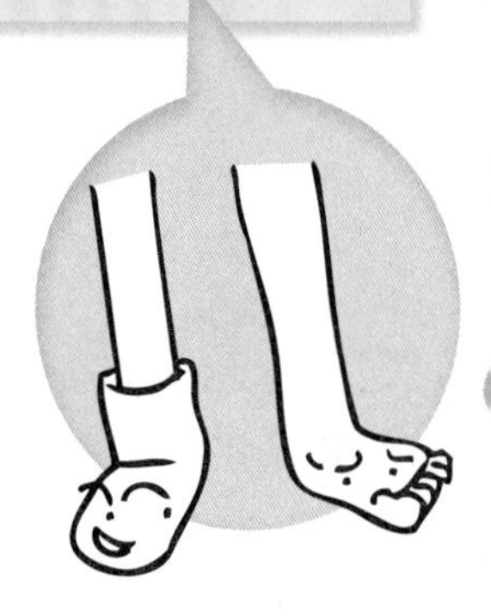

- I was his assistant, but now the shoe is on the other foot. I'm his supervisor.
  我以前是他助理，現在成了他的上司，真是十年河東十年河西。
- Forget your past glory for the shoe is on the other foot now.
  忘了過去的風光吧！今非昔比了。
- He turned the tables on the paparazzi when he started filming them.
  他反過來拍這些狗仔，將形勢逆轉。

Write your own sentence:

- When ______________________________, I learned what it was like to have the shoe on the other foot.

18

shoot oneself in the foot

朝自己的腳開槍，拿石頭砸自己的腳

to act against one's own interests by accident

沒事把槍拿在手上，一不小心開了槍，槍口竟朝著自己的腳。此慣用語意指說的話或做的事在無意間傷害了自己，沒想太多，卻招來罪受。難怪有諺語說：讓睡著的狗繼續睡（**let sleeping dogs lie**），意思是為免引起風波或麻煩，一動不如一靜。畢竟貿然行動的後果，很可能是驚動睡狗，咬傷自己，自惹一身腥。

- He really shot himself in the foot, telling his wife that he dreamed about his ex.
  他跟他太太說他夢到前女友，真是沒事找罪受。
- He must be mad to shoot himself in the foot. He got drunk before his finals.
  他八成是瘋了才會在期末考前喝醉，自討苦吃。
- He always shoots himself in the foot by saying the wrong thing.
  他總是說錯話，給自己找麻煩。
- He decided to let sleeping dogs lie and not report them to the teacher.
  他決定不要打草驚蛇，暫時不跟老師告他們的狀。

Write your own sentence:

- I shot myself in the foot when ______________________.

think on one's feet

站著思考，馬上作出反應，見招拆招

to think or react quickly in the middle of a process, activity, or conversation

支著下巴端坐是著名雕像「沈思者」的姿勢。思考需要安靜、放鬆，根據研究，最適合思考的姿勢是躺姿。因此，站著也能思考便意指反應敏快，或能即問即答，或能在做事當下機靈的應變，宛如武林高手，手出招、腳移動、眼觀四面、耳聽八方、腦做分析、嘴說道理，身手心口一次到位！

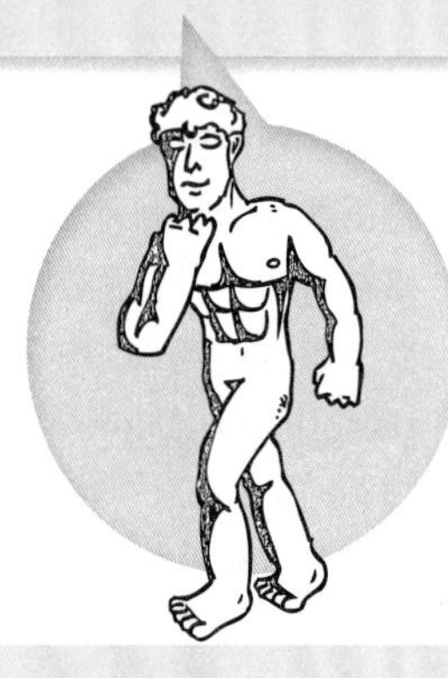

- He really thinks on his feet well. He is able to do live comedy shows.

  他腦子靈活嘴巴快，能即興演出脫口秀。

- He can think on his feet and answer reporters' questions without hesitating.

  他反應很快，記者問什麼他都能做出回答，毫不猶豫。

- He had to think on his feet when the flood waters approached his home.

  大水即將淹進他家，他必須當機立斷。

Write your own sentence:

- An ability to think on your feet is an advantage when ____.

20

vote with one's feet

用腳投票，用行動表達不滿

to express one's dissatisfaction by acting in a certain way

不論是用**ballot**（選票）勾出或寫下選項投進票箱，又或是**have a show of hands**（舉手表決），這兩種投票用的都是手。若是用腳投票，則表示以離開、出走、移民、拒買等行動，直接且具體地表達出對某人事物的不滿意、不支持、不喜歡。

- Many people are voting with their feet and leaving the country.

  許多人民紛紛出走，離開這個國家。

- The film was a big flop. The audience voted with their feet before the end.

  這部電影超難看，還沒演完觀眾都跑光了。

- The meeting was a waste of time so I voted with my feet.

  開這個會根本是浪費時間，所以我直接走人。

- Smoking indoors was allowed here so I voted with my feet and didn't patronize it again.

  這裡允許室內抽煙，我不喜歡，所以不再光顧。

Write your own sentence:

- I am prepared to vote with my feet if ____________.

dip one's toe in the water

把腳趾浸入水中，先試試（再決定是否深入、進一步）

to try something tentatively before deciding to make a serious commitment

只讓腳趾頭碰水，不想把腳弄溼，這表示連要不要下水都還不確定。因此這個慣用語表示不知喜不喜歡、會不會成功，總之先試了再說。想去歐洲玩，不確定是否真的要去，先找些資料瞭解就是先浸一下腳趾。又，**from head to toe**或**from top to toe**表示從頭到腳、全身上下、徹徹底底。

- Take a look at the brochure for Mexico and you may feel like dipping your toe in the water of working there.
  看看這本介紹墨西哥的小冊子，說不定你會想嘗試了解到那裡工作。
- I need an inexpensive camera to dip my toe in the water.
  我需要一台價格便宜的相機先試玩一下。
- He has dipped his toe in the water on asking them about rebidding.
  他已試著要他們重新招標，總之有問過了。
- She likes to be dressed in black from head to toe.
  她喜歡穿得一身黑。

Write your own sentence:

- I try to dip my toe in the water by ____________.

on one's toes

踮著腳尖站，保持警覺

to be alert

拳擊手或賽跑選手常以腳趾著地，保持備戰的姿勢。此慣用語意指全神貫注地警覺，一有動靜立可行動。**keep**某人**on toes**表示讓某人的注意力持續集中於當下的事。**step／tread on one's toes**（踩到某人腳趾）則表示踩到某人界線，以致冒犯、得罪、傷害了某人，使某人很不舒服。

- There was a bomb threat this morning. We need to stay on our toes.
  今早有炸彈恐嚇，我們得警覺點。
- You have to be on your toes all the time before you make your entrance.
  正式登台前，你得時時留神何時該上台。
- The teacher kept the students on their toes by telling a lot of jokes.
  老師拚命說笑話，以免學生的注意力跑掉。
- You will step on his toes if you talk directly to his supervisor.
  若你直接跟他上司說，這麼做可能會讓他很不爽。

Write your own sentence:

- We need to be on our toes all the while when ______________________.

blood 製造血親與血腥的血

& nerve 以及殺人不見血的神經

BLOOD流動、循環於身體周身，宛如一座城市的運輸系統，一旦中斷，該清理廢棄的運不出去、該補給輸送的運不進來，身體遲早會出問題。異常的**BLOOD**，會使人體氣血不足、臉色蒼白；失去**BLOOD**，會使生命隨著流失，沒了血、沒了生命的身體再無血色、再無體溫；也因此，戰鬥到最後一滴血就表示戰鬥到底，如：

They fought to the last drop of their blood. → 他們拚到最後。

BLOOD會一代傳一代，藉由**blood type**（血型）、甚至抽血檢查染色體，都可察知親屬關係。每當人們想表示與…有血緣關係，總會說「身上流著…的血」。英文諺語也有**Blood will tell.**（什麼樣的家庭生出什麼樣的孩子）以及**Blood is thicker than water.**（血濃於水，親人最親）。

因此，**BLOOD**不僅意指血液，也意謂著「血統、家世」。出身富貴既可說是**noble blood**，也可說**blue blood**（藍血）。雖說藍色在英文中常意謂著「憂鬱的」（**blue Monday**）、「下流猥褻的」（**blue movies**），但源自西班牙的**'sangre azul'**（藍血），乃是因為西班牙貴族皮膚白皙，靜脈的藍色血脈清晰可見，因此他們認為自己的血是藍的，藍血也就成了貴族的代稱。如：

His father asks him to marry a woman of blue blood.
→ 他父親要他娶貴族女子。

He is proud of his blue blood. → 他以出身貴族為榮。

精力旺盛、容易衝動的人常被形容為血氣方剛，因此**BLOOD**也意指脾氣、性子。熱血的人（**hot-blooded**）很熱情、但容易衝動；紅血之人（**red-blooded**）精力充沛、「性」緻旺盛。

失控或過多的精力容易造成流血事件，因此**BLOOD**也與「殺戮」有關，如：

His blood will be on your head. → 他的死算在你頭上。

The war shed the blood of thousands.
→ 這場戰爭使好幾千人傷亡。

以前的人還會以**God's blood**來發重誓，內容不離碎屍萬段、不得好死等暴力手段。為免褻瀆上帝或神明，人們把**God**說成諧音字**thunder**，於是**God's blood**輾轉成了**blood and thunder**，意指血腥暴力，尤指小說與電影中打打殺殺頭破血流的情節。

又如1862年，俾斯麥（Otto von Bismarck）以**iron**意謂強大的意志力與武力，以**blood**意指殺戮與犧牲，一席**"blood and iron" speech**（強調鐵血政策的演說），使人們為他冠上「鐵血宰相」的稱號。

---

bloodless revolution（不流血的革命）並不容易，但應是多數人的嚮往。**bloodless**也意指沒血色、很蒼白，**blood-sucker**則意指吸血動物或剝削別人利益的人。

形容詞**bloody**意指「流血的、沾血的、血腥的」，**give someone a bloody nose**（讓某人流鼻血）表示暫時領先某人或打倒某人，但後續如何仍未可知，畢竟對方只流了鼻血而已。

They gave their opponents a bloody nose in the debate.
→ 這場辯論他們暫時領先對手。

至於**bloody-minded**則意指故意刁難、作對的，存心找麻煩的。如：

He was excluded from the club. Somebody wad bloody-minded.
→ 社團不讓他加入，有人故意跟他作對。

流血事件令人怵目驚心，但不見血的殺人也不惶多讓。由神經纖維聚集成束的**NERVE**，負責傳導各種官能訊息，神經一受影響，又或肌肉痙攣、又或頭痛、又或心煩，不需任何人動手，痛苦自從體內竄出；倘若神經受損或病變，甚至會讓人麻木、癱瘓。因此所謂的「心理戰」（**war of nerves**），打擊的目標正是神經、心神，以無形的心理手段影響對手的精神狀態，達到自己的目的。因此**NERVE**採複數形**NERVES**時，表示神經紛亂，即「神經過敏、焦躁」。如：

She doesn't sleep or eat well.
She is really living on her nerves.
→ 她吃不好睡不著，經常處在焦慮中。

倘若能在心理戰中全身而退，想必**NERVE**堅固強韌，**NERVE**強或可意謂膽量大、勇氣足，無懼任何困難，也可意謂厚顏無恥、膽大妄為，一皮天下無難事。是大無畏還是厚臉皮，要依上下文判斷。如：

It must take plenty of nerve to transport explosives.
→ 運送炸藥膽子一定要大。

What a nerve! He walked off with my necklace.
→ 真不要臉！他居然悶不吭聲拿走我的項鍊。

1

bad blood

壞血，嫌隙、敵意、怨恨

enmity or hostility between persons or groups

日夜於各器官之間流動的血液，必須新鮮健康，才能確保器官有效運作。若人或團體機構之間有壞血，宛如器官之間有不良的血液，表示兩方結有恩怨，彼此不和、不信任。至於**new／fresh blood**（新鮮的血），則表示能增強能量的新進人員或新入會員。**sporting blood**則意指不怕冒險犯難、勇於嘗試新事物的天性。

- Bad blood between Ken and Joe might be a factor in delaying the project.
  Ken與Joe之間的樑子，可能是導致此案延遲的一個因素。
- A gorgeous girl caused bad blood between the two brothers.
  這兩兄弟因一貌美女孩彼此仇視。
- The publisher is badly in need of new blood to bring in new ideas.
  這家出版社急需新的人員帶進新的點子。
- His sporting blood tempted him to start an enterprise with little capital.
  他天不怕地不怕的個性，讓他以極少的資本創了業。

Write your own sentence:

- There has been bad blood between ______________ ______________________________ for years.

2

be out for blood

以血為目標，非報仇不可，絕不輕易放過

to be determined to attack or blame for something

與血有關的事，不是打殺、就是報仇。此慣用語意指由於憤怒、不甘心，一心一意要打倒、懲治別人，找別人算帳。但若有人 **scream／yell bloody murder**（嚷著要讓人流血送命），則表示此人透過叫囂、高分貝的咒罵表達不滿，重點是抱怨、抗議、倒不是真要拿刀砍人。

- He **was out for blood** when he found someone had stolen his trade secrets.

  他發現有人竊取商業機密，發誓非揪出此人、絕不善罷甘休。

- Be careful! That gang of hoodlums **is out for blood.**

  小心！那幫混混在找人算帳。

- If you increase class sizes from 20 to 30, parents will **scream bloody murder.**

  如果你把班級人數從20增加到30，家長恐怕會痛罵抗議。

Write your own sentence:

- _______________ is out for blood, but we ______________________.

3

blood and thunder

血與雷，（故事、影片中）暴力打鬥的情節

a speech or performance that is full of violence and bloodshed

此慣用語意指故事中殘暴、殺戮的情節。**blood-and-thunder**為形容詞，意指「暴力血腥的」，如：**a blood-and-thunder Western film**（充滿暴力、打殺情節的西部片）。**blood on the carpet**（地毯上的血）是另類暴力，以血來形容團體機構中迫使某些人去職的紛爭。**blood, sweat, and tears**（血、汗、淚）則意指努力，且是非常辛苦的努力。

- The detective novel is full of blood and thunder.

  這本偵探小說處處可見暴力打鬥的情節。

- There was much blood on the carpet after the meeting.

  這場會議之後，看來有一場人事大地震了。

- This gallery is the result of 5 years' blood, sweat and tears.

  這座美術館是五年辛苦努力的成果。

Write your own sentence:

- ______________________ usually have lots of blood and thunder.

4

can't get blood from a stone

石頭裡榨不出血，休想拿得到（錢）

impossible to get something from someone, especially money

這個慣用語意指要從某人身上拿到某物，就像要石頭流血一樣，有得等了，最常使用於錢的往來，因為不論是要真的沒錢的人、亦或小氣、賴皮的人掏錢，都像在以石頭榨血，不可能拿得到。同義的慣用語還有 **can't get／squeeze blood out of a turnip**（從蕪菁裡榨不出血來）。

- The bank asked him to pay for his loan, but he told them they can't get blood from a stone.
  銀行要他付貸款，但他跟他們說他就是拿不出來、有什麼辦法。
- You'll get blood from a stone before you get a contribution from your tight-fisted neighbor.
  等你從石頭榨出血來，你就拿得到你那吝嗇鄰居的捐款了。
- You can't increase the rent any further. We don't have the money. You can't squeeze blood out of a turnip.
  房租不能再漲了，我們沒錢，你漲也沒用。
- Getting overtime pay in the firm is like getting blood from a stone.
  在這家公司，要想拿到加班費，無異於緣木求魚。

Write your own sentence:

- I tried to ________________________________
  but it's just trying to get blood from a stone.

5

draw blood

抽血、放血，傷害某人使某人的身或心流血

to make a wound that bleeds; to injure someone physically or emotionally

draw blood 意指刻意使血流出，如抽血、放血，或以砍咬打揍等方式使人流血，又如以言語、行為傷害別人的心情感受，使心流血。此外，若在作戰或比賽中，有人 **draw first blood**（使別人流下第一滴血），表示此人初步領先或首度得分。

- The bullet skimmed his temple but it didn't draw blood.
  子彈擦過他太陽穴，但沒讓他流血。

- Slander can hardly draw blood from a man like him.
  毀謗傷不了像他這樣的人。

- He always knows how to draw blood with his cynical reviews.
  他總知道如何用挖苦、譏諷的評論傷害別人。

- He drew first blood in the match but in the end was defeated.
  他在比賽一開始領先，最後卻敗陣。

Write your own sentence:

- I won't allow ____________ to draw blood from me.

6

flesh and blood

肉與血，血肉之軀、凡人之身，親人

a human being; one's own relatives or kin

此慣用語以鮮血與肌肉表示人類，尤指有著極限、弱點以及七情六慾的凡夫俗子。**one's own flesh and blood**（某人自己的血肉），則如中文的「骨肉」、「骨血」，意指與某人有著血緣關係的親人。

- Many dolls are more popular than their flesh and blood counterparts.

  許多公仔比真實本尊還受歡迎。

- The many sorrows are more than flesh and blood can stand.

  這麼多令人傷痛的不幸，實非血肉之軀所能承受。

- He cut his own flesh and blood out of his will.

  他把親人全排除在他遺囑名單之外。

- I couldn't believe that someone so famous was my own flesh and blood.

  我真不敢相信那麼有名的人居然是我親戚。

Write your own sentence:

- I am not immune to ________________. I am only flesh and blood, after all.

7

have someone's blood on one's hands

手上沾有某人的血，要為某人的死傷負責

to be responsible for someone's death or violent injury

看到血，總令人想到受傷、死亡。此慣用語可依原意表示手上沾到某人的血、也可意指某人的死傷與沾血的手有直接或間接的關係。由此，**spill／shed blood**（流血）意指使人受傷或死亡，**no blood was spilt／shed**即表示沒有死傷，**a great deal of blood was spilt／shed**則為死傷慘重。

- On whose hands was the teenager's blood?
  誰該為這名少年的死負責？
- The driver has the boy's blood on his hands.
  這名駕駛應為這名少年的死負責。
- The leaders of the war have the blood of myriads of people on their hands.
  無數人的鮮血都為這場戰爭的領袖們而流。
- He did not want to see any innocent blood spilt.
  他不想看到無辜的人流血喪命。

Write your own sentence:

- ________________ have the blood of ____________ on their hands that will never wash off.

8

in one's blood

在血液之中，家族遺傳，生來就有

as a basic part of one's essential nature

如果某種長相特徵、個性特質、興趣專長存在於血液中，這表示它們渾然天成、不求自來，並非後天養成習得的（**acquired**）。若有人血是冷的（**in cold blood**），則表示行事冷酷、殘忍，**cold-blooded** 是形容詞，意指「冷血的、冷酷的、不帶感情的」。

- He has music in his blood and singing is as natural for him as breathing.

  他天生有音樂細胞，唱歌對他而言，有如呼吸般自然。

- Acting is in her blood. The happy-go-lucky trait runs in the blood, too.

  她生來帶演戲細胞，天性也豁達開朗。

- He was charged with killing his wife in cold blood.

  他被控蓄意殺妻。

- They were shot in cold blood.

  他們遭到殘酷地射殺。

Write your own sentence:

- __________ runs in my blood and __________ is as natural for me as breathing.

9

make one's blood boil

使某人血液沸騰，使某人怒從中來

to enrage one; to make one very angry

情緒會改變人的體溫，生氣時臉漲紅表示體溫上升，受驚嚇時臉發白表示體溫下降。由此，某事使人血液滾熱便意指某事使人憤怒，既氣事情本身、更氣道理說不清、又或無力改變。反之，**make one's blood run cold**（使人血液變冷）則表示使人恐懼、心生害怕，可參見BACK 14。

- Whenever I think of that self-righteous female teacher, it makes my blood boil.

  只要一想到那個自以為是的女老師我就一肚子火。

- It makes my blood boil to think of the amount of tax money that gets wasted.

  一想到納稅人的錢被浪費掉，我就怒火中燒。

- Cruelty and injustice often make our blood boil.

  殘暴與不公不義總使我們怒不可抑。

- He heard a ghostly laugh which made his blood run cold.

  他聽到幽幽的鬼笑聲，不禁全身發冷。

Write your own sentence:

- He told me ____________, which made my blood boil.

10

smell blood

聞到血的味道，發現下手的機會來了

to recognize an opportunity to be more successful; to be ready to act or fight

當鯊魚聞到血腥，牠們會非常興奮地朝著味道進攻廝殺。因此聞到血味便意指察覺到對手正處於弱勢，此時不動更待何時。**taste blood**（嘗到血味）則意指在冒險的行動中嘗到甜頭、或獲得初步優勢，使人更加躍躍欲試想繼續做下去。

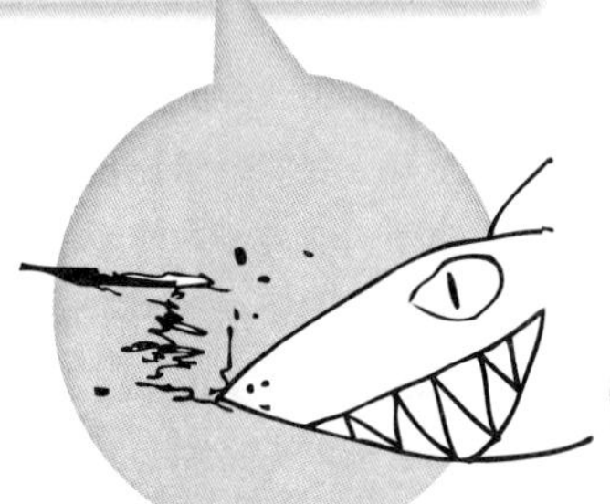

- When his supporters began to despair, his opponents began to smell blood.

  當他的支持者漸漸失去信心，他的對手意識到這正是反擊的好機會。

- The group smells blood and is starting a campaign against sex discrimination.

  這個團體覺得時機到了，開始發起反性別歧視運動。

- The reporter tasted blood when he had definite proof of Bob's love affair.

  這名記者拿到了Bob搞緋聞的確切證據，贏得初步勝利。

Write your own sentence:

- I could smell blood when ______________________.

11

a bundle of nerves

一束神經，高度緊張、神經兮兮的人

a very nervous, jittery person

當神經擴張到整個人只剩「神經束」，能適用於此人的形容詞自然也只剩「神經質」。**bundle**也可用**bag**。其實緊張時可藉由深呼吸來調整自己以**calm**／**steady one's nerves**（安定神經），神經穩定後，情緒自然可恢復平靜（**regain composure**）。

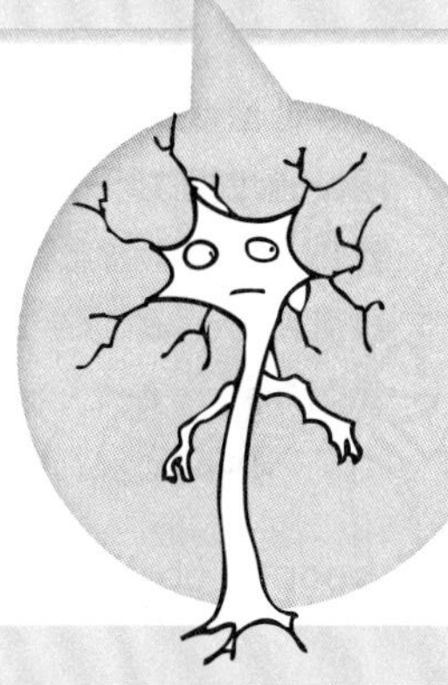

- I was a bundle of nerves before my dental appointment.
  看牙醫前我緊張得要命。
- For months after the disaster, he was a bundle of nerves.
  災難過後幾個月來，他終日惶惶不安。
- A sudden knock on the door at night is enough to make me a bag of nerves.
  夜裏突然聽到敲門聲，就會讓我驚恐不安。
- He steadied his nerves before he defended himself.
  他先鎮定自己的情緒，始而為自己辯護。

Write your own sentence:

- I was a bundle of nerves before ________________.

12

get on someone's nerves

爬上某人神經，弄得某人很煩

to annoy someone, especially by doing something again and again

神經被牽動，人的心神便難安穩。此慣用語意指某人事物持續反覆的狀態或行為弄得人很煩，就像持續聽到電鋸聲一樣，煩得人簡直快瘋了。**get** 也可用 **grate**（發出刺耳聲）。**get under someone's skin** 則是把別人惹惱，像蟲子一樣鑽到人家皮下，招人討厭。

- My wireless Internet connection is unstable and it's getting on my nerves.
  我的無線網路不太穩，煩死了。
- His fidgeting really gets on the teacher's nerves.
  他老坐不住，弄得老師很煩。
- He got on my nerves by asking me the same question repeatedly.
  他反覆問我同樣的問題，問得我煩死了。
- It really got under my skin when he said women were bad drivers.
  他說女生都不會開車，這話真的惹到我了。

Write your own sentence:

- ______________________ really gets on my nerves.

13

get up enough nerve

豎起足夠的神經，鼓足勇氣

to work up enough courage to do something

勇氣需要心給予意志、內臟給予能量、神經給予鎮定與沈著，因此**heart**／**guts**／**nerve**都可意指勇氣。由此，**lose nerve**表示失去勇氣、變得膽怯、害怕；**regain nerve**表示重拾信心、重振起來。此慣用語的**nerve**也可用**guts**／**courage**／**pluck**／**spunk**。

- I hope I can get enough nerve up to ask her for another date.
  我希望我能鼓足勇氣再邀她約會。
- He couldn't get up enough nerve to ask her autograph.
  他提不起勇氣去要她的簽名。
- He lost his nerve and would not try to swim across the lake.
  他突然恐慌起來，不願游過湖面。
- When investors have a yield of 10%, they will start to regain their nerve.
  當投資人能有10%的收益，他們就會重拾信心、穩定下來。

Write your own sentence:

- I hope I can get up enough nerve to

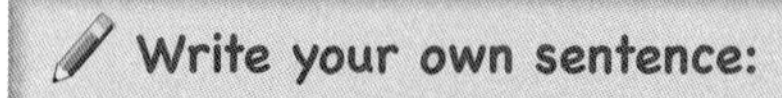.

14

hit a（raw）nerve

打到一根（疼痛的）神經，觸動敏感的神經、戳到痛處

to cause an emotional reaction

神經被打到，情緒肯定亂糟糟，此慣用語意指某事引起明顯的情緒反應，帶來刺激、刺痛；又或某人觸及敏感的話題，引人傷心、痛苦。**hit**也可用**touch**。打神經不會流血、卻會令人痛苦萬分，由此可知，**a war／battle of nerves**（心理戰）是多麼恐怖的戰術。

- The story has hit a nerve with Taiwan's aboriginal people.

  這篇報導令台灣原住民同胞感到受傷。

- I hit a nerve when I asked him if his son ever visited him. His face told me!

  我問他兒子是否來看過他，八成說到他傷心事，看他表情就知道。

- The legal team waged a war of nerves to persuade her to drop the case.

  該律師團運用心理戰，說服她撤銷告訴。

Write your own sentence:

- I am afraid I hit a nerve when I mentioned ________

  ____.

15

have a nerve

有一根神經，大膽、無恥、厚臉皮

to have audacity; to show effrontery

有一根神經特大條，行事就會鹵莽、不顧顏面，此慣用語意指某人大膽放肆、厚顏無恥。**a** 也可用 **some**。但神經大條的鹵莽，用對地方就成了勇氣，因此請小心：**have the nerve to V** 可意指有膽子做某事或竟膽敢做某事，請依上下文判斷。類似用語可參見 CHEST 07 與 FACE 18。

- She **has** such **a nerve**, always blaming me for things that are her fault.

  她好無恥，每次都把自己的錯推到我身上。

- You **have some nerve**! You put your tongue out at me!

  你真大膽，居然敢對我吐舌頭！

- He didn't **have the nerve to** sign the petition.

  他不敢參加簽名連署。

- He **had the nerve to** scold his boss in public.

  他竟敢當眾訓斥他的老闆。

Write your own sentence:

- __________ has a nerve to ask me ________________

  ______________________________.

16

strain every nerve
拉緊每一根神經，竭盡全力

to try extremely hard to do something

專注通常會使神經緊繃，因此，繃緊了所有神經，不容一點放鬆的空隙，就表示用盡全部的心力，盡其所能、竭力表現。但神經繃太緊或太久容易崩潰，若**have nerves of steel**（擁有鋼一般的神經叢），則表示心神經得起操磨，沈著鎮定、勇氣十足。

- They will strain every nerve to avoid military action.
  他們會竭盡所能，不讓軍事行動發生的。
- The bomb disposal expert is straining every nerve to dismantle a time bomb.
  這名拆彈專家正竭盡心思拆解一顆定時炸彈。
- We should strain every nerve to entertain our guests.
  我們應盡全力款待客人。
- You need to have nerves of steel to be a stunt performer.
  要當個特技演員一定要非常沈著果敢。

Write your own sentence:

- We should strain every nerve to ________________.

skin & bone 包著骨頭的皮

所有脊椎動物的軀體，都包覆在SKIN之下，雖只薄薄一層，卻十分重要，因為這一層正是軀體防禦外來影響的第一道防線。因此若有人救了我們的SKIN，便表示為我們解圍、幫我們脫離困境，可回頭參見NECK 07。

Sam always saves my skin whenever I get into trouble.
→ 每次我有麻煩，Sam都出手相救。

如果某事的發生不會讓鼻子掉皮，則表示此事沒什麼大不了，不會造成困擾，可見SKIN著實重要，掉了可不得了，可回頭參見NOSE 05。

It's no skin off my nose if you are going out with that guy.
→ 如果你要跟那傢伙出去，我無所謂。

又，若有外物鑽到SKIN底下，這表示異物入侵，一來意指某事惹惱了我們，二來也可意謂某人令我們深刻難忘。如Cole Porter曾寫過的一首歌，歌名正是"**I've Got You Under My Skin**"：

I've got you under my skin. → 無法忘了你

I've got you deep in the heart of me. → 心裡深深放著你

So deep in my heart that you're really a part of me.
→ 心裡深深放著你，你我合為一。

但若反過來，不是外物入侵，而是我們自己從SKIN裡跳了出來，則表示受到驚嚇，十分詫異或震驚，可回頭參見KNEE 05。

I heard a loud bang and nearly jumped out of my skin.
→ 我聽到砰一聲巨響，嚇得魂差點散了。

又若沒有外物入侵、也沒有魂從 **SKIN** 裡蹦出，但就是覺得有東西爬在 **SKIN** 上，毛毛麻麻的，還起了 **goose pimples**（雞皮疙瘩），這便表示心裡感到害怕、覺得恐怖，可回頭參見BACK 14。

Just to see snakes creeping along the trunk made my skin crawl.
→ 光是看到蛇沿著樹幹爬行，我就渾身不舒服。

其實 **SKIN** 不但有保護作用，還能為我們調溫，並且給予每個人不同的外型特徵。但 **SKIN** 再重要，它畢竟就只薄薄的一層，因此 **skin deep** 便意指「表面的、膚淺的」。如：

Their relationship is only skin deep. It won't last very long.
→ 他們的交情僅停留於表面，不會維持太久的。

SKIN 除了意指人的皮膚，也意指動物、蔬果的皮、或液體表面的薄膜，如：**a leopard skin**（豹皮）、**a banana skin**（香蕉皮）、**the skin on the pudding**（布丁上的那層膜）。

SKIN 當動詞用意指剝皮或擦破皮，如：**skin the deer**（剝下鹿皮）、**skin onions**（剝除洋蔥皮），又或以 **skin someone alive**（活剝某人的皮）誇張地表示嚴厲懲治。如：

He'll skin you alive if he knows you have double-crossed him.
→ 他要是知道你出賣了他，絕對會活剝你的皮。

I skinned my knee when I fell. → 我跌倒時擦傷了膝蓋。

由 **SKIN** 深入肉體到底部，會遇到硬梆梆的 **BONE**。硬硬的 **BONE** 很適合磨牙，難怪英文有句話這麼說：**Parents are the bones on which children**

sharpen their teeth.（父母是孩子磨牙的骨頭），這意謂著做父母的以犧牲付出、成就孩子長大茁壯，類似中文所說：孩子生來是向父母討債的。

BONE 是身體的基本架構，但若腦袋只長 **BONE**，不長腦，那就會變成 **bonehead**（呆子），很容易會 **pull a boner**（出紕漏、鬧笑話、犯下愚蠢的錯）。

身為基本架構的 **BONE** 除了意指骨頭，也可意指身體或屍骨，如：

Let me rest my weary old bones for a minute.
→ 讓我這把累壞了的老骨頭休息一下吧。

至於 **funny bone**，則是指手肘的尺骨端，按壓它會有刺痛的感覺，可為何這個按了會痛不會笑的部位會被叫做 **funny bone**（笑笑骨）呢？這是因為它的正式名稱 **humerus**，恰巧與 **humorous** 發音相同，因此該處就被視為 **humorous**（滑稽好笑的），俗語則稱之為 **funny bone**，而 **tickle someone's funny bone** 就被用來表示逗某人開心、使某人發笑。

如：

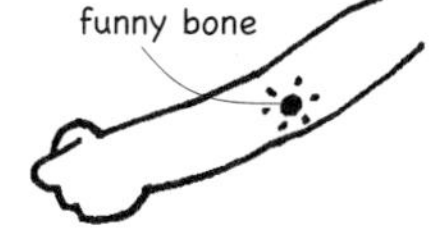

He always knows how to tickle my funny bone.
→ 他總知道怎麼逗我高興。

此外，由於以前的骰子是用 **BONE** 做的，因此 **roll the bones** 就表示擲骰子，尤其是指擲雙骰的賭博。如：

Let's go to the casino and roll the bones tonight.
→ 今晚到賭場賭兩把如何。

又由於以前的人會拿 **BONE** 來磨皮革，因此 **BONE** 當動詞用，便意指為考試而溫習、惡補，臨陣磨槍，一如把皮革磨新擦亮。如：

I need to bone up on my French grammar for the test.
→ 我得為考試趕快把法文文法複習得熟一點。

skin & bone

1

be skin and bones
只有皮和骨，瘦得可憐，骨瘦如柴

to be very thin; to be skinny and reduced to a skeleton; to be a size zero

一般而言，皮下有肉、肉下有骨，如果身體沒了肉，只剩皮包骨，身形肯定很瘦，甚至不成人形。此慣用語可形容體格很瘦、又或強調消瘦憔悴、形銷骨立。前面可加 **all** 或 **nothing but** 來強調。同義的慣用語還有 **a bag of bones**（一袋骨頭），亦即只剩一具裡頭裝著骨頭的皮囊。而所謂的「紙片人」，則是 **size zero model**（零尺寸模特兒）。

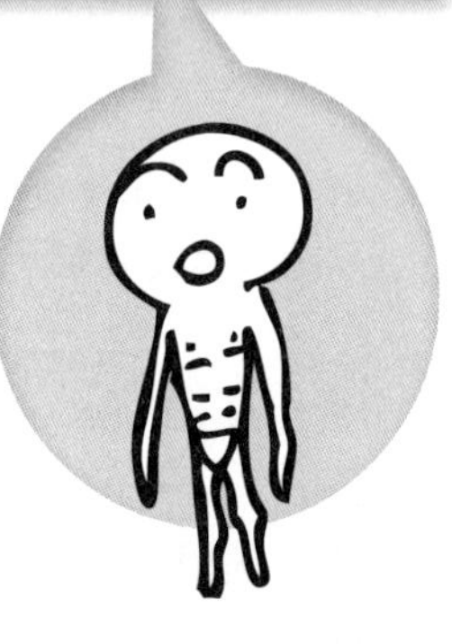

- He has taken off 30 pounds and now he is all skin and bones.
  他掉了三十磅，現在整個超瘦。
- That old horse is nothing but skin and bones. I won't ride it anymore.
  這匹老馬瘦巴巴的，我不會再騎牠了。
- If the model doesn't eat more, she will soon be just a bag of bones.
  如果這個模特兒再不多吃點，很快她就只剩皮包骨了。

Write your own sentence:

- __________ was skin and bones when __________ returned from __________.

have a thick skin

皮很厚，對別人的批評、侮辱等無感

to be insensitive to criticism or insult

此慣用語點出了「厚黑學」的「厚」，皮要厚如城牆、厚而硬、最厲害者還厚而無形。皮厚表示不在乎別人說什麼，不讓別人各種酸苦辣的言語穿透自己的皮囊進到腦子心裡、打到神經。**thick-skinned**為形容詞，將**thick**換成**thin**，則表示皮薄，別人稍微說什麼，情緒馬上有反應。

- Don't weep easily. You need to have a thick skin to survive.

  別動不動就哭。你得要無視別人的批評才能生存。

- You have to develop a thick skin as the spokesman for the workers on strike.

  身為罷工工人的發言人，你得讓自己臉皮厚些，禁得住別人的言語。

- You cannot be too thin-skinned if you are in the public eye.

  身為公眾人物，你不能太敏感、一點都說不得。

Write your own sentence:

- In addition to ________________, I need to have a thick skin.

3

be soaked to the skin

溼到皮膚，渾身溼透

to be extremely wet; to be wet through

soak意指「浸泡」，全身浸在水中、任水穿透衣服、直到皮膚，肯定一身溼嗒嗒。**soaked**也可用**drenched**或**wet**；**skin**也可用**bone**，溼到骨子裡，怎能不溼。骨子沒浸水則乾，**as dry as a bone**形容某物乾巴巴、全無水分。**as dry as dust**（如灰塵一樣無趣）則意指超級乏味。

- What a downpour! I am soaked to the skin.
  好大的一場雨，淋得我全身溼透透。
- Before I could find shelter, I got soaked to the bone.
  還來不及找到地方躲雨，我已變成落湯雞。
- The plant is as dry as a bone. Give it some water!
  這棵植物太乾了，澆點水吧！
- His lecture was (as) dry as dust – just like the subject.
  他的演講枯燥無味，就跟這個演講主題一樣。
- He was soaked to the skin after walking in the rain.
  他在雨中行走，淋得全身溼透。

Write your own sentence:

- ______________________________ and I was soaked to the skin.

4

a bone of contention

搶著要的骨頭，持續受到爭議的焦點

something that continues to be disputed

此慣用語以兩狗各咬骨頭一端僵持不下的畫面，形容意見紛歧、爭論不休的議題。至於女神爭搶的蘋果（**an apple of discord**）則意指爭鬥的禍根、不和的主因。在希臘神話中，女神維納斯為得這顆「給天下最美的女人」的蘋果，將希臘國王弟媳 **Helen** 送給特洛伊王子，以致於長達十年的特洛伊戰爭就這麼因一顆蘋果而展開。

- It is still a bone of contention whether to go on fighting.

  是否繼續作戰依然受到爭議。

- How to use the year-end bonus became a bone of contention between them.

  該如何使用這筆年終獎金，他們始終無法達成共識。

- The right to host the Olympic Games is an apple of discord between them.

  他們為了奧運主辦權而傷了和氣。

Write your own sentence:

- I would not have ________________ become a bone of contention between ________________.

5

feel it in one's bones

骨頭感覺得到，憑直覺，就是知道

to have an intuition or hunch about something

關節炎的人骨頭一痛，就知道快下雨了。此慣用語意指感覺到某事，唯沒有證據，好像關節炎的人以骨頭感應天氣一樣，**feel** 可用 **know**。同義詞有 **I have a hunch** 或參見 GUT 01。又，若 **be bred in the bone**，則表示某種信仰或教養所造成的習性已在骨子裡生根，根深蒂固、牢不可破。**bred-in-the-bone** 為形容詞，意為「根深蒂固的；難以根除的」。

- He is going to lose the election. I can feel it in my bones.
  他這次會落選，我有直覺。
- I am sure he'll achieve victory--I know it in my bones.
  我有把握他會贏得勝利——我就是知道。
- He is a bred-in-the-bone gambler. His gambling is bred in the bone.
  他嗜賭成性，他的好賭是改不了的了。

Write your own sentence:

- I know ________________________________.
  I can feel it in my bones.

6

have a bone to pick with someone

有根骨頭要找某人啃乾淨，非跟某人算清楚不可

to have a complaint, grievance or contentious issue to talk to someone

沒啃乾淨的骨頭上會有殘餘肉末，有的人可視而不見、有的人就非剔除不可。這個慣用語意指心有不滿、疑義，要找某人理個清楚。這種文縐縐的說法自十六世紀流傳至今多少已有些過時，如今遇有這類狀況，大多人會直接說：**I have problems／issues with you.**（我有問題要找你；我對你有點意見）。

- I have a bone to pick with you. Honestly, your messiness quite upsets me.
  我有件事得跟你抱怨一下，老實說，你的髒亂弄得我很煩。

- She no longer has a bone to pick with her husband after he tidied up his study.
  在她老公把書房收拾乾淨之後，她便沒再挑他毛病。

- I have a bone to pick with you about the assignment of jobs.
  對於工作的分配，我得跟你說我很不滿。

Write your own sentence:

- I have a bone to pick with __________ because ____.

skin & bone

7

make no bones about ...

沒放半點骨頭，坦率直接，毫無顧忌

to act or speak candidly about something; to have no scruples

喝湯時如果湯裡有骨頭，就得邊喝湯邊吐骨頭；若沒骨頭，就能暢快地讓湯直接入喉下肚。由此，此慣用語意指行事說話非常直接坦白，不拐彎抹角、不囉哩八嗦，不考慮丟不丟臉、傷不傷人，總之，就像喝碗沒骨頭的湯一樣，反正嘴一張開、喝下便是。

- He made no bones about wanting to marry into polite society.
  他毫不掩飾他想靠婚姻進入上流社會的念頭。
- He made no bones about how gross he thought the fashion show was.
  他不留情面地直言，他覺得這場時裝秀水準很差。
- I'll make no bones about it. I think you are a big phony.
  我就實話實說了，我覺得你很假。
- He is very talented. I make no bones about telling him so to his face every day.
  他很有才華，我每天都當著他的面直接這麼告訴他。

Write your own sentence:

- I made no bones about my dissatisfaction with ____________________.

8

to the bone

到骨子裡，徹底地，到最低限度

completely and thoroughly; to the minimum

皮在外、骨在內，因此來到骨子，便表示完完全全、十分徹底。由於骨裡還有 **marrow**（骨髓），也有人以 **to the marrow** 來表達。此慣用語常用來形容溼透（見 SKIN 03）、又或搭配 **chill**／**freeze** 形容冷得徹骨，又或搭配 **cut**／**pare down** 表示削減到最少 -- 只剩骨頭，當然少到不能再少。若是言論、批評等 **close to the bone**，則表示言詞太過露骨、雖是實話卻很傷人。

- The sight of copious bloodletting chilled me to the marrow.
  大量流血的畫面讓我全身冷到骨子裡。
- There is a cold front coming through. I am frozen to the bone.
  寒流來襲，我一整個凍僵、冷到不行。
- During the worst economic downturn, I cut my expenses to the bone.
  經濟衰退到極點時，我將開銷縮減到最低。
- Your comments about her figure were too close to the bone.
  你對她身材的評論也太直白毒蛇了。

Write your own sentence:

- After ________________, I was chilled to the bone.

9

a skeleton in the closet

衣櫥裡的骷髏，不可告人的秘密

a hidden secret that is shameful or embarrassing

此慣用語意指令人引以為恥、不堪回首的往事，一如藏在衣櫥裡的骨骸，就怕被發現後遭人質疑、唾棄。**come out of the closet**（出櫃）即由此衍生而出。**closet** 用 **cupboard** 是英式說法。又，**a skeleton at the feast**（宴席上的骷髏）意指令人掃興的人事物，但現今較常以 **damper** 來表示此義。**put a damper on** …即表示「令…大為掃興」。

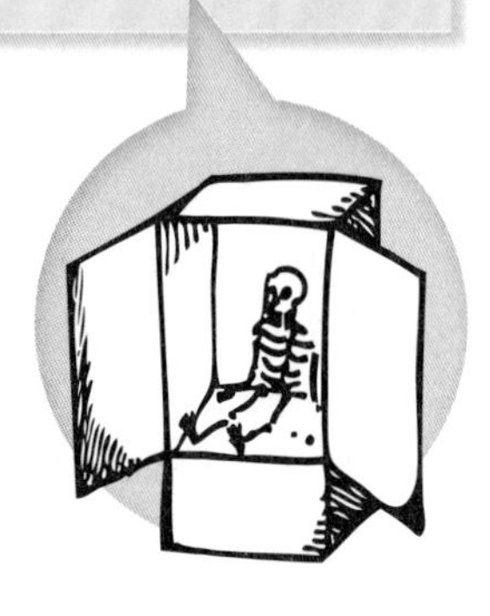

- His uncle was a barbarian brigand. That's his family's skeleton in the closet.

  他叔叔曾是殺人不眨眼的土匪，這是他們的家醜。

- I don't mind what skeletons he has in his closet.

  我不介意他有什麼不可告人的過去。

- The rainy weather put a damper on this year's New Year celebrations.

  下雨天讓今年跨年活動很掃興。

Write your own sentence:

- If you want ________________________, you can't afford to have too many skeletons in your closet.

flesh 肉體 & body 肉包著的身體

所謂身體、肉體，再瘦的身體也一定要有**FLESH**。組成**FLESH**的肌細胞內有收縮纖維，如此一來，身體內外大大小小、如心臟、腸胃、眼睛、大腿等等，才能透過收縮產生力量、運動並工作。

雖說**FLESH**很重要，但太多太少都不好，最好還是保持適中，別一會兒**put on flesh**（長肉、發胖）、一會兒**lose flesh**（肉不見了、消瘦）。

在莎士比亞的「威尼斯商人」裡，商人Shylock因Antonio還不出錢，要求他依照契約割下**one pound of flesh**（一磅肉）來償債。商人的要求於情於理都說不過去、唯獨於法有據，眼看Antonia就得忍受割肉之苦，幸好律師急智，要求商人依契約割下一磅肉，不能多也不能少，但就只能割肉，不能流下契約未載明的血（**blood**），一滴都不行，這才終於為Antonio解了圍。因此**pound of flesh**就被用來表示合法卻不合情理的要求，如：

His business is closed and the bank wants its pound of flesh.
→ 他的生意倒了，銀行絲毫不講情面地一直催債。

由上可知，**FLESH**與**blood**相依相存，而**flesh and blood**便意指著血肉之軀、活生生的凡人，可參見BLOOD 06。

He may be a priest, but he is only flesh and blood, like anybody else.
→ 他是神父沒錯，但他也和你我一樣，不過是具血肉之軀。

flesh & body

除了意指肉、肌肉，**FLESH** 也意指肉體、身體。如：

The spirit is willing, but the flesh is weak. → 心有餘而力不足。

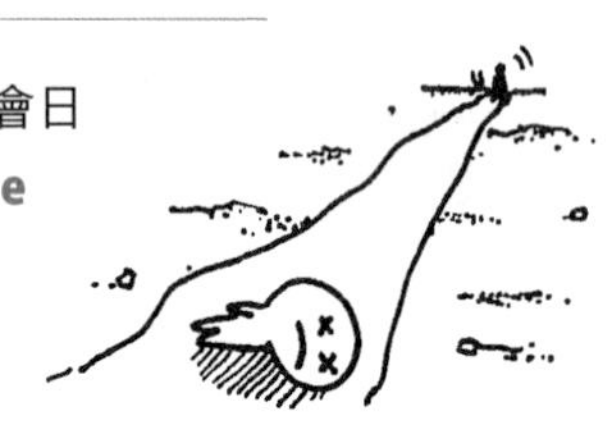

肉身在即代表生命在，生命一旦消逝，肉身便會日漸腐朽，化歸塵土，因此聖經裡這句話：**go the way of all the earth**（走上化塵之路）便意指死亡、歸天，是表示 **die** 較文雅的說法。但後來有人將 **earth** 誤寫為 **flesh**，人們便習慣了用 **go the way of all flesh** 來表達這個意思。如：

His uncle went the way of all flesh and he inherited the house.
→ 他叔叔羽化登仙，他便繼承了這棟房子。

FLESH 當動詞用，也與肉有關，意指「長肉」、「賦予實體」，如：

He began to flesh out at the age of fifteen.
→ 他十五歲才開始長肉。

You need to flesh out the third act.
→ 你得再充實一下第三幕的內容。

FLESH 是肉的廣義用詞，**muscle** 則意指由肌肉纖維聚集、可收縮、擴張的肌肉。因此 **FLESH+y** 成形容詞 **fleshy**，意指多肉的、肥胖的，而 **muscle** 的形容詞 **muscular** 則意指肌肉發達的、健壯的。而 **muscle** 當動詞，意思也都與強壯、勁力有關，如「用力搬動」:

The boss asked the guard to muscle him out of office.
→ 老闆叫警衛將他拉出辦公室。

又如「用強力手段拿走不屬於自己的東西」:

If you try to muscle in on his business, you'll be facing big trouble. → 如果你想強搶他的生意，你的麻煩可不小。

有了**FLESH**、有了**muscle**，**BODY**就有了實體。**BODY**除了可意指身體、軀幹、也意指屍體。如：

It is important to exercise our body and mind.
→ 身心的鍛鍊很重要。

The sword ran through his body.
→ 這劍刺穿了他的軀體。

His body was taken home for burial.
→ 他的屍體被送回家鄉埋葬。

若將**BODY**用於事物，則表示主體、主要部份；而**in a body**便意指全體一致。如：

Please type the body of the letter for me.
→ 請幫我把這信的本文部份打字出來。

The Cabinet resigned in a body.
→ 內閣集體總辭。

雖然**BODY**攸關人的存活，但別忘了無形的**soul**也很重要，沒有**soul**，人的生命就不能算完整，因此**person**（人）的另一種說法正是**living soul**。如：

Not a living soul on earth could cope with that spooky person.
→ 世上沒任何人有辦法對付那鬼氣森森的傢伙。

1

a thorn in one's flesh

肉中刺，時時令人頭大、煩惱的人事物，眼中釘

a constant bother or annoyance

肉裡有刺，當然很不舒服，這個慣用語意指煩惱的來源、持續令人傷腦筋的人事物。它源自聖經（Corinthians 12:7）：為人醫病的 **Paul** 有根刺在他身上，他三次請主將刺拔除卻未得恩准，終身與刺共處。畢竟人生之所以為人生，正在於它有悲有喜、禍福相依。**flesh** 也可用 **side**（側身）。又，背上的猴子也是煩惱，但不一樣，背上猴意指令人憂鬱，有形或無形的困擾。參見 BACK 07。

- Health inspectors are a thorn in the flesh of most restaurant owners.

  多數餐廳老闆都視衛生檢驗人員為頭痛人物。

- The notorious serial killer was the biggest thorn in the police's flesh.

  這個惡名滿天下的連續殺人犯是警方的頭號眼中釘。

- The town has long regarded the casino as a thorn in its side.

  小鎮的人一直都覺得這座賭場給他們帶來各種麻煩。

Write your own sentence:

- ________ was a thorn in the flesh of ____________.

2

in the flesh

以身體，親自，本人

in person; in one's physical presence

科技發達，透過照片、電視、電影出現在面前的人都活生生像真的一樣，透過視訊甚至還可通話，但再如何栩栩如生，都不可能碰觸得到真實的身體。此慣用語以身體表示本人、親自、亦即摸得到、觸得著的本尊。

- She appeared in the flesh, which ended the rumors about her death.
  她親自露面，使死亡的謠言不攻自破。
- I finally was able to see my favorite comedian in the flesh.
  我終於能見到最喜歡的喜劇演員本人。
- The winner must be there in the flesh to collect the prize.
  獲獎者需本人親自到場領獎。
- I have had a talk with him on the Internet, but I have never met him in the flesh.
  我和他在網路上交談過，但沒見過他本人。

Write your own sentence:

- I have never had the chance to meet ________________ in the flesh.

3

neither fish nor flesh

非魚也非肉，難以歸類，看不出是什麼

to be not recognizable; to be not fitting any category under discussion

此慣用語有多種版本，如：

neither fish nor fowl／**neither fish, flesh, nor fowl**／**neither fish, nor flesh, nor good red herring**。總之，**fish**是不吃**meat**的僧侶的食物、**fowl**（家禽肉）或**flesh**是一般人的肉食、**red herring**（燻鯡魚）是窮人的食物。如果非此三類，就表示無法分類或不倫不類。

- The cathedral has a baroque dome and a Gothic façade. It's neither fish nor flesh.

  這座大教堂有著巴洛克式的圓屋頂、哥德式的正面，無法歸在某類建築之下。

- This proposal is neither fish nor fowl. I can't tell what you're proposing.

  這個提案不倫不類，我實在看不出你想提的案是什麼。

- His dressing is neither fish, flesh, nor good red herring, raising a lot of eyebrows.

  他的穿著打扮不三不四，引起不少人側目。

Write your own sentence:

- The movie is neither fish nor flesh because ______________________.

4

press the flesh

把肉握緊壓一壓，（為選舉到處與人）握手

to shake hands with the public, especially when running for public office

此慣用語是種美式幽默，把握手（**shake hands**）形容成握住一團肉又壓又揉，這種握手在選舉時尤其常見。**the** 可省略。另有一種 **glad hand** 則意指熱情卻不帶感情的歡迎或問候，像是進商店或參加活動，通常就會 **get the glad hand**，得到熱情洋溢但未必誠心的歡迎光臨。

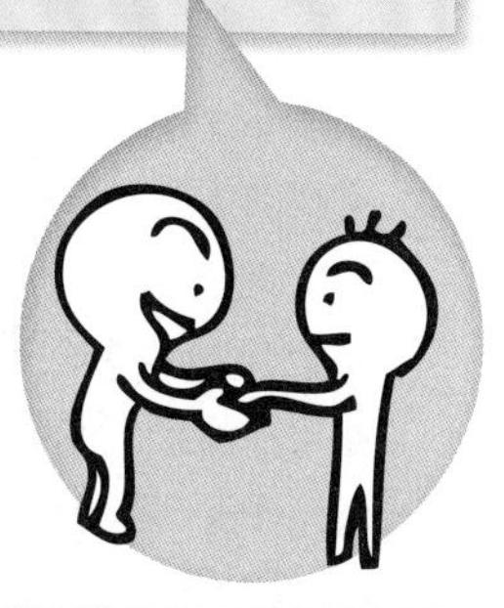

- Ann and Ben shook hands before their business negotiations.
  Ann與Ben先握手再進行商務談判。
- The candidate went through the crowd, pressing the flesh.
  這名候選人穿梭在群眾中，熱情地與大家握手。
- Whenever I go to a fundraising party, I get the glad hand.
  我每次參加募款餐會，都會受到熱烈歡迎。
- Politicians are apt to give the glad hand to one and all.
  政客通常來者不拒，一律給予熱情的問候。

Write your own sentence:

- __________ wanted to press the flesh,
  but I ______________________________.

5

flex one's muscles

屈縮肌肉，展示肌肉、實力、權力

to show off one's strength or power

flex意指屈曲四肢、使肌肉收縮，此慣用語原本意指有如**bodybuilder**（健美先生）般縮擠出大塊肌肉、展現肌力，後來也延伸用來表示展現勢力或影響力，並可自行加上形容詞，如：**flex political muscles**（展現政治上的實力）／**flex legal muscles**（展現司法上的權力）。

- The protests are their only chance to flex their muscles over the reform.

  抗議是他們唯一的機會，可以展現他們對改革的影響力。

- The bomb scare was an attempt by criminal gangs to flex their muscles and face down the police.

  此炸彈恐嚇事件是犯罪集團企圖展現勢力、與警方正面對戰。

- The successful movie actress decided to flex her muscles on the stage.

  這名成功的電影女星，決定站上舞台展現實力。

Write your own sentence:

- __________ are flexing their muscles in front of ______________________________.

6

body and soul

身體與靈魂，全心全意（地）

（with） physical and mental energy

完整的存活不只需要身體、也需要靈魂。此慣用語意指全心全意、用盡全部的自己去做某事，全心投入。由於存活需要身體與靈魂，**keep body and soul together**（讓身與靈還能湊在一起）便意指維持個溫飽、維持基本的需求勉強活下去。

- The pathologist puts body and soul into his cancer research.

  這名病理學家投下所有心思研究癌症。

- The architect threw himself into the project, body and soul.

  這名建築師全心投入在這個工程案上。

- I don't earn enough money to keep body and soul together.

  我賺的錢，連勉強餬口都不夠。

- He had to work very hard in order to keep body and soul together.

  他得要拼命工作，才能圖個溫飽。

Write your own sentence:

- I dedicate myself to ______________________, body and soul.

7

over my dead body

越過我的屍體，想都別想，除非我死

in no way; under no circumstances

此慣用語表達了強勢的反對，亦即要做…可以，等我死了再說、或我死都不會答應…這類表示「休想」的口氣。另一與屍體有關的慣用語為 **know where all the bodies are buried**（知道屍體都埋在哪裡），意指知道所有內情、秘密、醜聞、陰謀等不好的事情。

- 'Mom, I want to join the circus.' 'Over my dead body!'
  「媽，我想加入馬戲團。」「絕對不准！」
- If they demolish the house, they'll do it over my dead body.
  他們若敢拆這房子，我死給他們看。
- The only way you're going to have my permission is over my dead body.
  要我答應，門兒都沒有，除非我死。
- The personal assistant knows where all the bodies are buried in the company.
  這家公司的內幕秘密這名特助全都一清二楚。

Write your own sentence:

- You will ____________ over my dead body. No way.

8

bare one's soul

坦露靈魂，吐露心事

to reveal one's innermost private thoughts and feelings

bare意指揭露、使赤裸，**soul**（靈魂）則宛如心情感受的記憶卡，因此坦開靈魂就表示說出自己內心深處私密的心事或念頭，類似慣用語可參考CHEST&HEART的02與10。此外，既然**soul**連結著私人的內心深處，由此，**kindred soul／spirit**（同性質的靈魂／心靈）便意指志趣相投、信仰一致、合得來的人。

- Teenagers rarely bare their souls to their parents; they prefer their peers.

  青少年很少找父母說心事，他們較愛找同儕。

- He is not willing to bare his soul about his miseries on Cannibal Island.

  關於他在食人族島上的悲慘經歷，他並不想多談他的內心感受。

- Ben and I are kindred spirits when it comes to music. We both love jazz.

  說到音樂，Ben和我很合，我們都愛爵士樂。

Write your own sentence:

- I usually bare my soul to ______________ about ______________________________.

有關「HEAD」的諺語

A crown is no cure for the headache.
→ 王冠治不了頭痛。
→ 榮華富貴買不到平安的人生。

A good head and an industrious hand are worth gold in any land.
→ 腦袋聰明手也勤，天下無處不是金。

All the wit in the world is not in one head.
→ 世上所有的智慧不會只集中在一個腦袋。
→ 集思廣益；三個臭皮匠勝過一個諸葛亮。

Always hold your head up, but keep your nose at the friendly level.
→ 頭要抬高，但鼻子請保持在友善的高度。
→ 要俯仰無愧，但別自視太高瞧不起別人。

A still tongue makes a wise head.
→ 沈靜的舌造就睿智的頭。
→ 智者寡言。

Better an empty purse than an empty head.
→ 寧可錢袋扁，不要腦袋空。
→ 手中有錢，不如腦中有智慧。

Better be the head of an ass than the tail of a horse.
→ 寧為驢頭、不作馬尾。
→ 寧為雞首、不為牛後。

Don't put your head into the lion's mouth.
→ 不要把頭放進獅子的口裡。
→ 不要沒事冒沒必要的大險。

Fish begin to stink at the head.
→ 魚要腐爛頭先臭。
→ 上樑不正下樑歪。

He that has a head of glass must not throw stones at another.
→ 有著玻璃頭的人不該對別的玻璃頭丟石頭。
→ 別忘了自己的缺點，卻去說人長短。

He that has a tongue in his head may find his way anywhere.
→ 動腦想、開口問，不愁沒路走。

If a man empties his purse into his head, no man can take it away from him.
→ 若將錢包的錢放進腦袋，絕對沒人拿得走。
→ 智力投資最可靠。

One good head is better than a hundred strong hands.
→ 百雙有力的手，不如一個聰明的頭腦。

One way to keep your head above water is to avoid expensive dives.
→ 不想頭下沈（財務出問題），就不要花大錢玩跳水（遽然投資大筆金錢）。

The arrow shot upright falls on the shooter's head.
→ 對天射箭，打中自己。
→ 自作孽不可活；因果循環，報應不爽。

The heart sees further than the head.
→ 心的視野遠大於理智所見。

The real leaders do not always march at the head of the procession.
→ 真正的領導者大多不會率先走在隊伍最前面。

Those who can't use their head must use their back.
→ 不動腦的人就得用到背。
→ 不懂得思考判斷，那就等著扛苦果。

Too much bed makes a dull head.

→ 睡太多頭會鈍。

→ 不動會變笨。

Too much knowledge makes the head bald.

→ 知道得多，頭禿得快

→ 求知慾或好奇心都要適可而止；不要用腦過度。

Two heads are better than one.

→ 兩顆腦袋勝過一個。

→ 集思廣益；三個臭皮匠勝過一個諸葛亮。

Uneasy lies the head that wears a crown.

→ 戴著王冠的頭睡不穩。

→ 權位高、責任重、煩惱多。

有關「BRAIN／SKULL」的諺語

An idle brain is the devil's workshop.

→ 閒置的腦袋是魔鬼的工坊。

→ 遊手好閒乃萬惡之源。

Brain is better than brawn.

→ 腦比肌強。

→ 智慧勝於蠻力。

Full bellies make empty skulls.

→ 肚子滿滿，腦袋空空。

→ 物質生活好，人就不用腦。

If the brain sows not corn, it plants thistles.

→ 思想如田地，不種玉米就長薊。

Listen to the voice of experience, but also make use of your brain.

→ 傾聽經驗之談，自己也要動腦思索。

Money spent on the brain is never spent in vain.

→ 智力上的投資絕不會白費。

Silence is the best substitute for brains.

→ 沈默是腦子的最佳替代品。

→ 不聰明無妨，懂得安靜少言就好。

The brains don't lie in the beard.

→ 腦子又不長在鬍子裡。

→ 智慧無關乎年齡性別。

有關「HAIR」的諺語

Beauty draws us with a single hair.

→ 美女只需一根頭髮，就能拉動我們。

→ 美女不費吹灰之力即能呼風喚雨。

Care brings gray hair.

→ 憂煩帶來白頭髮。

→ 憂心催人老。

Experience is a comb which nature gives us when we are bald.

→ 經驗是上天在我們禿頭之後才贈予的梳子。

→ 亡羊補牢已太遲。

Gray hair is God's graffiti.
→ 白髮是上帝塗鴉的傑作。

Gray hair is a blessing – ask any bald man.
→ 擁有白髮是幸福的 —— 問問禿頭的人就知道。

Hair by hair you will put out the horse's tail.
→ 一根一根拔，必可拔光馬尾巴。
→ 滴水穿石；鐵杵磨成繡花針。

Take a hair of the dog that bit you.
→ 拿咬你的狗的毛來治咬傷。
→ 以毒攻毒；以酒解酒（尤指以酒解宿醉）。

有關「FACE／CHEEK／FOREHEAD／CHIN」的諺語

A fair face may hide a foul heart.
→ 美好的面孔也許藏著醜惡的心。
→ 人不可貌相；知人知面不知心。

Affectation is a greater injury to the face than small-pox.
→ 矯情比天花更傷臉。
→ 做作的人看起來比長天花的人還糟糕。

A good face is a letter of recommendation.
→ 好的相貌就是一封推薦介紹函。

A good face needs no paint.
→ 好的相貌無需擦脂抹粉。

A good fame is better than a good face.
→ 好的名聲勝於好的相貌。

Cheek brings success.
→ 臉皮厚才能成大事。

Don't cut off your nose to spite your face.
→ 別割自己的鼻毀自己的臉。
→ 不要跟自己過不去；賭氣無益。

Everyone's faults are not written in their foreheads.
→ 缺點或過錯不會寫在額頭上。
→ 知人知面不知心。

He may swim boldly who is held up by the chin.
→ 下巴被舉高，就會放膽游。
→ 有了安全感，就會放膽做。

Keep your face always toward the sunshine -- and shadows will fall behind you.
→ 永遠把臉迎向陽光，陰影自然落你身後。

The face is the index of the heart.
→ 臉是心的指標。
→ 相由心生。

有關「EYE」的諺語

An eye for an eye, and we will all go blind.
→ 以眼還眼，大家一起盲。
→ 以暴制暴，兩敗俱傷。

Avarice blinds our eyes.
→ 貪婪使眼盲。
→ 財迷心竅。

Beauty is in the eye of the beholder.
→ 美不美由看的人決定。
→ 美沒有絕對的標準；情人眼裡出西施。

Bring up a raven and he'll pick out your eyes.
→ 把渡鴉養大，他便會啄你的眼。
→ 養虎貽患。

Cry with one eye and laugh with the other.
→ 一眼哭、另一眼笑。
→ 心口不一；口是心非。

Far from eye, far from heart.
→ 遠離眼睛便遠離心。
→ 離久情疏。

Four eyes see more than two.
→ 四眼看得比兩眼多。
→ 人多辦法多；集思廣益。

Hawks will not pick hawks' eyes out.
→ 鷹不啄鷹的眼。
→ 同類不相殘。

Hedges have eyes, and walls have ears.

→ 籬笆有眼，隔牆有耳。

If the eye does not admire, the heart will not desire.

→ 眼不讚嘆，心不慾貪。

In the land of the blind, the one-eyed man is king.

→ 在盲人的國度，獨眼即稱王。

→ 山中無老虎，猴子做大王。

It is all fun and games until somebody loses an eye.

→ 玩到有人少了隻眼就知道不好玩了。

→ 貪玩易受傷；樂極易生悲。

It is easier for a camel to go through the eye of a needle than for a rich man to enter into the kingdom of God.

→ 有錢人要上天堂，比駱駝穿過針眼還難。

→ 有了財富難上天堂，為富易不仁。

Keep your eyes wide open before marriage, and half shut afterwards.

→ 婚前眼全開，婚後眼半閉。

Keep your mouth shut and your eyes open.

→ 嘴巴閉上眼睛睜開。

→ 少說多看。

The cat shuts its eyes while it steals cream.

→ 貓偷吃奶油的時候總閉上眼。

→ 掩耳盜鈴；自欺欺人。

The day has eyes, the night has ears.

→ 日有眼，夜有耳。

→ 若要人不知，除非己莫為。

The eye is blind if the mind is absent.

→ 心不專則眼不明。

有關「EYE」的諺語

有關「EAR」的諺語

The eye that sees all things else sees not itself.
→ 看得見一切的眼睛，偏偏看不見自己。

There's more to something (somebody) than meets the eye.
→ 某事（某人）絕不像表面所見那麼簡單。

When you go to buy, use your eyes not your ears.
→ 買東西，要用眼睛看（實物），莫用耳朵聽（人說）。

You can't expect people to see eye to eye with you if you look down on them.
→ 如果你看人低，如何要人與你眼對眼、意見一致。

You may force a man to shut his eyes, but you cannot make him sleep.
→ 你或可以強迫別人閉眼，卻不能使他睡。
→ 有些事勉強不得，只能順勢而為。

有關「EAR」的諺語

All asses wag their ears.
→ 驢子都愛搖耳朵。
→ 傻子總愛裝聰明；聽不懂偏愛裝懂的是笨蛋。

A man has two ears and one mouth that he may hear much and speak little.
→ 人有兩隻耳朵一張嘴，為的就是多聽少說話。

Choose a wife rather by your ear than your eye.
→ 選妻，最好用耳莫用眼。
→ 選妻，品行比容貌更重要。

Fields have eyes, and woods have ears.
→ 田地有眼、樹林有耳。
→ 說話要小心，隔牆有耳。

Give every man thy ear, but few thy voice.
→ 側耳傾聽少出聲。
→ 多聽少說。

Little pitchers have big ears.
→ 小水壺有大把手。
→ 小孩雖小，耳朵卻很靈；在小孩面前說話要謹慎。

No piper can please all ears.
→ 沒有風笛手能吹出眾耳都滿意的樂聲。
→ 要做到每個人都滿意是不可能的。

Nature has given us two ears, two eyes, and but one tongue--to the end that we should hear and see more than we speak.
→ 上天賜予我們耳一對，眼一雙，舌僅一根，終歸就是要我們多聽，多看，少說話。

The hungry belly has no ears.
→ 飢餓的肚子不長耳。
→ 餓了什麼都聽不進；饑寒起盜心；衣食足而後知榮辱。

The wise man has long ears and a short tongue.
→ 聰明人耳朵長，舌頭短。
→ 智者多聽少說。

Two sparrows on one ear of corn make an ill agreement.
→ 兩隻麻雀一支玉米穗，意見難一致。

You cannot make a silk purse out of a sow's ear.
→ 用母豬的耳朵做不出絲質的皮包。
→ 朽木不可雕；巧婦難為無米之炊。

有關「NOSE」的諺語

A big nose never spoiled a handsome face.
→ 大鼻子破壞不了好看的臉。

A dog's nose and a maid's knee are always cold.
→ 狗鼻子與少女的膝蓋總是冷的。

A person who looks down his nose at people will never see beyond that nose.
→ 目光老順著鼻子往下看（瞧不起別人）的人，目光永遠只到得了自己的鼻子尖。

A pig used to dirt turns its nose up at rice.
→ 習慣了爛泥的豬，對米飯嗤之以鼻。

Better a snotty child than his nose wiped off.
→ 寧願小孩滿是鼻涕，也不要擦得一乾二淨。
→ 治療有時比疾病本身更可怕。

He that has a great nose thinks everybody is speaking of it.
→ 愛打聽的人總覺得別人都在談論自己。
→ 做賊心虛。

Justice has a waxen nose. (The law has a nose of wax.)
→ 法律的鼻子是蠟做的。
→ 法律如蠟，任人玩弄沒原則。

Keep your nose out of other people's business.
→ 別把鼻子伸進別人的事裡。
→ 不要多管閒事。

有關「MOUTH」的諺語

A close mouth catches no flies.
→ 嘴巴閉起來，蒼蠅進不去。
→ 話少一點，禍遠一點。

A closed mouth gathers no feet.
→ 嘴巴閉起來就不會不小心把腳放進去。
→ 少說少出錯。

An enemy's mouth seldom speaks well.
→ 敵人嘴裡沒好話。
→ 狗嘴吐不出象牙來。

Bees that have honey in their mouths have stings in their tails.
→ 口中含蜜的蜜蜂，尾部有螫人的針。
→ 口蜜腹劍；笑裡藏刀。

Big mouthfuls often choke.
→ 大口大口吃容易嗆到。
→ 貪多嚼不爛；做事宜量力而為。

Bitter pills may have blessed effects.
→ 苦藥丸效果妙。
→ 良藥苦口；忠言逆耳。

Don't look a gift horse in the mouth.
→ 別人送你馬，莫去看馬嘴。
→ 餽贈之物切莫挑剔；要懂得感恩。

Good medicine is bitter in the mouth.
→ 好藥吃在嘴中總是苦。
→ 良藥苦口；忠言逆耳。

Let the hands get busy, not the mouth.
→ 手要勤勞，嘴莫多說。

Nothing is opened by mistake as often as one's mouth.
→ 最常在不該打開時卻打開的東西就是嘴巴。

Out of the mouth comes evil.
→ 禍從口出。

Quick feet and busy hands fill the mouth.
→ 手勤腳快，嘴吃得飽。

Wise men have their mouth in their heart, fools their heart in their mouth.
→ 智者嘴在心中，愚人心在嘴中。

The wise hand doth not all that the foolish mouth speaks.
→ 聰明人的手不做愚笨人說的事。

What the heart thinks, the mouth speaks.
→ 心想到什麼，嘴就說什麼。
→ 想到什麼說什麼；心直口快。

When the heart is afire, some sparks will fly out at the mouth.
→ 心中若著火，火花噴到嘴。
→ 心不靜，口隨便。

While the word is in your mouth, it is your own; when 'tis once spoken, 'tis another's.
→ 話未出口屬己身，話一出口屬別人。

有關「LIP」的諺語

Between the cup and the lip a morsel may slip.

→ 在杯與唇之間，也許就掉了一口。

→ 吃到嘴裡才算數；不小心則功虧一簣。

It is a dangerous crisis when a proud heart meets with flattering lips.

→ 驕傲的心遇上諂媚的唇，岌岌可危。

There's many a slip between cup and lip.

→ 在杯子還沒碰到嘴唇之前，仍大有可能失手掉杯。

→ 沒到最後，切不可掉以輕心。

有關「TOOTH」的諺語

A glutton may dig his grave with his teeth.

→ 貪吃的人以牙齒自掘墳墓。

→ 不節制飲食即自找死路。

If you can't bite, never show your teeth.

→ 咬不了人就別齜牙。

→ 沒本事就別叫囂。

The gods send nuts to those who have no teeth.

→ 神總把堅果送給沒牙的人。

→ 好運好事總來得不是時候。

The tongue always turns to an aching tooth.
→ 舌頭總愛跑去牙痛的地方。
→ 人們總愛拿自己的煩惱當話題。

有關「TONGUE」的諺語

A dog has many friends because he wags his tail instead of his tongue.
→ 狗的朋友很多，因為他搖尾巴不嚼舌。

A gossip is one who keeps a swivel tongue in her head.
→ 八卦有一條會迴轉的舌。
→ 說別人八卦，終會輪到自己。

A honey tongue, a heart of gall.
→ 甜蜜舌，怨毒心。
→ 口蜜腹劍；笑裡藏刀；佛口蛇心。

An ox is taken by the horns, and the man by the tongue.
→ 牛因角被擒，人因舌遭殃。

A silent tongue and true heart are the most admirable things on earth.
→ 緘默的舌，真誠的心，是世上最值得讚美之物。

Better the foot slip than the tongue .
→ 寧可腳滑跤，切莫口失言。

Govern your thoughts when alone, and your tongue when in company.
→ 獨自一人須慎思，與人相處須慎言。

He knows much who knows how to hold his tongue.
→ 懂得緘默的是明白人；智者寡言。

He that knows not how to hold his tongue knows not how to talk.
→ 懂得緘默才真懂什麼是說話。

His heart cannot be pure whose tongue is not clear.
→ 舌不乾淨，心不純潔。
→ 嘴不淨者心不純。

It is a good tongue that says no ill, and a better heart that thinks none.
→ 好舌不說惡言，好心不生邪念。

The tongue of idle persons is never idle.
→ 無所事事的人，舌頭忙得很。
→ 閒人最愛嚼舌根。

The tongue is not steel, yet it cuts.
→ 舌頭非鋼卻可傷人。

The tongue is but three inches long, yet it can kill a man six feet high.
→ 舌頭雖只三寸長，卻能殺死六尺漢。

The wise man's tongue is a shield, not a sword.
→ 智者的舌是盾、不是劍。
→ 智者用言語自保，不用言語傷人。

Turn your tongue seven times before speaking.
→ 舌頭轉七次，始而開口說。
→ 話到嘴邊留三分；言貴慎思。

有關「NECK」的諺語

Better a leg broken than the neck.

→ 寧可腿斷，不要脖子斷。

→ 留得青山在，不怕沒柴燒。

Everything may be repaired except the neckbone.

→ 壞了的東西也許還能修，唯獨頸子骨修不了。

→ 命只有一條，丟了就沒了。

Forget, when up to one's neck in alligators, that the mission is to drain the swamp.

→ 忙著應付鱷魚便忘了此行目的是排乾沼澤的水。

→ 忙一忙就忘了原先的目標。

He who looks up too much gets a pain in the neck.

→ 老往上看的人容易脖子痛。

→ 自視甚高的人招人厭。

Little thieves are hanged by the neck, great ones by the purse.

→ 被吊死的都是小賊偷，厲害的大盜再抓也只抓得到皮包。

One misfortune comes on the neck of another.

→ 倒霉事一件接一件來。

→ 禍不單行。

有關「THROAT」的諺語

A fool's tongue is long enough to cut his own throat.
→ 愚人的舌長到足以割自己的喉。
→ 聰明人不會亂說話害自己。

Save a thief from the gallows and he'll be the first who shall cut your throat.
→ 救下斷頭台上的小偷，日後他將割你的喉。
→ 縱虎歸山，後患無窮。

有關「SHOULDER」的諺語

A chip on the shoulder is a sure sign of wood higher up.
→ 肩上放有碎木塊，表示更高處有木頭。
→ 覺得別人對不起你，正表示別人也覺得你對不起他。

God gives burdens also shoulders.
→ 神給了重擔、也給了肩膀。

Responsibility must be shouldered; you cannot carry it under your arms.
→ 責任是扛在肩上的，不可挾在腋下。

Think of the devil and he's looking over your shoulders.
→ 正想著魔鬼，魔鬼就越過你肩膀看著你。
→ 說曹操，曹操到。

You can't put an old head on young shoulders.

→ 年輕的肩上不會有老成的頭。

→ 年輕人畢竟閱歷不足；嘴上無毛辦事不牢。

有關「ELBOW」的諺語

Elbow grease gives the best polish.

→ 用力擦，才能擦到最亮。

→ 要求完美，一定得下苦功。

The devil is always at the elbow of an idle man.

→ 懶人身邊必有魔鬼。

→ 懶必生惡。

有關「CHEST／BREAST」的諺語

A man's heart is indiscernible behind his chest.

→ 人心位在胸口後，看不清。

→ 人心難測。

Even if a chef cooks just a fly, he would keep the breast for himsel

→ 即便主廚只是料理一隻蒼蠅，他也會把胸肉留給自己。

→ 人不自私，天誅地滅。

Hope springs eternal in the human breast

→ 人的胸中永遠有希望源源不絕地躍動。

The cross on his breast and the devil in his heart.
→ 胸上有十字，心內住惡魔。
→ 面善心惡。

Where a chest lies open, a righteous man may sin.
→ 在胸膛（錢櫃）敞開之處，正直的人也可能犯罪。
→ 君子難過美色（金錢）關。

有關「HEART」的諺語

Absence makes the heart grow fonder.
→ 缺席不在，心愈充滿愛。
→ 小別勝新婚。

A good heart conquers ill fortune.
→ 好心能克服厄運。
→ 好人必多福；善人有善報。

A happy heart makes a blooming visage.
→ 快樂的心造就亮麗的容顏。

A heavy purse makes a light heart.
→ 荷包重，心輕鬆。
→ 錢多多，心不愁。

A light purse makes a heavy heart.
→ 荷包輕，心沈重。
→ 囊中無錢心事重。

A merry heart does good like a medicine.
→ 快樂的心正如一帖良藥。

A merry heart goes all the way.
→ 快樂的心，做什麼都順利。

As a man thinks in his heart, so is he.
→ 心想什麼，人就變成什麼。
→ 觀念造就一個人。

Busy hands and minds will not let a heart grow heavy.
→ 手忙腦動心情不沈重。

Every heart has its own sorrow.
→ 每顆心都有自己的苦處。
→ 誰無傷心事。

Faint heart never wins fair lady.
→ 膽小的人永遠難得美人心。
→ 不敢追就永遠追不到。

Home is where the heart is.
→ 家是心所在之處。
→ 心在哪，家就在哪。

Hope deferred makes the heart sick.
→ 遲未實現的希望，易使心煩亂絕望。

If it were not for hope, the heart would break.
→ 若沒希望，心早碎了。
→ 人是靠希望活著的。

Industry keeps the body healthy, the mind clear, the heart whole, the purse full.
→ 勤奮使身體健康，頭腦清楚，心思專注，荷包滿滿。

It is a poor heart that never rejoices.
→ 從不懂世間快樂的人太悲慘。
→ 再悲觀的人也總有高興的時候。

Joy puts heart into a man.
→ 喜悅使人有勁。
→ 人逢喜事精神爽。

Kind hearts are more than coronets.
→ 好心勝於冠冕。
→ 善良勝於顯貴；看人要看個性，別看地位。

Love makes all hard hearts gentle.
→ 愛能柔軟冷硬的心。

Music is the medicine of the breaking heart.
→ 音樂是醫治傷心的妙藥。

Nothing is impossible to a willing heart.
→ 有心的人，沒什麼不可能。
→ 有志者事竟成。

The best gifts are always tied with heartstrings.
→ 最棒的禮物總是以心弦捆紮。
→ 情意使禮重。

The best hearts are always the bravest.
→ 最好的心總是大無畏。
→ 善良的心無所不懼。

The mother's heart is the child's schoolroom.
→ 母親的心是孩子的課堂。
→ 什麼心腸的母親教出什麼樣的孩子。

To live in the hearts we leave behind is not to die.
→ 死後仍活在後人心中，雖死猶生。

Two things do prolong your life: a quiet heart and a loving wife.
→ 長壽有兩要訣：平靜的心、摯愛的妻。

Write it on your heart that every day is the best day of the year.
→ 要記住，每天都是一年中最好的一天。

有關「SPLEEN」的諺語

Even a fly has its spleen.
→ 就連蒼蠅都有脾臟（脾氣）。
→ 誰沒脾氣。

When the spleen increases, the body diminishes.
→ 脾愈多，身愈縮。
→ 脾氣少發為妙。

有關「BELLY／STOMACH」的諺語

A growing youth has a wolf in his belly.
→ 年輕人正在長，吃起飯來像虎狼。

Empty words will not fill an empty stomach.
→ 空洞的話語填不了空洞的胃。
→ 空話連篇，於事無補。

Guard lest the eyes be bigger than the stomach.
→ 小心別讓眼睛比胃大。
→ 不要吃不完還拚命拿；不要貪心。

It is hard to labor with an empty belly.
→ 空空的肚子幹不了活。
→ 人是鐵，飯是鋼；鐵打的身子也得吃飯。

Let your head be more than a funnel to your stomach.
→ 別讓頭淪落成胃的漏斗。
→ 要吃，也要動腦。

Poor men seek meat for their stomach, rich men stomach for their meat.
→ 窮人是設法找肉吃進肚子，有錢人是設法找肚子裝肉進去。

Sharp stomachs make short graces.
→ 尖扁的肚子沒教養。
→ 肚子餓便顧不了體面。

The way to a man's heart is through his stomach.
→ 要獲取男人的心，就要先獲取他的胃。

The belly has no conscience.
→ 肚子沒良知。
→ 肚子一餓就什麼也不顧；饑寒易起盜心。

To have a stomach and lack meat, to have meat and lack a stomach, to lie in bed and cannot rest, are great miseries.
→ 天下慘事莫過於：有胃口偏沒肉、沒胃口偏有肉、躺在床上難安歇。

When the belly is full, the bones would be at rest.
→ 肚子飽了，骨頭就想休息。
→ 肚飽思睡；飽暖圖安逸。

有關「BACK」的諺語

A good book is a best friend who never turns his back upon us.
→ 好書是永遠不會拒你我於門外的最好朋友。

He is a good friend that speaks well of us behind our backs.
→ 背後說好話的是真朋友。

He who blames one to his face is a hero, but he who backbites is a coward.
→ 當面指責是英雄，背後中傷是懦夫。

It is the last straw that breaks the camel's back.
→ 最後一根稻草，壓垮駱駝的背。
→ 凡是都有極限，超過分毫必敗。

Lying rides upon debt's back.
→ 謊言騎在債務的背上。
→ 欠債不還的人托辭多、難相信。

Misers put their back and their belly into their pockets.
→ 守財奴用背和肚子填滿荷包。
→ 守財奴為了錢，可以拚命做、不吃喝；愛財如命。

Poverty on an old man's back is a heavy burden.
→ 老而貧窮負擔重。

Patting yourself on the back is a poor way to get ahead.
→ 自己讚美自己，實非進步的好辦法。

Set a beggar on horseback and he'll ride to the devil.
→ 乞丐坐上馬背，便會奔向魔鬼。
→ 錢一多，人心便墮落。

When we are flat on our backs there is no way to look but up.
→ 仰面朝天、無助倒下時，目光哪都到不了、唯有往上看。

You scratch my back and I'll scratch yours.
→ 你幫我抓背，我也幫你抓。
→ 你幫過我、我也幫你；魚水相幫；朋比為奸。

有關「WAIST」的諺語

If you are up to your knees in pleasure, then you are up to your waist in grief.
→ 若你忙著貪歡，日後必忙著悲慘。

Middle age: when a narrow waist and a broad mind begin to change places.
→ 當窄細的腰、寬濶的心開始交換位置，即表示已進中年。

有關「ARM」的諺語

Forewarned is forearmed.
→ 預得警告即預先戒備。
→ 防患於未然。

Justice has long arms.
→ 正義的手臂很長。
→ 天網恢恢，疏而不漏。

Remember, if you ever need a helping hand, it's at the end of your arm.
→ 切記：需要幫手時，幫手就在自己手臂末端。

Stretch your arm no further than your sleeve will reach.
→ 別把手臂伸太長，以致袖子搆不著。
→ 要量入為出。

有關「HAND」的諺語

A bird in the hand is worth two in the bush.
→ 一鳥在手，勝於兩鳥在林。
→ 勿好高騖遠，手邊擁有的再微小卻真實。

A clean hand wants no washing.
→ 清白的手何需洗。
→ 身正不怕影子斜；問心無愧何所懼。

A handful of common sense is worth a bushel of learning.
→ 一小撮常識，與大把的學問有同等的價值。

An empty hand is no lure for a hawk.
→ 空手誘不來老鷹。
→ 捨不得下金鉤，哪能釣大魚。

A wise man will make tools of what comes to hand.
→ 聰明人懂得靈活運用手邊可得的一切。

Change lays not her hand upon truth.
→ 變化傷不了真理。
→ 真理恒不變。

Dogs that bark at a distance bite not at hand.

→ 在遠處咆哮的狗，不會近身來咬人。

→ 會咬人的狗未必會叫。

Gossiping and lying go hand in hand.

→ 流言蜚言總與謊言相伴相隨。

→ 是非八卦，必是謊話。

If you have no hand, you cannot make a fist.

→ 沒手如何握拳。

→ 巧婦難為無米之炊。

Industry is fortune's right hand, and frugality her left.

→ 勤勉是好運的右手，節儉是其左手。

It's all hands to the pumps.

→ 每隻手都該伸往泵浦幫忙抽水

→ 大家都該出把力。

Many hands make light work.

→ 手多工作輕。

→ 人多好辦事。

Nothing is stolen without hands.

→ 沒手何來偷。

→ 無風不起浪。

One can't hold two watermelons in one hand

→ 一手拿不了兩個西瓜。

→ 貪多嚼不爛；什麼都要，什麼都得不到。

Peace with sword in hand, 'tis safest making.

→ 和平時期手執劍，如此作法最安全。

→ 居安思危，為萬全之策。

Put not your hand between the bark and the tree.
→ 別把手放在樹皮與樹之間。
→ 不要侵犯他人隱私、管人閒事。

Put your hand in your pocket.
→ 把手放進口袋裡。
→ 慷慨解囊；樂善好施。

The devil finds work for idle hands to do.
→ 魔鬼愛替懶人找事做。
→ 閒散之人易行惡。

The hand that rocks the cradle is the hand that rules the world.
→ 搖動搖籃的手即統治世界的手。
→ 母親的影響力不容小覷。

The hand that gives, gathers.
→ 給予的手必有收獲。
→ 有捨必有得；給人方便，即給自己方便。

The left hand doesn't know what the right hand is doing.
→ 左手不知右手在做什麼。
→ 不溝通不協調，事情一團糟。

Wisdom in the mind is better than money in the hand.
→ 手中有錢財，不如腦中有智才。

You cannot clap with one hand.
→ 一隻手擊不出掌聲。
→ 孤掌難鳴；人多才好辦事。一個巴掌拍不響；紛爭兩端皆有責任。

有關「PALM」的諺語

An inch in a sword, or a palm in a lance, is a great advantage.

→ 劍進一吋、矛進掌尺，皆是大好機會。

No pain, no palm; no thorns, no throne; no gall, no glory; no cross, no crown.

→ 不經痛苦、何來勝利；未經惱人刺，何以登王座；沒有苦，沒榮耀；無十字架無王冠。

→ 吃得苦中苦，方為人上人。

有關「THUMB / FINGER / NAIL」的諺語

A person with a green thumb seldom paints a town red.

→ 綠拇指者鮮少會把滿城鎮畫得通紅。

→ 喜蒔花弄草者，通常不愛狂歡作樂。

Gain got by a lie will burn one's fingers.

→ 靠欺騙所得之物，必將燒到自己的手。

→ 騙來的利益，終害到自己。

He's an ill cook that cannot lick his own fingers.

→ 不舔自己手指的不是好廚師。

→ 不吃自己做的，絕非好廚師；要敢做敢當。

If all you have is a hammer, everything looks like a nail.
→ 手上只有鎚子，看什麼都是釘子。
→ 主觀偏執使心盲。

If I have lost the ring, I still have the fingers.
→ 就算掉了戒指，還有手指在。
→ 錢財本是身外物。

When the wise man points at the moon, the fool looks at the finger.
→ 智者指月亮，愚者看手指。
→ 文字指出真理所在，愚者卻只見文字不見真理。

Your fingers can't be of the same length.
→ 手指長短各有不同。
→ 人各有所長。

有關「KNEE／HEEL」的諺語

A beggar's knees are supple.
→ 乞丐的膝易彎曲。

Better to die on our feet than live on our knees.
→ 寧願站著死，不願跪著活。
→ 寧死不屈。

Don't let your sorrow come higher than your knees.
→ 別讓悲傷高過膝蓋。
→ 悲傷請適可而止。

One woe doth tread upon another's heels.
→ 禍事總是一個才走後面又來一個。
→ 禍不單行。

有關「LEG」的諺語

A lie has no legs.

→ 謊言沒有腿。

→ 謊言不會自己傳出去。

Lies have short legs.

→ 謊言有腿也是短腿。

→ 不實話語絕對站不住腳。

有關「FOOT」的諺語

A horse may stumble, though he has four feet.

→ 馬縱有四條腿，也有失蹄時。

→ 人有失手，馬有失蹄。

Always put your best foot forward, but don't step on other people's toes.

→ 全力表現自己最好的一面，但別踩到別人的腳趾（得罪人）。

A rabbit's foot is a poor substitute for horse sense.

→ 兔子腳取代不了馬的明智。

→ 身戴護身符，不如腦袋有智識。

A straight foot is not afraid of a crooked shoe.

→ 腳正不怕鞋歪。

→ 身正不怕影子斜；行事光明磊落，自不怕別人閒語。

Diseases（Misfortunes）come on horseback, but go away on foot.

→ 病（災）乘快馬來，徐徐步行去。

→ 病（災）總來得容易去得慢。

Every shoe fits not every foot.

→ 不同的腳需要不同的鞋。

→ 人人各有所需，切勿以己度人。

Footprints on the sands of time are not made by sitting down.

→ 坐著不動，無法在時間沙上留下腳印。

→ 努力活過，始為後世永誌不忘。

He who wants a mule without fault, must walk on foot.

→ 想乘不出錯的騾，勢必得靠自己走。

It's tough trying to keep your feet on the ground, your head above the clouds, your nose to the grindstone, your shoulder to the wheel, your finger on the pulse, your eye on the ball and your ear to the ground.

→ 天下之難在於：既要腳踏實地、又要持續保持夢想、願意苦幹實拚、努力不懈、清楚現況發展、看準後全力出手、並能掌握最新動態。

Not let the grass grow under one's feet.

→ 別讓腳底長出青草來。

→ 時間不等人；切勿蹉跎。

One foot is better than two crutches.

→ 一隻腳勝過兩根拐杖。

→ 聊勝於無。

Six feet of earth makes all men equal.

→ 六尺黃土下，人人皆平等。

→ 死亡面前無貴賤。

A beggar may sing before the footpad.

→ 乞丐遇劫匪，放膽高聲唱。

→ 光棍不怕人來偷。

The peacock has fair feathers, but foul feet.

→ 孔雀雖有華羽，卻有賤足。

→ 再美的人事物，也都有不堪的一面。

The shoemaker's children go barefoot.

→ 鞋匠的孩子總打赤腳沒鞋穿。

→ 愈是親近愈容易輕疏。

Where your will is ready, your feet are light.

→ 下定決心，腳步輕盈。

→ 天下無難事，只怕有心人。

有關「BLOOD」的諺語

Blood is thicker than water.

→ 血濃於水。

Blood will have blood.

→ 血債要用血來償。

Blood will tell.

→ 什麼樣的家庭生出什麼樣的孩子。

The soldiers' blood, the general's reputation.

→ 軍士的血，將軍的名。

→ 一將功成萬骨枯。

You cannot get blood from a stone.

→ 石頭裡抽不出血。

→ 沒有就是沒有。

有關「SKIN」的諺語

A cat has nine lives, as the onion seven skins.

→ 貓有九條命，洋蔥有七層皮。

→ 再卑微者也有想活下去的意志。

Beauty is only skin deep, but ugly goes straight to the bone.

→ 美色只是一層皮，醜陋深到骨子裡。

Catch the bear before you sell his skin.

→ 先抓到熊再賣熊的皮。

→ 八字少一撇就不能叫八。

The fox changes his skin but not his habit.

→ 狐狸改變得了毛皮，改不了習性。

→ 江山易改，本性難移。

There is more than one way to skin a cat.

→ 剝下貓皮的方法不只一種。

→ 解決問題、處理事情的方法多得很；辦法總是有的。

※此處cat應是指catfish（鯰魚），因為鯰魚的皮肉相連，去皮極不容易。

Tigers die and leave their skins; people die and leave their names.

→ 虎死留皮，人死留名。

有關「BONE」的諺語

A dog will not howl if you beat him with a bone.
→ 以骨打狗狗不嘷。

A good dog deserves a good bone.
→ 表現好的乖狗就該得好骨頭。
→ 有功者該賞。

Failure follows the man whose wishbone is where his backbone should be.
→ 背骨（堅毅）成了許願骨的人，後面必跟著失敗。

Hard words break no bones.
→ 惡言傷不到骨。
→ 笑罵由人，毋需放心上。

Two cats and a mouse, two wives in one house, two dogs and a bone, never agree in one.
→ 兩貓一鼠，兩妻一屋，兩狗一骨，最難同相處。

Two dogs strive for a bone, and a third runs away with it.
→ 兩狗爭一骨，第三方拿了骨頭跑。
→ 鷸蚌相爭，漁翁得利。

What is bred in the bone will come out in the flesh.
→ 根深於骨之物將形於肉之身。
→ 本性難移，積習難改。

有關「FLESH」的諺語

The nearer the bone, the sweeter the flesh.
→ 愈貼近骨頭的肉愈香；也當玩笑話，嘲笑某人妻子瘦如肉貼骨。

The spirit is willing but the flesh is weak.
→ 心有餘而力不足。

有關「BODY」的諺語

A good healthy body is worth more a crown in gold.
→ 健康的身體遠比黃金鑄成的王冠更有價值。

A little body often harbors a great soul.
→ 微小的身軀往往懷有偉大的靈魂。
→ 人小志氣高。

A sound mind lies in a sound body.
→ 健全的頭腦寓於健全的身體。

A true friend is one soul in two bodies.
→ 真正的朋友是兩個身子一條心。

Of all the possessions of this life, fame is the noblest; when the body has sunk into the dust, the great name still lives.
→ 活著時最可貴的財產是聲譽，死後入了土，高貴之名雖死猶存。

Reading is to the mind what exercise is to the body.

→ 閱讀之於心神，猶如運動之於身體。

→ 讀書可養神，運動可健身。

The pain of the mind is worse than the pain of the body.

→ 精神的痛苦遠比肉體的痛苦更惱人。

When riches increase, the body decreases.

→ 財富增，身軀減。

→ 財多往往體弱。

Wisdom is to the mind what health is to the body.

→ 智慧之於心靈，猶如健康之於身體。

有關「SOUL」的諺語

A good book is the purest essence of a human soul.

→ 好書是人類心靈最純淨的精髓。

Brevity is the soul of wit.

→ 言以簡潔為貴。

→ 把話說得好又少最難。

Confession may be good for the soul, but it's often bad for the reputation.

→ 坦白或有益於心靈，卻有害於聲譽。

Courage and resolution are the spirit and soul of virtue.

→ 勇氣與決心是美德的精魂。

Diseases of the soul are more dangerous than those of the body.

→ 心靈的疾病比肉體的疾病更危險。

Great souls suffer in silence.

→ 受苦時靜不出聲，是高貴的靈魂。

I count myself in nothing else so happy as in a soul remembering my good friends.

→ 我覺得再沒有什麼事比在靈魂深處想起好朋友們更快樂的了。

Music washes away from the soul the dust of everyday life.

→ 音樂能為心靈洗去凡塵瑣事所帶來的塵垢。

Open confession is good for the soul.

→ 坦白對心靈有益。

→ 坦白告罪，身心愉快。

Punctuality is the soul of business.

→ 守時是辦事的靈魂。

→ 行事一定要守時。

The soul is not where it lives, but where it loves.

→ 心靈不在它寓居何處，而在它所愛之處。

→ 靈魂因愛而存在。

To care for wisdom and truth and the improvement of the soul is far better than to seek money and honor and reputation.

→ 心繫智慧、真理、以及心靈的提昇，勝於追求金錢、面子與名望。

What sculpture is to a block of marble, education is to the soul.

→ 教育之於心靈，猶如雕刻之於大理石。

MEMO

國家圖書館出版品預行編目資料

用身體學慣用語像老外一樣說英文 / 于宥均，吳榮騰作．-- 初版．-- 新北市：楓書坊文化，2014.07 430 面；21 公分

ISBN 978-986-5775-82-7（平裝）

1. 英語　2. 慣用語

805.123　　103009220

出　　版／楓書坊文化出版社
地　　址／新北市板橋區信義路 163 巷 3 號 10 樓
郵政劃撥／19907596 楓書坊文化出版社
網　　址／www.maplebook.com.tw
電　　話／(02)2957-6096
傳　　真／(02)2957-6435
作　　者／于宥均
插　　畫／吳榮騰
總 經 銷／商流文化事業有限公司
地　　址／新北市中和區中正路 752 號 8 樓
網　　址／www.vdm.com.tw
電　　話／(02)2228-8841
傳　　真／(02)2228-6939
港澳經銷／泛華發行代理有限公司
定　　價／300 元
初版日期／2014 年 7 月